c.1 v.7

James, Henry
The complete tales of Henry James.

THE COMPLETE TALES OF HENRY JAMES
VOLUME SEVEN: 1888–1891

THE COMPLETE TALES OF

HENRY JAMES

EDITED WITH AN

INTRODUCTION BY

LEON EDEL

7

1888–1891

J. B. LIPPINCOTT COMPANY

PHILADELPHIA AND NEW YORK

CONTENTS

INTRODUCTION: 1888–1891

"A LONDON LIFE," the longest tale in this volume, was
begun during Henry James's "Italian phase," his memorable
sojourn in Tuscany and Venetia of 1886–87, which inspired
certain of the stories already published in this series and at
least three of those published here. The idea for the tale of
Laura Wing and her London experience was inscribed in
James's notebook in Venice, at the Palazzo Barbaro; it
stemmed from an incident told by the novelist's French admirer, Paul Bourget, who mentioned the suicide in Milan of
a young Frenchwoman, following her discovery (so Bourget
believed) that her mother had lovers. The predicament of a
girl in an acute state of anxiety seems to have had a particular
appeal to Henry James as a dramatic subject: and the form his
tale took was that her anxiety should be the consequence of
the adulteries, and the impending divorce, of an older sister,
an American, who has married into London society. Reflected in this tale is the evolution of James's moral view of the
European social scene. A decade earlier, in such tales as
"Daisy Miller," he had shown a young American innocent
refusing to conform to rigid Old World manners; in "The
Siege of London" he had also shown a divorcée shouldering
her way into the hierarchic social scale of Victorian England.
But in "A London Life" he is finally recognising that the
world of "society" is not as rigid as he had believed: that
social indiscretions are sometimes committed without tragic
consequences. All the personages in this tale try to explain
this to the puritanical American girl, who is determined to
prevent her sister from running away to the Continent with
her lover. "She exaggerates the badness of it," says the
seasoned old Lady Davenant. "Good heavens, at that rate

7

where should some of us be?" But Laura Wing, "bristling with righteousness," pursues her eloping sister to Belgium, and in her desperation even proposes marriage to a young American who has shown a friendly but aloof interest in her. She hopes in this way to shield herself from the impending scandal. Laura, with her inflexible conception of what is good and right, and her "high-strung" way of taking life, foreshadows James's panic-stricken governess of "The Turn of the Screw" and the despairing young woman of "The Visits." In the girl's proposal of marriage, James is recurring to the situation in the recently composed tale of the Aspern papers. But Laura has no valuable papers to offer as her "dowry." She can offer only a vision of her own strange torment to the bewildered young man to whom she appeals for rescue.

If, in this curious tale, James is still touching on the ways in which older sisters (or brothers) can pose a threat to the freedom of their siblings, he seems to say at the same time that the younger can sometimes be extremely meddlesome. And years later the novelist was to feel that there was a certain thinness of observation in his tale. He wondered why he had made the adulterous woman an American; nationality, he recognised, was not a part, in this story, of the "prime intention" as it had been in "Daisy Miller." Whether the woman was American or not seemed irrelevant; London society provided adulterous subjects in abundance. What had mattered was the puritanical stiffness of the girl, her "wild, vague, frantic, gesture." And this James conveys in a calm and unruffled prose that only heightens the tension of the story.

"The Modern Warning," "The Lesson of the Master," and "The Patagonia" were written in De Vere Gardens, when James was still experiencing the *élan* of his Italian experience. Of this group, "The Lesson of the Master" is best known, and has been many times reprinted. It was to be but

the first of a series of witty tales of the "literary life" which
James was to write during the next decade. Its subject is the
question of art and marriage—but treated largely as a joke. If
the great novelist in the tale, Henry St George, who speaks
for Henry James, pleads eloquently for celibacy, he does not
follow his own advice, and the reader feels almost as "sold"
as the young acolyte who, on his side, practised what the
master preached—to his own chagrin.

Less known, in this group, are "The Modern Warning"
and "The Patagonia." The heroine of "The Modern Warning" (originally titled "Two Countries" when it was serial-
ised) feels herself trapped between English and American
differences; but she is caught also in a psychological conflict
between her love for her brother, who symbolises her home-
land, and her loyalty to her English husband, who hates
America. The heroine of "The Patagonia" finds herself
trapped between loyalty to her fiancé, who awaits her in
Europe, and her feelings for a rich and spoiled young Bostonian, who trifles with her affections during a leisurely transatlantic voyage. Like Daisy Miller, young Grace Mavis aboard
the *Patagonia* is driven to desperate measures by the wagging
tongues of fellow-Americans. The issue in both "The Patagonia" and "The Modern Warning" is uncommonly violent
for a James story. The latter tale reflects the novelist's increasing sense that the lands of his birth and of his adoption are
"simply different chapters of the same general subject" and
his writings of this time suggest the futility of an endless
parade of transatlantic differences. "The Modern Warning" is a piece of hack-work when compared with the sharp-
ness and vigour of "The Patagonia," with its atmospheric
opening during the hot Boston midsummer, in which James
is recalling the discomfort of his own stay there five years
earlier. In narrative skill, the story of the voyage is one of
James's perfect examples of his use of the "indirect method."
We see Grace largely through the eyes of the narrator and of

her fellow-passengers; and it is through the narrator that we gain an acute sense of her painful dilemma.

"The Solution," the only tale which James wrote during 1889 (he was busy with his serialisation of *The Tragic Muse*), harks back to his long stay in Rome during the early 1870's when he rode horseback in the Campagna and led an agreeable life in the large salons of Roman palaces among American expatriates. There is an eloquent reminiscence of this period, wholly autobiographical, in the opening pages of the tale; and the lightness of the story—the joke played on the solemn and conscientious diplomat by his friends, and then their effort to disentangle him from his unwilling engagement—is forgotten in the singular suavity of the narration. James cultivates the memoir-writing manner of a seasoned man of the world, and if the episode is treated with high amusement it contains within it the recurring theme of the novelist's stories: the fear of entanglement and the fear of women. The joke, we must remember, is not at all funny to the victim who has to be liberated from the consequences of his indestructible gallantry. James was to refashion this tale into an inconsequential stage comedy, *Disengaged*, for Ada Rehan, but the play was never produced.

With "The Pupil," published in 1891, James began a productive period of work devoted to the short story and to the stage. He announced to his friends that he was abandoning the writing of novels; these yielded revenue during serialisation but had no sale in the bookshops. James would now write for the theatre in the hope of gaining a better livelihood; and by producing many tales, in the margin of his theatricals, he hoped to support himself adequately during this period. This explains the great variety of James's stories during the 1890's, and their appearance in periodicals as diverse as the *Yellow Book* and the *Illustrated London News*, the *New*

Review or *Black and White*. A good number were "contrived" and written in haste; they were intended exclusively for ephemeral reading. However, while the worldly success-seeking writer consciously worked for narrative superficiality, his other self, the artist, was busy sabotaging this effort and smuggling into the tales a considerable degree of subtle wit and complex characterisation. In seeking for the popular note and the readable subject, James brought into being, among his potboilers, several distinct masterpieces. One of these is "The Pupil."

This tale was derived from an anecdote told the novelist by Dr W. W. Baldwin, an expatriate American physician who practised in Florence, with whom James had undertaken in 1890 a little tour of out-of-the-way Tuscan towns. One day, in a hot uncomfortable railway carriage, which dragged itself from station to station, Baldwin told James of an American family he had known, "an odd adventurous, extravagant band, of high but rather unauthenticated pretensions" and their little boy who had a weak heart and was dragged about the Continent in a "prowling precarious" way. "Here was more than enough for a summer's day, even in old Italy— here was a thumping windfall," James later remembered. It was indeed a windfall: and we may well recognise the personal appeal of the anecdote. James himself had been dragged about the Continent as a boy, when he would have preferred to be in Newport; and he had been exposed to the vagueness and the uncertainties of the young pupil, Morgan Moreen. While James's parents in no way resembled the down-at-heel Moreens, James could depict their drifting life, rootlessness, and sense of change. He knew too what it was to have tutors and governesses; and the anxieties economic uncertainty could provoke in children. Even in his own comfortable childhood there had come a moment, during the American depression of 1856–57 (when he was thirteen), which caused his parents to beat a hurried retreat from a luxurious apartment in Paris to a modest residence at Boulogne-sur-Mer. Out of this personal past James could weave his delicate tale of a sensitive boy and his tutor, the first of the series of tales of the 1890's in which children suffer from parental indifference or hostility.

The tale was written rapidly and James sent it to the *Atlantic Monthly* which had published him regularly since the Civil War. Its new editor, Horace E. Scudder, promptly rejected the story. He may have been troubled by the picture of the child's attachment to the young man; more likely he was bothered by James's account of a mendacious American family which jumps its hotel bills and lives a hand-to-mouth existence. Unpublished letters testify to James's "shock of a perfectly honest surprise" at being turned down by the *Atlantic*. The novelist felt that responsibility to the readers, when it was a question of "an old and honourable reputation, [should] be left with the author himself." *Longman's Magazine* accepted the tale promptly in England.

Posterity has confirmed James's opinion of the story. A subtle portrait of a gifted adolescent, the tale has within it a double point of view—the boy's "troubled vision" of his family, "as reflected in the vision, also troubled enough, of his devoted friend." The tutor, who is seldom paid by the Moreens for his services, is called upon to supply the affection young Morgan would normally have expected from his parents. And he likes the boy so much that he stays on, in a perpetual conflict between his need for a livelihood and his feelings for his young charge. The life of the Moreens, their false standards and values, their façade of shabby arrogance and pride, their sublime belief in a providing world, their petty luxuries and pretence to style, and their strange helplessness—all this is shown as it affects the intensely aware young pupil. Quick of mind, and perceptive, he can only be ashamed of his family and thoroughly conscious of the shabby way in which it treats the tutor whom he adores. The ultimate parental decision to take advantage of this situation engenders a complex *dénouement*. Morgan's weak heart cannot tolerate the emotions aroused by parental indifference (however much this is inspired by desperation) and the willingness of his mother and father to "unload" him on his tutor.

James makes us suspect, however, that Morgan Moreen finds it no less difficult—and perhaps even more—to face the tutor's understandable hesitation—given his threadbare existence—to act out their dream of a life of freedom together. The dream had been exquisite. The prospect of reality has its terrors, and it is in some such conflict of loyalty and rejection that Morgan has his fatal moment of panic. He is solitary and betrayed; and his world suddenly becomes void and hopeless; like little Miles in "The Turn of the Screw," he can only be dispossessed of everything. He has been robbed even of his fantasy of flight. It is the last thing he learns in that "morning twilight of childhood" which James understood so well, in which there "was nothing at a given moment you could say a clever child didn't know."

"The Pupil" thus inaugurated James's most brilliant decade of short-story writing.

New York University   LEON EDEL

THE MODERN WARNING

I

WHEN he reached the hotel Macarthy Grice was apprised, to his great disappointment, of the fact that his mother and sister were absent for the day, and he reproached himself with not having been more definite in announcing his arrival to them in advance. It was a little his nature to expect people to know things about himself that he had not told them and to be vexed when he found they were ignorant of them. I will not go so far as to say that he was inordinately conceited, but he had a general sense that he himself knew most things without having them pumped into him. He had been uncertain about his arrival and, since he disembarked at Liverpool, had communicated his movements to the two ladies who after spending the winter in Rome were awaiting him at Cadenabbia only by notes as brief as telegrams and on several occasions by telegrams simply. It struck his mother that he spent a great deal of money on these latter missives—which were mainly negative, mainly to say that he could not yet say when he *should* be able to start for the Continent. He had had business in London and had apparently been a good deal vexed by the discovery that, most of the people it was necessary for him to see being out of town, the middle of August was a bad time for transacting it. Mrs Grice gathered that he had had annoyances and disappointments, but she hoped that by the time he should join them his serenity would have been restored. She had not seen him for a year and her heart hungered for her boy. Family feeling was strong among these three though Macarthy's manner of showing it was sometimes peculiar, and her affection for her son was jealous and passionate; but she and Agatha made no secret between themselves of the fact that the privilege of being his mother and his sister was mainly sensible when things were going well with him. They were a little afraid they were not going well just now and they asked each other why he could not leave his affairs alone for a few weeks anyway and treat his journey to Europe as a complete holiday —a course which would do him infinitely more good. He took life too hard and was overworked and overstrained. It was only to each other however that the anxious and affectionate women made these reflections, for they knew it was of no use to say such things to Macarthy. It was not that he answered them angrily; on the contrary he never noticed them at all. The answer was in the very essence of his nature: he was indomitably ambitious.

They had gone on the steamboat to the other end of the lake and could not possibly be back for several hours. There was a *festa* going on at one of the villages—in the hills, a little way from the lake—and several ladies and gentlemen had gone from the hotel to be present at it. They would find carriages at the landing and they would drive to the village, after which the same vehicles would bring them back to the boat. This information was given to Macarthy Grice by the secretary of the hotel, a young man with a very low shirt collar, whose nationality puzzled and even defied him by its indefiniteness (he liked to know whom he was talking to even when he could not have the satisfaction of feeling that it was an American), and who suggested to him that he might follow and overtake his friends in the next steamer. As however there appeared to be some danger that in this case he should cross them on their way back he determined simply to lounge about the lake-side and the grounds of the hotel. The place was lovely, the view magnificent, and there was a coming and going of little boats, of travellers of every nationality, of itinerant vendors of small superfluities. Macarthy observed these things as patiently as his native restlessness allowed—and indeed that quality was reinforced to-day by an inexplicable tendency to fidget. He changed his place twenty times; he lighted a cigar and threw it away; he ordered some luncheon and when it came had no appetite for it. He felt nervous and he wondered what he was nervous about; whether he were afraid that during their excursion an accident had befallen his mother or Agatha. He was not usually a prey to small timidities, and indeed it cost him a certain effort to admit that a little Italian lake could be deep enough to drown a pair of independent Americans or that Italian horses could have the high spirit to run away with them. He talked with no one, for the Americans seemed to him all taken up with each other and the English all taken up with themselves. He had a few elementary principles for use in travelling (he had travelled little, but he had an abundant supply of theory on the subject), and one of them was that with Englishmen an American should never open the conversation. It was his belief that in doing so an American was exposed to be snubbed, or even insulted, and this belief was unshaken by the fact that Englishmen very often spoke to him, Macarthy, first.

The afternoon passed, little by little, and at last, as he stood there with his hands in his pockets and his hat pulled over his nose to keep the western sun out of his eyes, he saw the boat that he was waiting for round a distant point. At this stage the little annoyance he had felt at the trick his relations had unwittingly played him passed completely away and there was nothing in his mind but the eagerness of affection, the joy of reunion—of the prospective embrace. This feeling was in his face, in the fixed smile with which he watched the boat grow larger and larger. If we watch the young man himself as he does so we shall perceive him to be a tallish, lean personage, with an excessive slope of the shoulders, a very thin neck, a short light beard and a bright, sharp, expressive eye. He almost always wore his hat too much behind or too much in front; in the former case it showed a very fine high forehead. He looked like a man of intellect whose body was not much to him and its senses and appetites not importunate. His feet were small and he always wore a double-breasted frockcoat, which he never buttoned. His mother and sister thought him very handsome. He had this appearance especially of course when, making them out on the deck of the steamer, he began to wave his hat and his hand to them. They responded in the most demonstrative manner and when they got near enough his mother called out to him over the water that she could not forgive herself for having lost so much of his visit. This was a bold proceeding for Mrs Grice, who usually held back. Only she had been uncertain—she had not expected him that day in particular. "It's my fault!—it's my fault!" exclaimed a gentleman beside her, whom our young man had not yet noticed, raising his hat slightly as he spoke. Agatha, on the other side, said nothing—she only smiled at her brother. He had not seen her for so many months that he had almost forgotten how pretty she was. She looked lovely, under the shadow of her hat and of the awning of the steamer, as she stood there with happiness in her face and a big bunch of familiar flowers in her hand. Macarthy was proud of many things, but on this occasion he was proudest of having such a charming sister. Before they all disembarked he had time to observe the gentleman who had spoken to him—an extraordinarily fair, clean-looking man, with a white waistcoat, a white hat, a glass in one eye and a flower in his buttonhole. Macarthy wondered who he was, but only vaguely, as it explained him sufficiently to suppose that he was a gentleman staying at the hotel who had made acquaintance with his mother and sister and taken part in the excursion. The only thing Grice had against him was that he had the air of an American who tried to look like an Englishman—a definite and conspicuous class to the young man's sense and one in regard to which he entertained a peculiar abhorrence. He was sorry his relatives should associate themselves with persons of that stamp; he would almost have preferred that they should become acquainted with the genuine English. He happened to perceive that the individual in question looked a good deal at him; but he disappeared instantly and discreetly when the boat drew up at the landing and the three Grices—I had almost written the three Graces— pressed each other in their arms.

Half an hour later Macarthy sat between the two ladies at the table d'hôte, where he had a hundred questions to answer and to ask. He was still more struck with Agatha's improvement; she was older, handsomer, brighter: she had turned completely into a young lady and into a very accomplished one. It seemed to him that there had been a change for the better in his mother as well, the only change of that sort of which the good lady was susceptible, an amelioration of health, a fresher colour and a less frequent cough. Mrs Grice was a gentle, sallow, serious little woman, the main principle of whose being was the habit of insisting that nothing that concerned herself was of the least consequence. She thought it indelicate to be ill and obtrusive even to be better, and discouraged all conversation of which she was in any degree the subject. Fortunately she had not been able to prevent her children from discussing her condition sufficiently to agree— it took but few words, for they agreed easily, that is Agatha always agreed with her brother—that she must have a change of climate and spend a winter or two in the south of Europe. Mrs Grice kept her son's birthday all the year and knew an extraordinary number of stitches in knitting. Her friends constantly received from her, by post, offerings of little mats for the table, done up in an envelope, usually without any writing. She could make little mats in forty or fifty different ways. Toward the end of the dinner Macarthy, who up to this moment had been wholly occupied with his companions, began to look around him and to ask questions about the people opposite. Then he leaned forward a little and turned his eye up and down the row of their fellow-tourists on the same side. It was in this way that he perceived the gentleman who had said from the steamer that it was *his* fault that Mrs Grice and her daughter had gone away for so many hours and who now was seated at some distance below the younger lady. At the moment Macarthy leaned forward this personage happened to be looking toward him, so that he caught his eye. The stranger smiled at him and nodded, as if an acquaintance might be considered to have been established between them, rather to Macarthy's surprise. He drew back and asked his sister who he was—the fellow who had been with them on the boat.

"He's an Englishman—Sir Rufus Chasemore," said the girl. Then she added, "Such a nice man."

"Oh, I thought he was an American making a fool of himself!" Macarthy rejoined.

"There's nothing of the fool about him," Agatha declared, laughing; and in a moment she added that Sir Rufus's usual place was beside hers, on her left hand. On this occasion he had moved away.

"What do you mean by this occasion?" her brother inquired.

"Oh, because you are here."

"And is he afraid of me?"

"Yes, I think he is."

"He doesn't behave so, anyway."

"Oh, he has very good manners," said the girl.

"Well, I suppose he's bound to do that. Isn't he a kind of nobleman?" Macarthy asked.

"Well no, not exactly a nobleman."

"Well, some kind of a panjandarum. Hasn't he got one of their titles?"

"Yes, but not a very high one," Agatha explained. "He's only a K.C.B. And also an M.P."

"A K.C.B. and an M.P.? What the deuce is all that?" And when Agatha had elucidated these mystic signs, as to which the young man's ignorance was partly simulated, he remarked that the Post-office ought to charge her friend double for his letters—for requiring that amount of stuff in his address. He also said that he owed him one for leading them astray at a time when they were bound to be on hand to receive one who was so dear to them. To this Agatha replied:

"Ah, you see, Englishmen are like that. They expect women to be so much honoured by their wanting them to do anything. And it must always be what *they* like, of course."

"What the men like? Well, that's all right, only they mustn't be Englishmen," said Macarthy Grice.

"Oh, if one is going to be a slave I don't know that the nationality of one's master matters!" his sister exclaimed. After which his mother began to ask him if he had seen anything during the previous months of their Philadelphia cousins—some cousins who wrote their name Gryce and for whom Macarthy had but a small affection.

After dinner the three sat out on the terrace of the hotel, in the delicious warmth of the September night. There were boats on the water, decked with coloured lanterns; music and song proceeded from several of them and every influence was harmonious. Nevertheless by the time Macarthy had finished a cigar it was judged best that the old lady should withdraw herself from the evening air. She went into the salon of the hotel, and her children accompanied her, against her protest, so that she might not be alone. Macarthy liked better to sit with his mother in a drawing-room which the lamps made hot than without her under the stars. At the end of a quarter of an hour he became aware that his sister had disappeared, and as some time elapsed without her returning he asked his mother what had become of her.

"I guess she has gone to walk with Sir Rufus," said the old lady, candidly.

"Why, you seem to do everything Sir Rufus wants, down here!" her son exclaimed. "How did he get such a grip on you?"

"Well, he has been most kind, Macarthy," Mrs Grice returned, not appearing to deny that the Englishman's influence was considerable.

"I have heard it stated that it's not the custom, down here, for young girls to walk round—at night—with foreign lords."

"Oh, he's not foreign and he's most reliable," said the old lady, very earnestly. It was not in her nature to treat such a question, or indeed any question, as unimportant.

"Well, that's all right," her son remarked, in a tone which implied that he was in good-humour and wished not to have his equanimity ruffled. Such accidents with Macarthy Grice were not light things. All the same at the end of five minutes more, as Agatha did not reappear, he expressed the hope that nothing of any kind had sprung up between her and the K.C.B.

"Oh, I guess they are just conversing by the lake. I'll go and find them if you like," said Mrs Grice.

"Well, haven't they been conversing by the lake—and on the lake—all day?" asked the young man, without taking up her proposal.

"Yes, of course we had a great deal of bright talk while we were out. It was quite enough for me to listen to it. But he is most kind—and he knows everything, Macarthy."

"Well, that's all right!" exclaimed the young man again. But a few moments later he returned to the charge and asked his mother if the Englishman were paying any serious attention—she knew what he meant—to Agatha. "Italian lakes and summer evenings and glittering titles and all that sort of thing—of course you know what they may lead to."

Mrs Grice looked anxious and veracious, as she always did, and appeared to consider a little. "Well, Macarthy, the truth is just this. Your sister is so attractive and so admired that it seems as if wherever she went there was a great interest taken in her. Sir Rufus certainly does like to converse with her, but so have many others—and so would any one in their place. And Agatha is full of conscience. For me that's her highest attraction."

"I'm very much pleased with her—she's a lovely creature," Macarthy remarked.

"Well, there's no one whose appreciation could gratify her more than yours. She has praised you up to Sir Rufus," added the old lady, simply.

"Dear mother, what has *he* got to do with it?" her son demanded, staring. "I don't care what Sir Rufus thinks of me."

Fortunately the good lady was left only for a moment confronted with this inquiry, for Agatha now re-entered the room, passing in from the terrace by one of the long windows and accompanied precisely by the gentleman whom her relatives had been discussing. She came toward them smiling and perhaps even blushing a little, but with an air of considerable resolution, and she said to Macarthy, "Brother, I want to make you acquainted with a good friend of ours, Sir Rufus Chasemore."

"Oh, I asked Miss Grice to be so good." The Englishman laughed, looking easy and genial.

Macarthy got up and extended his hand, with a "Very happy to know you, sir," and the two men stood a moment looking at each other while Agatha, beside them, bent her regard upon both. I shall not attempt to translate the reflections which rose in the young lady's mind as she did so, for they were complicated and subtle and it is quite difficult enough to reproduce our own more casual impression of the contrast between her companions. This contrast was extreme and complete, and it was not weakened by the fact that both the men had the signs of character and ability. The American was thin, dry, fine, with something in his face which seemed to say that there was more in him of the spirit than of the letter. He looked unfinished and yet somehow he looked mature, though he was not advanced in life. The Englishman had more detail about him, something stippled and retouched, an air of having been more artfully fashioned, in conformity with traditions and models. He wore old clothes which looked new, while his transatlantic brother wore new clothes which looked old. He thought he had never heard the American tone so marked as on the lips of Mr Macarthy Grice, who on his side found in the accent of his sister's friend a strange, exaggerated, even affected variation of the tongue in which he supposed himself to have been brought up. In general he was much irritated by the tricks which the English played with the English language, deprecating especially their use of familiar slang.

"Miss Grice tells me that you have just crossed the ditch, but I'm afraid you are not going to stay with us long," Sir Rufus remarked, with much pleasantness.

"Well, no, I shall return as soon as I have transacted my business," Macarthy replied. "That's all I came for."

"You don't do us justice; you ought to follow the example of your mother and sister and take a look round," Sir Rufus went on, with another laugh. He was evidently of a mirthful nature.

"Oh, I have been here before; I've seen the principal curiosities."

"He has seen everything thoroughly," Mrs Grice murmured over her crochet.

"Ah, I daresay you have seen much more than we poor natives. And your own country is so interesting. I have an immense desire to see that."

"Well, it certainly repays observation," said Macarthy Grice.

"You wouldn't like it at all; you would find it awful," his sister remarked, sportively, to Sir Rufus.

"Gracious, daughter!" the old lady exclaimed, trying to catch Agatha's eye.

"That's what she's always telling me, as if she were trying to keep me from going. I don't know what she has been doing over there that she wants to prevent me from finding out." Sir Rufus's eyes, while he made this observation, rested on the young lady in the most respectful yet at the same time the most complacent manner.

She smiled back at him and said with a laugh still clearer than his own, "I know the kind of people who will like America and the kind of people who won't."

"Do you know the kind who will like *you* and the kind who won't?" Sir Rufus Chasemore inquired.

"I don't know that in some cases it particularly matters what people like," Macarthy interposed, with a certain severity.

"Well, I must say I like people to like my country," said Agatha.

"You certainly take the best way to make them, Miss Grice!" Sir Rufus exclaimed.

"Do you mean by dissuading them from visiting it, sir?" Macarthy asked.

"Oh dear no; by being so charming a representative of it. But I shall most positively go on the first opportunity."

"I hope it won't be while we are on this side," said Mrs Grice, very civilly.

"You will need us over there to explain everything," her daughter added.

The Englishman looked at her a moment with his glass in his eye. "I shall certainly pretend to be very stupid." Then he went on, addressing himself to Macarthy: "I have an idea that you have some rocks ahead, but that doesn't diminish—in fact it increases—my curiosity to see the country."

"Oh, I suspect we'll scratch along all right," Macarthy replied, with rather a grim smile, in a tone which conveyed that the success of American institutions might not altogether depend on Sir Rufus's judgment of them. He was on the point of expressing his belief, further, that there were European countries which would be glad enough to exchange their "rocks" for those of the United States; but he kept back this reflection, as it might appear too pointed and he wished not to be rude to a man who seemed on such sociable terms with his mother and sister. In the course of a quarter of an hour the ladies took their departure for the upper regions and Macarthy Grice went off with them. The Englishman looked for him again however, as something had been said about their smoking a cigar together before they went to bed; but he never turned up, so that Sir Rufus puffed his own weed in solitude, strolling up and down the terrace without mingling with the groups that remained and looking much at the starlit lake and mountains.

II

THE next morning after breakfast Mrs Grice had a conversation with her son in her own room. Agatha had not yet appeared, and she explained that the girl was sleeping late, having been much fatigued by her excursion the day before as well as by the excitement of her brother's arrival. Macarthy thought it a little singular that she should bear her fatigue so much less well than her mother, but he understood everything in a moment, as soon as the old lady drew him toward her with her little conscious, cautious face, taking his hand in hers. She had had a long and important talk with Agatha the previous evening, after they went upstairs, and she had extracted from the girl some information which she had within a day or two begun very much to desire.

"It's about Sir Rufus Chasemore. I couldn't but think you would wonder—just as I was wondering myself," said Mrs Grice. "I felt as if I couldn't be satisfied till I had asked. I don't know how you will feel about it. I am afraid it will upset you a little; but anything that you may think—well, yes, it *is* the case."

"Do you mean she is engaged to be married to your Englishman?" Macarthy demanded, with a face that suddenly flushed.

"No, she's not engaged. I presume she wouldn't take that step without finding out how you'd feel. In fact that's what she said last night."

"I feel like thunder, I feel like hell!" Macarthy exclaimed; "and I hope you'll tell her so."

Mrs Grice looked frightened and pained. "Well, my son, I'm glad you've come, if there is going to be any trouble."

"Trouble—what trouble should there be? He can't marry her if she won't have him."

"Well, she didn't say she wouldn't have him; she said the question hadn't come up. But she thinks it would come up if she were to give him any sort of opening. That's what I thought and that's what I wanted to make sure of."

Macarthy looked at his mother for some moments in extreme seriousness; then he took out his watch and looked at that. "What time is the first boat?" he asked.

"I don't know—there are a good many."

"Well, we'll take the first—we'll quit this." And the young man put back his watch and got up with decision.

His mother sat looking at him rather ruefully. "Would you feel so badly if she were to do it?"

"She may do it without my consent; she shall never do it with," said Macarthy Grice.

"Well, I could see last evening, by the way you acted—" his mother murmured, as if she thought it her duty to try and enter into his opposition.

"How did I act, ma'am?"

"Well, you acted as if you didn't think much of the English."

"Well, I don't," said the young man.

"Agatha noticed it and she thought Sir Rufus noticed it too."

"They have such thick hides in general that they don't notice anything. But if he is more sensitive than the others perhaps it will keep him away."

"Would you like to wound him, Macarthy?" his mother inquired, with an accent of timid reproach.

"Wound him? I should like to kill him! Please to let Agatha know that we'll move on," the young man added.

Mrs Grice got up as if she were about to comply with this injunction, but she stopped in the middle of the room and asked of her son, with a quaint effort at conscientious impartiality which would have made him smile if he had been capable of smiling in such a connection, "Don't you think that in some respects the English are a fine nation?"

"Well, yes; I like them for pale ale and notepaper and umbrellas; and I got a firstrate trunk there the other day. But I want my sister to marry one of her own people."

"Yes, I presume it would be better," Mrs Grice remarked. "But Sir Rufus has occupied very high positions in his own country."

"I know the kind of positions he has occupied; I can tell what they were by looking at him. The more he has done of that the more intensely he represents what I don't like."

"Of course he would stand up for England," Mrs Grice felt herself compelled to admit.

"Then why the mischief doesn't he do so instead of running round after Americans?" Macarthy demanded.

"He doesn't run round after us; but we knew his sister, Lady Bolitho, in Rome. She is a most sweet woman and we saw a great deal of her; she took a great fancy to Agatha. I surmise that she mentioned us to him pretty often when she went back to England, and when he came abroad for his autumn holiday, as he calls it—he met us first in the Engadine, three or four weeks ago, and came down here with us—it seemed as if we already knew him and he knew us. He is very talented and he is quite well off."

"Mother," said Macarthy Grice, going close to the old lady and speaking very gravely, "why do you know so much about him? Why have you gone into it so?"

"I haven't gone into it; I only know what he has told us."

"But why have you given him the right to tell you? How does it concern you whether he is well off?"

The poor woman began to look flurried and scared. "My son, I have given him no right; I don't know what you mean. Besides, it wasn't he who told us he is well off; it was his sister."

"It would have been better if you hadn't known his sister," said the young man, gloomily.

"Gracious, Macarthy, we must know some one!" Mrs Grice rejoined, with a flicker of spirit.

"I don't see the necessity of your knowing the English."

"Why Macarthy, can't we even *know* them?" pleaded his mother.

"You see the sort of thing it gets you into."

"It hasn't got us into anything. Nothing has been done."

"So much the better, mother darling," said the young man. "In that case we will go on to Venice. Where is he going?"

"I don't know, but I suppose he won't come on to Venice if we don't ask him."

"I don't believe any delicacy would prevent him," Macarthy rejoined. "But he loathes me; that's an advantage."

"He *loathes* you—when he wanted so to know you?"

"Oh yes, I understand. Well, now he knows me! He knows he hates everything I like and I hate everything he likes."

"He doesn't imagine you hate your sister, I suppose!" said the old lady, with a little vague laugh.

"Mother," said Macarthy, still in front of her with his hands in his pockets, "I verily believe I should hate her if she were to marry him."

"Oh, gracious, my son, don't, don't!" cried Mrs Grice, throwing herself into his arms with a shudder of horror and burying her face on his shoulder.

Her son held her close and as he bent over her he went on: "Dearest mother, don't you see that we must remain together, that at any rate we mustn't be separated by different ideas, different associations and institutions? I don't believe any family has ever had more of the feeling that holds people closely together than we have had: therefore for heaven's sake let us keep it, let us find our happiness in it as we always have done. Of course Agatha will marry some day; but why need she marry in such a way as to make a gulf? You and she are all I have, and—I may be selfish—I should like very much to keep you."

"Of course I will let her know the way you feel," said the old lady, a moment later, rearranging her cap and her shawl and putting away her pocket-handkerchief.

"It's a matter she certainly ought to understand. She would wish to, unless she is very much changed," Macarthy added, as if he saw all this with high lucidity.

"Oh, she isn't changed—she'll never change!" his mother exclaimed, with rebounding optimism. She thought it wicked not to take cheerful views.

"She wouldn't if she were to marry an Englishman," he declared, as Mrs Grice left him to go to her daughter.

She told him an hour later that Agatha would be quite ready to start for Venice on the morrow and that she said he need have no fear that Sir Rufus Chasemore would follow them. He was naturally anxious to know from her what words she had had with Agatha, but the only very definite information he extracted was to the effect that the girl had declared with infinite feeling that she would never marry an enemy of her country. When he saw her later in the day he thought she had been crying; but there was nothing in her manner to show that she resented any pressure her mother might have

represented to her that he had put upon her or that she was
making a reluctant sacrifice. Agatha Grice was very fond of her
brother, whom she knew to be upright, distinguished and exceedingly mindful of the protection and support that he owed
her mother and herself. He was perverse and obstinate, but
she was aware that in essentials he was supremely tender, and
he had always been very much the most eminent figure in her
horizon.

No allusion was made between them to Sir Rufus Chasemore, though the silence on either side was rather a conscious
one, and they talked of the prospective pleasures of Venice
and of the arrangements Macarthy would be able to make in
regard to his mother's spending another winter in Rome. He
was to accompany them to Venice and spend a fortnight with
them there, after which he was to return to London to terminate his business and then take his way back to New York.
There was a plan of his coming to see them again later in the
winter, in Rome, if he should succeed in getting six weeks off.
As a man of energy and decision, though indeed of a somewhat irritable stomach, he made light of the Atlantic voyage:
it was a rest and a relief, alternating with his close attention to
business. That the disunion produced by the state of Mrs
Grice's health was a source of constant regret and even of
much depression to him was well known to his mother and
sister, who would not have broken up his home by coming
to live in Europe if he had not insisted upon it. Macarthy was
in the highest degree conscientious; he was capable of suffering the extremity of discomfort in a cause which he held to be
right. But his mother and sister *were* his home, all the same,
and in their absence he was perceptibly desolate. Fortunately
it had been hoped that a couple of southern winters would
quite set Mrs Grice up again and that then everything in
America would be as it had been before. Agatha's affection for
her brother was very nearly as great as his affection for herself; but it took the form of wishing that his loneliness might

be the cause of his marrying some thoroughly nice girl, inasmuch as after all her mother and she might not always be there. Fraternal tenderness in Macarthy's bosom followed a different logic. He was so fond of his sister that he had a secret hope that she would never marry at all. He had spoken otherwise to his mother, because that was the only way not to seem offensively selfish; but the essence of his thought was that on the day Agatha should marry she would throw him over. On the day she should marry an Englishman she would not throw him over—she would betray him. That is she would betray her country, and it came to the same thing. Macarthy's patriotism was of so intense a hue that to his own sense the national life and his own life flowed in an indistinguishable current.

The particular Englishman he had his eye upon now was not, as a general thing, visible before luncheon. He had told Agatha, who mentioned it to her brother, that in the morning he was immersed in work—in letter-writing. Macarthy wondered what his work might be, but did not condescend to inquire. He was enlightened however by happening by an odd chance to observe an allusion to Sir Rufus in a copy of the London *Times* which he took up in the reading-room of the hotel. This occurred in a letter to the editor of the newspaper, the writer of which accused Agatha's friend of having withheld from the public some information to which the public was entitled. The information had respect to "the situation in South Africa," and Sir Rufus was plainly an agent of the British government, the head of some kind of department or sub-department. This did not make Macarthy like him any better. He was displeased with the idea of England's possessing colonies at all and considered that she had acquired them by force and fraud and held them by a frail and unnatural tenure. It appeared to him that any man who occupied a place in this unrighteous system must have false, detestable views.

Sir Rufus Chasemore turned up on the terrace in the afternoon and bore himself with the serenity of a man unconscious of the damaging inferences that had been formed about him. Macarthy neither avoided him nor sought him out—he even relented a little toward him mentally when he thought of the loss he was about to inflict on him; but when the Englishman approached him and appeared to wish to renew their conversation of the evening before it struck him that he was wanting in delicacy. There was nothing strange in that however, for delicacy and tact were not the strong point of one's transatlantic cousins, with whom one had always to dot one's i's. It seemed to Macarthy that Sir Rufus Chasemore ought to have guessed that he cared little to keep up an acquaintance with him, though indeed the young American would have been at a loss to say how he was to guess it, inasmuch as he would have resented the imputation that he himself had been rude enough to make such a fact patent. The American ladies were in their apartments, occupied in some manner connected with their intended retreat, and there was nothing for Macarthy but to stroll up and down for nearly half an hour with the personage who was so provokingly the cause of it. It had come over him now that he should have liked extremely to spend several days on the lake of Como. The place struck him as much more delicious than it had done while he chafed the day before at the absence of his relations. He was angry with the Englishman for forcing him to leave it and still more angry with him for showing so little responsibility or even perception in regard to the matter. It occurred to him while he was in this humour that it might be a good plan to make himself so disagreeable that Sir Rufus would take to his heels and never reappear, fleeing before the portent of such an insufferable brother-in-law. But this plan demanded powers of execution which Macarthy did not flatter himself that he possessed: he felt that it was impossible to him to divest himself of his character of a polished American gentleman.

If he found himself dissenting from most of the judgments and opinions which Sir Rufus Chasemore happened to express

in the course of their conversation there was nothing perverse
in that: it was a simple fact apparently that the Englishman
had nothing in common with him and was predestined to
enunciate propositions to which it was impossible for him to
assent. Moreover how could he assent to propositions enun-
ciated in that short, offhand, clipping tone, with the words
running into each other and the voice rushing up and down
the scale? Macarthy, who spoke very slowly, with great distinctness and in general with great correctness, was annoyed
not only by his companion's intonation but by the odd and,
as it seemed to him, licentious application that he made of
certain words. He struck him as wanting in reverence for the
language, which Macarthy had an idea, not altogether unjust,
that he himself deeply cherished. He would have admitted
that these things were small and not great, but in the usual
relations of life the small things count more than the great,
and they sufficed at any rate to remind him of the essential
antipathy and incompatibility which he had always believed to
exist between an Englishman and an American. They were, in
the very nature of things, disagreeable to each other—both
mentally and physically irreconcilable. In cases where this
want of correspondence had been bridged over it was because
the American had made weak concessions, had been shame-
fully accommodating. That was a kind of thing the Englishman, to do him justice, never did; he had at least the courage
of his prejudices. It was not unknown to Macarthy that the
repugnance in question appeared to be confined to the American male, as was shown by a thousand international marriages,
which had transplanted as many of his countrywomen to unnatural British homes. That variation had to be allowed for,
and the young man felt that he was allowing for it when he
reflected that probably his own sister liked the way Sir Rufus
Chasemore spoke. In fact he was intimately convinced she
liked it, which was a reason the more for their quitting
Cadenabbia the next morning.

Sir Rufus took the opposite point of view quite as much as himself, only he took it gaily and familiarly and laughed about it, as if he were amused at the preferences his companion betrayed and especially amused that he should hold them so gravely, so almost gloomily. This sociable jocosity, as if they had known each other three months was what appeared to Macarthy so indelicate. They talked no politics and Sir Rufus said nothing more about America; but it stuck out of the Englishman at every pore that he was a resolute and consistent conservative, a prosperous, accomplished, professional, official Tory. It gave Macarthy a kind of palpitation to think that his sister had been in danger of associating herself with such arrogant doctrines. Not that a woman's political creed mattered; but that of her husband did. He had an impression that he himself was a passionate democrat, an unshrinking radical. It was a proof of how far Sir Rufus's manner was from being satisfactory to his companion that the latter was unable to guess whether he already knew of the sudden determination of his American friends to leave Cadenabbia or whether their intention was first revealed to him in Macarthy's casual mention of it, which apparently put him out not at all, eliciting nothing more than a frank, cheerful expression of regret. Macarthy somehow mistrusted a man who could conceal his emotions like that. How could he have known they were going unless Agatha had told him, and how could Agatha have told him, since she could not as yet have seen him? It did not even occur to the young man to suspect that she might have conveyed the unwelcome news to him by a letter. And if he had not known it why was he not more startled and discomfited when Macarthy dealt the blow? The young American made up his mind at last that the reason why Sir Rufus was not startled was that he had thought in advance it would be no more than natural that the newly-arrived brother should wish to spoil his game. But in that case why was he not angry with him for such a disposition? Why did he come after him

and insist on talking with him? There seemed to Macarthy
something impudent in this incongruity—as if to the mind of
an English statesman the animosity of a Yankee lawyer were
really of too little account.

III

IT may be intimated to the reader that Agatha Grice had written no note to her English friend, and she held no communication with him of any sort, till after she had left the table
d'hôte with her mother and brother in the evening. Sir Rufus
had seated himself at dinner in the same place as the night
before; he was already occupying it and he simply bowed to
her with a smile, from a distance, when she came into the
room. As she passed out to the terrace later with her companions he overtook her and said to her in a lower tone of
voice than usual that he had been exceedingly sorry to hear
that she was leaving Cadenabbia so soon. Was it really true?
could not they put it off a little? should not they find the
weather too hot in Venice and the mosquitoes too numerous?
Agatha saw that Sir Rufus asked these questions with the intention of drawing her away, engaging her in a walk, in some
talk to which they should have no listeners; and she resisted
him at first a little, keeping near the others because she had
made up her mind that morning in deep and solitary meditation that she would force him to understand that further
acquaintance could lead to nothing profitable for either party.
It presently came over her, however, that it would take some
little time to explain this truth and that the time might be
obtained by their walking a certain distance along the charming shore of the lake together. The windows of the hotel and
of the little water-side houses and villas projected over the
place long shafts of lamplight which shimmered on the water,

broken by the slow-moving barges laden with musicians, and gave the whole region the air of an illuminated garden surrounding a magnificent pond. Agatha made the further reflection that it would be only common kindness to give Sir Rufus an opportunity to say anything he wished to say; that is within the limits she was prepared to allow: they had been too good friends to separate without some of the forms of regret, without a backward look at least, since they might not enjoy a forward one. In short she had taken in the morning a resolution so virtuous, founded on so high and large a view of the whole situation, that she felt herself entitled to some reward, some present liberty of action. She turned away from her relatives with Sir Rufus—she observed that they paid no attention to her—and in a few moments she was strolling by his side at a certain distance from the hotel.

"I will tell you what I should like to do," he said, as they went; "I should like to turn up in Venice—about a week hence."

"I don't recommend you to do that," the girl replied, promptly enough; though as soon as she had spoken she bethought herself that she could give him no definite reason why he should not follow her; she could give him no reason at all that would not be singularly wanting in delicacy. She had a movement of vexation with her brother for having put her in a false position; it was the first, for in the morning when her mother repeated to her what Macarthy had said and she perceived all that it implied she had not been in the least angry with him—she sometimes indeed wondered why she was not —and she did not propose to become so for Sir Rufus Chasemore. What she had been was sad—touched too with a sense of horror—horror at the idea that she might be in danger of denying, under the influence of an insinuating alien, the pieties and sanctities in which she had been brought up. Sir Rufus *was* a tremendous conservative, though perhaps that did not matter so much, and he had let her know at an early stage of

their acquaintance that he had never liked Americans in the
least as a people. As it was apparent that he liked her—all
American and very American as she was—she had regarded
this shortcoming only in its minor bearings, and it had even
gratified her to form a private project of converting him to a
friendlier view. If she had not found him a charming man she
would not have cared what he thought about her countrypeople; but, as it happened, she did find him a charming man,
and it grieved her to see a mind that was really worthy of the
finest initiations (as regarded the American question) wasting
itself on poor prejudices. Somehow, by showing him how nice
she was herself she could make him like the people better with
whom she had so much in common, and as he admitted that
his observation of them had after all been very restricted she
would also make him know them better. This prospect drew
her on till suddenly her brother sounded the note of warning.
When it came she understood it perfectly; she could not pretend that she did not. If she were not careful she would give
her country away: in the privacy of her own room she had
coloured up to her hair at the thought. She had a lurid vision
in which the chance seemed to be greater that Sir Rufus Chasemore would bring her over to his side than that she should
make him like anything he had begun by disliking; so that she
resisted, with the conviction that the complications which
might arise from allowing a prejudiced Englishman to possess
himself, as he evidently desired to do, of her affections, would
be much greater than a sensitive girl with other loyalties to
observe might be able to manage. A moment after she had said
to her companion that she did not recommend him to come
to Venice she added that of course he was free to do as he
liked: only why should he come if he was sure the place was
so uncomfortable? To this Sir Rufus replied that it signified
little how uncomfortable it was if she should be there and that
there was nothing he would not put up with for the sake of a
few days more of her society.

"Oh, if it's for that you are coming," the girl replied, laughing and feeling nervous—feeling that something was in the air which she had wished precisely to keep out of it—"Oh, if it's for that you are coming you had very much better not take the trouble. You would have very little of my society. While my brother is with us all my time will be given up to him."

"Confound your brother!" Sir Rufus exclaimed. Then he went on: "You told me yourself he wouldn't be with you long. After he's gone you will be free again and you will still be in Venice, shan't you? I do want to float in a gondola with you."

"It's very possible my brother may be with us for weeks."

Sir Rufus hesitated a moment. "I see what you mean—that he won't leave you so long as I am about the place. In that case if you are so fond of him you ought to take it as a kindness of me to hover about." Before the girl had time to make a rejoinder to this ingenious proposition he added, "Why in the world has he taken such a dislike to me?"

"I know nothing of any dislike," Agatha said, not very honestly. "He has expressed none to me."

"He has to me then. He quite loathes me."

She was silent a little; then she inquired, "And do you like him very much?"

"I think he's immense fun! He's very clever, like most of the Americans I have seen, including yourself. I should like to show him I like him, and I have salaamed and kowtowed to him whenever I had a chance; but he won't let me get near him. Hang it, it's cruel!"

"It's not directed to you in particular, any dislike he may have. I have told you before that he doesn't like the English," Agatha remarked.

"Bless me—no more do I! But my best friends have been among them."

"I don't say I agree with my brother and I don't say I disagree with him," Sir Rufus's companion went on. "I have told you before that we are of Irish descent, on my mother's side. Her mother was a Macarthy. We have kept up the name and we have kept up the feeling."

"I see—so that even if the Yankee were to let me off the Paddy would come down! That's a most unholy combination. But you remember, I hope, what I have also told you— that I am quite as Irish as you can ever be. I had an Irish grandmother—a beauty of beauties, a certain Lady Laura Fitzgibbon, *qui vaut bien la vôtre.* A charming old woman she was."

"Oh, well, she wasn't of our kind!" the girl exclaimed, laughing.

"You mean that yours wasn't charming? In the presence of her granddaughter permit me to doubt it."

"Well, I suppose that those hostilities of race—transmitted and hereditary, as it were—are the greatest of all." Agatha Grice uttered this sage reflection by no means in the tone of successful controversy and with the faintest possible tremor in her voice.

"Good God! do you mean to say that an hostility of race, a legendary feud, is to prevent you and me from meeting again?" The Englishman stopped short as he made this inquiry, but Agatha continued to walk, as if that might help her to elude it. She had come out with a perfectly sincere determination to prevent Sir Rufus from saying what she believed he wanted to say, and if her voice had trembled just now it was because it began to come over her that her preventive measures would fail. The only tolerably efficacious one would be to turn straight round and go home. But there would be a rudeness in this course and even a want of dignity; and besides she did not wish to go home. She compromised by not answering her companion's question, and though she could not see him she was aware that he was looking after her with an expression in his face of high impatience momentarily baffled. She knew that expression and thought it handsome;

she knew all his expressions and thought them all handsome. He overtook her in a few moments and then she was surprised that he should be laughing as he exclaimed: "It's too absurd! —it's too absurd!" It was not long however before she understood the nature of his laughter, as she understood everything else. If she was nervous he was scarcely less so; his whole manner now expressed the temper of a man wishing to ascertain rapidly whether he may enjoy or must miss great happiness. Before she knew it he had spoken the words which she had flattered herself he should not speak; he had said that since there appeared to be a doubt whether they should soon meet again it was important he should seize the present occasion. He was very glad after all, because for several days he had been wanting to speak. He loved her as he had never loved any woman and he besought her earnestly to believe it. What was this crude stuff about disliking the English and disliking the Americans? what had questions of nationality to do with it any more than questions of ornithology? It was a question simply of being his wife, and that was rather between themselves, was it not? He besought her to consider it, as *he* had been turning it over from almost the first hour he met her. It was not in Agatha's power to go her way now, because he had laid his hand upon her in a manner that kept her motionless, and while he talked to her in low, kind tones, touching her face with the breath of supplication, she stood there in the warm darkness, very pale, looking as if she were listening to a threat of injury rather than to a declaration of love. "Of course I ought to speak to your mother," he said; "I ought to have spoken to her first. But your leaving at an hour's notice and apparently wishing to shake me off has given me no time. For God's sake give me your permission and I will do it to-night."

"Don't—don't speak to my mother," said Agatha, mournfully.

"Don't tell me to-morrow then that she won't hear of it!"

"She likes you, Sir Rufus," the girl rejoined, in the same singular, hopeless tone.

"I hope you don't mean to imply by that that you don't!"

"No; I like you of course; otherwise I should never have allowed myself to be in this position, because I hate it!" The girl uttered these last words with a sudden burst of emotion and an equally sudden failure of sequence, and turning round quickly began to walk in the direction from which they had come. Her companion, however, was again beside her, close to her, and he found means to prevent her from going as fast as she wished. History has lost the record of what at that moment he said to her; it was something that made her exclaim in a voice which seemed on the point of breaking into tears: "Please don't say that or anything like it again, Sir Rufus, or I shall have to take leave of you for ever this instant, on the spot." He strove to be obedient and they walked on a little in silence; after which she resumed, with a slightly different manner: "I am very sorry you have said this to-night. You have troubled and distressed me; it isn't a good time."

"I wonder if you would favour me with your idea of what might be a good time?"

"I don't know. Perhaps never. I am greatly obliged to you for the honour you have done me. I beg you to believe me when I say this. But I don't think I shall ever marry. I have other duties. I can't do what I like with my life."

At this Sir Rufus made her stop again, to tell him what she meant by such an extraordinary speech. What overwhelming duties had she, pray, and what restrictions upon her life that made her so different from other women? He could not, for his part, imagine a woman more free. She explained that she had her mother, who was terribly delicate and who must be her first thought and her first care. Nothing would induce her to leave her mother. She was all her mother had except Macarthy, and he was absorbed in his profession.

"What possible question need there be of your leaving

her?" the Englishman demanded. "What could be more delightful than that she should live with us and that we should take care of her together? You say she is so good as to like me, and I assure you I like *her*—most uncommonly."

"It would be impossible that we should take her away from my brother," said the girl, after an hesitation.

"Take her away?" And Sir Rufus Chasemore stood staring. "Well, if he won't look after her himself—you say he is so taken up with his work—he has no earthly right to prevent other people from doing so."

"It's not a man's business—it's mine—it's her daughter's."

"That's exactly what I think, and what in the world do I wish but to help you? If she requires a mild climate we will find some lovely place in the south of England and be as happy there as the day is long."

"So that Macarthy would have to come *there* to see his mother? Fancy Macarthy in the south of England—especially as happy as the day is long! He would find the day very long," Agatha Grice continued, with the strange little laugh which expressed—or rather which disguised—the mixture of her feelings. "He would never consent."

"Never consent to what? Is what you mean to say that he would never consent to your marriage? I certainly never dreamed that you would have to ask him. Haven't you defended to me again and again the freedom, the independence with which American girls marry? Where is the independence when it comes to your own case?" Sir Rufus Chasemore paused a moment and then he went on with bitterness: "Why don't you say outright that you are afraid of your brother? Miss Grice, I never dreamed that that would be your answer to an offer of everything that a man—and a man of some distinction, I may say, for it would be affectation in me to pretend that I consider myself a nonenity—can lay at the feet of a woman."

The girl did not reply immediately; she appeared to think

over intently what he had said to her, and while she did so she turned her white face and her charming serious eyes upon him. When at last she spoke it was in a very gentle, considerate tone. "You are wrong in supposing that I am afraid of my brother. How can I be afraid of a person of whom I am so exceedingly fond?"

"Oh, the two things are quite consistent," said Sir Rufus Chasemore, impatiently. "And is it impossible that I should ever inspire you with a sentiment which you would consent to place in the balance with this intense fraternal affection?" He had no sooner spoken those somewhat sarcastic words than he broke out in a different tone: "Oh Agatha, for pity's sake, don't make difficulties where there are no difficulties!"

"I don't make them; I assure you they exist. It is difficult to explain them, but I can see them, I can feel them. Therefore we mustn't talk this way any more. Please, please don't," the girl pursued, imploringly. "Nothing is possible to-day. Some day or other very likely there will be changes. Then we shall meet; then we shall talk again."

"I like the way you ask me to wait ten years. What do you mean by 'changes'? Before heaven, I shall never change," Sir Rufus declared.

Agatha Grice hesitated. "Well, perhaps you will like us better."

"Us? Whom do you mean by 'us'? Are you coming back to that beastly question of one's feelings—real or supposed it doesn't matter—about your great and glorious country? Good God, it's too monstrous! One tells a girl one adores her and she replies that she doesn't care so long as one doesn't adore her compatriots. What do you want me to do to them? What do you want me to say? I will say anything in the English language, or in the American, that you like. I'll say that they're the greatest of the great and have every charm and virtue under heaven. I'll go down on my stomach before them and remain there for ever. I can't do more than that!"

Whether this extravagant profession had the effect of making Agatha Grice ashamed of having struck that note in regard to her companion's international attitude, or whether her nerves were simply upset by his vehemence, his insistence, is more than I can say: what is certain is that her rejoinder to this last speech was a sudden burst of tears. They fell for a moment rapidly, soundlessly, but she was quicker still in brushing them away. "You may laugh at me or you may despise me," she said when she could speak, "and I daresay my state of mind is deplorably narrow. But I couldn't be happy with you if you hated my country."

"You would hate mine back and we should pass the live-liest, jolliest days!" returned the Englishman, gratified, soft-ened, enchanted by her tears. "My dear girl, what is a woman's country? It's her house and her garden, her children and her social world. You exaggerate immensely the difference which that part of the business makes. I assure you that if you were to marry me it would be the last thing you would find your-self thinking of. However, to prove how little I hate your country I am perfectly willing to go there and live with you."

"Oh, Sir Rufus Chasemore!" murmured Agatha Grice, protestingly.

"You don't believe me?"

She believed him not a bit and yet to hear him make such an offer was sweet to her, for it gave her a sense of the reality of his passion. "I shouldn't ask that—I shouldn't even like it," she said; and then he wished to know what she would like. "I should like you to let me go—not to press me, not to dis-tress me any more now. I shall think of everything—of course you know that. But it will take me a long time. That's all I can tell you now, but I think you ought to be content." He was obliged to say that he was content, and they resumed their walk in the direction of the hotel. Shortly before they reached it Agatha exclaimed with a certain irrelevance, "You ought to go there first; then you would know."

"Then I should know what?"

"Whether you would like it."

"Like your great country? Good Lord, what difference does it make whether I like it or not?"

"No—that's just it—you don't care," said Agatha; "yet you said to my brother that you wanted immensely to go."

"So I do; I am ashamed not to have been; that's an immense drawback to-day, in England, to a man in public life. Something has always stopped me off, tiresomely, from year to year. Of course I shall go the very first moment I can take the time."

"It's a pity you didn't go this year instead of coming down here," the girl observed, rather sententiously.

"I thank my stars I didn't!" he responded, in a very different tone.

"Well, I should try to make you like it," she went on. "I think it very probable I should succeed."

"I think it very probable you could do with me exactly whatever you might attempt."

"Oh, you hypocrite!" the girl exclaimed; and it was on this that she separated from him and went into the house. It soothed him to see her do so instead of rejoining her mother and brother, whom he distinguished at a distance sitting on the terrace. She had perceived them there as well, but she would go straight to her room; she preferred the company of her thoughts. It suited Sir Rufus Chasemore to believe that those thoughts would plead for him and eventually win his suit. He gave a melancholy, loverlike sigh, however, as he walked toward Mrs Grice and her son. He could not keep away from them, though he was so interested in being and appearing discreet. The girl had told him that her mother liked him, and he desired both to stimulate and to reward that inclination. Whatever he desired he desired with extreme definiteness and energy. He would go and sit down beside the little old lady (with whom hitherto he had no very direct conversation), and talk to her and be kind to her and amuse her. It must be added that he rather despaired of the success of these arts as he saw Macarthy Grice, on becoming aware of his approach, get up and walk away.

IV

"It sometimes seems to me as if he didn't marry on purpose to make me feel badly." That was the only fashion, as yet, in which Lady Chasemore had given away her brother to her husband. The words fell from her lips some five years after Macarthy's visit to the lake of Como—two years after her mother's death—a twelvemonth after her marriage. The same idea came into her mind—a trifle whimsically perhaps, only this time she forbore to express it—as she stood by her husband's side, on the deck of the steamer, half an hour before they reached the wharf at New York. Six years had elapsed between the scenes at Cadenabbia and their disembarkation in that city. Agatha knew that Macarthy would be on the wharf to meet them, and that he should be there alone was natural enough. But she had a prevision of their return with him—she also knew he expected that—to the house, so narrow but fortunately rather deep, in Thirty-seventh street, in which such a happy trio had lived in the old days before this unexpressed but none the less perceptible estrangement. As her marriage had taken place in Europe (Sir Rufus coming to her at Bologna, in the very midst of the Parliamentary session, the moment he heard, by his sister, of her mother's death: this was really the sign of devotion that had won her); as the ceremony of her nuptials, I say—a very simple one— had been performed in Paris, so that her absence from her native land had had no intermission, she had not seen the house since she left it with her mother for that remedial pilgrimage in the course of which poor Mrs Grice, travelling up from Rome in the spring, after her third winter there (two had been so far from sufficing), was to succumb, from one day to the other, to inflammation of the lungs. She saw it over again now, even before she left the ship, and felt in advance all that it would imply to find Macarthy living there as a bachelor, struggling with New York servants, unaided and unrelieved by the sister whose natural place might by many people have been thought to be the care of his establishment, as her natural reward would have been the honours of such a position. Lady Chasemore was prepared to feel pang upon pang when she should perceive how much less comfortably he lived than he would have lived if she had not quitted him. She knew that their second cousins in Boston, whose sense of duty was so terrible (even her poor mother, who never had a thought for herself, used to try as much as possible to conceal her life from them), considered that she had in a manner almost immoral deserted him for the sake of an English title. When they went ashore and drove home with Macarthy Agatha received exactly the impression she had expected: her brother's life struck her as bare, ungarnished, helpless, socially and domestically speaking. He had not the art of keeping house, naturally, and in New York, unless one were a good deal richer than he, it was very difficult to do that sort of thing by deputy. But Lady Chasemore made no further allusion to the idea that he remained single out of perversity. The situation was too serious for that or for any other flippant speech.

It was a delicate matter for the brothers-in-law to spend two or three weeks together; not however because when the moment for her own real decision came Macarthy had protested in vivid words against her marriage. By the time he arrived from America after his mother's death the Englishman was in possession of the field and it was too late to save her.

He had had the opportunity to show her kindness for which her situation made her extremely grateful—he had indeed rendered her services which Macarthy himself, though he knew they were the result of an interested purpose, could not but appreciate. When her brother met her in Paris he saw that she was already lost to him: she had ceased to struggle, she had accepted the fate of a Briton's bride. It appeared that she was much in love with her Briton—that was necessarily the end of it. Macarthy offered no opposition, and she would have liked it better if he had, as it would have given her a chance to put him in the wrong a little more than, formally at least, she had been able to do. He knew that she knew what he thought and how he felt, and there was no need of saying any more about it. No doubt he would not have accepted a sacrifice from her even if she had been capable of making it (there were moments when it seemed to her that even at the last, if he had appealed to her directly and with tenderness, she would have renounced); but it was none the less clear to her that he was deeply disappointed at her having found it in her heart to separate herself so utterly. And there was something in his whole attitude which seemed to say that it was not only from him that she separated herself, but from all her fellow-countrymen besides and from everything that was best and finest in American life. He regarded her marriage as an abjuration, an apostasy, a kind of moral treachery. It was of no use to say to him that she was doing nothing original or extraordinary, to ask him if he did not know that in England, at the point things had come to, American wives were as thick as blackberries, so that if she were doing wrong she was doing wrong with—well, almost the majority: for he had an answer to such cheap arguments, an answer according to which it appeared that the American girls who had done what she was about to do were notoriously poor specimens, the most frivolous and feather-headed young persons in the country. They had no conception of the great meaning of American institutions, no appreciation of their birthright, and they were doubtless very worthy recruits to a debauched and stultified aristocracy. The pity of Agatha's desertion was that *she* had been meant for better things, she had appreciated her birthright, or if she had not it had not been the fault of a brother who had taken so much pains to form her mind and character. The sentiment of her nationality had been cultivated in her; it was not a mere brute instinct or customary prejudice—it was a responsibility, a faith, a religion. She was not a poor specimen but a remarkably fine one; she was intelligent, she was clever, she was sensitive, she could understand difficult things and feel great ones.

Of course in those days of trouble in Paris, when it was arranged that she should be married immediately (as if there had really been an engagement to Sir Rufus from the night before their flight from Cadenabbia), of course she had had a certain amount of talk with Macarthy about the matter, and at such moments she had almost wished to drive him to protest articulately, so that she might as explicitly reassure him, endeavour to bring him round. But he had never said to her personally what he had said to her mother at Cadenabbia— what her mother, frightened and distressed, had immediately repeated to her. The most he said was that he hoped she was conscious of all the perfectly different and opposed things she and her husband would represent when they should find themselves face to face. He hoped she had measured in advance the strain that might arise from the fact that in so many ways her good would be his evil, her white his black and *vice versâ*— the fact in a word that by birth, tradition, convictions, she was the product of a democratic society, while the very breath of Sir Rufus's nostrils was the denial of human equality. She had replied, "Oh yes, I have thought of everything;" but in reality she had not thought that she was in any very aggressive manner a democrat or even that she had a representative function. She had not thought that Macarthy in his innermost

soul was a democrat either; and she had even wondered what
would happen if in regard to some of those levelling theories
he had suddenly been taken at his word. She knew however
that nothing would have made him more angry than to hint
that anything could happen which would find him unprepared, and she was ashamed to repudiate the opinions, the
general character her brother attributed to her, to fall below
the high standard he had set up for her. She had moreover no
wish to do so. She was well aware that there were many things
in English life that she should not like, and she was never a
more passionate American than the day she married Sir Rufus
Chasemore.

To what extent she remained one an observer of the deportment of this young lady would at first have had considerable
difficulty in judging. The question of the respective merits of
the institutions of the two countries came up very little in her
life. Her husband had other things to think of than the great
republic beyond the sea, and her horizon, social and political,
had practically the same large but fixed line as his. Sir Rufus
was immersed in politics and in administrative questions; but
these things belonged wholly to the domestic field; they were
embodied in big blue-books with terrible dry titles (Agatha
had tried conscientiously to acquaint herself with the contents
of some of them), which piled themselves up on the table of
his library. The conservatives had come into power just after
his marriage, and he had held honourable though not super-
eminent office. His duties had nothing to do with foreign
relations; they were altogether of an economical and statistical
kind. He performed them in a manner which showed perhaps
that he was conscious of some justice in the reproach usually
addressed to the Tories—the taunt that they always came to
grief in the department of industry and finance. His wife was
sufficiently in his confidence to know how much he had it at
heart to prove that a conservative administration could be
strong in ciphering. He never spoke to her of her own

country—they had so many other things to talk about—but if there was nothing in his behaviour to betray the assumption that she had given it up, so on the other hand there was nothing to show that he doubted of her having done so. What he had said about a woman's country being her husband and children, her house and garden and visiting list, was very considerably verified; for it was certain that her ladyship's new career gave her, though she had no children, plenty of occupation. Even if it had not however she would have found a good deal of work to her hand in loving her husband, which she continued to do with the most commendable zeal. He seemed to her a very magnificent person, bullying her not half so much as she expected. There were times when it even occurred to her that he really did not bully her enough, for she had always had an idea that it would be agreeable to be subjected to this probation by some one she should be very fond of.

After they had been married a year he became a permanent official, in succession to a gentleman who was made a peer on his retirement from the post to which Sir Rufus was appointed. This gave Lady Chasemore an opportunity to reflect that she might some day be a peeress, it being reasonable to suppose that the same reward would be meted out to her husband on the day on which, in the fulness of time and of credit, he also should retire. She was obliged to admit to herself that the reflection was unattended with any sense of horror; it exhilarated her indeed to the point of making her smile at the contingency of Macarthy's finding himself the brother of a member of the aristocracy. As a permanent official her husband was supposed to have no active political opinions; but she could not flatter herself that she perceived any diminution of his conservative zeal. Even if she had done so it would have made little difference, for it had not taken her long to discover that she had married into a tremendous Tory "set"—a set in which people took for granted she had feelings that she was not prepared to publish on the housetops. It was scarcely worth while however to explain at length that she had not been brought up in that way, partly because the people would not have understood and partly because really after all they did not care. How little it was possible in general to care her career in England helped her in due time to discover. The people who cared least appeared to be those who were most convinced that everything in the national life was going to the dogs. Lady Chasemore was not struck with this tendency herself; but if she had been the belief would have worried her more than it seemed to worry her friends. She liked most of them extremely and thought them very kind, very easy to live with; but she liked London much better than the country, rejoiced much when her husband's new post added to the number of months he would have annually to spend there (they ended by being there as much as any one), and had grave doubts as to whether she would have been able to "stand" it if her lot had been cast among those members of her new circle who lived mainly on their acres.

All the same, though what she had to bear she bore very easily, she indulged in a good deal of private meditation on some of the things that failed to catch her sympathy. She did not always mention them to her husband, but she always intended to mention them. She desired he should not think that she swallowed his country whole, that she was stupidly undiscriminating. Of course he knew that she was not stupid and of course also he knew that she could not fail to be painfully impressed by the misery and brutality of the British populace. She had never anywhere else seen anything like that. Of course, furthermore, she knew that Sir Rufus had given and would give in the future a great deal of thought to legislative measures directed to elevating gradually the condition of the lower orders. It came over Lady Chasemore at times that it would be well if some of these measures might arrive at maturity with as little delay as possible.

The night before she quitted England with her husband they slept at an hotel at Liverpool, in order to embark early on the morrow. Sir Rufus went out to attend to some business and, the evening being very close, she sat at the window of their sitting-room and looked out on a kind of square which stretched in front of the hotel. The night was muggy, the window was open and she was held there by a horrible fascination. Dusky forms of vice and wretchedness moved about in the stuffy darkness, visions of grimy, half-naked, whining beggary hovered before her, curses and the sound of blows came to her ears; there were young girls, frousy and violent, who evidently were drunk, as every one seemed to be, more or less, which was little wonder, as four public-houses flared into the impure night, visible from where Lady Chasemore sat, and they appeared to be gorged with customers, half of whom were women. The impression came back to her that the horrible place had made upon her and upon her mother when they landed in England years before, and as she turned from the window she liked to think that she was going to a country where, at any rate, there would be less of that sort of thing. When her husband came in he said it was of course a beastly place but much better than it used to be—which she was glad to hear. She made some allusion to the confidence they might have that they should be treated to no such scenes as that in *her* country: whereupon he remonstrated, jocosely expressing a hope that they should not be deprived of a glimpse of the celebrated American drinks and bar-room fights.

It must be added that in New York he made of his brother-in-law no inquiry about these phenomena—a reserve, a magnanimity keenly appreciated by his wife. She appreciated altogether the manner in which he conducted himself during their visit to the United States and felt that if she had not already known that she had married a perfect gentleman the fact would now have been revealed to her. For she had to

make up her mind to this, that after all (it was vain to shut
one's eyes to it) Sir Rufus personally did not like the United
States: he did not like them yet he made an immense effort to
behave as if he did. She was grateful to him for that; it
assuaged her nervousness (she was afraid there might be
"scenes" if he should break out with some of his displeasures);
so grateful that she almost forgot to be disappointed at the
failure of her own original intent, to be distressed at seeing or
rather at guessing (for he was reserved about it even to her),
that a nearer view of American institutions had not had the
effect which she once promised herself a nearer view should
have. She had married him partly to bring him over to an
admiration of her country (she had never told any one this,
for she was too proud to make the confidence to an English
person and if she had made it to an American the answer
would have been so prompt, "What on earth does it signify
what he thinks of it?" no one, of course, being obliged to
understand that it might signify to *her*); she had united herself to Sir Rufus in this missionary spirit and now not only
did her proselyte prove unamenable but the vanity of her
enterprise became a fact of secondary importance. She wondered a little that she did not suffer more from it, and this is
partly why she rejoiced that her husband kept most of his
observations to himself: it gave her a pretext for not being
ashamed. She had flattered herself before that in general he
had the manners of a diplomatist (she did not suspect that this
was not the opinion of all his contemporaries), and his behaviour during the first few weeks at least of their stay in the
western world struck her as a triumph of diplomacy. She had
really passed from caring whether he disliked American manners to caring primarily whether he showed he disliked them
—a transition which on her own side she was very sensible it
was important to conceal from Macarthy. To love a man who
could feel no tenderness for the order of things which had
encompassed her early years and had been intimately mixed

with her growth, which was a part of the conscience, the piety of many who had been most dear to her and whose memory would be dear to her always—that was an irregularity which was after all shut up in her own breast, where she could trust her dignity to get some way or other the upper hand of it. But to be pointed at as having such a problem as that on one's back was quite another affair; it was a kind of exposure of one's sanctities, a surrender of private judgment. Lady Chasemore had by this time known her husband long enough to enter into the logic of his preferences; if he disliked or disapproved what he saw in America his reasons for doing so had ceased to be a mystery. They were the very elements of his character, the joints and vertebration of his general creed. All the while she was absent from England with him (it was not very long, their whole tour, including the two voyages, being included in ten weeks), she knew more or less the impression that things would have made upon him; she knew that both in the generals and in the particulars American life would have gone against his grain, contradicted his traditions, violated his taste.

V

ALL the same he was determined to see it thoroughly, and this is doubtless one of the reasons why after the first few days she cherished the hope that they should be able to get off at the end without any collision with Macarthy. Of course it was to be taken into account that Macarthy's own demeanour was much more that of a man of the world than she had ventured to hope. He appeared for the time almost to have smothered his national consciousness, which had always been so acute, and to have accepted his sister's perfidious alliance. She could see that he was delighted that she should be near him again—

so delighted that he neglected to look for the signs of corruption in her or to manifest any suspicion that in fact, now that she was immersed in them again, she regarded her old associations with changed eyes. So, also, if she had not already been aware of how much Macarthy was a gentleman she would have seen it from the way he rose to the occasion. Accordingly they were all superior people and all was for the best in Lady Chasemore's simple creed. Her brother asked her no questions whatever about her life in England, but his letters had already enlightened her as to his determination to avoid that topic. They had hitherto not contained a single inquiry on the subject of her occupations and pursuits, and if she had been domiciled in the moon he could not have indulged in less reference to public or private events in the British islands. It was a tacit form of disapprobation of her being connected with that impertinent corner of the globe; but it had never prevented her from giving him the fullest information on everything he never asked about. He never took up her allusions, and when she poured forth information to him now in regard to matters concerning her life in her new home (on these points she was wilfully copious and appealing), he listened with a sort of exaggerated dumb deference, as if she were reciting a lesson and he must sit quiet till she should come to the end. Usually when she stopped he simply sighed, then directed the conversation to something as different as possible. It evidently pleased him however to see that she enjoyed her native air and her temporary reunion with some of her old familiars. This was a graceful inconsistency on his part: it showed that he had not completely given her up. Perhaps he thought Sir Rufus would die and that in this case she would come back and live in New York. She was careful not to tell him that such a calculation was baseless, that with or without Sir Rufus she should never be able to settle in her native city as Lady Chasemore. He was scrupulously polite to Sir Rufus, and this personage asked Agatha why he never by any chance addressed him save by his title. She could see what her husband meant, but even in the privacy of the conjugal chamber she was loyal enough to Macarthy not to reply, "Oh, it's a mercy he doesn't say simply 'Sir!'"

The English visitor was prodigiously active; he desired to leave nothing unexplored, unattempted; his purpose was to inspect institutions, to collect statistics, to talk with the principal people, to see the workings of the political machine, and Macarthy acquitted himself scrupulously, even zealously, in the way of giving him introductions and facilities. Lady Chasemore reflected with pleasure that it was in her brother's power to do the honours of his native land very completely. She suspected indeed that as he did not like her husband (he *couldn't* like him, in spite of Sir Rufus's now comporting himself so sweetly), it was a relief to him to pass him on to others —to work him off, as it were, into penitentiaries and chambers of commerce. Sir Rufus's frequent expeditions to these establishments and long interviews with local worthies of every kind kept him constantly out of the house and removed him from contact with his host, so that as Macarthy was extremely busy with his own profession (Sir Rufus was greatly struck with the way he worked; he had never seen a gentleman work so hard, without any shooting or hunting or fishing), it may be said, though it sounds odd, that the two men met very little directly—met scarcely more than in the evening or in other words always in company. During the twenty days the Chasemores spent together in New York they either dined out or were members of a party given at home by Macarthy, and on these occasions Sir Rufus found plenty to talk about with his new acquaintance. His wife flattered herself he was liked, he was so hilarious and so easy. He had a very appreciative manner, but she really wished sometimes that he might have subdued his hilarity a little; there were moments when perhaps it looked as if he took everything in the United States as if it were more than all else amusing. She knew exactly how it must privately affect Macarthy, this implication that it was merely a comical country; but after all it was not very easy to say how Macarthy would have preferred that a stranger, or that Sir Rufus in particular, should take the great republic. A cheerful view, yet untinged by the sense of drollery—that would have been the right thing if it could have been arrived at. At all events (and this was something gained), if Sir Rufus was in his heart a pessimist in regard to things he did not like he was not superficially sardonic. And then he asked questions by the million; and what was curiosity but an homage?

It will be inferred, and most correctly, that Macarthy Grice was not personally in any degree for his brother-in-law the showman of the exhibition. He caused him to be conducted, but he did not conduct him. He listened to his reports of what he had seen (it was at breakfast mainly that these fresh intimations dropped from Sir Rufus's lips), with very much the same cold patience (as if he were civilly forcing his attention) with which he listened to Agatha's persistent anecdotes of things that had happened to her in England. Of course with Sir Rufus there could be no question of persistence; he cared too little whether Macarthy cared or not and he did not stick to this everlasting subject of American institutions either to entertain him or to entertain himself—all he wanted was to lead on to further researches and discoveries. Macarthy always met him with the same response, "Oh, So-and-So is the man to tell you all about that. If you wish I will give you a letter to him." Sir Rufus always wished and certainly Macarthy wrote a prodigious number of letters. The inquiries and conclusions of his visitor (so far as Sir Rufus indulged in the latter) all bore on special points; he was careful to commit himself to no crude generalisations. He had to remember that he had still the rest of the country to see, and after a little discussion (which was confined to Lady Chasemore and her husband) it was decided that he should see it without his wife, who would await his return among her friends in New York.

This arrangement was much to her taste, but it gives again the
measure of the degree to which she had renounced her early
dream of interpreting the western world to Sir Rufus. If she
was not to be at his side at the moment, on the spot, of course
she could not interpret—he would get a tremendous start of
her. In short by staying quietly with Macarthy during his
absence she almost gave up the great advantage she had
hitherto had of knowing more about America than her husband could. She liked however to feel that she was making a
sacrifice—making one indeed both to Sir Rufus and to her
brother. The idea of giving up something for Macarthy (she
only wished it had been something more) did her great good
—sweetened the period of her husband's absence.

The whole season had been splendid, but at this moment
the golden days of the Indian summer descended upon the
shining city and steeped it in a kind of fragrant haze. For two
or three weeks New York seemed to Lady Chasemore
poetical; the marble buildings looked yellow in the sleeping
sunshine and her native land exhibited for the occasion an
atmosphere. Vague memories came back to her of her younger
years, of things that had to do somehow with the blurred
brightness of the late autumn in the country. She walked
about, she walked irresponsibly for hours; she did not care, as
she had to care in London. She met friends in the streets and
turned and walked with them; and pleasures as simple as this
acquired an exaggerated charm for her. She liked walking and
as an American girl had indulged the taste freely; but in London she had no time but to drive—besides which there were
other tiresome considerations. Macarthy came home from his
office earlier and she went to meet him in Washington Square
and walked up the Fifth Avenue with him in the rich afternoon. It was many years since she had been in New York and
she found herself taking a kind of relapsing interest in changes
and improvements. There were houses she used to know,
where friends had lived in the old days and where they lived

no more (no one in New York seemed to her to live where they used to live), which reminded her of incidents she had long ago forgotten, incidents that it pleased and touched her now to recall. Macarthy became very easy and sociable; he even asked her a few questions about her arrangements and habits in England and struck her (though she had never been particularly aware of it before) as having a great deal of the American humour. On one occasion he stayed away from work altogether and took her up the Hudson, on the steamer, to West Point—an excursion in which she found a peculiar charm. Every day she lunched intimately with a dozen ladies, at the house of one or other of them.

In due time Sir Rufus returned from Canada, the Mississippi, the Rocky Mountains and California; he had achieved marvels in the way of traversing distances and seeing manners and men with rapidity and facility. Everything had been settled in regard to their sailing for England almost directly after his return; there were only to be two more days in New York, then a rush to Boston, followed by another rush to Philadelphia and Washington. Macarthy made no inquiry whatever of his brother-in-law touching his impression of the great West; he neglected even to ask him if he had been favourably impressed with Canada. There would not have been much opportunity however, for Sir Rufus on his side was extremely occupied with the last things he had to do. He had not even time as yet to impart his impressions to his wife, and she forbore to interrogate him, feeling that the voyage close at hand would afford abundant leisure for the history of his adventures. For the moment almost the only light that he threw upon them was by saying to Agatha (not before Macarthy) that it was a pleasure to him to see a handsome woman again, as he had not had that satisfaction in the course of his travels. Lady Chasemore wondered, exclaimed, protested, eliciting from him the declaration that to his sense, and in the interior at least, the beauty of the women was, like a great many other things, a gigantic American fraud. Sir Rufus had looked for it in vain—he went so far as to say that he had, in the course of extensive wanderings about the world, seen no female type on the whole less to his taste than that of the ladies in whose society, in hundreds (there was no paucity of specimens), in the long, hot, heaving trains, he had traversed a large part of the American continent. His wife inquired whether by chance he preferred the young persons they had (or at least she had) observed at Liverpool the night before their departure; to which he replied that they were no doubt sad creatures, but that the looks of a woman mattered only so long as one lived with her, and he did not live, and never should live, with the daughters of that grimy seaport. With the women in the American cars he had been living—oh, tremendously! and they were deucedly plain. Thereupon Lady Chasemore wished to know whether he did not think Mrs Eugene had beauty, and Mrs Ripley, and her sister Mrs Redwood, and Mrs Long, and several other ornaments of the society in which they had mingled during their stay in New York. "Mrs Eugene is Mrs Eugene and Mrs Redwood is Mrs Redwood," Sir Rufus retorted; "but the women in the cars weren't either, and all the women I saw were like the women in the cars."—"Well, there may be something in the cars," said Lady Chasemore, pensively; and she mentioned that it was very odd that during her husband's absence, as she roamed about New York, she should have made precisely the opposite reflection and been struck with the number of pretty faces. "Oh, pretty faces, pretty faces, I daresay!" But Sir Rufus had no time to develop this vague rejoinder.

When they came back from Washington to sail Agatha told her brother that he was going to write a book about America: it was for this he had made so many inquiries and taken so many notes. She had not known it before; it was only while they were in Washington that he told her he had made up his mind to it. Something he saw or heard in Washington

appeared to have brought this resolution to a point. Lady
Chasemore privately thought it rather a formidable fact; her
husband had startled her a good deal in announcing his intention. She had said, "Of course it will be friendly—you'll say
nice things?" And he had replied, "My poor child, they will
abuse me like a pickpocket." This had scarcely been reassuring, so that she had had it at heart to probe the question
further, in the train, after they left Washington. But as it
happened, in the train, all the way, Sir Rufus was engaged in
conversation with a Democratic Congressman whom he had
picked up she did not know how—very certainly he had not
met him at any respectable house in Washington. They sat in
front of her in the car, with their heads almost touching, and
although she was a better American than her husband she
should not have liked hers to be so close to that of the Democratic Congressman. Now of course she knew that Sir Rufus
was taking in material for his book. This idea made her uncomfortable and she would have liked immensely to separate
him from his companion—she scarcely knew why, after all,
except that she could not believe the Representative represented anything very nice. She promised herself to ascertain
thoroughly, after they should be comfortably settled in the
ship, the animus with which the book was to be written.
She was a very good sailor and she liked to talk at sea; there
her husband would not be able to escape from her, and she
foresaw the manner in which she should catechise him. It
exercised her greatly in advance and she was more agitated
than she could easily have expressed by the whole question of
the book. Meanwhile, however, she was careful not to show
her agitation to Macarthy. She referred to her husband's project as casually as possible, and the reason she referred to it
was that this seemed more loyal—more loyal to Macarthy. If
the book, when written, should attract attention by the severity of its criticism (and that by many qualities it would attract
attention of the widest character Lady Chasemore could not

doubt), she should feel more easy not to have had the air of concealing from her brother that such a work was in preparation, which would also be the air of having a bad conscience about it. It was to prove, both to herself and Macarthy, that she had a good conscience that she told him of Sir Rufus's design. The habit of detachment from matters connected with his brother-in-law's activity was strong in him; nevertheless he was not able to repress some sign of emotion—he flushed very perceptibly. Quickly, however, he recovered his appearance of considering that the circumstance was one in which he could not hope to interest himself much; though the next moment he observed, with a certain inconsequence, "I am rather sorry to hear it."

"Why are you sorry?" asked Agatha. She was surprised and indeed gratified that he should commit himself even so far as to express regret. What she had supposed he would say, if he should say anything, was that he was obliged to her for the information, but that if it was given him with any expectation that he might be induced to read the book he must really let her know that such an expectation was extremely vain. He could have no more affinity with Sir Rufus's printed ideas than with his spoken ones.

"Well, it will be rather disagreeable for you," he said, in answer to her question. "Unless indeed you don't care what he says."

"But I do care. The book will be sure to be very able. Do you mean if it should be severe—that would be disagreeable for me? Very certainly it would; it would put me in a false, in a ridiculous position, and I don't see how I should bear it," Lady Chasemore went on, feeling that her candour was generous and wishing it to be. "But I shan't allow it to be severe. To prevent that, if it's necessary, I will write every word of it myself."

She laughed as she took this vow, but there was nothing in Macarthy's face to show that *he* could lend himself to a

mirthful treatment of the question. "I think an Englishman had
better look at home," he said, "and if he does so I don't easily
see how the occupation should leave him any leisure or any
assurance for reading lectures to other nations. The self-com-
placency of your husband's countrymen is colossal, imperturbable. Therefore, with the tight place they find themselves
in to-day and with the judgment of the rest of the world upon
them being what it is, it's grotesque to see them still sitting in
their old judgment-seat and pronouncing upon the short-
comings of people who are full of the life that has so long
since left *them*." Macarthy Grice spoke slowly, mildly, with a
certain dryness, as if he were delivering himself once for all
and would not return to the subject. The quietness of his
manner made the words solemn for his sister, and she stared
at him a moment, wondering, as if they pointed to strange
things which she had hitherto but imperfectly apprehended.

"The judgment of the rest of the world—what is that?"

"Why, that they are simply finished; that they don't
count."

"Oh, a nation must count which produces such men as my
husband," Agatha rejoined, with another laugh. Macarthy
was on the point of retorting that it counted as the laughing-
stock of the world (that of course was something), but he
checked himself and she moreover checked him by going on:
"Why Macarthy, you ought to come out with a book yourself about the English. You would steal my husband's
thunder."

"Nothing would induce me to do anything of the sort; I
pity them too much."

"You pity them?" Lady Chasemore exclaimed. "It would
amuse my husband to hear that."

"Very likely, and it would be exactly a proof of what is so
pitiable—the contrast between their gross pretensions and the
real facts of their condition. They have pressing upon them
at once every problem, every source of weakness, every

danger that can threaten the life of a people, and they have nothing to meet the situation with but their classic stupidity."

"Well, that has been useful to them before," said Lady Chasemore, smiling. Her smile was a little forced and she coloured as her brother had done when she first spoke to him. She found it impossible not to be impressed by what he said and yet she was vexed that she was, because this was far from her desire.

He looked at her as if he saw some warning in her face and continued: "Excuse my going so far. In this last month that we have spent together so happily for me I had almost forgotten that you are one of them."

Lady Chasemore said nothing—she did not deny that she was one of them. If her husband's country was denounced—after all he had not written his book yet—she felt as if such a denial would be a repudiation of one of the responsibilities she had taken in marrying him.

VI

THE postman was at the door in Grosvenor Crescent when she came back from her drive; the servant took the letters from his hand as she passed into the house. In the hall she stopped to see which of the letters were for her; the butler gave her two and retained those that were for Sir Rufus. She asked him what orders Sir Rufus had given about his letters and he replied that they were to be forwarded up to the following night. This applied only to letters, not to parcels, pamphlets and books. "But would he wish this to go, my lady?" the man asked, holding up a small packet; he added that it appeared to be a kind of document. She took it from him: her eye had caught a name printed on the wrapper and though she made no great profession of literature she recognised the name as

that of a distinguished publisher and the packet as a roll of
proof-sheets. She turned it up and down while the servant
waited; it had quite a different look from the bundles of
printed official papers which the postman was perpetually
leaving and which, when she scanned the array on the hall-
table in her own interest, she identified even at a distance.
They were certainly the sheets, at least the first, of her husband's book—those of which he had said to her on the
steamer, on the way back from New York a year before, "My
dear child, when I tell you that you shall see them—every
page of them—that you shall have complete control of them!"
Since she was to have complete control of them she began
with telling the butler not to forward them—to lay them on
the hall-table. She went upstairs to dress—she was dining out
in her husband's absence—and when she came down to re-
enter her carriage she saw the packet lying where it had been
placed. So many months had passed that she had ended by
forgetting that the book was on the stocks; nothing had happened to remind her of it. She had believed indeed that it was
not on the stocks and even that the project would die a
natural death. Sir Rufus would have no time to carry it out—
he had returned from America to find himself more than ever
immersed in official work—and if he did not put his hand to it
within two or three years at the very most he would never do
so at all, for he would have lost the freshness of his impressions, on which the success of the whole thing would
depend. He had his notes of course, but none the less a delay
would be fatal to the production of the volume (it was to be
only a volume and not a big one), inasmuch as by the time it
should be published it would have to encounter the objection that everything changed in America in two or three
years and no one wanted to know anything about a dead past.

Such had been the reflections with which Lady Chasemore
consoled herself for the results of those inquiries she had
promised herself, in New York, to make when once she

should be ensconced in a sea-chair by her husband's side and
which she had in fact made to her no small discomposure.
Meanwhile apparently he had stolen a march upon her, he
had put his hand to *The Modern Warning* (that was to be the
title, as she had learned on the ship), he had worked at it in
his odd hours, he had sent it to the printers and here were the
first-fruits of it. Had he had a bad conscience about it—was that
the reason he had been so quiet? She did not believe much in
his bad conscience, for he had been tremendously, formidably
explicit when they talked the matter over; had let her know
as fully as possible what he intended to do. Then it was that
he relieved himself, that in the long, unoccupied hours of their
fine voyage (he was in wonderful "form" at sea) he took her
into the confidence of his real impressions—made her understand how things had struck him in the United States. They
had not struck him well; oh no, they had not struck him well
at all! But at least he had prepared her and therefore since then
he had nothing to hide. It was doubtless an accident that he
appeared to have kept his work away from her, for sometimes, in other cases, he had paid her intelligence the compliment (was it not for that in part he had married her?) of supposing that she could enter into it. It was probable that in this
case he had wanted first to see for himself how his chapters
would look in print. Very likely even he had not written the
whole book, nor even half of it; he had only written the
opening pages and had them "set up": she remembered to
have heard him speak of this as a very convenient system. It
would be very convenient for her as well and she should also
be much interested in seeing how they looked. On the table,
in their neat little packet, they seemed half to solicit her, half
to warn her off.

They were still there of course when she came back from
her dinner, and this time she took possession of them. She
carried them upstairs and in her dressing-room, when she had
been left alone in her wrapper, she sat down with them under

the lamp. The packet lay in her lap a long time, however, before she decided to detach the envelope. Her hesitation came not from her feeling in any degree that this roll of printed sheets had the sanctity of a letter, a seal that she might not discreetly break, but from an insurmountable nervousness as to what she might find within. She sat there for an hour, with her head resting on the back of her chair and her eyes closed; but she had not fallen asleep—Lady Chasemore was very wide-awake indeed. She was living for the moment in a kind of concentration of memory, thinking over everything that had fallen from her husband's lips after he began, as I have said, to relieve himself. It turned out that the opinion he had formed of the order of society in the United States was even less favourable than she had had reason to fear. There were not many things it would have occurred to him to commend, and the few exceptions related to the matters that were not most characteristic of the country—not idiosyncrasies of American life. The idiosyncrasies he had held to be one and all detestable. The whole spectacle was a vivid warning, a consummate illustration of the horrors of democracy. The only thing that had saved the misbegotten republic as yet was its margin, its geographical vastness; but that was now discounted and exhausted. For the rest every democratic vice was in the ascendant and could be studied there *sur le vif;* he could not be too thankful that he had not delayed longer to go over and master the subject. He had come back with a head full of lessons and a heart fired with the resolve to enforce them upon his own people, who, as Agatha knew, had begun to move in the same lamentable direction. As she listened to him she perceived the mistake she had made in not going to the West with him, for it was from that part of the country that he had drawn his most formidable anecdotes and examples. Of these he produced a terrific array; he spoke by book, he overflowed with facts and figures, and his wife felt herself submerged by the deep, bitter waters. She even felt what a pity it was that she had not dragged him away from that vulgar little legislator whom he had stuck to so in the train, coming from Washington; yet it did not matter—a little more or a little less—the whole affair had rubbed him so the wrong way, exasperated his taste, confounded his traditions. He proved to have disliked quite unspeakably things that she supposed he liked, to have suffered acutely on occasions when she thought he was really pleased. It would appear that there had been no occasion, except once sitting at dinner between Mrs Redwood and Mrs Eugene, when he was really pleased. Even his long chat with the Pennsylvania representative had made him almost ill at the time. His wife could be none the less struck with the ability which had enabled him to absorb so much knowledge in so short a time; he had not only gobbled up facts, he had arranged them in a magnificent order, and she was proud of his being so clever even when he made her bleed by the way he talked. He had had no intention whatever of this, and he was as much surprised as touched when she broke out into a passionate appeal to him not to publish such horrible misrepresentations. She defended her country with exaltation, and so far as was possible in the face of his own flood of statistics, of anecdotes of "lobbying," of the corruption of public life, for which she was unprepared, endeavouring to gainsay him in the particulars as well as in the generals, she maintained that he had seen everything wrong, seen it through the distortion of prejudice, of a hostile temperament, in the light—or rather in the darkness—of wishing to find weapons to worry the opposite party in England. Of course America had its faults, but on the whole it was a much finer country than any other, finer even than his clumsy, congested old England, where there was plenty to do to sweep the house clean, if he would give a little more of his time to that. Scandals for scandals she had heard more since she came to England than all the years she had lived at home. She forbore to quote Macarthy to him (she had reasons for not

doing so), but something of the spirit of Macarthy flamed up
in her as she spoke.

Sir Rufus smiled at her vehemence; he took it in perfectly
good part, though it evidently left him not a little astonished.
He had forgotten that America was hers—that she had any
allegiance but the allegiance of her marriage. He had made her
his own and, being the intense Englishman that he was, it had
never occurred to him to doubt that she now partook of his
quality in the same degree as himself. He had assimilated her,
as it were, completely, and he had assumed that she had also
assimilated him and his country with him—a process which
would have for its consequence that the other country, the
ugly, vulgar, importunate one, would be, as he mentally
phrased it to himself, "shunted." That it had not been was the
proof of rather a morbid sensibility, which tenderness and
time would still assuage. Sir Rufus was tender, he reassured
his wife on the spot, in the first place by telling her that she
knew nothing whatever about the United States (it was
astonishing how little many of the people in the country itself
knew about them), and in the second by promising her that
he would not print a word to which her approval should not
be expressly given. She should countersign every page before
it went to press, and none should leave the house without her
visé. She wished to know if he possibly could have forgotten
—so strange would it be—that she had told him long ago, at
Cadenabbia, how horrible it would be to her to find herself
married to a man harbouring evil thoughts of her fatherland.
He remembered this declaration perfectly and others that had
followed it, but was prepared to ask if she on her side recol-
lected giving him notice that she should convert him into an
admirer of transatlantic peculiarities. She had had an excellent
opportunity, but she had not carried out her plan. He had been
passive in her hands, she could have done what she liked with
him (had not he offered, that night by the lake of Como, to
throw up his career and go and live with her in some beastly

American town? and he had really meant it—upon his honour he had!), so that if the conversion had not come off whose fault was it but hers? She had not gone to work with any sort of earnestness. At all events now it was too late; he had seen for himself—the impression was made. Two points were vivid beyond the others in Lady Chasemore's evocation of the scene on the ship; one was her husband's insistence on the fact that he had not the smallest animosity to the American people, but had only his own English brothers in view, wished only to protect and save them, to point a certain moral as it never had been pointed before; the other was his pledge that nothing should be made public without her assent.

As at last she broke the envelope of the packet in her lap she wondered how much she should find to assent to. More perhaps than a third person judging the case would have expected; for after what had passed between them Sir Rufus must have taken great pains to tone down his opinions—or at least the expression of them.

VII

HE came back to Grosvenor Place the next evening very late and on asking for his wife was told that she was in her apartments. He was furthermore informed that she was to have dined out but had given it up, countermanding the carriage at the last moment and despatching a note instead. On Sir Rufus's asking if she were ill it was added that she had seemed not quite right and had not left the house since the day before. A minute later he found her in her own sitting-room, where she appeared to have been walking up and down. She stopped when he entered and stood there looking at him; she was in her dressing-gown, very pale, and she received him without a smile. He went up to her, kissed her, saw something strange in her eyes and asked with eagerness if she had been suffering. "Yes, yes," she said, "but I have not been ill," and the next moment flung herself upon his neck and buried her face there, sobbing yet at the same time stifling her sobs. Inarticulate words were mingled with them and it was not till after a moment he understood that she was saying, "How could you? ah, how *could* you?" He failed to understand her allusion, and while he was still in the dark she recovered herself and broke away from him. She went quickly to a drawer and possessed herself of a parcel of papers which she held out to him, this time without meeting his eyes. "Please take them away—take them away for ever. It's your book—the things from the printers. I saw them on the table—I guessed what they were—I opened them to see. I read them—I read them. Please take them away."

He had by this time become aware that even though she had flung herself upon his breast his wife was animated by a spirit of the deepest reproach, an exquisite sense of injury. When he first saw the papers he failed to recognise his book: it had not been in his mind. He took them from her with an exclamation of wonder, accompanied by a laugh which was meant in kindness, and turned them over, glancing at page after page. Disconcerted as he was at the condition in which Agatha presented herself he was still accessible to that agreeable titillation which a man feels on seeing his prose "set up." Sir Rufus had been quoted and reported by the newspapers and had put into circulation several little pamphlets, but this was his first contribution to the regular literature of his country, and his publishers had given him a very handsome page. Its striking beauty held him a moment; then his eyes passed back to his wife, who with her grand, cold, wounded air was also very handsome. "My dear girl, do you think me an awful brute? have I made you ill?" he asked. He declared that he had no idea he had gone so far as to shock her—he had left out such a lot; he had tried to keep the sting out of everything; he had made it all butter and honey. But he begged her not to get into a state; he would go over the whole thing with her if she liked—make any changes she should require. It would spoil the book, but he would rather do that than spoil her perfect temper. It was in a highly jocular manner that he made this allusion to her temper, and it was impressed upon her that he was not too much discomposed by her discomposure to be able to joke. She took notice of two things: the first of which was that he had a perfectly good conscience and that no accusing eye that might have been turned upon him would have made him change colour. He had no sense that he had broken faith with her, and he really thought his horrible book was very mild. He spoke the simple truth in saying that for her sake he had endeavoured to qualify his strictures, and strange as it might appear he honestly believed he had succeeded. Later, at other times, Agatha wondered what he would have written if he had felt himself free. What she observed in the second place was that though he saw she was much upset he did not in the least sound the depth of her distress or, as she herself would have said, of her shame. He never would—he never would; he could not enter into her feelings, because he could not believe in them; they could only strike him as exaggerated and factitious. He had given her a country, a magnificent one, and why in the name of common sense was she making him a scene about another? It was morbid—it was mad.

When he accused her of this extravagance it was very simple for her to meet his surprise with a greater astonishment—astonishment at his being able to allow so little for her just susceptibility. He could not take it seriously that she had American feelings; he could not believe that it would make a terrible difference in her happiness to go about the world as the wife, the cynical, consenting wife of the author of a blow dealt with that brutality at a breast to which she owed filial honour. She did not say to him that she should never hold her

head up before Macarthy again (her strength had been that
hitherto, as against Macarthy, she was perfectly straight), but
it was in a great degree the prefigurement of her brother's
cold, lifelong scorn that had kindled in her, while she awaited
her husband's return, the passion with which she now protested. He would never read *The Modern Warning* but he
would hear all about it; he would meet it in the newspapers,
in every one's talk; the very voices of the air would distil the
worst pages into his ear and make the scandal of her participation even greater than—as heaven knew—it would deserve
to be. She thought of the month of renewed association, of
happy, pure impressions that she had spent a year before in
the midst of American kindness, in the midst of memories
more innocent than her visions of to-day; and the effect of this
retrospect was galling in the face of her possible shame.
Shame—shame: she repeated that word to Sir Rufus in a tone
which made him stare, as if it dawned upon him that her reason
was perhaps deserting her. That shame should attach itself
to his wife in consequence of any behaviour of *his* was an idea
that he had to make a very considerable effort to embrace; and
while his candour betrayed it his wife was touched even
through her resentment by seeing that she had not made him
angry. He thought she was strangely unreasonable, but he was
determined not to fall into that vice on his own side. She was
silent about Macarthy because Sir Rufus had accused her
before her marriage of being afraid of him, and she had then
resolved never again to incur such a taunt; but before things
had gone much further between them she reminded her husband that she had Irish blood, the blood of the people, in her
veins and that he must take that into account in measuring the
provocation he might think it safe to heap upon her. She was
far from being a fanatic on this subject, as he knew; but when
America was made out to be an object of holy horror to virtuous England she could not but remember that millions of
her Celtic cousins had found refuge there from the blessed

English dispensation and be struck with his recklessness in
challenging comparisons which were better left to sleep.

When his wife began to represent herself as Irish Sir Rufus
evidently thought her "off her head" indeed: it was the first
he had heard of it since she communicated the mystic fact to
him on the lake of Como. Nevertheless he argued with her for
half an hour as if she were sane, and before they separated he
made her a liberal concession, such as only a perfectly lucid
mind would be able to appreciate. This was a simple indulgence, at the end of their midnight discussion; it was not dic-
tated by any recognition of his having been unjust; for though
his wife reiterated this charge with a sacred fire in her eyes
which made them more beautiful than he had ever known
them he took his stand, in his own stubborn opinion, too
firmly upon piles of evidence, revelations of political fraud
and corruption, and the "whole tone of the newspapers"—
to speak only of that. He remarked to her that clearly he must
simply give way to her opposition. If she were going to suffer
so inordinately it settled the question. The book should not
be published and they would say no more about it. He would
put it away, he would burn it up and *The Modern Warning*
should be as if it had never been. Amen! amen! Lady Chasemore accepted this sacrifice with eagerness, although her husband (it must be added) did not fail to place before her the
exceeding greatness of it. He did not lose his temper, he was
not petulant nor spiteful, he did not throw up his project and
his vision of literary distinction in a huff; but he called her
attention very vividly and solemnly to the fact that in defer-
ring to the feelings she so uncompromisingly expressed he
renounced the dream of rendering a signal service to his
country. There was a certain bitterness in his smile as he told
her that *her* wish was the only thing in the world that could
have made him throw away such a golden opportunity. The
rest of his life would never offer him such another; but
patriotism might go to the dogs if only it were settled that she

should not have a grudge. He did not care what became of poor old England if once that precious result were obtained; poor old England might pursue impure delusions and rattle down hill as fast as she chose for want of the word his voice would have spoken—really inspired as he held it to be by the justice of his cause.

Lady Chasemore flattered herself that they did not drop the subject that night in acrimony; there was nothing of this in the long kiss which she took from her husband's lips, with wet eyes, with a grateful, comprehensive murmur. It seemed to her that nothing could be fairer or finer than their mutual confidence; her husband's concession was gallant in the extreme; but even more than this was it impressed upon her that her own affection was perfect, since it could accept such a renunciation without a fear of the aftertaste. She had been in love with Sir Rufus from the day he sought her hand at Cadenabbia, but she was never so much in love with him as during the weeks that immediately followed his withdrawal of his book. It was agreed between them that neither of them would speak of the circumstance again, but she at least, in private, devoted an immense deal of meditation to it. It gave her a tremendous reprieve, lifted a nightmare off her breast, and that in turn gave her freedom to reflect that probably few men would have made such a graceful surrender. She wanted him to understand, or at any rate she wanted to understand herself, that in all its particulars too she thoroughly appreciated it; if he really was unable to conceive how she could feel as she did, it was all the more generous of him to comply blindly, to take her at her word, little as he could make of it. It did not become less obvious to Lady Chasemore, but quite the contrary, as the weeks went on, that *The Modern Warning* would have been a masterpiece of its class. In her room, that evening, her husband had told her that the best of him intellectually had gone into it, that he believed he had uttered certain truths there as they never would be uttered again—contributed his grain of gold to the limited sum of human wisdom. He had done something to help his country, and then—to please her—he had undone it. Above all it was delightful to her that he had not been sullen or rancorous about it, that he never made her pay for his magnanimity. He neither sighed nor scowled nor took on the air of a domestic martyr; he came and went with his usual step and his usual smile, remaining to all appearance the same fresh-coloured, decided, accomplished high official.

Therefore it is that I find it difficult to explain how it was that Lady Chasemore began to feel at the end of a few months that their difficulties had after all not become the mere reminiscence of a flurry, making present security more deep. What if the flurry continued impalpably, insidiously, under the surface? She thought there had been no change, but now she suspected that there was at least a difference. She had read Tennyson and she knew the famous phrase about the little rift within the lute. It came back to her with a larger meaning, it haunted her at last, and she asked herself whether when she accepted her husband's relinquishment it had been her happiness and his that she staked and threw away. In the light of this fear she struck herself as having lived in a fool's paradise —a misfortune from which she had ever prayed to be delivered. She wanted in every situation to know the worst, and in this case she had not known it; at least she knew it only now, in the shape of the formidable fact that Sir Rufus's outward good manners misrepresented his real reaction. At present she began anxiously, broodingly to take this reaction for granted and to see signs of it in the very things which she had regarded at first as signs of resignation. She secretly watched his face; she privately counted his words. When she began to do this it was no very long time before she made up her mind that the latter had become much fewer—that Sir Rufus talked to her very much less than he had done of old. He took no revenge, but he was cold, and in his coldness there was something horribly inevitable. He looked at her less and less, whereas formerly his eyes had had no more agreeable occupation. She tried to teach herself that her suspicions were woven of air and were an offence to a just man's character; she remembered that Sir Rufus had told her she was morbid, and if the charge had not been true at the time it might very well be true now. But the effect of this reflection was only to suggest to her that Sir Rufus himself was morbid and that her behaviour had made him so. It was the last thing that would be in his nature, but she had subjected that nature to an injurious strain. He was feeling it now; he was feeling that he had failed in the duty of a good citizen: a good citizen being what he had ever most earnestly proposed to himself to be. Lady Chasemore pictured to herself that his cheek burned for this when it was turned away from her—that he ground his teeth with shame in the watches of the night. Then it came over her with unspeakable bitterness that there had been no real solution of their difficulty; that it was too great to be settled by so simple an arrangement as that—an arrangement too primitive for a complicated world. Nothing was less simple than to bury one's gold and live without the interest.

It is a singular circumstance, and suggesting perhaps a perversion of the imagination under the influence of distress, but Lady Chasemore at this time found herself thinking with a kind of baffled pride of the merits of *The Modern Warning* as a literary composition, a political essay. It would have been dreadful for her, but at least it would have been superb, and that was what was naturally enough present to the defeated author as he tossed through the sleepless hours. She determined at last to question him, to confess her fears, to make him tell her whether his weakness—if he considered it a weakness—really did rankle; though when he made the sacrifice months before (nearly a year had come round) he had let her know that he wished the subject buried between them for evermore. She approached it with some trepidation, and the

manner in which he looked at her as she stammered out her
inquiry was not such as to make the effort easier. He waited
in silence till she had expressed herself as she best could,
without helping her, without showing that he guessed her
trouble, her need to be assured that he did not feel her to have
been cruel. Did he?—*did* he? that was what she wanted to be
certain of. Sir Rufus's answer was in itself a question; he
demanded what she meant by imputing to him such hypocrisy, such bad faith. What did she take him for and what
right had he given her to make a new scene, when he flattered
himself the last pretext had been removed? If he had been
dissatisfied she might be very sure he would have told her so;
and as he had not told her she might pay him the compliment
to believe he was honest. He expressed the hope—and for the
first time in his life he was stern with her—that this would be
the last endeavour on her part to revive an odious topic. His
sternness was of no avail; it neither wounded her nor comforted her; it only had the effect of making her perfectly sure
that he suffered and that he regarded himself as a kind of
traitor. He was one more in the long list of those whom a
woman had ruined, who had sold themselves, sold their
honour and the commonwealth, for a fair face, a quiet life, a
show of tears, a bribe of caresses. The vision of this smothered
pain, which he tried to carry off as a gentleman should, only
ministered to the love she had ever borne him—the love that
had had the power originally to throw her into his arms in the
face of an opposing force. As month followed month all her
nature centred itself in this feeling; she loved him more than
ever and yet she had been the cause of the most tormenting
thing that had ever happened to him. This was a tragic contradiction, impossible to bear, and she sat staring at it with
tears of rage.

One day she had occasion to tell him that she had received
a letter from Macarthy, who announced that he should soon
sail for Europe, even intimated that he should spend two or

three weeks in London. He had been overworked, it was years since he had had a proper holiday, and the doctor threatened him with nervous prostration unless he very soon broke off everything. His sister had a vision of his reason for offering to let her see him in England; it was a piece of appreciation on Macarthy's part, a reward for their having behaved—that is, for Sir Rufus's having behaved, apparently under her influence—better than might have been expected. He had the good taste not to bring out his insolent book, and Macarthy gave this little sign, the most mollified thing he had done as yet, that he noticed. If Lady Chasemore had not at this moment been thinking of something else it might have occurred to her that nervous prostration, in her brother's organism, had already set in. The prospect of his visit held Sir Rufus's attention very briefly, and in a few minutes Agatha herself ceased to dwell upon it. Suddenly, illogically, fantastically, she could not have told why, at that moment and in that place, for she had had no such intention when she came into the room, she broke out: "My own darling, do you know what has come over me? I have changed entirely—I see it differently; I want you to publish that grand thing." And she stood there smiling at him, expressing the transformation of her feeling so well that he might have been forgiven for not doubting it.

Nevertheless he did doubt it, especially at first. But she repeated, she pressed, she insisted; once she had spoken in this sense she abounded and overflowed. It went on for several days (he had begun by refusing to listen to her, for even in touching the question she had violated his express command), and by the end of a week she persuaded him that she had really come round. She was extremely ingenious and plausible in tracing the process by which she had done so, and she drew from him the confession (they kissed a great deal after it was made) that the manuscript of *The Modern Warning* had not been destroyed at all, but was safely locked up in a cabinet, together with the interrupted proofs. She doubtless placed her tergiversation in a more natural light than her biographer has been able to do: he however will spare the reader the exertion of following the impalpable clue which leads to the heart of the labyrinth. A month was still to elapse before Macarthy would show himself, and during this time she had the leisure and freedom of mind to consider the sort of face with which she should meet him, her husband having virtually promised that he would send the book back to the printers. Now, of course, she renounced all pretension of censorship; she had nothing to do with it; it might be whatever he liked; she gave him formal notice that she should not even look at it after it was printed. It was his affair altogether now—it had ceased to be hers. A hard crust had formed itself in the course of a year over a sensibility that was once so tender; this she admitted was very strange, but it would be stranger still if (with the value that he had originally set upon his opportunity) he should fail to feel that he might hammer away at it. In this case would not the morbidness be quite on *his* side? Several times, during the period that preceded Macarthy's arrival, Lady Chasemore saw on the table in the hall little packets which reminded her of the roll of proofs she had opened that evening in her room. Her courage never failed her, and an observer of her present relations with her husband might easily have been excused for believing that the solution which at one time appeared so illusory was now valid for earthly purposes. Sir Rufus was immensely taken up with the resumption of his task; the revision of his original pages went forward the more rapidly that in fact, though his wife was unaware of it, they had repeatedly been in his hands since he put them away. He had retouched and amended them, by the midnight lamp, disinterestedly, platonically, hypothetically; and the alterations and improvements which suggest them-selves when valuable ideas are laid by to ripen, like a row of pears on a shelf, started into life and liberty. Sir Rufus was as

happy as a man who after having been obliged for a long time
to entertain a passion in secret finds it recognised and legitimated, finds that the obstacles are removed and he may
conduct his beloved to the altar.

Nevertheless when Macarthy Grice alighted at the door of
his sister's house—he had assented at the last to her urgent
request that he would make it his habitation during his stay in
London—he stepped into an atmosphere of sudden alarm and
dismay. It was late in the afternoon, a couple of hours before
dinner, and it so happened that Sir Rufus drove up at the
moment the American traveller issued from the carriage that
had been sent for him. The two men exchanged greetings on
the steps of the house, but in the next breath Macarthy's host
asked what had become of Agatha, whether she had not gone
to the station to meet him, as she had announced at noon,
when Sir Rufus saw her last, that she intended.

It appeared that she had not accompanied the carriage;
Macarthy had been met only by one of the servants, who had
been with the Chasemores to America and was therefore in a
position to recognise him. This functionary said to Sir Rufus
that her ladyship had sent him down word an hour before the
carriage started that she had altered her intention and he was
to go on without her. By this time the door of the house had
been thrown open; the butler and the other footman had come
to the front. They had not, however, their usual perpendicular
demeanour, and the master's eye immediately saw that there
was something wrong in the house. This apprehension was
confirmed by the butler on the instant, before he had time to
ask a question. "We are afraid her ladyship is ill, sir; rather
seriously, sir; we have but this moment discovered it, sir; her
maid is with her, sir, and the other women."

Sir Rufus started; he paused but a single instant, looking
from one of the men to the other. Their faces were very white;
they had a strange, scared expression. "What do you mean
by rather seriously?—what the devil has happened?" But he

had sprung to the stairs—he was half-way up before they could answer.

"You had better go up, sir, really," said the butler to Macarthy, who was planted there and had turned as white as himself. "We are afraid she has taken something."

"Taken something?"

"By mistake, sir, you know, sir," quavered the footman, looking at his companion. There were tears in the footman's eyes. Macarthy felt sick.

"And there's no doctor? You don't send? You stand gaping?"

"We are going, sir—we have already gone!" cried both the men together. "He'll come from the hospital, round the corner; he'll be here by the time you're upstairs. It was but this very moment, sir, just before you rang the bell," one of them went on. The footman who had come with Macarthy from Euston dashed out of the house and he himself followed the direction his brother-in-law had taken. The butler was with him, saying he didn't know what—that it was only while they were waiting—that it would be a stroke for Sir Rufus. He got before him, on the upper landing; he led the way to Lady Chasemore's room, the door of which was open, revealing a horrible hush and, beyond the interior, a flurried, gasping flight of female domestics. Sir Rufus was there, he was at the bed still; he had cleared the room; two of the women had remained, they had hold of Lady Chasemore, who lay there passive, with a lifeless arm that caught Macarthy's eye—calling her, chafing her, pushing each other, saying that she would come to in a minute. Sir Rufus had apparently been staring at his wife in stupefaction and horror, but as Macarthy came to the bed he caught her up in his arms, pressing her to his bosom, and the American visitor met his face glaring at him over her shoulder, convulsed and transformed. "She has taken something, but only by mistake:" he was conscious that the butler was saying that again, behind him, in his ear.

"By God, you have killed her! it's *your* infernal work!" cried Sir Rufus, in a voice that matched his terrible face.

"*I* have killed her?" answered Macarthy, bewildered and appalled.

"Your damned fantastic opposition—the fear of meeting you," Sir Rufus went on. But his words lost themselves, as he bent over her, in violent kisses and imprecations, in demands whether nothing could be done, why the doctor was not there; in clumsy passionate attempts to arouse, to revive.

"Oh, I am sure she wanted you to come. She was very well this morning, sir," the waiting-maid broke out, to Macarthy, contradicting Sir Rufus in her fright and protesting again that it was nothing, that it was a faint, for the very pleasure, that her ladyship would come round. The other woman had picked up a little phial. She thrust it at Macarthy with the boldness of their common distress, and as he took it from her mechanically he perceived that it was empty and had a strange odour. He sniffed it—then with a shout of horror flung it away. He rushed at his sister and for a moment almost had a struggle with her husband for the possession of her body, in which, as soon as he touched it, he felt the absence of life. Then she was on the bed again, beautiful, irresponsive, inanimate, and they were both beside her for an instant, after which Sir Rufus broke away and staggered out of the room. It seemed an eternity to Macarthy while he waited, though it had already come over him that he was waiting only for something still worse. The women talked, tried to tell him things; one of them said something about the pity of his coming all the way from America on purpose. Agatha was beautiful; there was no disfigurement. The butler had gone out with Sir Rufus and he came back with him, reappearing first, and with the doctor. Macarthy did not even heed what the doctor said. By this time he knew it all for himself. He flung himself into a chair, overwhelmed, covering his face with the cape of his ulster. The odour of the little phial was in his nostrils. He let the doctor lead him out without resistance, scarcely with consciousness, after some minutes.

Lady Chasemore had taken something—the doctor gave it a name—but it was not by mistake. In the hall, downstairs, he stood looking at Macarthy, kindly, soothingly, tentatively, with his hand on his shoulder. "Had she—a—had she some domestic grief?" Macarthy heard him ask. He could not stay in the house—not with Chasemore. The servant who had brought him from the station took him to an hotel, with his luggage, in the carriage, which was still at the door—a horrible hotel where, in a dismal, dingy back room, with chimney-pots outside, he spent a night of unsurpassable anguish. He could not understand, and he howled to himself, "Why, *why*, just now?" Sir Rufus, in the other house, had exactly such another vigil: it was plain enough that this was the case when, the next morning, he came to the hotel. He held out his hand to Macarthy—he appeared to take back his monstrous words of the evening before. He made him return to Grosvenor Crescent; he made him spend three days there, three days during which the two men scarcely exchanged a word. But the rest of the holiday that Macarthy had undertaken for the benefit of his health was passed upon the Continent, with little present evidence that he should find what he had sought. *The Modern Warning* has not yet been published, but it may still appear. This doubtless will depend upon whether, this time, the sheets have really been destroyed—buried in Lady Chasemore's grave or only put back into the cabinet.

A LONDON LIFE

I

IT was raining, apparently, but she didn't mind—she would put on stout shoes and walk over to Plash. She was restless and so fidgety that it was a pain; there were strange voices that frightened her—they threw out the ugliest intimations—in the empty rooms at home. She would see old Mrs Berrington, whom she liked because she was so simple, and old Lady Davenant, who was staying with her and who was interesting for reasons with which simplicity had nothing to do. Then she would come back to the children's tea—she liked even better the last half-hour in the schoolroom, with the bread and butter, the candles and the red fire, the little spasms of confidence of Miss Steet the nursery-governess, and the society of Scratch and Parson (their nicknames would have made you think they were dogs) her small, magnificent nephews, whose flesh was so firm yet so soft and their eyes so charming when they listened to stories. Plash was the dower-house and about a mile and a half, through the park, from Mellows. It was not raining after all, though it had been; there was only a grayness in the air, covering all the strong, rich green, and a pleasant damp, earthy smell, and the walks were smooth and hard, so that the expedition was not arduous.

The girl had been in England more than a year, but there were some satisfactions she had not got used to yet nor ceased to enjoy, and one of these was the accessibility, the convenience of the country. Within the lodge-gates or without them it seemed all alike a park—it was all so intensely "property." The very name of Plash, which was quaint and old, had not lost its effect upon her, nor had it become indifferent to her that the place was a dower-house—the little red-walled, ivied asylum to which old Mrs Berrington had retired when, on his father's death, her son came into the estates. Laura Wing thought very ill of the custom of the expropriation of the widow in the evening of her days, when honour and abundance should attend her more than ever; but her condemnation of this wrong forgot itself when so many of the consequences looked right—barring a little dampness: which was the fate sooner or later of most of her unfavourable judgments of English institutions. Iniquities in such a country somehow always made pictures; and there had been dower-houses in the novels, mainly of fashionable life, on which her later childhood was fed. The iniquity did not as a general thing prevent these retreats from being occupied by old ladies with wonderful reminiscences and rare voices, whose reverses had not deprived them of a great deal of becoming hereditary lace. In the park, half-way, suddenly, Laura stopped, with a pain—a moral pang—that almost took away her breath; she looked at the misty glades and the dear old beeches (so familiar they were now and loved as much as if she owned them); they seemed in their unlighted December bareness conscious of all the trouble, and they made her conscious of all the change. A year ago she knew nothing, and now she knew almost everything; and the worst of her knowledge (or at least the worst of the fears she had raised upon it) had come to her in that beautiful place, where everything was so full of peace and purity, of the air of happy submission to immemorial law. The place was the same but her eyes were different: they had seen such sad, bad things in so short a time. Yes, the time was short and everything was strange. Laura Wing was too uneasy even to sigh, and as she walked on she lightened her tread almost as if she were going on tiptoe.

At Plash the house seemed to shine in the wet air—the tone of the mottled red walls and the limited but perfect lawn to be the work of an artist's brush. Lady Davenant was in the drawing-room, in a low chair by one of the windows, reading the second volume of a novel. There was the same look of crisp chintz, of fresh flowers wherever flowers could be put, of a wall-paper that was in the bad taste of years before, but had been kept so that no more money should be spent, and was almost covered over with amateurish drawings and superior engravings, framed in narrow gilt with large margins. The room had its bright, durable, sociable air, the air that Laura Wing liked in so many English things—that of being meant for daily life, for long periods, for uses of high decency. But more than ever to-day was it incongruous that such an habitation, with its chintzes and its British poets, its well-worn carpets and domestic art—the whole aspect so unmeretricious and sincere—should have to do with lives that were not right. Of course however it had to do only indirectly, and the wrong life was not old Mrs Berrington's nor yet Lady Davenant's. If Selina and Selina's doings were not an implication of such an interior any more than it was for them an explication, this was because she had come from so far off, was a foreign element altogether. Yet it was there she had found her occasion, all the influences that had altered her so (her sister had a theory that she was metamorphosed, that when she was young she seemed born for innocence) if not at Plash at least at Mellows, for the two places after all had ever so much in common, and there were rooms at the great house that looked remarkably like Mrs Berrington's parlour.

Lady Davenant always had a head-dress of a peculiar style, original and appropriate—a sort of white veil or cape which came in a point to the place on her forehead where her smooth hair began to show and then covered her shoulders. It was always exquisitely fresh and was partly the reason why she struck the girl rather as a fine portrait than as a living person. And yet she was full of life, old as she was, and had been made finer, sharper and more delicate, by nearly eighty years of it.

It was the hand of a master that Laura seemed to see in her face, the witty expression of which shone like a lamp through the ground-glass of her good breeding; nature was always an artist, but not so much of an artist as that. Infinite knowledge the girl attributed to her, and that was why she liked her a little fearfully. Lady Davenant was not as a general thing fond of the young or of invalids; but she made an exception as regards youth for the little girl from America, the sister of the daughter-in-law of her dearest friend. She took an interest in Laura partly perhaps to make up for the tepidity with which she regarded Selina. At all events she had assumed the general responsibility of providing her with a husband. She pretended to care equally little for persons suffering from other forms of misfortune, but she was capable of finding excuses for them when they had been sufficiently to blame. She expected a great deal of attention, always wore gloves in the house and never had anything in her hand but a book. She neither embroidered nor wrote—only read and talked. She had no special conversation for girls but generally addressed them in the same manner that she found effective with her contemporaries. Laura Wing regarded this as an honour, but very often she didn't know what the old lady meant and was ashamed to ask her. Once in a while Lady Davenant was ashamed to tell. Mrs Berrington had gone to a cottage to see an old woman who was ill—an old woman who had been in her service for years, in the old days. Unlike her friend she was fond of young people and invalids, but she was less interesting to Laura, except that it was a sort of fascination to wonder how she could have such abysses of placidity. She had long cheeks and kind eyes and was devoted to birds; somehow she always made Laura think secretly of a tablet of fine white soap—nothing else was so smooth and clean.

"And what's going on *chez vous*—who is there and what are they doing?" Lady Davenant asked, after the first greetings.

"There isn't any one but me—and the children—and the governess."

"What, no party—no private theatricals? How do you live?"

"Oh, it doesn't take so much to keep me going," said Laura. "I believe there were some people coming on Saturday, but they have been put off, or they can't come. Selina has gone to London."

"And what has she gone to London for?"

"Oh, I don't know—she has so many things to do."

"And where is Mr Berrington?"

"He has been away somewhere; but I believe he is coming back to-morrow—or next day."

"Or the day after?" said Lady Davenant. "And do they never go away together?" she continued after a pause.

"Yes, sometimes—but they don't come back together."

"Do you mean they quarrel on the way?"

"I don't know what they do, Lady Davenant—I don't understand," Laura Wing replied, with an unguarded tremor in her voice. "I don't think they are very happy."

"Then they ought to be ashamed of themselves. They have got everything so comfortable—what more do they want?"

"Yes, and the children are such dears!"

"Certainly—charming. And is she a good person, the present governess? Does she look after them properly?"

"Yes—she seems very good—it's a blessing. But I think she's unhappy too."

"Bless us, what a house! Does she want some one to make love to her?"

"No, but she wants Selina to see—to appreciate," said the young girl.

"And doesn't she appreciate—when she leaves them that way quite to the young woman?"

"Miss Steet thinks she doesn't notice how they come on—she is never there."

"And has she wept and told you so? You know they are always crying, governesses—whatever line you take. You shouldn't draw them out too much—they are always looking for a chance. She ought to be thankful to be let alone. You mustn't be too sympathetic—it's mostly wasted," the old lady went on.

"Oh, I'm not—I assure you I'm not," said Laura Wing. "On the contrary, I see so much about me that I don't sympathise with."

"Well, you mustn't be an impertinent little American either!" her interlocutress exclaimed. Laura sat with her for half an hour and the conversation took a turn through the affairs of Plash and through Lady Davenant's own, which were visits in prospect and ideas suggested more or less directly by them as well as by the books she had been reading, a heterogeneous pile on a table near her, all of them new and clean, from a circulating library in London. The old woman had ideas and Laura liked them, though they often struck her as very sharp and hard, because at Mellows she had no diet of that sort. There had never been an idea in the house, since she came at least, and there was wonderfully little reading. Lady Davenant still went from country-house to country-house all winter, as she had done all her life, and when Laura asked her she told her the places and the people she probably should find at each of them. Such an enumeration was much less interesting to the girl than it would have been a year before: she herself had now seen a great many places and people and the freshness of her curiosity was gone. But she still cared for Lady Davenant's descriptions and judgments, because they were the thing in her life which (when she met the old woman from time to time) most represented talk—the rare sort of talk that was not mere chaff. That was what she had dreamed of before she came to England, but in Selina's set the dream had not come true. In Selina's set people only harried each other from morning till night with extravagant accusations—

it was all a kind of horse-play of false charges. When Lady Davenant was accusatory it was within the limits of perfect verisimilitude.

Laura waited for Mrs Berrington to come in but she failed to appear, so that the girl gathered her waterproof together with an intention of departure. But she was secretly reluctant, because she had walked over to Plash with a vague hope that some soothing hand would be laid upon her pain. If there was no comfort at the dower-house she knew not where to look for it, for there was certainly none at home—not even with Miss Steet and the children. It was not Lady Davenant's leading characteristic that she was comforting, and Laura had not aspired to be coaxed or coddled into forgetfulness: she wanted rather to be taught a certain fortitude—how to live and hold up one's head even while knowing that things were very bad. A brazen indifference—it was not exactly that that she wished to acquire; but were there not some sorts of indifference that were philosophic and noble? Could Lady Davenant not teach them, if she should take the trouble? The girl remembered to have heard that there had been years before some disagreeable occurrences in *her* family; it was not a race in which the ladies inveterately turned out well. Yet who to-day had the stamp of honour and credit—of a past which was either no one's business or was part and parcel of a fair public record—and carried it so much as a matter of course? She herself had been a good woman and that was the only thing that told in the long run. It was Laura's own idea to be a good woman and that this would make it an advantage for Lady Davenant to show her how not to feel too much. As regards feeling enough, that was a branch in which she had no need to take lessons.

The old woman liked cutting new books, a task she never remitted to her maid, and while her young visitor sat there she went through the greater part of a volume with the paper-knife. She didn't proceed very fast—there was a kind of patient, awkward fumbling of her aged hands; but as she passed her knife into the last leaf she said abruptly—"And how is your sister going on? She's very light!" Lady Davenant added before Laura had time to reply.

"Oh, Lady Davenant!" the girl exclaimed, vaguely, slowly, vexed with herself as soon as she had spoken for having uttered the words as a protest, whereas she wished to draw her companion out. To correct this impression she threw back her waterproof.

"Have you ever spoken to her?" the old woman asked.

"Spoken to her?"

"About her behaviour. I daresay you haven't—you Americans have such a lot of false delicacy. I daresay Selina wouldn't speak to you if you were in her place (excuse the supposition!) and yet she is capable——" But Lady Davenant paused, preferring not to say of what young Mrs Berrington was capable. "It's a bad house for a girl."

"It only gives me a horror," said Laura, pausing in turn.

"A horror of your sister? That's not what one should aim at. You ought to get married—and the sooner the better. My dear child, I have neglected you dreadfully."

"I am much obliged to you, but if you think marriage looks to me happy!" the girl exclaimed, laughing without hilarity.

"Make it happy for some one else and you will be happy enough yourself. You ought to get out of your situation."

Laura Wing was silent a moment, though this was not a new reflection to her. "Do you mean that I should leave Selina altogether? I feel as if I should abandon her—as if I should be a coward."

"Oh, my dear, it isn't the business of little girls to serve as parachutes to fly-away wives! That's why if you haven't spoken to her you needn't take the trouble at this time of day. Let her go—let her go!"

"Let her go?" Laura repeated, staring.

Her companion gave her a sharper glance. "Let her stay, then! Only get out of the house. You can come to me, you know, whenever you like. I don't know another girl I would say that to."

"Oh, Lady Davenant," Laura began again, but she only got as far as this; in a moment she had covered her face with her hands—she had burst into tears.

"Ah my dear, don't cry or I shall take back my invitation! It would never do if you were to *larmoyer*. If I have offended you by the way I have spoken of Selina I think you are too sensitive. We shouldn't feel more for people than they feel for themselves. She has no tears, I'm sure."

"Oh, she has, she has!" cried the girl, sobbing with an odd effect as she put forth this pretension for her sister.

"Then she's worse than I thought. I don't mind them so much when they are merry but I hate them when they are sentimental."

"She's so changed—so changed!" Laura Wing went on.

"Never, never, my dear: *c'est de naissance*."

"You never knew my mother," returned the girl; "when I think of mother——" The words failed her while she sobbed.

"I daresay she was very nice," said Lady Davenant gently. "It would take that to account for you: such women as Selina are always easily enough accounted for. I didn't mean it was inherited—for that sort of thing skips about. I daresay there was some improper ancestress—except that you Americans don't seem to have ancestresses."

Laura gave no sign of having heard these observations; she was occupied in brushing away her tears. "Everything is so changed—you don't know," she remarked in a moment. "Nothing could have been happier—nothing could have been sweeter. And now to be so dependent—so helpless—so poor!"

"Have you nothing at all?" asked Lady Davenant, with simplicity.

"Only enough to pay for my clothes."

"That's a good deal, for a girl. You are uncommonly dressy, you know."

"I'm sorry I seem so. That's just the way I don't want to look."

"You Americans can't help it; you 'wear' your very features and your eyes look as if they had just been sent home. But I confess you are not so smart as Selina."

"Yes, isn't she splendid?" Laura exclaimed, with proud inconsequence. "And the worse she is the better she looks."

"Oh my child, if the bad women looked as bad as they are——! It's only the good ones who can afford that," the old lady murmured.

"It was the last thing I ever thought of—that I should be ashamed," said Laura.

"Oh, keep your shame till you have more to do with it. It's like lending your umbrella—when you have only one."

"If anything were to happen—publicly—I should die, I should die!" the girl exclaimed passionately and with a motion that carried her to her feet. This time she settled herself for departure. Lady Davenant's admonition rather frightened than sustained her.

The old woman leaned back in her chair, looking up at her. "It would be very bad, I daresay. But it wouldn't prevent me from taking you in."

Laura Wing returned her look, with eyes slightly distended, musing. "Think of having to come to that!"

Lady Davenant burst out laughing. "Yes, yes, you must come; you are so original!"

"I don't mean that I don't feel your kindness," the girl broke out, blushing. "But to be only protected—always protected: is that a life?"

"Most women are only too thankful and I am bound to

say I think you are *difficile*." Lady Davenant used a good many French words, in the old-fashioned manner and with a pronunciation not perfectly pure: when she did so she reminded Laura Wing of Mrs Gore's novels. "But you shall be better protected than even by me. *Nous verrons cela.* Only you must stop crying—this isn't a crying country."

"No, one must have courage here. It takes courage to marry for such a reason."

"Any reason is good enough that keeps a woman from being an old maid. Besides, you will like him."

"He must like me first," said the girl, with a sad smile.

"There's the American again! It isn't necessary. You are too proud—you expect too much."

"I'm proud for what I am—that's very certain. But I don't expect anything," Laura Wing declared. "That's the only form my pride takes. Please give my love to Mrs Berrington. I am so sorry—so sorry," she went on, to change the talk from the subject of her marrying. She wanted to marry but she wanted also not to want it, and, above all, not to appear to. She lingered in the room, moving about a little; the place was always so pleasant to her that to go away—to return to her own barren home—had the effect of forfeiting a sort of privilege of sanctuary. The afternoon had faded but the lamps had been brought in, the smell of flowers was in the air and the old house of Plash seemed to recognise the hour that suited it best. The quiet old lady in the firelight, encompassed with the symbolic security of chintz and water-colour, gave her a sudden vision of how blessed it would be to jump all the middle dangers of life and have arrived at the end, safely, sensibly, with a cap and gloves and consideration and memories. "And, Lady Davenant, what does *she* think?" she asked abruptly, stopping short and referring to Mrs Berrington.

"Think? Bless your soul, she doesn't do that! If she did, the things she says would be unpardonable."

"The things she says?"

"That's what makes them so beautiful—that they are not spoiled by preparation. You could never think of them *for* her." The girl smiled at this description of the dearest friend of her interlocutress, but she wondered a little what Lady Davenant would say to visitors about *her* if she should accept a refuge under her roof. Her speech was after all a flattering proof of confidence. "She wishes it had been you—I happen to know that," said the old woman.

"It had been me?"

"That Lionel had taken a fancy to."

"I wouldn't have married him," Laura rejoined after a moment.

"Don't say that or you will make me think it won't be easy to help you. I shall depend upon you not to refuse anything so good."

"I don't call him good. If he were good his wife would be better."

"Very likely; and if you had married him *he* would be better, and that's more to the purpose. Lionel is as idiotic as a comic song, but you have cleverness for two."

"And you have it for fifty, dear Lady Davenant. Never, never—I shall never marry a man I can't respect!" Laura Wing exclaimed.

She had come a little nearer her old friend and taken her hand; her companion held her a moment and with the other hand pushed aside one of the flaps of the waterproof. "And what is it your clothing costs you?" asked Lady Davenant, looking at the dress underneath and not giving any heed to this declaration.

"I don't exactly know: it takes almost everything that is sent me from America. But that is dreadfully little—only a few pounds. I am a wonderful manager. Besides," the girl added, "Selina wants one to be dressed."

"And doesn't she pay any of your bills?"

"Why, she gives me everything—food, shelter, carriages."

"Does she never give you money?"

"I wouldn't take it," said the girl. "They need everything they have—their life is tremendously expensive."

"That I'll warrant!" cried the old woman. "It was a most beautiful property, but I don't know what has become of it now. *Ce n'est pas pour vous blesser*, but the hole you Americans *can* make——"

Laura interrupted immediately, holding up her head; Lady Davenant had dropped her hand and she had receded a step. "Selina brought Lionel a very considerable fortune and every penny of it was paid."

"Yes, I know it was; Mrs Berrington told me it was most satisfactory. That's not always the case with the fortunes you young ladies are supposed to bring!" the old lady added, smiling.

The girl looked over her head a moment. "Why do your men marry for money?"

"Why indeed, my dear? And before your troubles what used your father to give you for your personal expenses?"

"He gave us everything we asked—we had no particular allowance."

"And I daresay you asked for everything?" said Lady Davenant.

"No doubt we were very dressy, as you say."

"No wonder he went bankrupt—for he did, didn't he?"

"He had dreadful reverses but he only sacrificed himself—he protected others."

"Well, I know nothing about these things and I only ask *pour me renseigner*," Mrs Berrington's guest went on. "And after their reverses your father and mother lived I think only a short time?"

Laura Wing had covered herself again with her mantle; her eyes were now bent upon the ground and, standing there before her companion with her umbrella and her air of momentary submission and self-control, she might very well have been a young person in reduced circumstances applying for a place. "It was short enough but it seemed—some parts of it—terribly long and painful. My poor father—my dear father," the girl went on. But her voice trembled and she checked herself.

"I feel as if I were cross-questioning you, which God forbid!" said Lady Davenant. "But there is one thing I should really like to know. Did Lionel and his wife, when you were poor, come freely to your assistance?"

"They sent us money repeatedly—it was *her* money of course. It was almost all we had."

"And if you have been poor and know what poverty is tell me this: has it made you afraid to marry a poor man?"

It seemed to Lady Davenant that in answer to this her young friend looked at her strangely; and then the old woman heard her say something that had not quite the heroic ring she expected. "I am afraid of so many things to-day that I don't know where my fears end."

"I have no patience with the highstrung way you take things. But I have to know, you know."

"Oh, don't try to know any more shames—any more horrors!" the girl wailed with sudden passion, turning away.

Her companion got up, drew her round again and kissed her. "I think you would fidget me," she remarked as she released her. Then, as if this were too cheerless a leave-taking, she added in a gayer tone, as Laura had her hand on the door: "Mind what I tell you, my dear; let her go!" It was to this that the girl's lesson in philosophy reduced itself, she reflected, as she walked back to Mellows in the rain, which had now come on, through the darkening park.

II

THE children were still at tea and poor Miss Steet sat between them, consoling herself with strong cups, crunching melancholy morsels of toast and dropping an absent gaze on her little companions as they exchanged small, loud remarks. She always sighed when Laura came in—it was her way of expressing appreciation of the visit—and she was the one person whom the girl frequently saw who seemed to her more unhappy than herself. But Laura envied her—she thought her position had more dignity than that of her employer's dependent sister. Miss Steet had related her life to the children's pretty young aunt and this personage knew that though it had had painful elements nothing so disagreeable had ever befallen her or was likely to befall her as the odious possibility of her sister's making a scandal. She had two sisters (Laura knew all about them) and one of them was married to a clergyman in Staffordshire (a very ugly part) and had seven children and four hundred a year; while the other, the eldest, was enormously stout and filled (it was a good deal of a squeeze) a position as matron in an orphanage at Liverpool. Neither of them seemed destined to go into the English divorce-court, and such a circumstance on the part of one's near relations struck Laura as in itself almost sufficient to constitute happiness. Miss Steet never lived in a state of nervous anxiety—everything about her was respectable. She made the girl almost angry sometimes, by her drooping, martyr-like air; Laura was near breaking out at her with, "Dear me, what have *you* got to complain of? Don't you earn your living like an honest girl and are you obliged to see things going on about you that you hate?"

But she could not say things like that to her, because she

had promised Selina, who made a great point of this, that she
would never be too familiar with her. Selina was not without
her ideas of decorum—very far from it indeed; only she
erected them in such queer places. She was not familiar with
her children's governess; she was not even familiar with the
children themselves. That was why after all it was impossible
to address much of a remonstrance to Miss Steet when she sat
as if she were tied to the stake and the fagots were being
lighted. If martyrs in this situation had tea and cold meat
served them they would strikingly have resembled the provoking young woman in the schoolroom at Mellows. Laura
could not have denied that it was natural she should have
liked it better if Mrs Berrington would *sometimes* just look in
and give a sign that she was pleased with her system; but poor
Miss Steet only knew by the servants or by Laura whether
Mrs Berrington were at home or not: she was for the most
part not, and the governess had a way of silently intimating
(it was the manner she put her head on one side when she
looked at Scratch and Parson—of course *she* called them
Geordie and Ferdy) that she was immensely handicapped and
even that they were. Perhaps they were, though they certainly showed it little in their appearance and manner, and
Laura was at least sure that if Selina had been perpetually
dropping in Miss Steet would have taken that discomfort even
more tragically. The sight of this young woman's either real
or fancied wrongs did not diminish her conviction that she
herself would have found courage to become a governess.
She would have had to teach very young children, for she
believed she was too ignorant for higher flights. But Selina
would never have consented to that—she would have considered it a disgrace or even worse—a *pose*. Laura had proposed to her six months before that she should dispense with
a paid governess and suffer *her* to take charge of the little
boys: in that way she should not feel so completely dependent—she should be doing something in return. "And pray

what would happen when you came to dinner? Who would look after them then?" Mrs Berrington had demanded, with a very shocked air. Laura had replied that perhaps it was not absolutely necessary that she should come to dinner—she could dine early, with the children; and that if her presence in the drawing-room should be required the children had their nurse—and what did they have their nurse for? Selina looked at her as if she was deplorably superficial and told her that they had their nurse to dress them and look after their clothes —did she wish the poor little ducks to go in rags? She had her own ideas of thoroughness and when Laura hinted that after all at that hour the children were in bed she declared that even when they were asleep she desired the governess to be at hand—that was the way a mother felt who really took an interest. Selina was wonderfully thorough; she said something about the evening hours in the quiet schoolroom being the proper time for the governess to "get up" the children's lessons for the next day. Laura Wing was conscious of her own ignorance; nevertheless she presumed to believe that she could have taught Geordie and Ferdy the alphabet without anticipatory nocturnal researches. She wondered what her sister supposed Miss Steet taught them—whether she had a cheap theory that they were in Latin and algebra.

The governess's evening hours in the quiet schoolroom would have suited Laura well—so at least she believed; by touches of her own she would make the place even prettier than it was already, and in the winter nights, near the bright fire, she would get through a delightful course of reading. There was the question of a new piano (the old one was pretty bad—Miss Steet had a finger!) and perhaps she should have to ask Selina for that—but it would be all. The schoolroom at Mellows was not a charmless place and the girl often wished that she might have spent her own early years in so dear a scene. It was a sort of panelled parlour, in a wing, and looked out on the great cushiony lawns and a part of the terrace where the peacocks used most to spread their tails. There were quaint old maps on the wall, and "collections"—birds and shells—under glass cases, and there was a wonderful pictured screen which old Mrs Berrington had made when Lionel was young out of primitive wood-cuts illustrative of nursery-tales. The place was a setting for rosy childhood, and Laura believed her sister never knew how delightful Scratch and Parson looked there. Old Mrs Berrington had known in the case of Lionel—it had all been arranged for him. That was the story told by ever so many other things in the house, which portrayed the full perception of a comfortable, liberal, deeply domestic effect, addressed to eternities of possession, characteristic thirty years before of the unquestioned and unquestioning old lady whose sofas and "corners" (she had perhaps been the first person in England to have corners) demonstrated the most of her cleverness.

Laura Wing envied English children, the boys at least, and even her own chubby nephews, in spite of the cloud that hung over them; but she had already noted the incongruity that appeared to-day between Lionel Berrington at thirty-five and the influences that had surrounded his younger years. She did not dislike her brother-in-law, though she admired him scantily, and she pitied him; but she marvelled at the waste involved in some human institutions (the English country gentry for instance) when she perceived that it had taken so much to produce so little. The sweet old wainscoted parlour, the view of the garden that reminded her of scenes in Shakespeare's comedies, all that was exquisite in the home of his forefathers—what visible reference was there to these fine things in poor Lionel's stable-stamped composition? When she came in this evening and saw his small sons making competitive noises in their mugs (Miss Steet checked this impropriety on her entrance) she asked herself what *they* would have to show twenty years later for the frame that made them just then a picture. Would they be wonderfully ripe and noble,

the perfection of human culture? The contrast was before her
again, the sense of the same curious duplicity (in the literal
meaning of the word) that she had felt at Plash—the way the
genius of such an old house was all peace and decorum and
the spirit that prevailed there, outside of the schoolroom,
was contentious and impure. She had often been struck with
it before—with that perfection of machinery which can still
at certain times make English life go on of itself with a stately
rhythm long after there is corruption within it.

She had half a purpose of asking Miss Steet to dine with
her that evening downstairs, so absurd did it seem to her that
two young women who had so much in common (enough at
least for that) should sit feeding alone at opposite ends of the
big empty house, melancholy on such a night. She would not
have cared just now whether Selina did think such a course
familiar: she indulged sometimes in a kind of angry humility,
placing herself near to those who were laborious and sordid.
But when she observed how much cold meat the governess
had already consumed she felt that it would be a vain form
to propose to her another repast. She sat down with her and
presently, in the firelight, the two children had placed themselves in position for a story. They were dressed like the
mariners of England and they smelt of the ablutions to which
they had been condemned before tea and the odour of which
was but partly overlaid by that of bread and butter. Scratch
wanted an old story and Parson a new, and they exchanged
from side to side a good many powerful arguments. While
they were so engaged Miss Steet narrated at her visitor's
invitation the walk she had taken with them and revealed that
she had been thinking for a long time of asking Mrs Berrington—if she only had an opportunity—whether she should
approve of her giving them a few elementary notions of
botany. But the opportunity had not come—she had had the
idea for a long time past. She was rather fond of the study
herself; she had gone into it a little—she seemed to intimate

that there had been times when she extracted a needed comfort from it. Laura suggested that botany might be a little dry for such young children in winter, from text-books—that the better way would be perhaps to wait till the spring and show them out of doors, in the garden, some of the peculiarities of plants. To this Miss Steet rejoined that her idea had been to teach some of the general facts slowly—it would take a long time—and then they would be all ready for the spring. She spoke of the spring as if it would not arrive for a terribly long time. She had hoped to lay the question before Mrs Berrington that week—but was it not already Thursday? Laura said, "Oh yes, you had better do anything with the children that will keep them profitably occupied;" she came very near saying anything that would occupy the governess herself.

She had rather a dread of new stories—it took the little boys so long to get initiated and the first steps were so terribly bestrewn with questions. Receptive silence, broken only by an occasional rectification on the part of the listener, never descended until after the tale had been told a dozen times. The matter was settled for "Riquet with the Tuft," but on this occasion the girl's heart was not much in the entertainment. The children stood on either side of her, leaning against her, and she had an arm round each; their little bodies were thick and strong and their voices had the quality of silver bells. Their mother had certainly gone too far; but there was nevertheless a limit to the tenderness one could feel for the neglected, compromised bairns. It was difficult to take a sentimental view of them—they would never take such a view of themselves. Geordie would grow up to be a master-hand at polo and care more for that pastime than for anything in life, and Ferdy perhaps would develop into "the best shot in England." Laura felt these possibilities stirring within them; they were in the things they said to her, in the things they said to each other. At any rate they would never reflect upon anything in the world. They contradicted each other on a question of ancestral history to which their attention apparently had been drawn by their nurse, whose people had been tenants for generations. Their grandfather had had the hounds for fifteen years—Ferdy maintained that he had always had them. Geordie ridiculed this idea, like a man of the world; he had had them till he went into volunteering—then he had got up a magnificent regiment, he had spent thousands of pounds on it. Ferdy was of the opinion that this was wasted money—he himself intended to have a real regiment, to be a colonel in the Guards. Geordie looked as if he thought that a superficial ambition and could see beyond it; his own most definite view was that he would have back the hounds. He didn't see why papa didn't have them—unless it was because he wouldn't take the trouble.

"I know—it's because mamma is an American!" Ferdy announced, with confidence.

"And what has that to do with it?" asked Laura.

"Mamma spends so much money—there isn't any more for anything!"

This startling speech elicited an alarmed protest from Miss Steet; she blushed and assured Laura that she couldn't imagine where the child could have picked up such an extraordinary idea. "I'll look into it—you may be sure I'll look into it," she said; while Laura told Ferdy that he must never, never, never, under any circumstances, either utter or listen to a word that should be wanting in respect to his mother.

"If any one should say anything against any of my people I would give him a good one!" Geordie shouted, with his hands in his little blue pockets.

"I'd hit him in the eye!" cried Ferdy, with cheerful inconsequence.

"Perhaps you don't care to come to dinner at half-past seven," the girl said to Miss Steet; "but I should be very glad—I'm all alone."

"Thank you so much. All alone, really?" murmured the governess.

"Why don't you get married? then you wouldn't be alone," Geordie interposed, with ingenuity.

"Children, you are really too dreadful this evening!" Miss Steet exclaimed.

"I shan't get married—I want to have the hounds," proclaimed Geordie, who had apparently been much struck with his brother's explanation.

"I will come down afterwards, about half-past eight, if you will allow me," said Miss Steet, looking conscious and responsible.

"Very well—perhaps we can have some music; we will try something together."

"Oh, music—*we* don't go in for music!" said Geordie, with clear superiority; and while he spoke Laura saw Miss Steet get up suddenly, looking even less alleviated than usual. The door of the room had been pushed open and Lionel Berrington stood there. He had his hat on and a cigar in his mouth and his face was red, which was its common condition. He took off his hat as he came into the room, but he did not stop smoking and he turned a little redder than before. There were several ways in which his sister-in-law often wished he had been very different, but she had never disliked him for a certain boyish shyness that was in him, which came out in his dealings with almost all women. The governess of his children made him uncomfortable and Laura had already noticed that he had the same effect upon Miss Steet. He was fond of his children, but he saw them hardly more frequently than their mother and they never knew whether he were at home or away. Indeed his goings and comings were so frequent that Laura herself scarcely knew: it was an accident that on this occasion his absence had been marked for her. Selina had had her reasons for wishing not to go up to town while her husband was still at Mellows, and she cherished the irritating belief that he stayed at home on purpose to watch her—to keep her from going away. It was her theory that she herself was perpetually at home—that few women were more domestic, more glued to the fireside and absorbed in the duties belonging to it; and unreasonable as she was she recognised the fact that for her to establish this theory she must make her husband sometimes see her at Mellows. It was not enough for her to maintain that he would see her if he were sometimes there himself. Therefore she disliked to be caught in the crude fact of absence—to go away under his nose; what she preferred was to take the next train after his own and return an hour or two before him. She managed this often with great ability, in spite of her not being able to be sure when he *would* return. Of late however she had ceased to take so much trouble, and Laura, by no desire of the girl's own, was enough in the confidence of her impatiences and perversities to know that for her to have wished (four days before the moment I write of) to put him on a wrong scent—or to keep him at least off the right one—she must have had something more dreadful than usual in her head. This was why the girl had been so nervous and why the sense of an impending catastrophe, which had lately gathered strength in her mind, was at present almost intolerably pressing: she knew how little Selina could afford to be more dreadful than usual.

Lionel startled her by turning up in that unexpected way, though she could not have told herself when it would have been natural to expect him. This attitude, at Mellows, was left to the servants, most of them inscrutable and incommunicative and erect in a wisdom that was founded upon telegrams— you couldn't speak to the butler but he pulled one out of his pocket. It was a house of telegrams; they crossed each other a dozen times an hour, coming and going, and Selina in particular lived in a cloud of them. Laura had but vague ideas as to what they were all about; once in a while, when they fell under her eyes, she either failed to understand them or judged

them to be about horses. There were an immense number of
horses, in one way and another, in Mrs Berrington's life.
Then she had so many friends, who were always rushing
about like herself and making appointments and putting them
off and wanting to know if she were going to certain places
or whether she would go if they did or whether she would
come up to town and dine and "do a theatre." There were
also a good many theatres in the existence of this busy lady.
Laura remembered how fond their poor father had been of
telegraphing, but it was never about the theatre: at all events
she tried to give her sister the benefit or the excuse of heredity. Selina had her own opinions, which were superior to
this: she once remarked to Laura that it was idiotic for a
woman to write—to telegraph was the only way not to get
into trouble. If doing so sufficed to keep a lady out of it Mrs
Berrington's life should have flowed like the rivers of Eden.

III

LAURA, as soon as her brother-in-law had been in the room
a moment, had a particular fear; she had seen him twice
noticeably under the influence of liquor; she had not liked it
at all and now there were some of the same signs. She was
afraid the children would discover them, or at any rate Miss
Steet, and she felt the importance of not letting him stay in the
room. She thought it almost a sign that he should have come
there at all—he was so rare an apparition. He looked at her
very hard, smiling as if to say, "No, no, I'm not—not if you
think it!" She perceived with relief in a moment that he was
not very bad, and liquor disposed him apparently to tenderness, for he indulged in an interminable kissing of Geordie
and Ferdy, during which Miss Steet turned away delicately,
looking out of the window. The little boys asked him no

questions to celebrate his return—they only announced that
they were going to learn botany, to which he replied: "Are
you, really? Why, I never did," and looked askance at the
governess, blushing as if to express the hope that she would
let him off from carrying that subject further. To Laura and
to Miss Steet he was amiably explanatory, though his explanations were not quite coherent. He had come back an
hour before—he was going to spend the night—he had driven
over from Churton—he was thinking of taking the last train
up to town. Was Laura dining at home? Was any one coming? He should enjoy a quiet dinner awfully.

"Certainly I'm alone," said the girl. "I suppose you know
Selina is away."

"Oh yes—I know where Selina is!" And Lionel Berrington looked round, smiling at every one present, including
Scratch and Parson. He stopped while he continued to smile
and Laura wondered what he was so much pleased at. She
preferred not to ask—she was sure it was something that
wouldn't give *her* pleasure; but after waiting a moment her
brother-in-law went on: "Selina's in Paris, my dear; that's
where Selina is!"

"In Paris?" Laura repeated.

"Yes, in Paris, my dear—God bless her! Where else do
you suppose? Geordie my boy, where should *you* think your
mummy would naturally be?"

"Oh, I don't know," said Geordie, who had no reply ready
that would express affectingly the desolation of the nursery.
"If I were mummy I'd travel."

"Well now that's your mummy's idea—she has gone to
travel," returned the father. "Were you ever in Paris, Miss
Steet?"

Miss Steet gave a nervous laugh and said No, but she had
been to Boulogne; while to her added confusion Ferdy
announced that he knew where Paris was—it was in America.
"No, it ain't—it's in Scotland!" cried Geordie; and Laura

asked Lionel how he knew—whether his wife had written to him.

"Written to me? when did she ever write to me? No, I saw a fellow in town this morning who saw her there—at breakfast yesterday. He came over last night. That's how I know my wife's in Paris. You can't have better proof than that!"

"I suppose it's a very pleasant season there," the governess murmured, as if from a sense of duty, in a distant, discomfortable tone.

"I daresay it's very pleasant indeed—I daresay it's awfully amusing!" laughed Mr Berrington. "Shouldn't you like to run over with me for a few days, Laura—just to have a go at the theatres? I don't see why we should always be moping at home. We'll take Miss Steet and the children and give mummy a pleasant surprise. Now who do you suppose she was with, in Paris—who do you suppose she was seen with?"

Laura had turned pale, she looked at him hard, imploringly, in the eyes: there was a name she was terribly afraid he would mention. "Oh sir, in that case we had better go and get ready!" Miss Steet quavered, betwixt a laugh and a groan, in a spasm of discretion; and before Laura knew it she had gathered Geordie and Ferdy together and swept them out of the room. The door closed behind her with a very quick softness and Lionel remained a moment staring at it.

"I say, what does she mean?—ain't that damned impertinent?" he stammered. "What did she think I was going to say? Does she suppose I would say any harm before—before *her?* Dash it, does she suppose I would give away my wife to the servants?" Then he added, "And I wouldn't say any harm before you, Laura. You are too good and too nice and I like you too much!"

"Won't you come downstairs? won't you have some tea?" the girl asked, uneasily.

"No, no, I want to stay here—I like this place," he replied, very gently and reasonably. "It's a deuced nice place—it's

an awfully jolly room. It used to be this way—always—when
I was a little chap. I was a rough one, my dear; I wasn't a
pretty little lamb like that pair. I think it's because you look
after them—that's what makes 'em so sweet. The one in my
time—what was her name? I think it was Bald or Bold—I
rather think she found me a handful. I used to kick her shins
—I was decidedly vicious. And do *you* see it's kept so well,
Laura?" he went on, looking round him. "'Pon my soul, it's
the prettiest room in the house. What does she want to go to
Paris for when she has got such a charming house? Now can
you answer me that, Laura?"

"I suppose she has gone to get some clothes; her dressmaker lives in Paris, you know."

"Dressmaker? Clothes? Why, she has got whole rooms full
of them. Hasn't she got whole rooms full of them?"

"Speaking of clothes, I must go and change mine," said
Laura. "I have been out in the rain—I have been to Plash—
I'm decidedly damp."

"Oh, you have been to Plash? You have seen my mother?
I hope she's in very good health." But before the girl could
reply to this he went on: "Now, I want you to guess who
she's in Paris with. Motcomb saw them together—at that
place, what's his name? close to the Madeleine." And as Laura
was silent, not wishing at all to guess, he continued—"It's
the ruin of any woman, you know; I can't think what she has
got in her head." Still Laura said nothing, and as he had hold
of her arm, she having turned away, she led him this time out
of the room. She had a horror of the name, the name that was
in her mind and that was apparently on his lips, though his
tone was so singular, so contemplative. "My dear girl, she's
with Lady Ringrose—what do you say to that?" he exclaimed,
as they passed along the corridor to the staircase.

"With Lady Ringrose?"

"They went over on Tuesday—they are knocking about
there alone."

"I don't know Lady Ringrose," Laura said, infinitely relieved that the name was not the one she had feared. Lionel leaned on her arm as they went downstairs.

"I rather hope not—I promise you she has never put her foot in this house! If Selina expects to bring her here I should like half an hour's notice; yes, half an hour would do. She might as well be seen with——" And Lionel Berrington checked himself. "She has had at least fifty——" And again he stopped short. "You must pull me up, you know, if I say anything you don't like!"

"I don't understand you—let me alone, please!" the girl broke out, disengaging herself with an effort from his arm. She hurried down the rest of the steps and left him there looking after her, and as she went she heard him give an irrelevant laugh.

IV

SHE determined not to go to dinner—she wished for that day not to meet him again. He would drink more—he would be worse—she didn't know what he might say. Besides she was too angry—not with him but with Selina—and in addition to being angry she was sick. She knew who Lady Ringrose was; she knew so many things to-day that when she was younger —and only a little—she had not expected ever to know. Her eyes had been opened very wide in England and certainly they had been opened to Lady Ringrose. She had heard what she had done and perhaps a good deal more, and it was not very different from what she had heard of other women. She knew Selina had been to her house; she had an impression that her ladyship had been to Selina's, in London, though she herself had not seen her there. But she had not known they were so intimate as that—that Selina would rush over to Paris with her. What they had gone to Paris for was not necessarily criminal; there were a hundred reasons, familiar to ladies who were fond of change, of movement, of the theatres and of new bonnets; but nevertheless it was the fact of this little excursion quite as much as the companion that excited Laura's disgust. She was not ready to say that the companion was any worse, though Lionel appeared to think so, than twenty other women who were her sister's intimates and whom she herself had seen in London, in Grosvenor Place, and even under the motherly old beeches at Mellows. But she thought it unpleasant and base in Selina to go abroad that way, like a commercial traveller, capriciously, clandestinely, without giving notice, when she had left her to understand that she was simply spending three or four days in town. It was bad taste and bad form, it was *cabotin* and had the mark of Selina's complete, irremediable frivolity—the worst accusation (Laura tried to cling to that opinion) that she laid herself open to. Of course frivolity that was never ashamed of itself was like a neglected cold—you could die of it morally as well as of anything else. Laura knew this and it was why she was inexpressibly vexed with her sister. She hoped she should get a letter from Selina the next morning (Mrs Berrington would show at least that remnant of propriety) which would give her a chance to despatch her an answer that was already writing itself in her brain. It scarcely diminished Laura's eagerness for such an opportunity that she had a vision of Selina's showing her letter, laughing, across the table, at the place near the Madeleine, to Lady Ringrose (who would be painted—Selina herself, to do her justice, was not yet) while the French waiters, in white aprons, contemplated *ces dames*. It was new work for our young lady to judge of these shades—the gradations, the probabilities of license, and of the side of the line on which, or rather how far on the wrong side, Lady Ringrose was situated.

A quarter of an hour before dinner Lionel sent word to her

room that she was to sit down without him—he had a headache and wouldn't appear. This was an unexpected grace and it simplified the position for Laura; so that, smoothing her ruffles, she betook herself to the table. Before doing this however she went back to the schoolroom and told Miss Steet she must contribute her company. She took the governess (the little boys were in bed) downstairs with her and made her sit opposite, thinking she would be a safeguard if Lionel were to change his mind. Miss Steet was more frightened than herself—she was a very shrinking bulwark. The dinner was dull and the conversation rare; the governess ate three olives and looked at the figures on the spoons. Laura had more than ever her sense of impending calamity; a draught of misfortune seemed to blow through the house; it chilled her feet under her chair. The letter she had in her head went out like a flame in the wind and her only thought now was to telegraph to Selina the first thing in the morning, in quite different words. She scarcely spoke to Miss Steet and there was very little the governess could say to her: she had already related her history so often. After dinner she carried her companion into the drawing-room, by the arm, and they sat down to the piano together. They played duets for an hour, mechanically, violently; Laura had no idea what the music was—she only knew that their playing was execrable. In spite of this—"That's a very nice thing, that last," she heard a vague voice say, behind her, at the end; and she became aware that her brother-in-law had joined them again.

Miss Steet was pusillanimous—she retreated on the spot, though Lionel had already forgotten that he was angry at the scandalous way she had carried off the children from the schoolroom. Laura would have gone too if Lionel had not told her that he had something very particular to say to her. That made her want to go more, but she had to listen to him when he expressed the hope that she hadn't taken offence at anything he had said before. He didn't strike her as tipsy now;

he had slept it off or got rid of it and she saw no traces of his headache. He was still conspicuously cheerful as if he had got some good news and were very much encouraged. She knew the news he had got and she might have thought, in view of his manner, that it could not really have seemed to him so bad as he had pretended to think it. It was not the first time however that she had seen him pleased that he had a case against his wife, and she was to learn on this occasion how extreme a satisfaction he could take in his wrongs. She would not sit down again; she only lingered by the fire, pretending to warm her feet, and he walked to and fro in the long room, where the lamplight to-night was limited, stepping on certain figures of the carpet as if his triumph were alloyed with hesitation.

"I never know how to talk to you—you are so beastly clever," he said. "I can't treat you like a little girl in a pinafore—and yet of course you are only a young lady. You're so deuced good—that makes it worse," he went on, stopping in front of her with his hands in his pockets and the air he himself had of being a good-natured but dissipated boy; with his small stature, his smooth, fat, suffused face, his round, watery, light-coloured eyes and his hair growing in curious infantile rings. He had lost one of his front teeth and always wore a stiff white scarf, with a pin representing some symbol of the turf or the chase. "I don't see why *she* couldn't have been a little more like you. If I could have had a shot at you first!"

"I don't care for any compliments at my sister's expense," Laura said, with some majesty.

"Oh I say, Laura, don't put on so many frills, as Selina says. You know what your sister is as well as I do!" They stood looking at each other a moment and he appeared to see something in her face which led him to add—"You know, at any rate, how little we hit it off."

"I know you don't love each other—it's too dreadful."

"Love each other? she hates me as she'd hate a hump on her back. She'd do me any devilish turn she could. There isn't a feeling of loathing that she doesn't have for me! She'd like to stamp on me and hear me crack, like a black beetle, and she never opens her mouth but she insults me." Lionel Berrington delivered himself of these assertions without violence, without passion or the sting of a new discovery; there was a familiar gaiety in his trivial little tone and he had the air of being so sure of what he said that he did not need to exaggerate in order to prove enough.

"Oh, Lionel!" the girl murmured, turning pale. "Is that the particular thing you wished to say to me?"

"And you can't say it's my fault—you won't pretend to do that, will you?" he went on. "Ain't I quiet, ain't I kind, don't I go steady? Haven't I given her every blessed thing she has ever asked for?"

"You haven't given her an example!" Laura replied, with spirit. "You don't care for anything in the wide world but to amuse yourself, from the beginning of the year to the end. No more does she—and perhaps it's even worse in a woman. You are both as selfish as you can live, with nothing in your head or your heart but your vulgar pleasure, incapable of a concession, incapable of a sacrifice!" She at least spoke with passion; something that had been pent up in her soul broke out and it gave her relief, almost a momentary joy.

It made Lionel Berrington stare; he coloured, but after a moment he threw back his head with laughter. "Don't you call me kind when I stand here and take all that? If I'm so keen for my pleasure what pleasure do *you* give me? Look at the way I take it, Laura. You ought to do me justice. Haven't I sacrificed my home? and what more can a man do?"

"I don't think you care any more for your home than Selina does. And it's so sacred and so beautiful, God forgive you! You are all blind and senseless and heartless and I don't know what poison is in your veins. There is a curse on you and there will be a judgment!" the girl went on, glowing like a young prophetess.

"What do you want me to do? Do you want me to stay at home and read the Bible?" her companion demanded with an effect of profanity, confronted with her deep seriousness.

"It wouldn't do you any harm, once in a while."

"There will be a judgment on *her*—that's very sure, and I know where it will be delivered," said Lionel Berrington, indulging in a visible approach to a wink. "Have I done the half to her she has done to me? I won't say the half but the hundredth part? Answer me truly, my dear!"

"I don't know what she has done to you," said Laura, impatiently.

"That's exactly what I want to tell you. But it's difficult. I'll bet you five pounds she's doing it now!"

"You are too unable to make yourself respected," the girl remarked, not shrinking now from the enjoyment of an advantage—that of feeling herself superior and taking her opportunity.

Her brother-in-law seemed to feel for the moment the prick of this observation. "What has such a piece of nasty boldness as that to do with respect? She's the first that ever defied me!" exclaimed the young man, whose aspect somehow scarcely confirmed this pretension. "You know all about her—don't make believe you don't," he continued in another tone. "You see everything—you're one of the sharp ones. There's no use beating about the bush, Laura—you've lived in this precious house and you're not so green as that comes to. Besides, you're so good yourself that you needn't give a shriek if one is obliged to say what one means. Why didn't you grow up a little sooner? Then, over there in New York, it would certainly have been you I would have made up to. *You* would have respected me—eh? now don't say you wouldn't." He rambled on, turning about the room again, partly like a person whose sequences were naturally slow but also a little as if, though he knew what he had in mind, there were still a scruple attached to it that he was trying to rub off.

"I take it that isn't what I must sit up to listen to, Lionel, is it?" Laura said, wearily.

"Why, you don't want to go to bed at nine o'clock, do you? That's all rot, of course. But I want you to help me."

"To help you—how?"

"I'll tell you—but you must give me my head. I don't know what I said to you before dinner—I had had too many brandy and sodas. Perhaps I was too free; if I was I beg your pardon. I made the governess bolt—very proper in the super-intendent of one's children. Do you suppose they saw any-thing? I shouldn't care for that. I did take half a dozen or so; I was thirsty and I was awfully gratified."

"You have little enough to gratify you."

"Now that's just where you are wrong. I don't know when I've fancied anything so much as what I told you."

"What you told me?"

"About her being in Paris. I hope she'll stay a month!"

"I don't understand you," Laura said.

"Are you very sure, Laura? My dear, it suits my book! Now you know yourself he's not the first."

Laura was silent; his round eyes were fixed on her face and she saw something she had not seen before—a little shining point which on Lionel's part might represent an idea, but which made his expression conscious as well as eager. "He?" she presently asked. "Whom are you speaking of?"

"Why, of Charley Crispin, G——" And Lionel Berring-ton accompanied this name with a startling imprecation.

"What has he to do——?"

"He has everything to do. Isn't he with her there?"

"How should I know? You said Lady Ringrose."

"Lady Ringrose is a mere blind—and a devilish poor one at that. I'm sorry to have to say it to you, but he's her lover. I mean Selina's. And he ain't the first."

There was another short silence while they stood opposed,

and then Laura asked—and the question was unexpected—
"Why do you call him Charley?"

"Doesn't he call me Lion, like all the rest?" said her
brother-in-law, staring.

"You're the most extraordinary people. I suppose you
have a certain amount of proof before you say such things
to me?"

"Proof, I've oceans of proof! And not only about Crispin,
but about Deepmere."

"And pray who is Deepmere?"

"Did you never hear of Lord Deepmere? He has gone to
India. That was before you came. I don't say all this for my
pleasure, Laura," Mr Berrington added.

"Don't you, indeed?" asked the girl with a singular laugh.
"I thought you were so glad."

"I'm glad to know it but I'm not glad to tell it. When I say
I'm glad to know it I mean I'm glad to be fixed at last. Oh,
I've got the tip! It's all open country now and I know just
how to go. I've gone into it most extensively; there's nothing
you can't find out to-day—if you go to the right place. I've—
I've——" He hesitated a moment, then went on: "Well, it's
no matter what I've done. I know where I am and it's a great
comfort. She's up a tree, if ever a woman was. Now we'll see
who's a beetle and who's a toad!" Lionel Berrington concluded, gaily, with some incongruity of metaphor.

"It's not true—it's not true—it's not true," Laura said,
slowly.

"That's just what she'll say—though that's not the way
she'll say it. Oh, if she could get off by your saying it for her!
—for you, my dear, would be believed."

"Get off—what do you mean?" the girl demanded, with a
coldness she failed to feel, for she was tingling all over with
shame and rage.

"Why, what do you suppose I'm talking about? I'm going
to haul her up and to have it out."

"You're going to make a scandal?"

"*Make* it? Bless my soul, it isn't me! And I should think it was made enough. I'm going to appeal to the laws of my country—that's what I'm going to do. She pretends I'm stopped, whatever she does. But that's all gammon—I ain't!"

"I understand—but you won't do anything so horrible," said Laura, very gently.

"Horrible as you please, but less so than going on in this way; I haven't told you the fiftieth part—you will easily understand that I can't. They are not nice things to say to a girl like you—especially about Deepmere, if you didn't know it. But when they happen you've got to look at them, haven't you? That's the way I look at it."

"It's not true—it's not true—it's not true," Laura Wing repeated, in the same way, slowly shaking her head.

"Of course you stand up for your sister—but that's just what I wanted to say to you, that you ought to have some pity for *me* and some sense of justice. Haven't I always been nice to you? Have you ever had so much as a nasty word from me?"

This appeal touched the girl; she had eaten her brother-in-law's bread for months, she had had the use of all the luxuries with which he was surrounded, and to herself personally she had never known him anything but good-natured. She made no direct response however; she only said—"Be quiet, be quiet and leave her to me. I will answer for her."

"Answer for her—what do you mean?"

"She shall be better—she shall be reasonable—there shall be no more talk of these horrors. Leave her to me—let me go away with her somewhere."

"Go away with her? I wouldn't let you come within a mile of her, if you were *my* sister!"

"Oh, shame, shame!" cried Laura Wing, turning away from him.

She hurried to the door of the room, but he stopped her

before she reached it. He got his back to it, he barred her way and she had to stand there and hear him. "I haven't said what I wanted—for I told you that I wanted you to help me. I ain't cruel—I ain't insulting—you can't make out that against me; I'm sure you know in your heart that I've swallowed what would sicken most men. Therefore I will say that you ought to be fair. You're too clever not to be; *you* can't pretend to swallow——" He paused a moment and went on, and she saw it was his idea—an idea very simple and bold. He wanted her to side with him—to watch for him—to help him to get his divorce. He forbore to say that she owed him as much for the hospitality and protection she had in her poverty enjoyed, but she was sure that was in his heart. "Of course she's your sister, but when one's sister's a perfect bad 'un there's no law to force one to jump into the mud to save her. It *is* mud, my dear, and mud up to your neck. You had much better think of her children—you had much better stop in *my* boat."

"Do you ask me to help you with evidence against her?" the girl murmured. She had stood there passive, waiting while he talked, covering her face with her hands, which she parted a little, looking at him.

He hesitated a moment. "I ask you not to deny what you have seen—what you feel to be true."

"Then of the abominations of which you say you have proof, you haven't proof."

"Why haven't I proof?"

"If you want *me* to come forward!"

"I shall go into court with a strong case. You may do what you like. But I give you notice and I expect you not to forget that I have given it. Don't forget—because you'll be asked—that I have told you to-night where she is and with whom she is and what measures I intend to take."

"Be asked—be asked?" the girl repeated.

"Why, of course you'll be cross-examined."

"Oh, mother, mother!" cried Laura Wing. Her hands were over her face again and as Lionel Berrington, opening the door, let her pass, she burst into tears. He looked after her, distressed, compunctious, half-ashamed, and he exclaimed to himself—"The bloody brute, the bloody brute!" But the words had reference to his wife.

V

"And are you telling me the perfect truth when you say that Captain Crispin was not there?"

"The perfect truth?" Mrs Berrington straightened herself to her height, threw back her head and measured her interlocutress up and down; it is to be surmised that this was one of the many ways in which she knew she looked very handsome indeed. Her interlocutress was her sister, and even in a discussion with a person long since initiated she was not incapable of feeling that her beauty was a new advantage. On this occasion she had at first the air of depending upon it mainly to produce an effect upon Laura; then, after an instant's reflection, she determined to arrive at her result in another way. She exchanged her expression of scorn (of resentment at her veracity's being impugned) for a look of gentle amusement; she smiled patiently, as if she remembered that of course Laura couldn't understand of what an impertinence she had been guilty. There was a quickness of perception and lightness of hand which, to her sense, her American sister had never acquired: the girl's earnest, almost barbarous probity blinded her to the importance of certain pleasant little forms. "My poor child, the things you do say! One doesn't put a question about the perfect truth in a manner that implies that a person is telling a perfect lie. However, as it's only you, I don't mind satisfying your clumsy curiosity.

I haven't the least idea whether Captain Crispin was there or not. I know nothing of his movements and he doesn't keep me informed—why should he, poor man?—of his whereabouts. He was not there for me—isn't that all that need interest you? As far as I was concerned he might have been at the North Pole. I neither saw him nor heard of him. I didn't see the end of his nose!" Selina continued, still with her wiser, tolerant brightness, looking straight into her sister's eyes. Her own were clear and lovely and she was but little less handsome than if she had been proud and freezing. Laura wondered at her more and more; stupefied suspense was now almost the girl's constant state of mind.

Mrs Berrington had come back from Paris the day before but had not proceeded to Mellows the same night, though there was more than one train she might have taken. Neither had she gone to the house in Grosvenor Place but had spent the night at an hotel. Her husband was absent again; he was supposed to be in Grosvenor Place, so that they had not yet met. Little as she was a woman to admit that she had been in the wrong she was known to have granted later that at this moment she had made a mistake in not going straight to her own house. It had given Lionel a degree of advantage, made it appear perhaps a little that she had a bad conscience and was afraid to face him. But she had had her reasons for putting up at an hotel, and she thought it unnecessary to express them very definitely. She came home by a morning train, the second day, and arrived before luncheon, of which meal she partook in the company of her sister and in that of Miss Steet and the children, sent for in honour of the occasion. After luncheon she let the governess go but kept Scratch and Parson—kept them on ever so long in the morning-room where she remained; longer than she had ever kept them before. Laura was conscious that she ought to have been pleased at this, but there was a perversity even in Selina's manner of doing right; for she wished immensely now to see her alone—she had something so serious to say to her. Selina hugged her children repeatedly, encouraging their sallies; she laughed extravagantly at the artlessness of their remarks, so that at table Miss Steet was quite abashed by her unusual high spirits. Laura was unable to question her about Captain Crispin and Lady Ringrose while Geordie and Ferdy were there: they would not understand, of course, but names were always reflected in their limpid little minds and they gave forth the image later —often in the most extraordinary connections. It was as if Selina knew what she was waiting for and were determined to make her wait. The girl wished her to go to her room, that she might follow her there. But Selina showed no disposition to retire, and one could never entertain the idea for her, on any occasion, that it would be suitable that she should change her dress. The dress she wore—whatever it was—was too becoming to her, and to the moment, for that. Laura noticed how the very folds of her garment told that she had been to Paris; she had spent only a week there but the mark of her *couturière* was all over her; it was simply to confer with this great artist that, from her own account, she had crossed the Channel. The signs of the conference were so conspicuous that it was as if she had said, "Don't you see the proof that it was for nothing but *chiffons?*" She walked up and down the room with Geordie in her arms, in an access of maternal tenderness; he was much too big to nestle gracefully in her bosom, but that only made her seem younger, more flexible, fairer in her tall, strong slimness. Her distinguished figure bent itself hither and thither, but always in perfect freedom, as she romped with her children; and there was another moment, when she came slowly down the room, holding one of them in each hand and singing to them while they looked up at her beauty, charmed and listening and a little surprised at such new ways—a moment when she might have passed for some grave, antique statue of a young matron, or even for a picture of Saint Cecilia. This morning, more than ever, Laura was struck with her air of youth, the inextinguishable freshness that would have made any one exclaim at her being the mother of such bouncing little boys. Laura had always admired her, thought her the prettiest woman in London, the beauty with the finest points; and now these points were so vivid (especially her finished slenderness and the grace, the natural elegance of every turn—the fall of her shoulders had never looked so perfect) that the girl almost detested them: they appeared to her a kind of advertisement of danger and even of shame.

Miss Steet at last came back for the children, and as soon as she had taken them away Selina observed that she would go over to Plash—just as she was: she rang for her hat and jacket and for the carriage. Laura could see that she would not give her just yet the advantage of a retreat to her room. The hat and jacket were quickly brought, but after they were put on Selina kept her maid in the drawing-room, talking to her a long time, telling her elaborately what she wished done with the things she had brought from Paris. Before the maid departed the carriage was announced, and the servant, leaving the door of the room open, hovered within earshot. Laura then, losing patience, turned out the maid and closed the door; she stood before her sister, who was prepared for her drive. Then she asked her abruptly, fiercely, but colouring with her question, whether Captain Crispin had been in Paris. We have heard Mrs Berrington's answer, with which her strenuous sister was imperfectly satisfied; a fact the perception of which it doubtless was that led Selina to break out, with a greater show of indignation: "I never heard of such extraordinary ideas for a girl to have, and such extraordinary things for a girl to talk about! My dear, you have acquired a freedom—you have emancipated yourself from conventionality—and I suppose I must congratulate you." Laura only stood there, with her eyes fixed, without answering the sally, and Selina went on, with another change of tone: "And pray if he *was*

there, what is there so monstrous? Hasn't it happened that
he is in London when I am there? Why is it then so awful that
he should be in Paris?"

"Awful, awful, too awful," murmured Laura, with intense
gravity, still looking at her—looking all the more fixedly that
she knew how little Selina liked it.

"My dear, you do indulge in a style of innuendo, for a
respectable young woman!" Mrs Berrington exclaimed, with
an angry laugh. "You have ideas that when I was a girl——"
She paused, and her sister saw that she had not the assurance
to finish her sentence on that particular note.

"Don't talk about my innuendoes and my ideas—you
might remember those in which I have heard you indulge!
Ideas? what ideas did I ever have before I came here?" Laura
Wing asked, with a trembling voice. "Don't pretend to be
shocked, Selina; that's too cheap a defence. You have said
things to me—if you choose to talk of freedom! What is the
talk of your house and what does one hear if one lives with
you? I don't care what I hear now (it's all odious and there's
little choice and my sweet sensibility has gone God knows
where!) and I'm very glad if you understand that I don't care
what I say. If one talks about your affairs, my dear, one
mustn't be too particular!" the girl continued, with a flash of
passion.

Mrs Berrington buried her face in her hands. "Merciful
powers, to be insulted, to be covered with outrage, by one's
wretched little sister!" she moaned.

"I think you should be thankful there is one human being
—however wretched—who cares enough for you to care
about the truth in what concerns you," Laura said. "Selina,
Selina—are you hideously deceiving us?"

"Us?" Selina repeated, with a singular laugh. "Whom do
you mean by us?"

Laura Wing hesitated; she had asked herself whether it
would be best she should let her sister know the dreadful

scene she had had with Lionel; but she had not, in her mind, settled that point. However, it was settled now in an instant. "I don't mean your friends—those of them that I have seen. I don't think *they* care a straw—I have never seen such people. But last week Lionel spoke to me—he told me he *knew* it, as a certainty."

"Lionel spoke to you?" said Mrs Berrington, holding up her head with a stare. "And what is it that he knows?"

"That Captain Crispin was in Paris, and that you were with him. He believes you went there to meet him."

"He said this to *you?*"

"Yes, and much more—I don't know why I should make a secret of it."

"The disgusting beast!" Selina exclaimed slowly, solemnly. "He enjoys the right—the legal right—to pour forth his vileness upon *me;* but when he is so lost to every feeling as to begin to talk to you in such a way——!" And Mrs Berrington paused, in the extremity of her reprobation.

"Oh, it was not his talk that shocked me—it was his believing it," the girl replied. "That, I confess, made an impression on me."

"Did it indeed? I'm infinitely obliged to you! You are a tender, loving little sister."

"Yes, I am, if it's tender to have cried about you—all these days—till I'm blind and sick!" Laura replied. "I hope you are prepared to meet him. His mind is quite made up to apply for a divorce."

Laura's voice almost failed her as she said this—it was the first time that in talking with Selina she had uttered that horrible word. She had heard it however, often enough on the lips of others; it had been bandied lightly enough in her presence under those somewhat austere ceilings of Mellows, of which the admired decorations and mouldings, in the taste of the middle of the last century, all in delicate plaster and reminding her of Wedgwood pottery, consisted of slim festoons, urns and trophies and knotted ribbons, so many symbols of domestic affection and irrevocable union. Selina herself had flashed it at her with light superiority, as if it were some precious jewel kept in reserve, which she could convert at any moment into specie, so that it would constitute a happy provision for her future. The idea—associated with her own point of view—was apparently too familiar to Mrs Berrington to be the cause of her changing colour; it struck her indeed, as presented by Laura, in a ludicrous light, for her pretty eyes expanded a moment and she smiled pityingly. "Well, you are a poor dear innocent, after all. Lionel would be about as able to divorce me—even if I were the most abandoned of my sex—as he would be to write a leader in the *Times*."

"I know nothing about that," said Laura.

"So I perceive—as I also perceive that you must have shut your eyes very tight. Should you like to know a few of the reasons—heaven forbid I should attempt to go over them all; there are millions!—why his hands are tied?"

"Not in the least."

"Should you like to know that his own life is too base for words and that his impudence in talking about me would be sickening, if it weren't grotesque?" Selina went on, with increasing emotion. "Should you like me to tell you to what he has stooped—to the very gutter—and the charming history of his relations with——"

"No, I don't want you to tell me anything of the sort," Laura interrupted. "Especially as you were just now so pained by the license of my own allusions."

"You listen to him then—but it suits your purpose not to listen to me!"

"Oh, Selina, Selina!" the girl almost shrieked, turning away.

"Where have your eyes been, or your senses, or your powers of observation? You can be clever enough when it suits you!" Mrs Berrington continued, throwing off another ripple of derision. "And now perhaps, as the carriage is waiting, you will let me go about my duties."

Laura turned again and stopped her, holding her arm as she passed toward the door. "Will you swear—will you swear by everything that is most sacred?"

"Will I swear what?" And now she thought Selina visibly blanched.

"That you didn't lay eyes on Captain Crispin in Paris."

Mrs Berrington hesitated, but only for an instant. "You are really too odious, but as you are pinching me to death I will swear, to get away from you. I never laid eyes on him."

The organs of vision which Mrs Berrington was ready solemnly to declare that she had not misapplied were, as her sister looked into them, an abyss of indefinite prettiness. The girl had sounded them before without discovering a conscience at the bottom of them, and they had never helped any one to find out anything about their possessor except that she was one of the beauties of London. Even while Selina spoke Laura had a cold, horrible sense of not believing her, and at the same time a desire, colder still, to extract a reiteration of the pledge. Was it the asseveration of her innocence that she wished her to repeat, or only the attestation of her falsity? One way or the other it seemed to her that this would settle something, and she went on inexorably—"By our dear mother's memory—by our poor father's?"

"By my mother's, by my father's," said Mrs Berrington, "and by that of any other member of the family you like!" Laura let her go; she had not been pinching her, as Selina described the pressure, but had clung to her with insistent hands. As she opened the door Selina said, in a changed voice: "I suppose it's no use to ask you if you care to drive to Plash."

"No, thank you, I don't care—I shall take a walk."

"I suppose, from that, that your friend Lady Davenant has gone."

"No, I think she is still there."

"That's a bore!" Selina exclaimed, as she went off.

VI

LAURA WING hastened to her room to prepare herself for her walk; but when she reached it she simply fell on her knees, shuddering, beside her bed. She buried her face in the soft counterpane of wadded silk; she remained there a long time, with a kind of aversion to lifting it again to the day. It burned with horror and there was coolness in the smooth glaze of the silk. It seemed to her that she had been concerned in a hideous transaction, and her uppermost feeling was, strangely enough, that she was ashamed—not of her sister but of herself. She did not believe her—that was at the bottom of everything, and she had made her lie, she had brought out her perjury, she had associated it with the sacred images of the dead. She took no walk, she remained in her room, and quite late, towards six o'clock, she heard on the gravel, outside of her windows, the wheels of the carriage bringing back Mrs Berrington. She had evidently been elsewhere as well as to Plash; no doubt she had been to the vicarage—she was capable even of that. She could pay "duty-visits," like that (she called at the vicarage about three times a year), and she could go and be nice to her mother-in-law with her fresh lips still fresher for the lie she had just told. For it was as definite as an aching nerve to Laura that she did not believe her, and if she did not believe her the words she had spoken were a lie. It was the lie, the lie to *her* and which she had dragged out of her that seemed to the girl the ugliest thing. If she had admitted her folly, if she had explained, attenuated, sophisticated, there would have been a difference in her favour; but now she was bad because she was hard. She had a surface of polished metal. And she could make plans and calculate, she could act and do things for a particular effect. She could go straight to old Mrs Berrington and to the parson's wife and his many daughters (just as she had kept the children after luncheon, on purpose, so long) because that looked innocent and domestic and denoted a mind without a feather's weight upon it.

A servant came to the young lady's door to tell her that tea was ready; and on her asking who else was below (for she had heard the wheels of a second vehicle just after Selina's return), she learned that Lionel had come back. At this news she requested that some tea should be brought to her room—she determined not to go to dinner. When the dinner-hour came she sent down word that she had a headache, that she was going to bed. She wondered whether Selina would come to her (she could forget disagreeable scenes amazingly); but her fervent hope that she would stay away was gratified. Indeed she would have another call upon her attention if her meeting with her husband was half as much of a concussion as was to have been expected. Laura had found herself listening hard, after knowing that her brother-in-law was in the house: she half expected to hear indications of violence—loud cries or the sound of a scuffle. It was a matter of course to her that some dreadful scene had not been slow to take place, something that discretion should keep her out of even if she had not been too sick. She did not go to bed—partly because she didn't know what might happen in the house. But she was restless also for herself: things had reached a point when it seemed to her that she must make up her mind. She left her candles unlighted—she sat up till the small hours, in the glow of the fire. What had been settled by her scene with Selina was that worse things were to come (looking into her fire, as the night went on, she had a rare prevision of the catastrophe that hung over the house), and she considered, or tried to consider, what it would be best for her, in anticipation, to do. The first thing was to take flight.

It may be related without delay that Laura Wing did not take flight and that though the circumstance detracts from the interest that should be felt in her character she did not even make up her mind. That was not so easy when action had to ensue. At the same time she had not the excuse of a conviction that by not acting—that is by not withdrawing from her brother-in-law's roof—she should be able to hold Selina up to her duty, to drag her back into the straight path. The hopes connected with that project were now a phase that she had left behind her; she had not to-day an illusion about her sister large enough to cover a sixpence. She had passed through the period of superstition, which had lasted the longest—the time when it seemed to her, as at first, a kind of profanity to doubt of Selina and judge her, the elder sister whose beauty and success she had ever been proud of and who carried herself, though with the most good-natured fraternisings, as one native to an upper air. She had called herself in moments of early penitence for irrepressible suspicion a little presumptuous prig: so strange did it seem to her at first, the impulse of criticism in regard to her bright protectress. But the revolution was over and she had a desolate, lonely freedom which struck her as not the most cynical thing in the world only because Selina's behaviour was more so. She supposed she should learn, though she was afraid of the knowledge, what had passed between that lady and her husband while her vigil ached itself away. But it appeared to her the next day, to her surprise, that nothing was changed in the situation save that Selina knew at present how much more she was suspected. As this had not a chastening effect upon Mrs Berrington nothing had been gained by Laura's appeal to her. Whatever Lionel had said to his wife he said nothing to Laura: he left her at perfect liberty to forget the subject he had opened up to her so luminously. This was very characteristic of his good-nature; it had come over him that after all she wouldn't like it, and if the free use of the gray ponies could make up to her for the shock she might order them every day in the week and banish the unpleasant episode from her mind.

Laura ordered the gray ponies very often: she drove herself all over the country. She visited not only the neighbouring but the distant poor, and she never went out without stopping for one of the vicar's fresh daughters. Mellows was now half the time full of visitors and when it was not its master and mistress were staying with their friends either together or singly. Sometimes (almost always when she was asked) Laura Wing accompanied her sister and on two or three occasions she paid an independent visit. Selina had often told her that she wished her to have her own friends, so that the girl now felt a great desire to show her that she had them. She had arrived at no decision whatever; she had embraced in intention no particular course. She drifted on, shutting her eyes, averting her head and, as it seemed to herself, hardening her heart. This admission will doubtless suggest to the reader that she was a weak, inconsequent, spasmodic young person, with a standard not really, or at any rate not continuously, high; and I have no desire that she shall appear anything but what she was. It must even be related of her that since she could not escape and live in lodgings and paint fans (there were reasons why this combination was impossible) she determined to try and be happy in the given circumstances—to float in shallow, turbid water. She gave up the attempt to understand the cynical *modus vivendi* at which her companions seemed to have arrived; she knew it was not final but it served them sufficiently for the time; and if it served them why should it not serve her, the dependent, impecunious, tolerated little sister, representative of the class whom it behoved above all to mind their own business? The time was coming round when they would all move up to town, and there, in the crowd, with the added movement, the strain would be less and indifference easier.

Whatever Lionel had said to his wife that evening she had found something to say to him: that Laura could see, though not so much from any change in the simple expression of his little red face and in the vain bustle of his existence as from the grand manner in which Selina now carried herself. She was "smarter" than ever and her waist was smaller and her back straighter and the fall of her shoulders finer; her long eyes were more oddly charming and the extreme detachment of her elbows from her sides conduced still more to the exhibition of her beautiful arms. So she floated, with a serenity not disturbed by a general tardiness, through the interminable succession of her engagements. Her photographs were not to be purchased in the Burlington Arcade—she had kept out of that; but she looked more than ever as they would have represented her if they had been obtainable there. There were times when Laura thought her brother-in-law's formless desistence too frivolous for nature; it even gave her a sense of deeper dangers. It was as if he had been digging away in the dark and they would all tumble into the hole. It happened to her to ask herself whether the things he had said to her the afternoon he fell upon her in the schoolroom had not all been a clumsy practical joke, a crude desire to scare, that of a schoolboy playing with a sheet in the dark; or else brandy and soda, which came to the same thing. However this might be she was obliged to recognise that the impression of brandy and soda had not again been given her. More striking still however was Selina's capacity to recover from shocks and condone imputations; she kissed again—kissed Laura—without tears, and proposed problems connected with the rearrangement of trimmings and of the flowers at dinner, as candidly—as earnestly—as if there had never been an intenser question between them. Captain Crispin was not mentioned; much less of course, so far as Laura was concerned, was he seen. But Lady Ringrose appeared; she came down for two days, during an absence of Lionel's. Laura, to her surprise, found her no such Jezebel but a clever little woman with a single eye-glass and short hair who had read Lecky and could give her useful hints about water-colours; a reconciliation that encouraged the girl, for this was the direction in which it now seemed to her best that she herself should grow.

VII

In Grosvenor Place, on Sunday afternoon, during the first weeks of the season, Mrs Berrington was usually at home: this indeed was the only time when a visitor who had not made an appointment could hope to be admitted to her presence. Very few hours in the twenty-four did she spend in her own house. Gentlemen calling on these occasions rarely found her sister: Mrs Berrington had the field to herself. It was understood between the pair that Laura should take this time for going to see her old women: it was in that manner that Selina qualified the girl's independent social resources. The old women however were not a dozen in number; they consisted mainly of Lady Davenant and the elder Mrs Berrington, who had a house in Portman Street. Lady Davenant lived at Queen's Gate and also was usually at home of a Sunday afternoon: her visitors were not all men, like Selina Berrington's, and Laura's maidenly bonnet was not a false note in her drawing-room. Selina liked her sister, naturally enough, to make herself useful, but of late, somehow, they had grown rarer, the occasions that depended in any degree upon her aid, and she had never been much appealed to—though it would have seemed natural she should be—on behalf of the weekly chorus of gentlemen. It came to be recognised on Selina's part that nature had dedicated her more to the relief of old women than to that of young men. Laura had a distinct sense of interfering with the free interchange of anecdote and pleasantry that went on at her sister's fireside: the anecdotes were mostly such an immense secret that they could not be told fairly if she were there, and she had their privacy on her conscience. There was an exception however; when Selina expected Americans she naturally asked her to stay at home; not apparently so much because their conversation would be good for her as because hers would be good for them.

One Sunday, about the middle of May, Laura Wing prepared herself to go and see Lady Davenant, who had made a long absence from town at Easter but would now have returned. The weather was charming, she had from the first established her right to tread the London streets alone (if she was a poor girl she could have the detachment as well as the helplessness of it) and she promised herself the pleasure of a walk along the park, where the new grass was bright. A moment before she quitted the house her sister sent for her to the drawing-room; the servant gave her a note scrawled in pencil: "That man from New York is here—Mr Wendover, who brought me the introduction the other day from the Schoolings. He's rather a dose—you must positively come down and talk to him. Take him out with you if you can." The description was not alluring, but Selina had never made a request of her to which the girl had not instantly responded: it seemed to her she was there for that. She joined the circle in the drawing-room and found that it consisted of five persons, one of whom was Lady Ringrose. Lady Ringrose was at all times and in all places a fitful apparition; she had described herself to Laura during her visit at Mellows as "a bird on the branch." She had no fixed habit of receiving on Sunday, she was in and out as she liked, and she was one of the few specimens of her sex who, in Grosvenor Place, ever turned up, as she said, on the occasions to which I allude. Of the three gentlemen two were known to Laura; she could have told you at least that the big one with the red hair was in the Guards and the other in the Rifles; the latter looked like a rosy child and as if he ought to be sent up to play with Geordie and Ferdy: his social nickname indeed was the Baby. Selina's admirers were of all ages—they ranged from infants to octogenarians.

She introduced the third gentleman to her sister; a tall, fair, slender young man who suggested that he had made a mistake in the shade of his tight, perpendicular coat, ordering it of too heavenly a blue. This added however to the candour of his appearance, and if he was a dose, as Selina had described him, he could only operate beneficently. There were moments when Laura's heart rather yearned towards her countrymen, and now, though she was preoccupied and a little disappointed at having been detained, she tried to like Mr Wendover, whom her sister had compared invidiously, as it seemed to her, with her other companions. It struck her that his surface at least was as glossy as theirs. The Baby, whom she remembered to have heard spoken of as a dangerous flirt, was in conversation with Lady Ringrose and the guardsman with Mrs Berrington; so she did her best to entertain the American visitor, as to whom any one could easily see (she thought) that he had brought a letter of introduction—he wished so to maintain the credit of those who had given it to him. Laura scarcely knew these people, American friends of her sister who had spent a period of festivity in London and gone back across the sea before her own advent; but Mr Wendover gave her all possible information about them. He lingered upon them, returned to them, corrected statements he had made at first, discoursed upon them earnestly and exhaustively. He seemed to fear to leave them, lest he should find nothing again so good, and he indulged in a parallel that was almost elaborate between Miss Fanny and Miss Katie. Selina told her sister afterwards that she had overheard him—

that he talked of them as if he had been a nursemaid; upon
which Laura defended the young man even to extravagance.
She reminded her sister that people in London were always
saying Lady Mary and Lady Susan: why then shouldn't
Americans use the Christian name, with the humbler prefix
with which they had to content themselves? There had been
a time when Mrs Berrington had been happy enough to be
Miss Lina, even though she was the elder sister; and the girl
liked to think there were still old friends—friends of the
family, at home, for whom, even should she live to sixty years
of spinsterhood, she would never be anything but Miss
Laura. This was as good as Donna Anna or Donna Elvira:
English people could never call people as other people did, for
fear of resembling the servants.

Mr Wendover was very attentive, as well as communicative; however his letter might be regarded in Grosvenor Place
he evidently took it very seriously himself; but his eyes wandered considerably, none the less, to the other side of the
room, and Laura felt that though he had often seen persons
like her before (not that he betrayed this too crudely) he had
never seen any one like Lady Ringrose. His glance rested also
on Mrs Berrington, who, to do her justice, abstained from
showing, by the way she returned it, that she wished her sister
to get him out of the room. Her smile was particularly pretty
on Sunday afternoons and he was welcome to enjoy it as a
part of the decoration of the place. Whether or no the young
man should prove interesting he was at any rate interested;
indeed she afterwards learned that what Selina deprecated in
him was the fact that he would eventually display a fatiguing
intensity of observation. He would be one of the sort who
noticed all kinds of little things—things she never saw or
heard of—in the newspapers or in society, and would call
upon her (a dreadful prospect) to explain or even to defend
them. She had not come there to explain England to the
Americans; the more particularly as her life had been a

burden to her during the first years of her marriage through her having to explain America to the English. As for defending England to her countrymen she had much rather defend it *from* them: there were too many—too many for those who were already there. This was the class she wished to spare— she didn't care about the English. They could obtain an eye for an eye and a cutlet for a cutlet by going over there; which she had no desire to do—not for all the cutlets in Christendom!

When Mr Wendover and Laura had at last cut loose from the Schoolings he let her know confidentially that he had come over really to see London: he had time, that year; he didn't know when he should have it again (if ever, as he said) and he had made up his mind that this was about the best use he could make of four months and a half. He had heard so much of it; it was talked of so much to-day; a man felt as if he ought to know something about it. Laura wished the others could hear this—that England was coming up, was making her way at last to a place among the topics of societies more universal. She thought Mr Wendover after all remarkably like an Englishman, in spite of his saying that he believed she had resided in London quite a time. He talked a great deal about things being characteristic, and wanted to know, lowering his voice to make the inquiry, whether Lady Ringrose were not particularly so. He had heard of her very often, he said; and he observed that it was very interesting to see her: he could not have used a different tone if he had been speaking of the prime minister or the laureate. Laura was ignorant of what he had heard of Lady Ringrose; she doubted whether it could be the same as what she had heard from her brother-in-law: if this had been the case he never would have mentioned it. She foresaw that his friends in London would have a good deal to do in the way of telling him whether this or that were characteristic or not; he would go about in much the same way that English travellers did in America, fixing his attention mainly on society (he let Laura know that this was especially what he wished to go into) and neglecting the antiquities and sights, quite as if he failed to believe in their importance. He would ask questions it was impossible to answer; as to whether for instance society were very different in the two countries. If you said yes you gave a wrong impression and if you said no you didn't give a right one: that was the kind of thing that Selina had suffered from. Laura found her new acquaintance, on the present occasion and later, more philosophically analytic of his impressions than those of her countrymen she had hitherto encountered in her new home; the latter, in regard to such impressions, usually exhibited either a profane levity or a tendency to mawkish idealism.

Mrs Berrington called out at last to Laura that she must not stay if she had prepared herself to go out: whereupon the girl, having nodded and smiled good-bye at the other members of the circle, took a more formal leave of Mr Wendover —expressed the hope, as an American girl does in such a case, that they should see him again. Selina asked him to come and dine three days later; which was as much as to say that relations might be suspended till then. Mr Wendover took it so, and having accepted the invitation he departed at the same time as Laura. He passed out of the house with her and in the street she asked him which way he was going. He was too tender, but she liked him; he appeared not to deal in chaff and that was a change that relieved her—she had so often had to pay out that coin when she felt wretchedly poor. She hoped he would ask her leave to go with her the way she was going —and this not on particular but on general grounds. It would be American, it would remind her of old times; she should like him to be as American as that. There was no reason for her taking so quick an interest in his nature, inasmuch as she had not fallen under his spell; but there were moments when she felt a whimsical desire to be reminded of the way people felt and acted at home. Mr Wendover did not disappoint her, and the bright chocolate-coloured vista of the Fifth Avenue seemed to surge before her as he said, "May I have the pleasure of making my direction the same as yours?" and moved round, systematically, to take his place between her and the curbstone. She had never walked much with young men in America (she had been brought up in the new school, the school of attendant maids and the avoidance of certain streets) and she had very often done so in England, in the country; yet, as at the top of Grosvenor Place she crossed over to the park, proposing they should take that way, the breath of her native land was in her nostrils. It was certainly only an American who could have the tension of Mr Wendover; his solemnity almost made her laugh, just as her eyes grew dull when people "slanged" each other hilariously in her sister's house; but at the same time he gave her a feeling of high respectability. It would be respectable still if she were to go on with him indefinitely—if she never were to come home at all. He asked her after a while, as they went, whether he had violated the custom of the English in offering her his company; whether in that country a gentleman might walk with a young lady—the first time he saw her—not because their roads lay together but for the sake of the walk.

"Why should it matter to me whether it is the custom of the English? I am not English," said Laura Wing. Then her companion explained that he only wanted a general guidance —that with her (she was so kind) he had not the sense of having taken a liberty. The point was simply—and rather comprehensively and strenuously he began to set forth the point. Laura interrupted him; she said she didn't care about it and he almost irritated her by telling her she was kind. She was, but she was not pleased at its being recognised so soon; and he was still too importunate when he asked her whether she continued to go by American usage, didn't find that if one lived there one had to conform in a great many ways to the English. She was weary of the perpetual comparison, for she not only heard it from others—she heard it a great deal from herself. She held that there were certain differences you felt, if you belonged to one or the other nation, and that was the end of it: there was no use trying to express them. Those you *could* express were not real or not important ones and were not worth talking about. Mr Wendover asked her if she liked English society and if it were superior to American; also if the tone were very high in London. She thought his questions "academic"—the term she used to see applied in the *Times* to certain speeches in Parliament. Bending his long leanness over her (she had never seen a man whose material presence was so insubstantial, so unoppressive) and walking almost sidewise, to give her a proper attention, he struck her as innocent, as incapable of guessing that she had had a certain observation of life. They were talking about totally different things: English society, as he asked her judgment upon it and she had happened to see it, was an affair that he didn't suspect. If she were to give him that judgment it would be more than he doubtless bargained for; but she would do it not to make him open his eyes—only to relieve herself. She had thought of that before in regard to two or three persons she had met—of the satisfaction of breaking out with some of her feelings. It would make little difference whether the person understood her or not; the one who should do so best would be far from understanding everything. "I want to get out of it, please—out of the set I live in, the one I have tumbled into through my sister, the people you saw just now. There are thousands of people in London who are different from that and ever so much nicer; but I don't see them, I don't know how to get at them; and after all, poor dear man, what power have you to help me?" That was in the last analysis the gist of what she had to say.

Mr Wendover asked her about Selina in the tone of a person who thought Mrs Berrington a very important phenomenon, and that by itself was irritating to Laura Wing.

Important—gracious goodness, no! She might have to live
with her, to hold her tongue about her; but at least she was
not bound to exaggerate her significance. The young man
forbore decorously to make use of the expression, but she
could see that he supposed Selina to be a professional beauty
and she guessed that as this product had not yet been domes-
ticated in the western world the desire to behold it, after
having read so much about it, had been one of the motives of
Mr Wendover's pilgrimage. Mrs Schooling, who must have
been a goose, had told him that Mrs Berrington, though
transplanted, was the finest flower of a rich, ripe society and
as clever and virtuous as she was beautiful. Meanwhile Laura
knew what Selina thought of Fanny Schooling and her
incurable provinciality. "Now was that a good example of
London talk—what I heard (I only heard a little of it, but the
conversation was more general before you came in) in your
sister's drawing-room? I don't mean literary, intellectual
talk—I suppose there are special places to hear that; I mean—
I mean——" Mr Wendover went on with a deliberation
which gave his companion an opportunity to interrupt him.
They had arrived at Lady Davenant's door and she cut his
meaning short. A fancy had taken her, on the spot, and the
fact that it was whimsical seemed only to recommend it.

"If you want to hear London talk there will be some very
good going on in here," she said. "If you would like to come
in with me——?"

"Oh, you are very kind—I should be delighted," replied
Mr Wendover, endeavouring to emulate her own more rapid
processes. They stepped into the porch and the young man,
anticipating his companion, lifted the knocker and gave a
postman's rap. She laughed at him for this and he looked
bewildered; the idea of taking him in with her had become
agreeably exhilarating. Their acquaintance, in that moment,
took a long jump. She explained to him who Lady Davenant
was and that if he was in search of the characteristic it would

be a pity he shouldn't know her; and then she added, before
he could put the question:

"And what I am doing is *not* in the least usual. No, it is
not the custom for young ladies here to take strange gentlemen off to call on their friends the first time they see them."

"So that Lady Davenant will think it rather extraordinary?" Mr Wendover eagerly inquired; not as if that idea
frightened him, but so that his observation on this point
should also be well founded. He had entered into Laura's
proposal with complete serenity.

"Oh, most extraordinary!" said Laura, as they went in.
The old lady however concealed such surprise as she may
have felt, and greeted Mr Wendover as if he were any one of
fifty familiars. She took him altogether for granted and asked
him no questions about his arrival, his departure, his hotel or
his business in England. He noticed, as he afterwards confided to Laura, her omission of these forms; but he was not
wounded by it—he only made a mark against it as an illustration of the difference between English and American
manners: in New York people always asked the arriving
stranger the first thing about the steamer and the hotel. Mr
Wendover appeared greatly impressed with Lady Davenant's
antiquity, though he confessed to his companion on a subsequent occasion that he thought her a little flippant, a little
frivolous even for her years. "Oh yes," said the girl, on that
occasion, "I have no doubt that you considered she talked
too much, for one so old. In America old ladies sit silent and
listen to the young." Mr Wendover stared a little and replied
to this that with her—with Laura Wing—it was impossible
to tell which side she was on, the American or the English:
sometimes she seemed to take one, sometimes the other. At
any rate, he added, smiling, with regard to the other great
division it was easy to see—she was on the side of the old.
"Of course I am," she said; "when one *is* old!" And then he
inquired, according to his wont, if she were thought so in

England; to which she answered that it was England that had made her so.

Lady Davenant's bright drawing-room was filled with mementoes and especially with a collection of portraits of distinguished people, mainly fine old prints with signatures, an array of precious autographs. "Oh, it's a cemetery," she said, when the young man asked her some question about one of the pictures; "they are my contemporaries, they are all dead and those things are the tombstones, with the inscriptions. I'm the grave-digger, I look after the place and try to keep it a little tidy. I have dug my own little hole," she went on, to Laura, "and when you are sent for you must come and put me in." This evocation of mortality led Mr Wendover to ask her if she had known Charles Lamb; at which she stared for an instant, replying: "Dear me, no—one didn't meet him."

"Oh, I meant to say Lord Byron," said Mr Wendover.

"Bless me, yes; I was in love with him. But he didn't notice me, fortunately—we were so many. He was very nice-looking but he was very vulgar." Lady Davenant talked to Laura as if Mr Wendover had not been there; or rather as if his interests and knowledge were identical with hers. Before they went away the young man asked her if she had known Garrick, and she replied: "Oh, dear, no, we didn't have them in our houses, in those days."

"He must have been dead long before you were born!" Laura exclaimed.

"I daresay; but one used to hear of him."

"I think I meant Edmund Kean," said Mr Wendover.

"You make little mistakes of a century or two," Laura Wing remarked, laughing. She felt now as if she had known Mr Wendover a long time.

"Oh, he was very clever," said Lady Davenant.

"Very magnetic, I suppose," Mr Wendover went on.

"What's that? I believe he used to get tipsy."

"Perhaps you don't use that expression in England?"
Laura's companion inquired.

"Oh, I daresay we do, if it's American; we talk American
now. You seem very good-natured people, but such a jargon
as you *do* speak!"

"I like *your* way, Lady Davenant," said Mr Wendover,
benevolently, smiling.

"You might do worse," cried the old woman; and then she
added: "Please go out!" They were taking leave of her but
she kept Laura's hand and, for the young man, nodded with
decision at the open door. "Now, wouldn't *he* do?" she asked,
after Mr Wendover had passed into the hall.

"Do for what?"

"For a husband, of course."

"For a husband—for whom?"

"Why—for me," said Lady Davenant.

"I don't know—I think he might tire you."

"Oh—if he's tiresome!" the old lady continued, smiling
at the girl.

"I think he is very good," said Laura.

"Well then, he'll do."

"Ah, perhaps *you* won't!" Laura exclaimed smiling back
at her and turning away.

VIII

SHE was of a serious turn by nature and unlike many serious
people she made no particular study of the art of being gay.
Had her circumstances been different she might have done so,
but she lived in a merry house (heaven save the mark! as she
used to say) and therefore was not driven to amuse herself for
conscience sake. The diversions she sought were of a serious
cast and she liked those best which showed most the note of

difference from Selina's interests and Lionel's. She felt that she was most divergent when she attempted to cultivate her mind, and it was a branch of such cultivation to visit the curiosities, the antiquities, the monuments of London. She was fond of the Abbey and the British Museum—she had extended her researches as far as the Tower. She read the works of Mr John Timbs and made notes of the old corners of history that had not yet been abolished—the houses in which great men had lived and died. She planned a general tour of inspection of the ancient churches of the City and a pilgrimage to the queer places commemorated by Dickens. It must be added that though her intentions were great her adventures had as yet been small. She had wanted for opportunity and independence; people had other things to do than to go with her, so that it was not till she had been some time in the country and till a good while after she had begun to go out alone that she entered upon the privilege of visiting public institutions by herself. There were some aspects of London that frightened her, but there were certain spots, such as the Poets' Corner in the Abbey or the room of the Elgin marbles, where she liked better to be alone than not to have the right companion. At the time Mr Wendover presented himself in Grosvenor Place she had begun to put in, as they said, a museum or something of that sort whenever she had a chance. Besides her idea that such places were sources of knowledge (it is to be feared that the poor girl's notions of knowledge were at once conventional and crude) they were also occasions for detachment, an escape from worrying thoughts. She forgot Selina and she "qualified" herself a little—though for what she hardly knew.

The day Mr Wendover dined in Grosvenor Place they talked about St Paul's, which he expressed a desire to see, wishing to get some idea of the great past, as he said, in England as well as of the present. Laura mentioned that she had spent half an hour the summer before in the big black temple on Ludgate Hill; whereupon he asked her if he might entertain the hope that—if it were not disagreeable to her to go again—she would serve as his guide there. She had taken him to see Lady Davenant, who was so remarkable and worth a long journey, and now he should like to pay her back—to show *her* something. The difficulty would be that there was probably nothing she had not seen; but if she could think of anything he was completely at her service. They sat together at dinner and she told him she would think of something before the repast was over. A little while later she let him know that a charming place had occurred to her—a place to which she was afraid to go alone and where she should be grateful for a protector: she would tell him more about it afterwards. It was then settled between them that on a certain afternoon of the same week they would go to St Paul's together, extending their ramble as much further as they had time. Laura lowered her voice for this discussion, as if the range of allusion had had a kind of impropriety. She was now still more of the mind that Mr Wendover was a good young man—he had such worthy eyes. His principal defect was that he treated all subjects as if they were equally important; but that was perhaps better than treating them with equal levity. If one took an interest in him one might not despair of teaching him to discriminate.

Laura said nothing at first to her sister about her appointment with him: the feelings with which she regarded Selina were not such as to make it easy for her to talk over matters of conduct, as it were, with this votary of pleasure at any price, or at any rate to report her arrangements to her as one would do to a person of fine judgment. All the same, as she had a horror of positively hiding anything (Selina herself did that enough for two) it was her purpose to mention at luncheon on the day of the event that she had agreed to accompany Mr Wendover to St Paul's. It so happened however that Mrs Berrington was not at home at this repast; Laura partook of it in the company of Miss Steet and her young charges. It very often happened now that the sisters failed to meet in the morning, for Selina remained very late in her room and there had been a considerable intermission of the girl's earlier custom of visiting her there. It was Selina's habit to send forth from this fragrant sanctuary little hieroglyphic notes in which she expressed her wishes or gave her directions for the day. On the morning I speak of her maid put into Laura's hand one of these communications, which contained the words: "Please be sure and replace me with the children at lunch—I meant to give them that hour to-day. But I have a frantic appeal from Lady Watermouth; she is worse and beseeches me to come to her, so I rush for the 12.30 train." These lines required no answer and Laura had no questions to ask about Lady Watermouth. She knew she was tiresomely ill, in exile, condemned to forego the diversions of the season and calling out to her friends, in a house she had taken for three months at Weybridge (for a certain particular air) where Selina had already been to see her. Selina's devotion to her appeared commendable—she had her so much on her mind. Laura had observed in her sister in relation to other persons and objects these sudden intensities of charity, and she had said to herself, watching them—"Is it because she is bad?— does she want to make up for it somehow and to buy herself off from the penalties?"

Mr Wendover called for his *cicerone* and they agreed to go in a romantic, Bohemian manner (the young man was very docile and appreciative about this), walking the short distance to the Victoria station and taking the mysterious underground railway. In the carriage she anticipated the inquiry that she figured to herself he presently would make and said, laughing: "No, no, this is very exceptional; if we were both English—and both what we are, otherwise—we wouldn't do this."

"And if only one of us were English?"

"It would depend upon which one."

"Well, say me."

"Oh, in that case I certainly—on so short an acquaintance —would not go sight-seeing with you."

"Well, I am glad I'm American," said Mr Wendover, sitting opposite to her.

"Yes, you may thank your fate. It's much simpler," Laura added.

"Oh, you spoil it!" the young man exclaimed—a speech of which she took no notice but which made her think him brighter, as they used to say at home. He was brighter still after they had descended from the train at the Temple station (they had meant to go on to Blackfriars, but they jumped out on seeing the sign of the Temple, fired with the thought of visiting that institution too) and got admission to the old garden of the Benchers, which lies beside the foggy, crowded river, and looked at the tombs of the crusaders in the low Romanesque church, with the cross-legged figures sleeping so close to the eternal uproar, and lingered in the flagged, homely courts of brick, with their much-lettered door-posts, their dull old windows and atmosphere of consultation— lingered to talk of Johnson and Goldsmith and to remark how London opened one's eyes to Dickens; and he was brightest of all when they stood in the high, bare cathedral, which suggested a dirty whiteness, saying it was fine but wondering why it was not finer and letting a glance as cold as the dusty, colourless glass fall upon epitaphs that seemed to make most of the defunct bores even in death. Mr Wendover was decorous but he was increasingly gay, and these qualities appeared in him in spite of the fact that St Paul's was rather a disappointment. Then they felt the advantage of having the other place—the one Laura had had in mind at dinner—to fall back upon: that perhaps would prove a compensation. They entered a hansom now (they had to come to that, though they had walked also from the Temple to St Paul's) and drove to

Lincoln's Inn Fields, Laura making the reflection as they
went that it was really a charm to roam about London under
valid protection—such a mixture of freedom and safety—and
that perhaps she had been unjust, ungenerous to her sister. A
good-natured, positively charitable doubt came into her mind
—a doubt that Selina might have the benefit of. What she
liked in her present undertaking was the element of the
imprévu that it contained, and perhaps it was simply the same
happy sense of getting the laws of London—once in a way—
off her back that had led Selina to go over to Paris to ramble
about with Captain Crispin. Possibly they had done nothing
worse than go together to the Invalides and Notre Dame; and
if any one were to meet *her* driving that way, so far from
home, with Mr Wendover—Laura, mentally, did not finish
her sentence, overtaken as she was by the reflection that she
had fallen again into her old assumption (she had been in and
out of it a hundred times), that Mrs Berrington *had* met
Captain Crispin—the idea she so passionately repudiated.
She at least would never deny that she had spent the afternoon
with Mr Wendover: she would simply say that he was an
American and had brought a letter of introduction.

The cab stopped at the Soane Museum, which Laura Wing
had always wanted to see, a compatriot having once told her
that it was one of the most curious things in London and one
of the least known. While Mr Wendover was discharging the
vehicle she looked over the important old-fashioned square
(which led her to say to herself that London was endlessly big
and one would never know all the places that made it up) and
saw a great bank of cloud hanging above it—a definite portent of a summer storm. "We are going to have thunder; you
had better keep the cab," she said; upon which her companion told the man to wait, so that they should not afterwards, in the wet, have to walk for another conveyance. The
heterogeneous objects collected by the late Sir John Soane are
arranged in a fine old dwelling-house, and the place gives one

the impression of a sort of Saturday afternoon of one's youth
—a long, rummaging visit, under indulgent care, to some
eccentric and rather alarming old travelled person. Our young
friends wandered from room to room and thought everything
queer and some few objects interesting; Mr Wendover said it
would be a very good place to find a thing you couldn't find
anywhere else—it illustrated the prudent virtue of keeping.
They took note of the sarcophagi and pagodas, the artless old
maps and medals. They admired the fine Hogarths; there were
uncanny, unexpected objects that Laura edged away from,
that she would have preferred not to be in the room with.
They had been there half an hour—it had grown much
darker—when they heard a tremendous peal of thunder and
became aware that the storm had broken. They watched it a
while from the upper windows—a violent June shower, with
quick sheets of lightning and a rainfall that danced on the
pavements. They took it sociably, they lingered at the window, inhaling the odour of the fresh wet that splashed over
the sultry town. They would have to wait till it had passed,
and they resigned themselves serenely to this idea, repeating
very often that it would pass very soon. One of the keepers
told them that there were other rooms to see—that there were
very interesting things in the basement. They made their way
down—it grew much darker and they heard a great deal of
thunder—and entered a part of the house which presented
itself to Laura as a series of dim, irregular vaults—passages
and little narrow avenues—encumbered with strange vague
things, obscured for the time but some of which had a wicked,
startling look, so that she wondered how the keepers could
stay there. "It's very fearful—it looks like a cave of idols!"
she said to her companion; and then she added—"Just look
there—is that a person or a thing?" As she spoke they drew
nearer to the object of her reference—a figure in the middle of
a small vista of curiosities, a figure which answered her question by uttering a short shriek as they approached. The

immediate cause of this cry was apparently a vivid flash of lightning, which penetrated into the room and illuminated both Laura's face and that of the mysterious person. Our young lady recognised her sister, as Mrs Berrington had evidently recognised her. "Why, Selina!" broke from her lips before she had time to check the words. At the same moment the figure turned quickly away, and then Laura saw that it was accompanied by another, that of a tall gentleman with a light beard which shone in the dusk. The two persons retreated together—dodged out of sight, as it were, disappearing in the gloom or in the labyrinth of the objects exhibited. The whole encounter was but the business of an instant.

"Was it Mrs Berrington?" Mr Wendover asked with interest while Laura stood staring.

"Oh no, I only thought it was at first," she managed to reply, very quickly. She had recognised the gentleman—he had the fine fair beard of Captain Crispin—and her heart seemed to her to jump up and down. She was glad her companion could not see her face, and yet she wanted to get out, to rush up the stairs, where he would see it again, to escape from the place. She wished not to be there with *them*—she was overwhelmed with a sudden horror. "She has lied—she has lied again—she has lied!" that was the rhythm to which her thought began to dance. She took a few steps one way and then another: she was afraid of running against the dreadful pair again. She remarked to her companion that it was time they should go off, and then when he showed her the way back to the staircase she pleaded that she had not half seen the things. She pretended suddenly to a deep interest in them, and lingered there roaming and prying about. She was flurried still more by the thought that he would have seen her flurry, and she wondered whether he believed the woman who had shrieked and rushed away was *not* Selina. If she was not Selina why had she shrieked? and if she was Selina what would Mr Wendover think of her behaviour, and of her own, and of the strange accident of their meeting? What must she herself think of that? so astonishing it was that in the immensity of London so infinitesimally small a chance should have got itself enacted. What a queer place to come to—for people like them! They would get away as soon as possible, of that she could be sure; and she would wait a little to give them time.

Mr Wendover made no further remark—that was a relief; though his silence itself seemed to show that he was mystified. They went upstairs again and on reaching the door found to their surprise that their cab had disappeared—a circumstance the more singular as the man had not been paid. The rain was still coming down, though with less violence, and the square had been cleared of vehicles by the sudden storm. The doorkeeper, perceiving the dismay of our friends, explained that the cab had been taken up by another lady and another gentleman who had gone out a few minutes before; and when they inquired how he had been induced to depart without the money they owed him the reply was that there evidently had been a discussion (he hadn't heard it, but the lady seemed in a fearful hurry) and the gentleman had told him that they would make it all up to him and give him a lot more into the bargain. The doorkeeper hazarded the candid surmise that the cabby would make ten shillings by the job. But there were plenty more cabs; there would be one up in a minute and the rain moreover was going to stop. "Well, that *is* sharp practice!" said Mr Wendover. He made no further allusion to the identity of the lady.

IX

THE rain did stop while they stood there, and a brace of hansoms was not slow to appear. Laura told her companion that he must put her into one—she could go home alone: she had taken up enough of his time. He deprecated this course very respectfully; urged that he had it on his conscience to deliver her at her own door; but she sprang into the cab and closed the apron with a movement that was a sharp prohibition. She wanted to get away from him—it would be too awkward, the long, pottering drive back. Her hansom started off while Mr Wendover, smiling sadly, lifted his hat. It was not very comfortable, even without him; especially as before she had gone a quarter of a mile she felt that her action had been too marked—she wished she had let him come. His puzzled, innocent air of wondering what was the matter annoyed her; and she was in the absurd situation of being angry at a desistence which she would have been still angrier if he had been guiltless of. It would have comforted her (because it would seem to share her burden) and yet it would have covered her with shame if he had guessed that what she saw was wrong. It would not occur to him that there was a scandal so near her, because he thought with no great promptitude of such things; and yet, since there was—but since there was after all Laura scarcely knew what attitude would sit upon him most gracefully. As to what he might be prepared to suspect by having heard what Selina's reputation was in London, of that Laura was unable to judge, not knowing what was said, because of course it was not said to *her*. Lionel would undertake to give her the benefit of this any moment she would allow him, but how in the world could *he* know either, for how could things be said to him? Then, in the rattle of the hansom, passing through streets for which the girl had no eyes, "She has lied, she has lied, she has lied!" kept repeating itself. Why had she written and signed that wanton falsehood about her going down to Lady Watermouth? How could she have gone to Lady Watermouth's when she was making so very different and so extraordinary a use of the hours she had announced her intention of spending there? What had been the need of that misrepresentation and why did she lie before she was driven to it?

It was because she was false altogether and deception came out of her with her breath; she was so depraved that it was easier to her to fabricate than to let it alone. Laura would not have asked her to give an account of her day, but she would ask her now. She shuddered at one moment, as she found herself saying—even in silence—such things of her sister, and the next she sat staring out of the front of the cab at the stiff problem presented by Selina's turning up with the partner of her guilt at the Soane Museum, of all places in the world. The girl shifted this fact about in various ways, to account for it—not unconscious as she did so that it was a pretty exercise of ingenuity for a nice girl. Plainly, it was a rare accident: if it had been their plan to spend the day together the Soane Museum had not been in the original programme. They had been near it, they had been on foot and they had rushed in to take refuge from the rain. But how did they come to be near it and above all to be on foot? How could Selina do anything so reckless from her own point of view as to walk about the town—even an out-of-the-way part of it—with her suspected lover? Laura Wing felt the want of proper knowledge to explain such anomalies. It was too little clear to her where ladies went and how they proceeded when they consorted with gentlemen in regard to their meetings with whom they had to lie. She knew nothing of where Captain Crispin lived; very possibly—for she vaguely remembered having heard Selina say of him that he was very poor—he had chambers in that part of the town, and they were either going to them or coming from them. If Selina had neglected to take her way in a four-wheeler with the glasses up it was through some chance that would not seem natural till it was explained, like that of their having darted into a public institution. Then no doubt it would hang together with the rest only too well. The explanation most exact would probably be that the pair had snatched a walk together (in the course of a day of many edifying episodes) for the "lark" of it, and for the sake of the walk had taken the risk, which in that part of London, so detached from all gentility, had appeared to them small. The last thing Selina could have expected was to meet her sister in such a strange corner—her sister with a young man of her own!

She was dining out that night with both Selina and Lionel —a conjunction that was rather rare. She was by no means always invited with them, and Selina constantly went without her husband. Appearances, however, sometimes got a sop thrown them; three or four times a month Lionel and she entered the brougham together like people who still had forms, who still said "my dear." This was to be one of those occasions, and Mrs Berrington's young unmarried sister was included in the invitation. When Laura reached home she learned, on inquiry, that Selina had not yet come in, and she went straight to her own room. If her sister had been there she would have gone to hers instead—she would have cried out to her as soon as she had closed the door: "Oh, stop, stop —in God's name, stop before you go any further, before exposure and ruin and shame come down and bury us!" That was what was in the air—the vulgarest disgrace, and the girl, harder now than ever about her sister, was conscious of a more passionate desire to save herself. But Selina's absence made the difference that during the next hour a certain chill fell upon this impulse from other feelings: she found suddenly that she was late and she began to dress. They were to go together after dinner to a couple of balls; a diversion which struck her as ghastly for people who carried such horrors in their breasts. Ghastly was the idea of the drive of husband, wife and sister in pursuit of pleasure, with falsity and detection and hate between them. Selina's maid came to her door to tell her that she was in the carriage—an extraordinary piece of punctuality, which made her wonder, as Selina was always dreadfully late for everything. Laura went down as quickly as she could, passed through the open door, where the servants were grouped in the foolish majesty of their superfluous attendance, and through the file of dingy gazers who had paused at the sight of the carpet across the pavement and the waiting carriage, in which Selina sat in pure white splendour. Mrs Berrington had a tiara on her head and a proud patience in her face, as if her sister were really a sore trial. As soon as the girl had taken her place she said to the footman: "Is Mr Berrington there?"—to which the man replied: "No ma'am, not yet." It was not new to Laura that if there was any one later as a general thing than Selina it was Selina's husband. "Then he must take a hansom. Go on." The footman mounted and they rolled away.

There were several different things that had been present to Laura's mind during the last couple of hours as destined to mark—one or the other—this present encounter with her sister; but the words Selina spoke the moment the brougham began to move were of course exactly those she had not foreseen. She had considered that she might take this tone or that tone or even no tone at all; she was quite prepared for her presenting a face of blankness to any form of interrogation and saying, "What on earth are you talking about?" It was in short conceivable to her that Selina would deny absolutely that she had been in the museum, that they had stood face to face and that she had fled in confusion. She was capable of explaining the incident by an idiotic error on Laura's part, by her having seized on another person, by her seeing Captain

Crispin in every bush; though doubtless she would be taxed (of course she would say *that* was the woman's own affair) to supply a reason for the embarrassment of the other lady. But she was not prepared for Selina's breaking out with: "Will you be so good as to inform me if you are engaged to be married to Mr Wendover?"

"Engaged to him? I have seen him but three times."

"And is that what you usually do with gentlemen you have seen three times?"

"Are you talking about my having gone with him to see some sights? I see nothing wrong in that. To begin with you see what he is. One might go with him anywhere. Then he brought us an introduction—we have to do something for him. Moreover you threw him upon me the moment he came—you asked me to take charge of him."

"I didn't ask you to be indecent! If Lionel were to know it he wouldn't tolerate it, so long as you live with us."

Laura was silent a moment. "I shall not live with you long." The sisters, side by side, with their heads turned, looked at each other, a deep crimson leaping into Laura's face. "I wouldn't have believed it—that you are so bad," she said. "You are horrible!" She saw that Selina had not taken up the idea of denying—she judged that would be hopeless: the recognition on either side had been too sharp. She looked radiantly handsome, especially with the strange new expression that Laura's last word brought into her eyes. This expression seemed to the girl to show her more of Selina morally than she had ever yet seen—something of the full extent and the miserable limit.

"It's different for a married woman, especially when she's married to a cad. It's in a girl that such things are odious—scouring London with strange men. I am not bound to explain to you—there would be too many things to say. I have my reasons—I have my conscience. It was the oddest of all things, our meeting in that place—I know that as well as you,"

Selina went on, with her wonderful affected clearness; "but
it was not your finding me that was out of the way; it was my
finding you—with your remarkable escort! That was incredible. I pretended not to recognise you, so that the gentleman who was with me shouldn't see you, shouldn't know you.
He questioned me and I repudiated you. You may thank me
for saving you! You had better wear a veil next time—one
never knows what may happen. I met an acquaintance at
Lady Watermouth's and he came up to town with me. He
happened to talk about old prints; I told him how I have
collected them and we spoke of the bother one has about the
frames. He insisted on my going with him to that place—from
Waterloo—to see such an excellent model."

Laura had turned her face to the window of the carriage
again; they were spinning along Park Lane, passing in the
quick flash of other vehicles an endless succession of ladies
with "dressed" heads, of gentlemen in white neckties. "Why,
I thought your frames were all so pretty!" Laura murmured.
Then she added: "I suppose it was your eagerness to save
your companion the shock of seeing me—in my dishonour—
that led you to steal our cab."

"Your cab?"

"Your delicacy was expensive for you!"

"You don't mean you were knocking about in *cabs* with
him!" Selina cried.

"Of course I know that you don't really think a word of
what you say about me," Laura went on; "though I don't
know that that makes your saying it a bit less unspeakably
base."

The brougham pulled up in Park Lane and Mrs Berrington bent herself to have a view through the front glass. "We
are there, but there are two other carriages," she remarked,
for all answer. "Ah, there are the Collingwoods."

"Where are you going—where are you going—where are
you going?" Laura broke out.

The carriage moved on, to set them down, and while the footman was getting off the box Selina said: "I don't pretend to be better than other women, but you do!" And being on the side of the house she quickly stepped out and carried her crowned brilliancy through the long-lingering daylight and into the open portals.

X

"WHAT do you intend to do? You will grant that I have a right to ask you that."

"To do? I shall do, as I have always done—not so badly, as it seems to me."

This colloquy took place in Mrs Berrington's room, in the early morning hours, after Selina's return from the entertainment to which reference was last made. Her sister came home before her—she found herself incapable of "going on" when Selina quitted the house in Park Lane at which they had dined. Mrs Berrington had the night still before her, and she stepped into her carriage with her usual air of graceful resignation to a brilliant lot. She had taken the precaution, however, to provide herself with a defence, against a little sister bristling with righteousness, in the person of Mrs Collingwood, to whom she offered a lift, as they were bent upon the same business and Mr Collingwood had a use of his own for his brougham. The Collingwoods were a happy pair who could discuss such a divergence before their friends candidly, amicably, with a great many "My loves" and "Not for the worlds." Lionel Berrington disappeared after dinner, without holding any communication with his wife, and Laura expected to find that he had taken the carriage, to repay her in kind for her having driven off from Grosvenor Place without him. But it was not new to the girl that he really spared his

wife more than she spared him; not so much perhaps because
he wouldn't do the "nastiest" thing as because he couldn't.
Selina could always be nastier. There was ever a whimsicality
in her actions: if two or three hours before it had been her
fancy to keep a third person out of the carriage she had now
her reasons for bringing such a person in. Laura knew that she
would not only pretend, but would really believe, that her
vindication of her conduct on their way to dinner had been
powerful and that she had won a brilliant victory. What need,
therefore, to thresh out further a subject that she had chopped
into atoms? Laura Wing, however, had needs of her own, and
her remaining in the carriage when the footman next opened
the door was intimately connected with them.

"I don't care to go in," she said to her sister. "If you will
allow me to be driven home and send back the carriage for
you, that's what I shall like best."

Selina stared and Laura knew what she would have said
if she could have spoken her thought. "Oh, you are furious
that I haven't given you a chance to fly at me again, and you
must take it out in sulks!" These were the ideas—ideas of
"fury" and sulks—into which Selina could translate feelings
that sprang from the pure depths of one's conscience. Mrs
Collingwood protested—she said it was a shame that Laura
shouldn't go in and enjoy herself when she looked so lovely.
"Doesn't she look lovely?" She appealed to Mrs Berrington.
"Bless us, what's the use of being pretty? Now, if she had
my face!"

"I think she looks rather cross," said Selina, getting out
with her friend and leaving her sister to her own inventions.
Laura had a vision, as the carriage drove away again, of what
her situation would have been, or her peace of mind, if Selina
and Lionel had been good, attached people like the Collingwoods, and at the same time of the singularity of a good
woman's being ready to accept favours from a person as to
whose behaviour she had the lights that must have come to the

lady in question in regard to Selina. She accepted favours herself and she only wanted to be good: that was oppressively
true; but if she had not been Selina's sister she would never
drive in her carriage. That conviction was strong in the girl as
this vehicle conveyed her to Grosvenor Place; but it was not
in its nature consoling. The prevision of disgrace was now so
vivid to her that it seemed to her that if it had not already
overtaken them she had only to thank the loose, mysterious,
rather ignoble tolerance of people like Mrs Collingwood.
There were plenty of that species, even among the good;
perhaps indeed exposure and dishonour would begin only
when the bad had got hold of the facts. Would the bad be
most horrified and do most to spread the scandal? There
were, in any event, plenty of them too.

Laura sat up for her sister that night, with that nice question to help her to torment herself—whether if she was hard
and merciless in judging Selina it would be with the bad too
that she would associate herself. Was she all wrong after all—
was she cruel by being too rigid? Was Mrs Collingwood's
attitude the right one and ought she only to propose to herself
to "allow" more and more, and to allow ever, and to smooth
things down by gentleness, by sympathy, by not looking at
them too hard? It was not the first time that the just measure
of things seemed to slip from her hands as she became
conscious of possible, or rather of very actual, differences of
standard and usage. On this occasion Geordie and Ferdy
asserted themselves, by the mere force of lying asleep upstairs in their little cribs, as on the whole the proper measure.
Laura went into the nursery to look at them when she came
home—it was her habit almost any night—and yearned over
them as mothers and maids do alike over the pillow of rosy
childhood. They were an antidote to all casuistry; for Selina
to forget *them*—that was the beginning and the end of shame.
She came back to the library, where she should best hear the
sound of her sister's return; the hours passed as she sat there,

without bringing round this event. Carriages came and went all night; the soft shock of swift hoofs was on the wooden roadway long after the summer dawn grew fair—till it was merged in the rumble of the awakening day. Lionel had not come in when she returned, and he continued absent, to Laura's satisfaction; for if she wanted not to miss Selina she had no desire at present to have to tell her brother-in-law why she was sitting up. She prayed Selina might arrive first: then she would have more time to think of something that harassed her particularly—the question of whether she ought to tell Lionel that she had seen her in a far-away corner of the town with Captain Crispin. Almost impossible as she found it now to feel any tenderness for her, she yet detested the idea of bearing witness against her: notwithstanding which it appeared to her that she could make up her mind to do this if there were a chance of its preventing the last scandal—a catastrophe to which she saw her sister rushing straight. That Selina was capable at a given moment of going off with her lover, and capable of it precisely because it was the greatest ineptitude as well as the greatest wickedness—there was a voice of prophecy, of warning, to this effect in the silent, empty house. If repeating to Lionel what she had seen would contribute to prevent anything, or to stave off the danger, was it not her duty to denounce his wife, flesh and blood of her own as she was, to his further reprobation? This point was not intolerably difficult to determine, as she sat there waiting, only because even what was righteous in that probation could not present itself to her as fruitful or efficient. What could Lionel frustrate, after all, and what intelligent or authoritative step was he capable of taking? Mixed with all that now haunted her was her consciousness of what his own absence at such an hour represented in the way of the unedifying. He might be at some sporting club or he might be anywhere else; at any rate he was not where he ought to be at three o'clock in the morning. Such the husband such the wife, she said to herself; and she felt that Selina would have a kind of advantage, which she grudged her, if she should come in and say: "And where is *he*, please—where is he, the exalted being on whose behalf you have undertaken to preach so much better than he himself practises?"

But still Selina failed to come in—even to take that advantage; yet in proportion as her waiting was useless did the girl find it impossible to go to bed. A new fear had seized her, the fear that she would never come back at all—that they were already in the presence of the dreaded catastrophe. This made her so nervous that she paced about the lower rooms, listening to every sound, roaming till she was tired. She knew it was absurd, the image of Selina taking flight in a ball-dress; but she said to herself that she might very well have sent other clothes away, in advance, somewhere (Laura had her own ripe views about the maid); and at any rate, for herself, that was the fate she had to expect, if not that night then some other one soon, and it was all the same: to sit counting the hours till a hope was given up and a hideous certainty remained. She had fallen into such a state of apprehension that when at last she heard a carriage stop at the door she was almost happy, in spite of her prevision of how disgusted her sister would be to find her. They met in the hall—Laura went out as she heard the opening of the door. Selina stopped short, seeing her, but said nothing—on account apparently of the presence of the sleepy footman. Then she moved straight to the stairs, where she paused again, asking the footman if Mr Berrington had come in.

"Not yet, ma'am," the footman answered.

"Ah!" said Mrs Berrington, dramatically, and ascended the stairs.

"I have sat up on purpose—I want particularly to speak to you," Laura remarked, following her.

"Ah!" Selina repeated, more superior still. She went fast, almost as if she wished to get to her room before her sister could overtake her. But the girl was close behind her, she passed into the room with her. Laura closed the door; then she told her that she had found it impossible to go to bed without asking her what she intended to do.

"Your behaviour is too monstrous!" Selina flashed out. "What on earth do you wish to make the servants suppose?"

"Oh, the servants—in *this* house; as if one could put any idea into their heads that is not there already!" Laura thought. But she said nothing of this—she only repeated her question: aware that she was exasperating to her sister but also aware that she could not be anything else. Mrs Berrington, whose maid, having outlived surprises, had gone to rest, began to divest herself of some of her ornaments, and it was not till after a moment, during which she stood before the glass, that she made that answer about doing as she had always done. To this Laura rejoined that she ought to put herself in her place enough to feel how important it was to *her* to know what was likely to happen, so that she might take time by the forelock and think of her own situation. If anything should happen she would infinitely rather be out of it—be as far away as possible. Therefore she must take her measures.

It was in the mirror that they looked at each other—in the strange, candle-lighted duplication of the scene that their eyes met. Selina drew the diamonds out of her hair, and in this occupation, for a minute, she was silent. Presently she asked: "What are you talking about—what do you allude to as happening?"

"Why, it seems to me that there is nothing left for you but to go away with him. If there is a prospect of that insanity——" But here Laura stopped; something so unexpected was taking place in Selina's countenance—the movement that precedes a sudden gush of tears. Mrs Berrington dashed down the glittering pins she had detached from her tresses, and the next moment she had flung herself into an armchair and was weeping profusely, extravagantly. Laura forbore to go to her;

she made no motion to soothe or reassure her, she only stood
and watched her tears and wondered what they signified.
Somehow even the slight refreshment she felt at having
affected her in that particular and, as it had lately come to
seem, improbable way did not suggest to her that they were
precious symptoms. Since she had come to disbelieve her
word so completely there was nothing precious about Selina
any more. But she continued for some moments to cry
passionately, and while this lasted Laura remained silent. At
last from the midst of her sobs Selina broke out, "Go away,
go away—leave me alone!"

"Of course I infuriate you," said the girl; "but how can
I see you rush to your ruin—to that of all of us—without
holding on to you and dragging you back?"

"Oh, you don't understand anything about anything!"
Selina wailed, with her beautiful hair tumbling all over her.

"I certainly don't understand how you can give such a
tremendous handle to Lionel."

At the mention of her husband's name Selina always gave
a bound, and she sprang up now, shaking back her dense
braids. "I give him no handle and you don't know what you
are talking about! I know what I am doing and what becomes
me, and I don't care if I do. He is welcome to all the handles
in the world, for all that he can do with them!"

"In the name of common pity think of your children!"
said Laura.

"Have I ever thought of anything else? Have you sat up
all night to have the pleasure of accusing me of cruelty? Are
there sweeter or more delightful children in the world, and
isn't that a little *my* merit, pray?" Selina went on, sweeping
away her tears. "Who has made them what they are, pray?—
is it their lovely father? Perhaps you'll say it's you! Certainly
you have been nice to them, but you must remember that
you only came here the other day. Isn't it only for them that
I am trying to keep myself alive?"

This formula struck Laura Wing as grotesque, so that she replied with a laugh which betrayed too much her impression, "Die for them—that would be better!"

Her sister, at this, looked at her with an extraordinary cold gravity. "Don't interfere between me and my children. And for God's sake cease to harry me!"

Laura turned away: she said to herself that, given that intensity of silliness, of course the worst would come. She felt sick and helpless, and, practically, she had got the certitude she both wanted and dreaded. "I don't know what has become of your mind," she murmured; and she went to the door. But before she reached it Selina had flung herself upon her in one of her strange but, as she felt, really not encouraging revulsions. Her arms were about her, she clung to her, she covered Laura with the tears that had again begun to flow. She besought her to save her, to stay with her, to help her against herself, against *him*, against Lionel, against everything—to forgive her also all the horrid things she had said to her. Mrs Berrington melted, liquefied, and the room was deluged with her repentance, her desolation, her confession, her promises and the articles of apparel which were detached from her by the high tide of her agitation. Laura remained with her for an hour, and before they separated the culpable woman had taken a tremendous vow—kneeling before her sister with her head in her lap—never again, as long as she lived, to consent to see Captain Crispin or to address a word to him, spoken or written. The girl went terribly tired to bed.

A month afterwards she lunched with Lady Davenant, whom she had not seen since the day she took Mr Wendover to call upon her. The old woman had found herself obliged to entertain a small company, and as she disliked set parties she sent Laura a request for sympathy and assistance. She had disencumbered herself, at the end of so many years, of the burden of hospitality; but every now and then she invited people, in order to prove that she was not too old. Laura suspected her of choosing stupid ones on purpose to prove it better—to show that she could submit not only to the extraordinary but, what was much more difficult, to the usual. But when they had been properly fed she encouraged them to disperse; on this occasion as the party broke up Laura was the only person she asked to stay. She wished to know in the first place why she had not been to see her for so long, and in the second how that young man had behaved—the one she had brought that Sunday. Lady Davenant didn't remember his name, though he had been so good-natured, as she said, since then, as to leave a card. If he had behaved well that was a very good reason for the girl's neglect and Laura need give no other. Laura herself would not have behaved well if at such a time she had been running after old women. There was nothing, in general, that the girl liked less than being spoken of, off-hand, as a marriageable article—being planned and arranged for in this particular. It made too light of her independence, and though in general such inventions passed for benevolence they had always seemed to her to contain at bottom an impertinence—as if people could be moved about like a game of chequers. There was a liberty in the way Lady Davenant's imagination disposed of her (with such an *insouciance* of her own preferences), but she forgave that, because after all this old friend was not obliged to think of her at all.

"I knew that you were almost always out of town now, on Sundays—and so have we been," Laura said. "And then I have been a great deal with my sister—more than before."

"More than before what?"

"Well, a kind of estrangement we had, about a certain matter."

"And now you have made it all up?"

"Well, we have been able to talk of it (we couldn't before —without painful scenes), and that has cleared the air. We have gone about together a good deal," Laura went on. "She has wanted me constantly with her."

"That's very nice. And where has she taken you?" asked the old lady.

"Oh, it's I who have taken her, rather." And Laura hesitated.

"Where do you mean?—to say her prayers?"

"Well, to some concerts—and to the National Gallery."

Lady Davenant laughed, disrespectfully, at this, and the girl watched her with a mournful face. "My dear child, you are too delightful! You are trying to reform her? by Beethoven and Bach, by Rubens and Titian?"

"She is very intelligent, about music and pictures—she has excellent ideas," said Laura.

"And you have been trying to draw them out? that is very commendable."

"I think you are laughing at me, but I don't care," the girl declared, smiling faintly.

"Because you have a consciousness of success?—in what do they call it?—the attempt to raise her tone? You have been trying to wind her up, and you *have* raised her tone?"

"Oh, Lady Davenant, I don't know and I don't understand!" Laura broke out. "I don't understand anything any more—I have given up trying."

"That's what I recommended you to do last winter. Don't you remember that day at Plash?"

"You told me to let her go," said Laura.

"And evidently you haven't taken my advice."

"How can I—how can I?"

"Of course, how can you? And meanwhile if she doesn't go it's so much gained. But even if she should, won't that nice young man remain?" Lady Davenant inquired. "I hope very much Selina hasn't taken you altogether away from him."

Laura was silent a moment; then she returned: "What nice

young man would ever look at me, if anything bad should happen?"

"I would never look at *him* if he should let that prevent him!" the old woman cried. "It isn't for your sister he loves you, I suppose; is it?"

"He doesn't love me at all."

"Ah, then he does?" Lady Davenant demanded, with some eagerness, laying her hand on the girl's arm. Laura sat near her on her sofa and looked at her, for all answer to this, with an expression of which the sadness appeared to strike the old woman freshly. "Doesn't he come to the house—doesn't he say anything?" she continued, with a voice of kindness.

"He comes to the house—very often."

"And don't you like him?"

"Yes, very much—more than I did at first."

"Well, as you liked him at first well enough to bring him straight to see me, I suppose that means that now you are immensely pleased with him."

"He's a gentleman," said Laura.

"So he seems to me. But why then doesn't he speak out?"

"Perhaps that's the very reason! Seriously," the girl added, "I don't know what he comes to the house for."

"Is he in love with your sister?"

"I sometimes think so."

"And does she encourage him?"

"She detests him."

"Oh, then, I like him! I shall immediately write to him to come and see me: I shall appoint an hour and give him a piece of my mind."

"If I believed that, I should kill myself," said Laura.

"You may believe what you like; but I wish you didn't show your feelings so in your eyes. They might be those of a poor widow with fifteen children. When I was young I managed to be happy, whatever occurred; and I am sure I looked so."

"Oh yes, Lady Davenant—for you it was different. You were safe, in so many ways," Laura said. "And you were surrounded with consideration."

"I don't know; some of us were very wild, and exceedingly ill thought of, and I didn't cry about it. However, there are natures and natures. If you will come and stay with me to-morrow I will take you in."

"You know how kind I think you, but I have promised Selina not to leave her."

"Well, then, if she keeps you she must at least go straight!" cried the old woman, with some asperity. Laura made no answer to this and Lady Davenant asked, after a moment: "And what is Lionel doing?"

"I don't know—he is very quiet."

"Doesn't it please him—his wife's improvement?" The girl got up; apparently she was made uncomfortable by the ironical effect, if not by the ironical intention, of this question. Her old friend was kind but she was penetrating; her very next words pierced further. "Of course if you are really protecting her I can't count upon you": a remark not adapted to enliven Laura, who would have liked immensely to transfer herself to Queen's Gate and had her very private ideas as to the efficacy of her protection. Lady Davenant kissed her and then suddenly said—"Oh, by the way, his address; you must tell me that."

"His address?"

"The young man's whom you brought here. But it's no matter," the old woman added; "the butler will have entered it—from his card."

"Lady Davenant, you won't do anything so loathsome!" the girl cried, seizing her hand.

"Why is it loathsome, if he comes so often? It's rubbish, his caring for Selina—a married woman—when you are there."

"Why is it rubbish—when so many other people do?"

"Oh, well, he is different—I could see that; or if he isn't
he ought to be!"

"He likes to observe—he came here to take notes," said
the girl. "And he thinks Selina a very interesting London
specimen."

"In spite of her dislike of him?"

"Oh, he doesn't know that!" Laura exclaimed.

"Why not? he isn't a fool."

"Oh, I have made it seem——" But here Laura stopped;
her colour had risen.

Lady Davenant stared an instant. "Made it seem that she
inclines to him? Mercy, to do that how fond of him you must
be!" An observation which had the effect of driving the girl
straight out of the house.

XI

On one of the last days of June Mrs Berrington showed her
sister a note she had received from "your dear friend," as she
called him, Mr Wendover. This was the manner in which she
usually designated him, but she had naturally, in the present
phase of her relations with Laura, never indulged in any
renewal of the eminently perverse insinuations by means of
which she had attempted, after the incident at the Soane
Museum, to throw dust in her eyes. Mr Wendover proposed
to Mrs Berrington that she and her sister should honour with
their presence a box he had obtained for the opera three nights
later—an occasion of high curiosity, the first appearance of a
young American singer of whom considerable things were
expected. Laura left it to Selina to decide whether they should
accept this invitation, and Selina proved to be of two or three
differing minds. First she said it wouldn't be convenient to
her to go, and she wrote to the young man to this effect.

Then, on second thoughts, she considered she might very well go, and telegraphed an acceptance. Later she saw reason to regret her acceptance and communicated this circumstance to her sister, who remarked that it was still not too late to change. Selina left her in ignorance till the next day as to whether she had retracted; then she told her that she had let the matter stand—they would go. To this Laura replied that she was glad—for Mr Wendover. "And for yourself," Selina said, leaving the girl to wonder why every one (this universality was represented by Mrs Lionel Berrington and Lady Davenant) had taken up the idea that she entertained a passion for her compatriot. She was clearly conscious that this was not the case; though she was glad her esteem for him had not yet suffered the disturbance of her seeing reason to believe that Lady Davenant had already meddled, according to her terrible threat. Laura was surprised to learn afterwards that Selina had, in London parlance, "thrown over" a dinner in order to make the evening at the opera fit in. The dinner would have made her too late, and she didn't care about it: she wanted to hear the whole opera.

The sisters dined together alone, without any question of Lionel, and on alighting at Covent Garden found Mr Wendover awaiting them in the portico. His box proved commodious and comfortable, and Selina was gracious to him: she thanked him for his consideration in not stuffing it full of people. He assured her that he expected but one other inmate —a gentleman of a shrinking disposition, who would take up no room. The gentleman came in after the first act; he was introduced to the ladies as Mr Booker, of Baltimore. He knew a great deal about the young lady they had come to listen to, and he was not so shrinking but that he attempted to impart a portion of his knowledge even while she was singing. Before the second act was over Laura perceived Lady Ringrose in a box on the other side of the house, accompanied by a lady unknown to her. There was apparently another person in the box, behind the two ladies, whom they turned round from time to time to talk with. Laura made no observation about Lady Ringrose to her sister, and she noticed that Selina never resorted to the glass to look at her. That Mrs Berrington had not failed to see her, however, was proved by the fact that at the end of the second act (the opera was Meyerbeer's *Huguenots*) she suddenly said, turning to Mr Wendover: "I hope you won't mind very much if I go for a short time to sit with a friend on the other side of the house." She smiled with all her sweetness as she announced this intention, and had the benefit of the fact that an apologetic expression is highly becoming to a pretty woman. But she abstained from looking at her sister, and the latter, after a wondering glance at her, looked at Mr Wendover. She saw that he was disappointed—even slightly wounded: he had taken some trouble to get his box and it had been no small pleasure to him to see it graced by the presence of a celebrated beauty. Now his situation collapsed if the celebrated beauty were going to transfer her light to another quarter. Laura was unable to imagine what had come into her sister's head—to make her so inconsiderate, so rude. Selina tried to perform her act of defection in a soothing, conciliating way, so far as appealing eyebeams went; but she gave no particular reason for her escapade, withheld the name of the friends in question and betrayed no consciousness that it was not usual for ladies to roam about the lobbies. Laura asked her no question, but she said to her, after an hesitation: "You won't be long, surely. You know you oughtn't to leave me here." Selina took no notice of this—excused herself in no way to the girl. Mr Wendover only exclaimed, smiling in reference to Laura's last remark: "Oh, so far as leaving you here goes——!" In spite of his great defect (and it was his only one, that she could see) of having only an ascending scale of seriousness, she judged him interestedly enough to feel a real pleasure in noticing that though he was annoyed at Selina's going away and not saying that she would come back soon, he conducted himself as a gentleman should, submitted respectfully, gallantly, to her wish. He suggested that her friends might perhaps, instead, be induced to come to his box, but when she had objected, "Oh, you see, there are too many," he put her shawl on her shoulders, opened the box, offered her his arm. While this was going on Laura saw Lady Ringrose studying them with her glass. Selina refused Mr Wendover's arm; she said, "Oh no, you stay with *her*—I daresay *he'll* take me:" and she gazed inspiringly at Mr Booker. Selina never mentioned a name when the pronoun would do. Mr Booker of course sprang to the service required and led her away, with an injunction from his friend to bring her back promptly. As they went off Laura heard Selina say to her companion—and she knew Mr Wendover could also hear it—"Nothing would have induced me to leave her alone with *you!*" She thought this a very extraordinary speech—she thought it even vulgar; especially considering that she had never seen the young man till half an hour before and since then had not exchanged twenty words with him. It came to their ears so distinctly that Laura was moved to notice it by exclaiming, with a laugh: "Poor Mr Booker, what does she suppose I would do to him?"

"Oh, it's for you she's afraid," said Mr Wendover.

Laura went on, after a moment: "She oughtn't to have left me alone with you, either."

"Oh yes, she ought—after all!" the young man returned.

The girl had uttered these words from no desire to say something flirtatious, but because they simply expressed a part of the judgment she passed, mentally, on Selina's behaviour. She had a sense of wrong—of being made light of; for Mrs Berrington certainly knew that honourable women didn't (for the appearance of the thing) arrange to leave their unmarried sister sitting alone, publicly, at the playhouse, with a couple of young men—the couple that there would be as soon as Mr Booker should come back. It displeased her that the people in the opposite box, the people Selina had joined, should see her exhibited in this light. She drew the curtain of the box a little, she moved a little more behind it, and she heard her companion utter a vague appealing, protecting sigh, which seemed to express his sense (her own corresponded with it) that the glory of the occasion had somehow suddenly departed. At the end of some minutes she perceived among Lady Ringrose and her companions a movement which appeared to denote that Selina had come in. The two ladies in front turned round—something went on at the back of the box. "She's there," Laura said, indicating the place; but Mrs Berrington did not show herself—she remained masked by the others. Neither was Mr Booker visible; he had not, seemingly, been persuaded to remain, and indeed Laura could see that there would not have been room for him. Mr Wendover observed, ruefully, that as Mrs Berrington evidently could see nothing at all from where she had gone she had exchanged a very good place for a very bad one. "I can't imagine—I can't imagine——" said the girl; but she paused, losing herself in reflections and wonderments, in conjectures that soon became anxieties. Suspicion of Selina was now so rooted in her heart that it could make her unhappy even when it pointed no-where, and by the end of half an hour she felt how little her fears had really been lulled since that scene of dishevelment and contrition in the early dawn.

The opera resumed its course, but Mr Booker did not come back. The American singer trilled and warbled, executed remarkable flights, and there was much applause, every symptom of success; but Laura became more and more un-aware of the music—she had no eyes but for Lady Ringrose and her friend. She watched them earnestly—she tried to sound with her glass the curtained dimness behind them. Their attention was all for the stage and they gave no present sign of having any fellow-listeners. These others had either gone away or were leaving them very much to themselves.

Laura was unable to guess any particular motive on her sister's part, but the conviction grew within her that she had not put such an affront on Mr Wendover simply in order to have a little chat with Lady Ringrose. There was something else, there was some one else, in the affair; and when once the girl's idea had become as definite as that it took but little longer to associate itself with the image of Captain Crispin. This image made her draw back further behind her curtain, because it brought the blood to her face; and if she coloured for shame she coloured also for anger. Captain Crispin was there, in the opposite box; those horrible women concealed him (she forgot how harmless and well-read Lady Ringrose had appeared to her that time at Mellows); they had lent themselves to this abominable proceeding. Selina was nestling there in safety with him, by their favour, and she had had the baseness to lay an honest girl, the most loyal, the most unselfish of sisters, under contribution to the same end. Laura crimsoned with the sense that she had been, unsuspectingly, part of a scheme, that she was being used as the two women opposite were used, but that she had been outraged into the bargain, inasmuch as she was not, like them, a conscious accomplice and not a person to be given away in that manner before hundreds of people. It came back to her how bad Selina had been the day of the business in Lincoln's Inn Fields, and how in spite of intervening comedies the woman who had then found such words of injury would be sure to break out in a new spot with a new weapon. Accordingly, while the pure music filled the place and the rich picture of the stage glowed beneath it, Laura found herself face to face with the strange inference that the evil of Selina's nature made her wish—since she had given herself to it—to bring her sister to her own colour by putting an appearance of "fastness" upon her. The girl said to herself that she would have succeeded, in the cynical view of London; and to her troubled spirit the immense theatre had a myriad eyes, eyes that she knew, eyes that would know her,

that would see her sitting there with a strange young man.
She had recognised many faces already and her imagination
quickly multiplied them. However, after she had burned a
while with this particular revolt she ceased to think of herself
and of what, as regarded herself, Selina had intended: all her
thought went to the mere calculation of Mrs Berrington's
return. As she did not return, and still did not, Laura felt a
sharp constriction of the heart. She knew not what she feared
—she knew not what she supposed. She was so nervous (as
she had been the night she waited, till morning, for her sister
to re-enter the house in Grosvenor Place) that when Mr
Wendover occasionally made a remark to her she failed to
understand him, was unable to answer him. Fortunately he
made very few; he was preoccupied—either wondering also
what Selina was "up to" or, more probably, simply absorbed
in the music. What she *had* comprehended, however, was
that when at three different moments she had said, restlessly,
"Why doesn't Mr Booker come back?" he replied, "Oh,
there's plenty of time—we are very comfortable." These
words she was conscious of; she particularly noted them
and they interwove themselves with her restlessness. She
also noted, in her tension, that after her third inquiry Mr
Wendover said something about looking up his friend, if she
didn't mind being left alone a moment. He quitted the box
and during this interval Laura tried more than ever to see with
her glass what had become of her sister. But it was as if the
ladies opposite had arranged themselves, had arranged their
curtains, on purpose to frustrate such an attempt: it was impossible to her even to assure herself of what she had begun to
suspect, that Selina was now not with them. If she was not
with them where in the world had she gone? As the moments
elapsed, before Mr Wendover's return, she went to the door
of the box and stood watching the lobby, for the chance that
he would bring back the absentee. Presently she saw him
coming alone, and something in the expression of his face

made her step out into the lobby to meet him. He was smiling, but he looked embarrassed and strange, especially when he saw her standing there as if she wished to leave the place.

"I hope you don't want to go," he said, holding the door for her to pass back into the box.

"Where are they—where are they?" she demanded, remaining in the corridor.

"I saw our friend—he has found a place in the stalls, near the door by which you go into them—just here under us."

"And does he like that better?"

Mr Wendover's smile became perfunctory as he looked down at her. "Mrs Berrington has made such an amusing request of him."

"An amusing request?"

"She made him promise not to come back."

"Made him promise——?" Laura stared.

"She asked him—as a particular favour to her—not to join us again. And he said he wouldn't."

"Ah, the monster!" Laura exclaimed, blushing crimson.

"Do you mean poor Mr Booker?" Mr Wendover asked. "Of course he had to assure her that the wish of so lovely a lady was law. But he doesn't understand!" laughed the young man.

"No more do I. And where is the lovely lady?" said Laura, trying to recover herself.

"He hasn't the least idea."

"Isn't she with Lady Ringrose?"

"If you like I will go and see."

Laura hesitated, looking down the curved lobby, where there was nothing to see but the little numbered doors of the boxes. They were alone in the lamplit bareness; the *finale* of the act was ringing and booming behind them. In a moment she said: "I'm afraid I must trouble you to put me into a cab."

"Ah, you won't see the rest? *Do* stay—what difference does it make?" And her companion still held open the door of the box. Her eyes met his, in which it seemed to her that as well as in his voice there was conscious sympathy, entreaty, vindication, tenderness. Then she gazed into the vulgar corridor again; something said to her that if she should return she would be taking the most important step of her life. She considered this, and while she did so a great burst of applause filled the place as the curtain fell. "See what we are losing! And the last act is so fine," said Mr Wendover. She returned to her seat and he closed the door of the box behind them.

Then, in this little upholstered receptacle which was so public and yet so private, Laura Wing passed through the strangest moments she had known. An indication of their strangeness is that when she presently perceived that while she was in the lobby Lady Ringrose and her companion had quite disappeared, she observed the circumstance without an exclamation, holding herself silent. Their box was empty, but Laura looked at it without in the least feeling this to be a sign that Selina would now come round. She would never come round again, nor would she have gone home from the opera. That was by this time absolutely definite to the girl, who had first been hot and now was cold with the sense of what Selina's injunction to poor Mr Booker exactly meant. It was worthy of her, for it was simply a vicious little kick as she took her flight. Grosvenor Place would not shelter her that night and would never shelter her more: that was the reason she tried to spatter her sister with the mud into which she herself had jumped. She would not have dared to treat her in such a fashion if they had had a prospect of meeting again. The strangest part of this remarkable juncture was that what ministered most to our young lady's suppressed emotion was not the tremendous reflection that this time Selina had really "bolted" and that on the morrow all London would know it: all that had taken the glare of certainty (and a very

hideous hue it was), whereas the chill that had fallen upon the
girl now was that of a mystery which waited to be cleared
up. Her heart was full of suspense—suspense of which she
returned the pressure, trying to twist it into expectation.
There was a certain chance in life that sat there beside her, but
it would go for ever if it should not move nearer that night;
and she listened, she watched, for it to move. I need not inform the reader that this chance presented itself in the person
of Mr Wendover, who more than any one she knew had it in
his hand to transmute her detestable position. To-morrow he
would know, and would think sufficiently little of a young
person of *that* breed: therefore it could only be a question of
his speaking on the spot. That was what she had come back
into the box for—to give him his opportunity. It was open to
her to think he had asked for it—adding everything together.

The poor girl added, added, deep in her heart, while she
said nothing. The music was not there now, to keep them
silent; yet he remained quiet, even as she did, and that for
some minutes was a part of her addition. She felt as if she were
running a race with failure and shame; she would get in first
if she should get in before the degradation of the morrow. But
this was not very far off, and every minute brought it nearer.
It would be there in fact, virtually, that night, if Mr Wendover
should begin to realise the brutality of Selina's not turning up
at all. The comfort had been, hitherto, that he didn't realise
brutalities. There were certain violins that emitted tentative
sounds in the orchestra; they shortened the time and made her
uneasier—fixed her idea that he could lift her out of her mire
if he would. It didn't appear to prove that he would, his also
observing Lady Ringrose's empty box without making an
encouraging comment upon it. Laura waited for him to remark that her sister obviously would turn up now; but no
such words fell from his lips. He must either like Selina's being
away or judge it damningly, and in either case why didn't he
speak? If he had nothing to say, why *had* he said, why had he

done, what did he mean——? But the girl's inward challenge to him lost itself in a mist of faintness; she was screwing herself up to a purpose of her own, and it hurt almost to anguish, and the whole place, around her, was a blur and swim, through which she heard the tuning of fiddles. Before she knew it she had said to him, "Why have you come so often?"

"So often? To see you, do you mean?"

"To see *me*—it was for that? Why have you come?" she went on. He was evidently surprised, and his surprise gave her a point of anger, a desire almost that her words should hurt him, lash him. She spoke low, but she heard herself, and she thought that if what she said sounded to *him* in the same way——! "You have come very often—too often, too often!"

He coloured, he looked frightened, he was, clearly, extremely startled. "Why, you have been so kind, so delightful," he stammered.

"Yes, of course, and so have you! Did you come for Selina? She is married, you know, and devoted to her husband." A single minute had sufficed to show the girl that her companion was quite unprepared for her question, that he was distinctly not in love with her and was face to face with a situation entirely new. The effect of this perception was to make her say wilder things.

"Why, what is more natural, when one likes people, than to come often? Perhaps I have bored you—with our American way," said Mr Wendover.

"And is it because you like me that you have kept me here?" Laura asked. She got up, leaning against the side of the box; she had pulled the curtain far forward and was out of sight of the house.

He rose, but more slowly; he had got over his first confusion. He smiled at her, but his smile was dreadful. "Can you have any doubt as to what I have come for? It's a pleasure to me that you have liked me well enough to ask."

For an instant she thought he was coming nearer to her, but he didn't: he stood there twirling his gloves. Then an unspeakable shame and horror—horror of herself, of him, of everything—came over her, and she sank into a chair at the back of the box, with averted eyes, trying to get further into her corner. "Leave me, leave me, go away!" she said, in the lowest tone that he could hear. The whole house seemed to her to be listening to her, pressing into the box.

"Leave you alone—in this place—when I love you? I can't do that—indeed I can't."

"You don't love me—and you torture me by staying!" Laura went on, in a convulsed voice. "For God's sake go away and don't speak to me, don't let me see you or hear of you again!"

Mr Wendover still stood there, exceedingly agitated, as well he might be, by this inconceivable scene. Unaccustomed feelings possessed him and they moved him in different directions. Her command that he should take himself off was passionate, yet he attempted to resist, to speak. How would she get home—would she see him to-morrow—would she let him wait for her outside? To this Laura only replied: "Oh dear, oh dear, if you would only go!" and at the same instant she sprang up, gathering her cloak around her as if to escape from him, to rush away herself. He checked this movement, however, clapping on his hat and holding the door. One moment more he looked at her—her own eyes were closed; then he exclaimed, pitifully, "Oh Miss Wing, oh Miss Wing!" and stepped out of the box.

When he had gone she collapsed into one of the chairs again and sat there with her face buried in a fold of her mantle. For many minutes she was perfectly still—she was ashamed even to move. The one thing that could have justified her, blown away the dishonour of her monstrous overture, would have been, on his side, the quick response of unmistakable passion. It had not come, and she had nothing left but to loathe herself. She did so violently, for a long time, in the dark corner of the box, and she felt that he loathed her too. "I love you!"—how pitifully the poor little make-believe words had quavered out and how much disgust they must have represented! "Poor man—poor man!" Laura Wing suddenly found herself murmuring: compassion filled her mind at the sense of the way she had used him. At the same moment a flare of music broke out: the last act of the opera had begun and she had sprung up and quitted the box.

The passages were empty and she made her way without trouble. She descended to the vestibule; there was no one to stare at her and her only fear was that Mr Wendover would be there. But he was not, apparently, and she saw that she should be able to go away quickly. Selina would have taken the carriage—she could be sure of that; or if she hadn't it wouldn't have come back yet; besides, she couldn't possibly wait there so long as while it was called. She was in the act of asking one of the attendants, in the portico, to get her a cab, when some one hurried up to her from behind overtaking her—a gentleman in whom, turning round, she recognised Mr Booker. He looked almost as bewildered as Mr Wendover, and his appearance disconcerted her almost as much as that of his friend would have done. "Oh, are you going away, alone? What must you think of me?" this young man exclaimed; and he began to tell her something about her sister and to ask her at the same time if he might not go with her—help her in some way. He made no inquiry about Mr Wendover, and she afterwards judged that that distracted gentleman had sought him out and sent him to her assistance; also that he himself was at that moment watching them from behind some column. He would have been hateful if he had shown himself; yet (in this later meditation) there was a voice in her heart which commended his delicacy. He effaced himself to look after her—he provided for her departure by proxy.

"A cab, a cab—that's all I want!" she said to Mr Booker;

and she almost pushed him out of the place with the wave of the hand with which she indicated her need. He rushed off to call one, and a minute afterwards the messenger whom she had already despatched rattled up in a hansom. She quickly got into it, and as she rolled away she saw Mr Booker returning in all haste with another. She gave a passionate moan—this common confusion seemed to add a grotesqueness to her predicament.

XII

THE next day, at five o'clock, she drove to Queen's Gate, turning to Lady Davenant in her distress in order to turn somewhere. Her old friend was at home and by extreme good fortune alone; looking up from her book, in her place by the window, she gave the girl as she came in a sharp glance over her glasses. This glance was acquisitive; she said nothing, but laying down her book stretched out her two gloved hands. Laura took them and she drew her down toward her, so that the girl sank on her knees and in a moment hid her face, sobbing, in the old woman's lap. There was nothing said for some time: Lady Davenant only pressed her tenderly—stroked her with her hands. "Is it very bad?" she asked at last. Then Laura got up, saying as she took a seat, "Have you heard of it and do people know it?"

"I haven't heard anything. Is it very bad?" Lady Davenant repeated.

"We don't know where Selina is—and her maid's gone."

Lady Davenant looked at her visitor a moment. "Lord, what an ass!" she then ejaculated, putting the paper-knife into her book to keep her place. "And whom has she persuaded to take her—Charles Crispin?" she added.

"We suppose—we suppose——" said Laura.

"And he's another," interrupted the old woman. "And who supposes—Geordie and Ferdy?"

"I don't know; it's all black darkness!"

"My dear, it's a blessing, and now you can live in peace."

"In peace!" cried Laura; "with my wretched sister leading such a life?"

"Oh, my dear, I daresay it will be very comfortable; I am sorry to say anything in favour of such doings, but it very often is. Don't worry; you take her too hard. Has she gone abroad?" the old lady continued. "I daresay she has gone to some pretty, amusing place."

"I don't know anything about it. I only know she is gone. I was with her last evening and she left me without a word."

"Well, that was better. I hate 'em when they make parting scenes; it's too mawkish!"

"Lionel has people watching them," said the girl; "agents, detectives, I don't know what. He has had them for a long time; I didn't know it."

"Do you mean you would have told her if you had? What is the use of detectives now? Isn't he rid of her?"

"Oh, I don't know, he's as bad as she; he talks too horribly—he wants every one to know it," Laura groaned.

"And has he told his mother?"

"I suppose so: he rushed off to see her at noon. She'll be overwhelmed."

"Overwhelmed? Not a bit of it!" cried Lady Davenant, almost gaily. "When did anything in the world overwhelm her and what do you take her for? She'll only make some delightful odd speech. As for people knowing it," she added, "they'll know it whether he wants them or not. My poor child, how long do you expect to make believe?"

"Lionel expects some news to-night," Laura said. "As soon as I know where she is I shall start."

"Start for where?"

"To go to her—to do something."

"Something preposterous, my dear. Do you expect to bring her back?"

"He won't take her in," said Laura, with her dried, dismal eyes. "He wants his divorce—it's too hideous!"

"Well, as she wants hers what is simpler?"

"Yes, she wants hers. Lionel swears by all the gods she can't get it."

"Bless me, won't one do?" Lady Davenant asked. "We shall have some pretty reading."

"It's awful, awful, awful!" murmured Laura.

"Yes, they oughtn't to be allowed to publish them. I wonder if we couldn't stop that. At any rate he had better be quiet: tell him to come and see me."

"You won't influence him; he's dreadful against her. Such a house as it is to-day!"

"Well, my dear, naturally."

"Yes, but it's terrible for me: it's all more sickening than I can bear."

"My dear child, come and stay with me," said the old woman, gently.

"Oh, I can't desert her; I can't abandon her!"

"Desert—abandon? What a way to put it! Hasn't she abandoned you?"

"She has no heart—she's too base!" said the girl. Her face was white and the tears now began to rise to her eyes again.

Lady Davenant got up and came and sat on the sofa beside her: she put her arms round her and the two women embraced. "Your room is all ready," the old lady remarked. And then she said, "When did she leave you? When did you see her last?"

"Oh, in the strangest, maddest, cruelest way, the way most insulting to me. We went to the opera together and she left me there with a gentleman. We know nothing about her since."

"With a gentleman?"

"With Mr Wendover—that American, and something too dreadful happened."

"Dear me, did he kiss you?" asked Lady Davenant.

Laura got up quickly, turning away. "Good-bye, I'm going, I'm going!" And in reply to an irritated, protesting exclamation from her companion she went on, "Anywhere—anywhere to get away!"

"To get away from your American?"

"I asked him to marry me!" The girl turned round with her tragic face.

"He oughtn't to have left that to you."

"I knew this horror was coming, and it took possession of me, there in the box, from one moment to the other—the idea of making sure of some other life, some protection, some respectability. First I thought he liked me, he had behaved as if he did. And I like him, he is a very good man. So I asked him, I couldn't help it, it was too hideous—I offered myself!" Laura spoke as if she were telling that she had stabbed him, standing there with dilated eyes.

Lady Davenant got up again and went to her; drawing off her glove she felt her cheek with the back of her hand. "You are ill, you are in a fever. I'm sure that whatever you said it was very charming."

"Yes, I am ill," said Laura.

"Upon my honour you shan't go home, you shall go straight to bed. And what did he say to you?"

"Oh, it was too miserable!" cried the girl, pressing her face again into her companion's kerchief. "I was all, all mistaken; he had never thought!"

"Why the deuce then did he run about that way after you? He was a brute to say it!"

"He didn't say it and he never ran about. He behaved like a perfect gentleman."

"I've no patience—I wish I had seen him that time!" Lady Davenant declared.

"Yes, that would have been nice! You'll never see him; if
he *is* a gentleman he'll rush away."

"Bless me, what a rushing away!" murmured the old
woman. Then passing her arm round Laura she added,
"You'll please to come upstairs with me."

Half an hour later she had some conversation with her
butler which led to his consulting a little register into which
it was his law to transcribe with great neatness, from their
cards, the addresses of new visitors. This volume, kept in the
drawer of the hall table, revealed the fact that Mr Wendover
was staying in George Street, Hanover Square. "Get into a
cab immediately and tell him to come and see me this evening,"
Lady Davenant said. "Make him understand that it interests
him very nearly, so that no matter what his engagements may
be he must give them up. Go quickly and you'll just find him:
he'll be sure to be at home to dress for dinner." She had cal-
culated justly, for a few minutes before ten o'clock the door
of her drawing-room was thrown open and Mr Wendover
was announced.

"Sit there," said the old lady; "no, not that one, nearer to
me. We must talk low. My dear sir, I won't bite you!"

"Oh, this is very comfortable," Mr Wendover replied
vaguely, smiling through his visible anxiety. It was no more
than natural that he should wonder what Laura Wing's
peremptory friend wanted of him at that hour of the night;
but nothing could exceed the gallantry of his attempt to
conceal the symptoms of alarm.

"You ought to have come before, you know," Lady
Davenant went on. "I have wanted to see you more than
once."

"I have been dining out—I hurried away. This was the first
possible moment, I assure you."

"I too was dining out and I stopped at home on purpose to
see you. But I didn't mean to-night, for you have done very
well. I was quite intending to send for you—the other day.

But something put it out of my head. Besides, I knew she wouldn't like it."

"Why, Lady Davenant, I made a point of calling, ever so long ago—after that day!" the young man exclaimed, not reassured, or at any rate not enlightened.

"I daresay you did—but you mustn't justify yourself; that's just what I don't want; it isn't what I sent for you for. I have something very particular to say to you, but it's very difficult. Voyons un peu!"

The old woman reflected a little, with her eyes on his face, which had grown more grave as she went on; its expression intimated that he failed as yet to understand her and that he at least was not exactly trifling. Lady Davenant's musings apparently helped her little, if she was looking for an artful approach; for they ended in her saying abruptly, "I wonder if you know what a capital girl she is."

"Do you mean—do you mean———?" stammered Mr Wendover, pausing as if he had given her no right not to allow him to conceive alternatives.

"Yes, I do mean. She's upstairs, in bed."

"Upstairs in bed!" The young man stared.

"Don't be afraid—I'm not going to send for her!" laughed his hostess; "her being here, after all, has nothing to do with it, except that she *did* come—yes, certainly, she did come. But my keeping her—that was my doing. My maid has gone to Grosvenor Place to get her things and let them know that she will stay here for the present. Now am I clear?"

"Not in the least," said Mr Wendover, almost sternly.

Lady Davenant, however, was not of a composition to suspect him of sternness or to care very much if she did, and she went on, with her quick discursiveness: "Well, we must be patient; we shall work it out together. I was afraid you would go away, that's why I lost no time. Above all I want you to understand that she has not the least idea that I have sent for you, and you must promise me never, never, never

to let her know. She would be monstrous angry. It is quite
my own idea—I have taken the responsibility. I know very
little about you of course, but she has spoken to me well of
you. Besides, I am very clever about people, and I liked you
that day, though you seemed to think I was a hundred and
eighty."

"You do me great honour," Mr Wendover rejoined.

"I'm glad you're pleased! You must be if I tell you that I
like you now even better. I see what you are, except for the
question of fortune. It doesn't perhaps matter much, but have
you any money? I mean have you a fine income?"

"No, indeed I haven't!" And the young man laughed in
his bewilderment. "I have very little money indeed."

"Well, I daresay you have as much as I. Besides, that
would be a proof she is not mercenary."

"You haven't in the least made it plain whom you are
talking about," said Mr Wendover. "I have no right to
assume anything."

"Are you afraid of betraying her? I am more devoted to her
even than I want you to be. She has told me what happened
between you last night—what she said to you at the opera.
That's what I want to talk to you about."

"She was very strange," the young man remarked.

"I am not so sure that she was strange. However, you are
welcome to think it, for goodness knows she says so herself.
She is overwhelmed with horror at her own words; she is
absolutely distracted and prostrate."

Mr Wendover was silent a moment. "I assured her that I
admire her—beyond every one. I was most kind to her."

"Did you say it in that tone? You should have thrown
yourself at her feet! From the moment you didn't—surely
you understand women well enough to know."

"You must remember where we were—in a public place,
with very little room for throwing!" Mr Wendover exclaimed.

"Ah, so far from blaming you she says your behaviour was

perfect. It's only I who want to have it out with you," Lady
Davenant pursued. "She's so clever, so charming, so good
and so unhappy."

"When I said just now she was strange, I meant only in
the way she turned against me."

"She turned against you?"

"She told me she hoped she should never see me again."

"And you, should you like to see her?"

"Not now—not now!" Mr Wendover exclaimed, eagerly.

"I don't mean now, I'm not such a fool as that. I mean
some day or other, when she has stopped accusing herself, if
she ever does."

"Ah, Lady Davenant, you must leave that to me," the
young man returned, after a moment's hesitation.

"Don't be afraid to tell me I'm meddling with what doesn't
concern me," said his hostess. "Of course I know I'm meddling; I sent for you here to meddle. Who wouldn't, for that
creature? She makes one melt."

"I'm exceedingly sorry for her. I don't know what she
thinks she said."

"Well, that she asked you why you came so often to
Grosvenor Place. I don't see anything so awful in that, if you
did go."

"Yes, I went very often. I liked to go."

"Now, that's exactly where I wish to prevent a miscon-
ception," said Lady Davenant. "If you liked to go you had a
reason for liking, and Laura Wing was the reason, wasn't
she?"

"I thought her charming, and I think her so now more
than ever."

"Then you are a dear good man. Vous faisiez votre cour, in
short."

Mr Wendover made no immediate response: the two sat
looking at each other. "It isn't easy for me to talk of these
things," he said at last; "but if you mean that I wished to

ask her to be my wife I am bound to tell you that I had no such intention."

"Ah, then I'm at sea. You thought her charming and you went to see her every day. What then did you wish?"

"I didn't go every day. Moreover I think you have a very different idea in this country of what constitutes—well, what constitutes making love. A man commits himself much sooner."

"Oh, I don't know what *your* odd ways may be!" Lady Davenant exclaimed, with a shade of irritation.

"Yes, but I was justified in supposing that those ladies did: they at least are American."

"'They,' my dear sir! For heaven's sake don't mix up that nasty Selina with it!"

"Why not, if I admired her too? I do extremely, and I thought the house most interesting."

"Mercy on us, if that's your idea of a nice house! But I don't know—I have always kept out of it," Lady Davenant added, checking herself. Then she went on, "If you are so fond of Mrs Berrington I am sorry to inform you that she is absolutely good-for-nothing."

"Good-for-nothing?"

"Nothing to speak of! I have been thinking whether I would tell you, and I have decided to do so because I take it that your learning it for yourself would be a matter of but a very short time. Selina has bolted, as they say."

"Bolted?" Mr Wendover repeated.

"I don't know what you call it in America."

"In America we don't do it."

"Ah, well, if they stay, as they do usually abroad, that's better. I suppose you didn't think her capable of behaving herself, did you?"

"Do you mean she has left her husband—with some one else?"

"Neither more nor less; with a fellow named Crispin. It

appears it all came off last evening, and she had her own
reasons for doing it in the most offensive way—publicly,
clumsily, with the vulgarest bravado. Laura has told me what
took place, and you must permit me to express my surprise
at your not having divined the miserable business."

"I saw something was wrong, but I didn't understand. I'm
afraid I'm not very quick at these things."

"Your state is the more gracious; but certainly you are not
quick if you could call there so often and not see through
Selina."

"Mr Crispin, whoever he is, was never there," said the
young man.

"Oh, she was a clever hussy!" his companion rejoined.

"I knew she was fond of amusement, but that's what I liked
to see. I wanted to see a house of that sort."

"Fond of amusement is a very pretty phrase!" said Lady
Davenant, laughing at the simplicity with which her visitor
accounted for his assiduity. "And did Laura Wing seem to you
in her place in a house of that sort?"

"Why, it was natural she should be with her sister, and
she always struck me as very gay."

"That was your enlivening effect! And did she strike
you as very gay last night, with this scandal hanging over
her?"

"She didn't talk much," said Mr Wendover.

"She knew it was coming—she felt it, she saw it, and that's
what makes her sick now, that at *such* a time she should have
challenged you, when she felt herself about to be associated
(in people's minds, of course) with such a vile business. In
people's minds and in yours—when you should know what
had happened."

"Ah, Miss Wing isn't associated——" said Mr Wendover.
He spoke slowly, but he rose to his feet with a nervous
movement that was not lost upon his companion: she noted it
indeed with a certain inward sense of triumph. She was very

deep, but she had never been so deep as when she made up her mind to mention the scandal of the house of Berrington to her visitor and intimated to him that Laura Wing regarded herself as near enough to it to receive from it a personal stain. "I'm extremely sorry to hear of Mrs Berrington's misconduct," he continued gravely, standing before her. "And I am no less obliged to you for your interest."

"Don't mention it," she said, getting up too and smiling. "I mean my interest. As for the other matter, it will all come out. Lionel will haul her up."

"Dear me, how dreadful!"

"Yes, dreadful enough. But don't betray me."

"Betray you?" he repeated, as if his thoughts had gone astray a moment.

"I mean to the girl. Think of her shame!"

"Her shame?" Mr Wendover said, in the same way.

"It seemed to her, with what was becoming so clear to her, that an honest man might save her from it, might give her his name and his faith and help her to traverse the bad place. She exaggerates the badness of it, the stigma of her relationship. Good heavens, at that rate where would some of us be? But those are her ideas, they are absolutely sincere, and they had possession of her at the opera. She had a sense of being lost and was in a real agony to be rescued. She saw before her a kind gentleman who had seemed—who had certainly seemed ——" And Lady Davenant, with her fine old face lighted by her bright sagacity and her eyes on Mr Wendover's, paused, lingering on this word. "Of course she must have been in a state of nerves."

"I am very sorry for her," said Mr Wendover, with his gravity that committed him to nothing.

"So am I! And of course if you were not in love with her you weren't, were you?"

"I must bid you good-bye, I am leaving London." That was the only answer Lady Davenant got to her inquiry.

"Good-bye then. She is the nicest girl I know. But once more, mind you don't let her suspect!"

"How can I let her suspect anything when I shall never see her again?"

"Oh, don't say that," said Lady Davenant, very gently.

"She drove me away from her with a kind of ferocity."

"Oh, gammon!" cried the old woman.

"I'm going home," he said, looking at her with his hand on the door.

"Well, it's the best place for you. And for her too!" she added as he went out. She was not sure that the last words reached him.

XIII

LAURA WING was sharply ill for three days, but on the fourth she made up her mind she was better, though this was not the opinion of Lady Davenant, who would not hear of her getting up. The remedy she urged was lying still and yet lying still; but this specific the girl found well-nigh intolerable—it was a form of relief that only ministered to fever. She assured her friend that it killed her to do nothing: to which her friend replied by asking her what she had a fancy to do. Laura had her idea and held it tight, but there was no use in producing it before Lady Davenant, who would have knocked it to pieces. On the afternoon of the first day Lionel Berrington came, and though his intention was honest he brought no healing. Hearing she was ill he wanted to look after her—he wanted to take her back to Grosvenor Place and make her comfortable: he spoke as if he had every convenience for producing that condition, though he confessed there was a little bar to it in his own case. This impediment was the "cheeky" aspect of Miss Steet, who went sniffing about as if she knew a lot, if she should only condescend to tell it. He saw more of the children now; "I'm going to have 'em in every day, poor little devils," he said; and he spoke as if the discipline of suffering had already begun for him and a kind of holy change had taken place in his life. Nothing had been said yet in the house, of course, as Laura knew, about Selina's disappearance, in the way of treating it as irregular; but the servants pretended so hard not to be aware of anything in particular that they were like pickpockets looking with unnatural interest the other way after they have cribbed a fellow's watch. To a certainty, in a day or two, the governess would give him warning: she would come and tell him she couldn't stay in such a place, and he would tell her, in return, that she was a little donkey for not knowing that the place was much more respectable now than it had ever been.

This information Selina's husband imparted to Lady Davenant, to whom he discoursed with infinite candour and humour, taking a highly philosophical view of his position and declaring that it suited him down to the ground. His wife couldn't have pleased him better if she had done it on purpose; he knew where she had been every hour since she quitted Laura at the opera—he knew where she was at that moment and he was expecting to find another telegram on his return to Grosvenor Place. So if it suited *her* it was all right, wasn't it? and the whole thing would go as straight as a shot. Lady Davenant took him up to see Laura, though she viewed their meeting with extreme disfavour, the girl being in no state for talking. In general Laura had little enough mind for it, but she insisted on seeing Lionel: she declared that if this were not allowed her she would go after him, ill as she was— she would dress herself and drive to his house. She dressed herself now, after a fashion; she got upon a sofa to receive him. Lady Davenant left him alone with her for twenty minutes, at the end of which she returned to take him away. This interview was not fortifying to the girl, whose idea

—the idea of which I have said that she was tenacious—
was to go after her sister, to take possession of her, cling to
her and bring her back. Lionel, of course, wouldn't hear of
taking her back, nor would Selina presumably hear of coming; but this made no difference in Laura's heroic plan. She
would work it, she would compass it, she would go down on
her knees, she would find the eloquence of angels, she would
achieve miracles. At any rate it made her frantic not to try,
especially as even in fruitless action she should escape from
herself—an object of which her horror was not yet extinguished.

As she lay there through inexorably conscious hours the
picture of that hideous moment in the box alternated with the
vision of her sister's guilty flight. She wanted to fly, herself—
to go off and keep going for ever. Lionel was fussily kind to
her and he didn't abuse Selina—he didn't tell her again how
that lady's behaviour suited his book. He simply resisted, with
a little exasperating, dogged grin, her pitiful appeal for knowledge of her sister's whereabouts. He knew what she wanted
it for and he wouldn't help her in any such game. If she would
promise, solemnly, to be quiet, he would tell her when she
got better, but he wouldn't lend her a hand to make a fool of
herself. Her work was cut out for her—she was to stay and
mind the children: if she was so keen to do her duty she
needn't go further than that for it. He talked a great deal
about the children and figured himself as pressing the little
deserted darlings to his bosom. He was not a comedian, and
she could see that he really believed he was going to be better
and purer now. Laura said she was sure Selina would make an
attempt to get them—or at least one of them; and he replied,
grimly, "Yes, my dear, she had better try!" The girl was so
angry with him, in her hot, tossing weakness, for refusing to
tell her even whether the desperate pair had crossed the
Channel, that she was guilty of the immorality of regretting
that the difference in badness between husband and wife was

so distinct (for it was distinct, she could see that) as he made his dry little remark about Selina's trying. He told her he had already seen his solicitor, the clever Mr Smallshaw, and she said she didn't care.

On the fourth day of her absence from Grosvenor Place she got up, at an hour when she was alone (in the afternoon, rather late), and prepared herself to go out. Lady Davenant had admitted in the morning that she was better, and fortunately she had not the complication of being subject to a medical opinion, having absolutely refused to see a doctor. Her old friend had been obliged to go out—she had scarcely quitted her before—and Laura had requested the hovering, rustling lady's-maid to leave her alone; she assured her she was doing beautifully. Laura had no plan except to leave London that night; she had a moral certainty that Selina had gone to the Continent. She had always done so whenever she had a chance, and what chance had ever been larger than the present? The Continent was fearfully vague, but she would deal sharply with Lionel—she would show him she had a right to knowledge. He would certainly be in town; he would be in a complacent bustle with his lawyers. She had told him that she didn't believe he had yet gone to them, but in her heart she believed it perfectly. If he didn't satisfy her she would go to Lady Ringrose, odious as it would be to her to ask a favour of this depraved creature: unless indeed Lady Ringrose had joined the little party to France, as on the occasion of Selina's last journey thither. On her way downstairs she met one of the footmen, of whom she made the request that he would call her a cab as quickly as possible— she was obliged to go out for half an hour. He expressed the respectful hope that she was better and she replied that she was perfectly well—he would please tell her ladyship when she came in. To this the footman rejoined that her ladyship *had* come in—she had returned five minutes before and had gone to her room. "Miss Frothingham told her you were asleep, Miss," said the man, "and her ladyship said it was a blessing and you were not to be disturbed."

"Very good, I will see her," Laura remarked, with dissimulation: "only please let me have my cab."

The footman went downstairs and she stood there listening; presently she heard the house-door close—he had gone out on his errand. Then she descended very softly—she prayed he might not be long. The door of the drawing-room stood open as she passed it, and she paused before it, thinking she heard sounds in the lower hall. They appeared to subside and then she found herself faint—she was terribly impatient for her cab. Partly to sit down till it came (there was a seat on the landing, but another servant might come up or down and see her), and partly to look, at the front window, whether it were not coming, she went for a moment into the drawing-room. She stood at the window, but the footman was slow; then she sank upon a chair—she felt very weak. Just after she had done so she became aware of steps on the stairs and she got up quickly, supposing that her messenger had returned, though she had not heard wheels. What she saw was not the footman she had sent out, but the expansive person of the butler, followed apparently by a visitor. This functionary ushered the visitor in with the remark that he would call her ladyship, and before she knew it she was face to face with Mr Wendover. At the same moment she heard a cab drive up, while Mr Wendover instantly closed the door.

"Don't turn me away; do see me—do see me!" he said. "I asked for Lady Davenant—they told me she was at home. But it was you I wanted, and I wanted her to help me. I was going away—but I couldn't. You look very ill—do listen to me! You don't understand—I will explain everything. Ah, how ill you look!" the young man cried, as the climax of this sudden, soft, distressed appeal. Laura, for all answer, tried to push past him, but the result of this movement was that she found herself enclosed in his arms. He stopped her, but she disengaged herself, she got her hand upon the door. He was leaning against it, so she couldn't open it, and as she stood there panting she shut her eyes, so as not to see him. "If you would let me tell you what I think—I would do anything in the world for you!" he went on.

"Let me go—you persecute me!" the girl cried, pulling at the handle.

"You don't do me justice—you are too cruel!" Mr Wendover persisted.

"Let me go—let me go!" she only repeated, with her high, quavering, distracted note; and as he moved a little she got the door open. But he followed her out: would she see him that night? Where was she going? might he not go with her? would she see him to-morrow?

"Never, never, never!" she flung at him as she hurried away. The butler was on the stairs, descending from above; so he checked himself, letting her go. Laura passed out of the house and flew into her cab with extraordinary speed, for Mr Wendover heard the wheels bear her away while the servant was saying to him in measured accents that her ladyship would come down immediately.

Lionel was at home, in Grosvenor Place: she burst into the library and found him playing papa. Geordie and Ferdy were sporting around him, the presence of Miss Steet had been dispensed with, and he was holding his younger son by the stomach, horizontally, between his legs, while the child made little sprawling movements which were apparently intended to represent the act of swimming. Geordie stood impatient on the brink of the imaginary stream, protesting that it was his turn now, and as soon as he saw his aunt he rushed at her with the request that she would take him up in the same fashion. She was struck with the superficiality of their childhood; they appeared to have no sense that she had been away and no care that she had been ill. But Lionel made up for this; he greeted her with affectionate jollity, said it was a good job she had come back, and remarked to the children that they would have great larks now that auntie was home again. Ferdy asked if she had been with mummy, but didn't wait for an answer, and she observed that they put no question about their mother and made no further allusion to her while they remained in the room. She wondered whether their father had enjoined upon them not to mention her, and reflected that even if he had such a command would not have been efficacious. It added to the ugliness of Selina's flight that even her children didn't miss her, and to the dreariness, somehow, to Laura's sense, of the whole situation, that one could neither spend tears on the mother and wife, because she was not worth it, nor sentimentalise about the little boys, because they didn't inspire it. "Well, you do look seedy—I'm bound to say that!" Lionel exclaimed; and he recommended strongly a glass of port, while Ferdy, not seizing this reference, suggested that daddy should take her by the waistband and teach her to "strike out." He represented himself in the act of drowning, but Laura interrupted this entertainment, when the servant answered the bell (Lionel having rung for the port), by requesting that the children should be conveyed to Miss Steet. "Tell her she must never go away again," Lionel said to Geordie, as the butler took him by the hand; but the only touching consequence of this injunction was that the child piped back to his father, over his shoulder, "Well, you mustn't either, you know!"

"You must tell me or I'll kill myself—I give you my word!" Laura said to her brother-in-law, with unnecessary violence, as soon as they had left the room.

"I say, I say," he rejoined, "you *are* a wilful one! What do you want to threaten me for? Don't you know me well enough to know that ain't the way? That's the tone Selina used to take. Surely you don't want to begin and imitate her!" She only sat there, looking at him, while he leaned against the chimney-piece smoking a short cigar. There was a silence, during which she felt the heat of a certain irrational anger at the thought that a little ignorant, red-faced jockey should have the luck to be in the right as against her flesh and blood. She considered him helplessly, with something in her eyes that had never been there before—something that, apparently, after a moment, made an impression on him. Afterwards, however, she saw very well that it was not her threat that had moved him, and even at the moment she had a sense, from the way he looked back at her, that this was in no manner the first time a baffled woman had told him that she would kill herself. He had always accepted his kinship with her, but even in her trouble it was part of her consciousness that he now lumped her with a mixed group of female figures, a little wavering and dim, who were associated in his memory with "scenes," with importunities and bothers. It is apt to be the disadvantage of women, on occasions of measuring their strength with men, that they may perceive that the man has a larger experience and that they themselves are a part of it. It is doubtless as a provision against such emergencies that nature has opened to them operations of the mind that are independent of experience. Laura felt the dishonour of her race the more that her brother-in-law seemed so gay and bright about it: he had an air of positive prosperity, as if his misfortune had turned into that. It came to her that he really liked the idea of the public *éclaircissement*—the fresh occupation, the bustle and importance and celebrity of it. That was sufficiently incredible, but as she was on the wrong side it was also humiliating. Besides, higher spirits always suggest finer wisdom, and such an attribute on Lionel's part was most humiliating of all. "I haven't the least objection at present to telling you what you want to know. I shall have made my little arrangements very soon and you will be subpœnaed."

"Subpœnaed?" the girl repeated, mechanically.

"You will be called as a witness on my side."

"On your side."

"Of course you're on my side, ain't you?"

"Can they force me to come?" asked Laura, in answer to this.

"No, they can't force you, if you leave the country."

"That's exactly what I want to do."

"That will be idiotic," said Lionel, "and very bad for your sister. If you don't help me you ought at least to help her."

She sat a moment with her eyes on the ground. "Where is she—where is she?" she then asked.

"They are at Brussels, at the Hôtel de Flandres. They appear to like it very much."

"Are you telling me the truth?"

"Lord, my dear child, *I* don't lie!" Lionel exclaimed. "You'll make a jolly mistake if you go to her," he added. "If you have seen her with him how can you speak for her?"

"I won't see her with him."

"That's all very well, but he'll take care of that. Of course if you're ready for perjury——!" Lionel exclaimed.

"I'm ready for anything."

"Well, I've been kind to you, my dear," he continued, smoking, with his chin in the air.

"Certainly you have been kind to me."

"If you want to defend her you had better keep away from her," said Lionel. "Besides for yourself, it won't be the best thing in the world—to be known to have been in it."

"I don't care about myself," the girl returned, musingly.

"Don't you care about the children, that you are so ready to throw them over? For you would, my dear, you know. If you go to Brussels you never come back here—you never cross this threshold—you never touch them again!"

Laura appeared to listen to this last declaration, but she made no reply to it; she only exclaimed after a moment, with a certain impatience, "Oh, the children will do anyway!" Then she added passionately, "You *won't*, Lionel; in mercy's name tell me that you won't!"

"I won't what?"

"Do the awful thing you say."

"Divorce her? The devil I won't!"

"Then why do you speak of the children—if you have no pity for them?"

Lionel stared an instant. "I thought you said yourself that they would do anyway!"

Laura bent her head, resting it on the back of her hand, on the leathern arm of the sofa. So she remained, while Lionel stood smoking; but at last, to leave the room, she got up with an effort that was a physical pain. He came to her, to detain her, with a little good intention that had no felicity for her, trying to take her hand persuasively. "Dear old girl, don't try and behave just as *she* did! If you'll stay quietly here I won't call you, I give you my honour I won't; there! You want to see the doctor—that's the fellow you want to see. And what good will it do you, even if you bring her home in pink paper? Do you candidly suppose I'll ever look at her—except across the court-room?"

"I must, I must, I must!" Laura cried, jerking herself away from him and reaching the door.

"Well then, good-bye," he said, in the sternest tone she had ever heard him use.

She made no answer, she only escaped. She locked herself in her room; she remained there an hour. At the end of this time she came out and went to the door of the schoolroom, where she asked Miss Steet to be so good as to come and speak to her. The governess followed her to her apartment, and there Laura took her partly into her confidence. There were things she wanted to do before going, and she was too weak to act without assistance. She didn't want it from the servants, if only Miss Steet would learn from them whether Mr Berrington were dining at home. Laura told her that her sister was ill and she was hurrying to join her abroad. It had to be mentioned, that way, that Mrs Berrington had left the country,

though of course there was no spoken recognition between
the two women of the reasons for which she had done so.
There was only a tacit hypocritical assumption that she was
on a visit to friends and that there had been nothing queer
about her departure. Laura knew that Miss Steet knew the
truth, and the governess knew that she knew it. This young
woman lent a hand, very confusedly, to the girl's preparations;
she ventured not to be sympathetic, as that would point too
much to badness, but she succeeded perfectly in being dismal.
She suggested that Laura was ill herself, but Laura replied
that this was no matter when her sister was so much worse.
She elicited the fact that Mr Berrington was dining out—the
butler believed with his mother—but she was of no use when
it came to finding in the "Bradshaw" which she brought up
from the hall the hour of the night-boat to Ostend. Laura
found it herself; it was conveniently late, and it was a gain to
her that she was very near the Victoria station, where she
would take the train for Dover. The governess wanted to go
to the station with her, but the girl would not listen to this—
she would only allow her to see that she had a cab. Laura let
her help her still further; she sent her down to talk to Lady
Davenant's maid when that personage arrived in Grosvenor
Place to inquire, from her mistress, what in the world had
become of poor Miss Wing. The maid intimated, Miss Steet
said on her return, that her ladyship would have come herself,
only she was too angry. She was very bad indeed. It was an
indication of this that she had sent back her young friend's
dressing-case and her clothes. Laura also borrowed money
from the governess—she had too little in her pocket. The
latter brightened up as the preparations advanced; she had
never before been concerned in a flurried night-episode, with
an unavowed clandestine side; the very imprudence of it (for
a sick girl alone) was romantic, and before Laura had gone
down to the cab she began to say that foreign life must be
fascinating and to make wistful reflections. She saw that the

coast was clear, in the nursery—that the children were
asleep, for their aunt to come in. She kissed Ferdy while her
companion pressed her lips upon Geordie, and Geordie while
Laura hung for a moment over Ferdy. At the door of the cab
she tried to make her take more money, and our heroine had
an odd sense that if the vehicle had not rolled away she would
have thrust into her hand a keepsake for Captain Crispin.

A quarter of an hour later Laura sat in the corner of a
railway-carriage, muffled in her cloak (the July evening was
fresh, as it so often is in London—fresh enough to add to her
sombre thoughts the suggestion of the wind in the Channel),
waiting in a vain torment of nervousness for the train to set
itself in motion. Her nervousness itself had led her to come
too early to the station, and it seemed to her that she had
already waited long. A lady and a gentleman had taken their
place in the carriage (it was not yet the moment for the outward crowd of tourists) and had left their appurtenances there
while they strolled up and down the platform. The long
English twilight was still in the air, but there was dusk under
the grimy arch of the station and Laura flattered herself that
the off-corner of the carriage she had chosen was in shadow.
This, however, apparently did not prevent her from being
recognised by a gentleman who stopped at the door, looking
in, with the movement of a person who was going from
carriage to carriage. As soon as he saw her he stepped quickly
in, and the next moment Mr Wendover was seated on the edge
of the place beside her, leaning toward her, speaking to her
low, with clasped hands. She fell back in her seat, closing her
eyes again. He barred the way out of the compartment.

"I have followed you here—I saw Miss Steet—I want to
implore you not to go! Don't, don't! I know what you're
doing. Don't go, I beseech you. I saw Lady Davenant, I
wanted to ask her to help me, I could bear it no longer. I
have thought of you, night and day, these four days. Lady
Davenant has told me things, and I entreat you not to go!"

Laura opened her eyes (there was something in his voice, in his pressing nearness), and looked at him a moment: it was the first time she had done so since the first of those detestable moments in the box at Covent Garden. She had never spoken to him of Selina in any but an honourable sense. Now she said, "I'm going to my sister."

"I know it, and I wish unspeakably you would give it up—it isn't good—it's a great mistake. Stay here and let me talk to you."

The girl raised herself, she stood up in the carriage. Mr Wendover did the same; Laura saw that the lady and gentleman outside were now standing near the door. "What have you to say? It's my own business!" she returned, between her teeth. "Go out, go out, go out!"

"Do you suppose I would speak if I didn't care—do you suppose I would care if I didn't love you?" the young man murmured, close to her face.

"What is there to care about? Because people will know it and talk? If it's bad it's the right thing for me! If I don't go to her where else shall I go?"

"Come to me, dearest, dearest!" Mr Wendover went on. "You are ill, you are mad! I love you—I assure you I do!"

She pushed him away with her hands. "If you follow me I will jump off the boat!"

"Take your places, take your places!" cried the guard, on the platform. Mr Wendover had to slip out, the lady and gentleman were coming in. Laura huddled herself into her corner again and presently the train drew away.

Mr Wendover did not get into another compartment; he went back that evening to Queen's Gate. He knew how interested his old friend there, as he now considered her, would be to hear what Laura had undertaken (though, as he learned, on entering her drawing-room again, she had already heard of it from her maid), and he felt the necessity to tell her once more how her words of four days before had fructified in his heart, what a strange, ineffaceable impression she had made upon him: to tell her in short and to repeat it over and over, that he had taken the most extraordinary fancy——! Lady Davenant was tremendously vexed at the girl's perversity, but she counselled him patience, a long, persistent patience. A week later she heard from Laura Wing, from Antwerp, that she was sailing to America from that port—a letter containing no mention whatever of Selina or of the reception she had found at Brussels. To America Mr Wendover followed his young compatriot (that at least she had no right to forbid), and there, for the moment, he has had a chance to practise the humble virtue recommended by Lady Davenant. He knows she has no money and that she is staying with some distant relatives in Virginia; a situation that he—perhaps too superficially— figures as unspeakably dreary. He knows further that Lady Davenant has sent her fifty pounds, and he himself has ideas of transmitting funds, not directly to Virginia but by the roundabout road of Queen's Gate. Now, however, that Lionel Berrington's deplorable suit is coming on he reflects with some satisfaction that the Court of Probate and Divorce is far from the banks of the Rappahannock. "Berrington *versus* Berrington and Others" is coming on—but these are matters of the present hour.

THE LESSON OF THE MASTER

I

HE had been informed that the ladies were at church, but that was corrected by what he saw from the top of the steps (they descended from a great height in two arms, with a circular sweep of the most charming effect) at the threshold of the door which, from the long, bright gallery, overlooked the immense lawn. Three gentlemen, on the grass, at a distance, sat under the great trees; but the fourth figure was not a gentleman, the one in the crimson dress which made so vivid a spot, told so as a "bit of colour" amid the fresh, rich green. The servant had come so far with Paul Overt to show him the way and had asked him if he wished first to go to his room. The young man declined this privilege, having no disorder to repair after so short and easy a journey and liking to take a general perceptive possession of the new scene immediately, as he always did. He stood there a little with his eyes on the group and on the admirable picture—the wide grounds of an old country-house near London (that only made it better,) on a splendid Sunday in June. "But that lady, who is she?" he said to the servant before the man went away.

"I think it's Mrs St George, sir."

"Mrs St George, the wife of the distinguished——" Then Paul Overt checked himself, doubting whether the footman would know.

"Yes, sir—probably, sir," said the servant, who appeared to wish to intimate that a person staying at Summersoft would naturally be, if only by alliance, distinguished. His manner, however, made poor Overt feel for the moment as if he himself were but little so.

"And the gentlemen?" he inquired.

"Well, sir, one of them is General Fancourt."

"Ah yes, I know; thank you." General Fancourt was distinguished, there was no doubt of that, for something he had done, or perhaps even had not done (the young man could not remember which) some years before in India. The servant went away, leaving the glass doors open into the gallery, and Paul Overt remained at the head of the wide double staircase, saying to himself that the place was sweet and promised a pleasant visit, while he leaned on the balustrade of fine old ironwork which, like all the other details, was of the same period as the house. It all went together and spoke in one voice—a rich English voice of the early part of the eighteenth century. It might have been church-time on a summer's day in the reign of Queen Anne; the stillness was too perfect to be modern, the nearness counted so as distance and there was something so fresh and sound in the originality of the large smooth house, the expanse of whose beautiful brickwork, which had been kept clear of messy creepers (as a woman with a rare complexion disdains a veil,) was pink rather than red. When Paul Overt perceived that the people under the trees were noticing him he turned back through the open doors into the great gallery which was the pride of the place. It traversed the mansion from end to end and seemed—with its bright colours, its high panelled windows, its faded, flowered chintzes, its quickly-recognised portraits and pictures, the blue and white china of its cabinets and the attenuated festoons and rosettes of its ceiling—a cheerful upholstered avenue into the other century.

The young man was slightly nervous; that belonged in general to his disposition as a student of fine prose, with his dose of the artist's restlessness; and there was a particular excitement in the idea that Henry St George might be a member of the party. For the younger writer he had remained a high literary figure, in spite of the lower range of production to which he had fallen after his three first great successes, the comparative absence of quality in his later work. There had been moments when Paul Overt almost shed tears upon this; but now that he was near him (he had never met him,) he was conscious only of the fine original source and of his own immense debt. After he had taken a turn or two up and down the gallery he came out again and descended the steps. He was but slenderly supplied with a certain social boldness (it was really a weakness in him,) so that, conscious of a want of acquaintance with the four persons in the distance, he indulged in a movement as to which he had a certain safety in feeling that it did not necessarily appear to commit him to an attempt to join them. There was a fine English awkwardness in it—he felt this too as he sauntered vaguely and obliquely across the lawn, as if to take an independent line. Fortunately there was an equally fine English directness in the way one of the gentlemen presently rose and made as if to approach him, with an air of conciliation and reassurance. To this demonstration Paul Overt instantly responded, though he knew the gentleman was not his host. He was tall, straight and elderly, and had a pink, smiling face and a white moustache. Our young man met him half way while he laughed and said: "A—— Lady Watermouth told us you were coming; she asked me just to look after you." Paul Overt thanked him (he liked him without delay,) and turned round with him, walking toward the others. "They've all gone to church—all except us," the stranger continued as they went; "we're just sitting here—it's so jolly." Overt rejoined that it was jolly indeed—it was such a lovely place; he mentioned that he had not seen it before—it was a charming impression.

"Ah, you've not been here before?" said his companion. "It's a nice little place—not much to *do*, you know." Overt wondered what he wanted to "do"—he felt as if he himself were doing a good deal. By the time they came to where the others sat he had guessed his initiator was a military man, and (such was the turn of Overt's imagination,) this made him still more sympathetic. He would naturally have a passion for activity—for deeds at variance with the pacific, pastoral scene. He was evidently so good-natured, however, that he accepted the inglorious hour for what it was worth. Paul Overt shared it with him and with his companions for the next twenty minutes; the latter looked at him and he looked at them without knowing much who they were, while the talk went on without enlightening him much as to what it was about. It was indeed about nothing in particular, and wandered, with casual, pointless pauses and short terrestrial flights, amid the names of persons and places—names which, for him, had no great power of evocation. It was all sociable and slow, as was right and natural on a warm Sunday morning.

Overt's first attention was given to the question, privately considered, of whether one of the two younger men would be Henry St George. He knew many of his distinguished contemporaries by their photographs, but he had never, as it happened, seen a portrait of the great misguided novelist. One of the gentlemen was out of the question—he was too young; and the other scarcely looked clever enough, with such mild, undiscriminating eyes. If those eyes were St George's, the problem presented by the ill-matched parts of his genius was still more difficult of solution. Besides, the deportment of the personage possessing them was not, as regards the lady in the red dress, such as could be natural, towards his wife, even to a writer accused by several critics of sacrificing too much to manner. Lastly, Paul Overt had an indefinite feeling that if the gentleman with the sightless eyes bore the name that had set his heart beating faster (he also had contradictory, conventional whiskers—the young admirer of the celebrity had never in a mental vision seen *his* face in so vulgar a frame), he would have given him a sign of recognition or of friendliness—would have heard of him a little, would know something about *Ginistrella*, would have gathered at least that that

recent work of fiction had made an impression on the discern-
ing. Paul Overt had a dread of being grossly proud, but it
seemed to him that his self-consciousness took no undue
license in thinking that the authorship of *Ginistrella* con-
stituted a degree of identity. His soldierly friend became clear
enough; he was "Fancourt," but he was also the General; and
he mentioned to our young man in the course of a few
moments that he had but lately returned from twenty years'
service abroad.

"And do you mean to remain in England?" Overt asked.

"Oh yes, I have bought a little house in London."

"And I hope you like it," said Overt, looking at Mrs St
George.

"Well, a little house in Manchester Square—there's a limit
to the enthusiasm that that inspires."

"Oh, I meant being at home again—being in London."

"My daughter likes it—that's the main thing. She's very
fond of art and music and literature and all that kind of thing.
She missed it in India and she finds it in London, or she hopes
she will find it. Mr St George has promised to help her—he
has been awfully kind to her. She has gone to church—she's
fond of that too—but they'll all be back in a quarter of an
hour. You must let me introduce you to her—she will be so
glad to know you. I dare say she has read every word you
have written."

"I shall be delighted—I haven't written very many," said
Overt, who felt without resentment that the General at least
was very vague about that. But he wondered a little why, since
he expressed this friendly disposition, it did not occur to him
to pronounce the word which would put him in relation with
Mrs St George. If it was a question of introductions Miss
Fancourt (apparently she was unmarried,) was far away and
the wife of his illustrious *confrère* was almost between them.
This lady struck Paul Overt as a very pretty woman, with a
surprising air of youth and a high smartness of aspect which

seemed to him (he could scarcely have said why,) a sort of
mystification. St George certainly had every right to a charming wife, but he himself would never have taken the important little woman in the aggressively Parisian dress for the
domestic partner of a man of letters. That partner in general,
he knew, was far from presenting herself in a single type: his
observation had instructed him that she was not inveterately,
not necessarily dreary. But he had never before seen her look
so much as if her prosperity had deeper foundations than an
ink-spotted study-table littered with proof-sheets. Mrs St
George might have been the wife of a gentleman who "kept"
books rather than wrote them, who carried on great affairs in
the City and made better bargains than those that poets make
with publishers. With this she hinted at a success more personal, as if she had been the most characteristic product of an
age in which society, the world of conversation, is a great
drawing-room with the City for its antechamber. Overt
judged her at first to be about thirty years of age; then, after a
while, he perceived that she was much nearer fifty. But she
juggled away the twenty years somehow—you only saw
them in a rare glimpse, like the rabbit in the conjurer's sleeve.
She was extraordinarily white, and everything about her was
pretty—her eyes, her ears, her hair, her voice, her hands, her
feet (to which her relaxed attitude in her wicker chair gave a
great publicity,) and the numerous ribbons and trinkets with
which she was bedecked. She looked as if she had put on her
best clothes to go to church and then had decided that they
were too good for that and had stayed at home. She told a
story of some length about the shabby way Lady Jane had
treated the Duchess, as well as an anecdote in relation to a
purchase she had made in Paris (on her way back from
Cannes,) for Lady Egbert, who had never refunded the money.
Paul Overt suspected her of a tendency to figure great people
as larger than life, until he noticed the manner in which she
handled Lady Egbert, which was so subversive that it reassured

him. He felt that he should have understood her better if he
might have met her eye; but she scarcely looked at him.
"Ah, here they come—all the good ones!" she said at last;
and Paul Overt saw in the distance the return of the church-
goers—several persons, in couples and threes, advancing in a
flicker of sun and shade at the end of a large green vista
formed by the level grass and the overarching boughs.

"If you mean to imply that we are bad, I protest," said one
of the gentlemen—"after making oneself agreeable all the
morning!"

"Ah, if they've found you agreeable!" Mrs St George
exclaimed, smiling. "But if we are good the others are
better."

"They must be angels then," observed the General.

"Your husband was an angel, the way he went off at your
bidding," the gentleman who had first spoken said to Mrs St
George.

"At my bidding?"

"Didn't you make him go to church?"

"I never made him do anything in my life but once, when
I made him burn up a bad book. That's all!" At her "That's
all!" Paul broke into an irrepressible laugh; it lasted only a
second, but it drew her eyes to him. His own met them, but
not long enough to help him to understand her; unless it were
a step towards this that he felt sure on the instant that the
burnt book (the way she alluded to it!) was one of her
husband's finest things.

"A bad book?" her interlocutor repeated.

"I didn't like it. He went to church because your daughter
went," she continued, to General Fancourt. "I think it my
duty to call your attention to his demeanour to your daughter."

"Well, if you don't mind it, I don't," the General laughed.

"*Il s'attache à ses pas.* But I don't wonder—she's so
charming."

"I hope she won't make him burn any books!" Paul Overt ventured to exclaim.

"If she would make him write a few it would be more to the purpose," said Mrs St George. "He has been of an indolence this year!"

Our young man stared—he was so struck with the lady's phraseology. Her "Write a few" seemed to him almost as good as her "That's all." Didn't she, as the wife of a rare artist, know what it was to produce *one* perfect work of art? How in the world did she think they were turned off? His private conviction was that admirably as Henry St George wrote, he had written for the last ten years, and especially for the last five, only too much, and there was an instant during which he felt the temptation to make this public. But before he had spoken a diversion was effected by the return of the absent guests. They strolled up dispersedly—there were eight or ten of them—and the circle under the trees rearranged itself as they took their place in it. They made it much larger; so that Paul Overt could feel (he was always feeling that sort of thing, as he said to himself,) that if the company had already been interesting to watch it would now become a great deal more so. He shook hands with his hostess, who welcomed him without many words, in the manner of a woman able to trust him to understand—conscious that, in every way, so pleasant an occasion would speak for itself. She offered him no particular facility for sitting by her, and when they had all subsided again he found himself still next General Fancourt, with an unknown lady on his other flank.

"That's my daughter—that one opposite," the General said to him without loss of time. Overt saw a tall girl, with magnificent red hair, in a dress of a pretty grey-green tint and of a limp silken texture, in which every modern effect had been avoided. It had therefore somehow the stamp of the latest thing, so that Overt quickly perceived she was eminently a contemporary young lady.

"She's very handsome—very handsome," he repeated, looking at her. There was something noble in her head, and she appeared fresh and strong.

Her father surveyed her with complacency; then he said: "She looks too hot—that's her walk. But she'll be all right presently. Then I'll make her come over and speak to you."

"I should be sorry to give you that trouble; if you were to take me over there—" the young man murmured.

"My dear sir, do you suppose I put myself out that way? I don't mean for you, but for Marian," the General added.

"*I* would put myself out for her, soon enough," Overt replied; after which he went on: "Will you be so good as to tell me which of those gentlemen is Henry St George?"

"The fellow talking to my girl. By Jove, he *is* making up to her—they're going off for another walk."

"Ah, is that he, really?" The young man felt a certain surprise, for the personage before him contradicted a preconception which had been vague only till it was confronted with the reality. As soon as this happened the mental image, retiring with a sigh, became substantial enough to suffer a slight wrong. Overt, who had spent a considerable part of his short life in foreign lands, made now, but not for the first time, the reflection that whereas in those countries he had almost always recognised the artist and the man of letters by his personal "type," the mould of his face, the character of his head, the expression of his figure and even the indications of his dress, in England this identification was as little as possible a matter of course, thanks to the greater conformity, the habit of sinking the profession instead of advertising it, the general diffusion of the air of the gentleman—the gentleman committed to no particular set of ideas. More than once, on returning to his own country, he had said to himself in regard to the people whom he met in society: "One sees them about and one even talks with them; but to find out what they *do* one would really have to be a detective." In respect to several individuals whose work he was unable to like (perhaps he was wrong) he found himself adding, "No wonder they conceal it—it's so bad!" He observed that oftener than in France and in Germany his artist looked like a gentleman (that is, like an English one,) while he perceived that outside of a few exceptions his gentleman didn't look like an artist. St George was not one of the exceptions; that circumstance he definitely apprehended before the great man had turned his back to walk off with Miss Fancourt. He certainly looked better behind than any foreign man of letters, and beautifully correct in his tall black hat and his superior frock coat. Somehow, all the same, these very garments (he wouldn't have minded them so much on a weekday,) were disconcerting to Paul Overt, who forgot for the moment that the head of the profession was not a bit better dressed than himself. He had caught a glimpse of a regular face, with a fresh colour, a brown moustache and a pair of eyes surely never visited by a fine frenzy, and he promised himself to study it on the first occasion. His temporary opinion was that St George looked like a lucky stockbroker—a gentleman driving eastward every morning from a sanitary suburb in a smart dog-cart. That carried out the impression already derived from his wife. Paul Overt's glance, after a moment, travelled back to this lady, and he saw that her own had followed her husband as he moved off with Miss Fancourt. Overt permitted himself to wonder a little whether she were jealous when another woman took him away. Then he seemed to perceive that Mrs St George was not glaring at the indifferent maiden—her eyes rested only on her husband, and with unmistakable serenity. That was the way she wanted him to be—she liked his conventional uniform. Overt had a great desire to hear more about the book she had induced him to destroy.

II

As they all came out from luncheon General Fancourt took hold of Paul Overt and exclaimed, "I say, I want you to know my girl!" as if the idea had just occurred to him and he had not spoken of it before. With the other hand he possessed himself of the young lady and said: "You know all about him. I've seen you with his books. She reads everything—everything!" he added to the young man. The girl smiled at him and then laughed at her father. The General turned away and his daughter said:

"Isn't papa delightful?"

"He is indeed, Miss Fancourt."

"As if I read you because I read 'everything'!"

"Oh, I don't mean for saying that," said Paul Overt. "I liked him from the moment he spoke to me. Then he promised me this privilege."

"It isn't for you he means it, it's for me. If you flatter yourself that he thinks of anything in life but me you'll find you are mistaken. He introduces every one to me. He thinks me insatiable."

"You speak like him," said Paul Overt, laughing.

"Ah, but sometimes I want to," the girl replied, colouring. "I don't read everything—I read very little. But I *have* read you."

"Suppose we go into the gallery," said Paul Overt. She pleased him greatly, not so much because of this last remark (though that of course was not disagreeable to him,) as because, seated opposite to him at luncheon, she had given him for half an hour the impression of her beautiful face. Something else had come with it—a sense of generosity, of an enthusiasm which, unlike many enthusiasms, was not all manner. That was not spoiled for him by the circumstance that the repast had placed her again in familiar contact with Henry St George. Sitting next to her he was also opposite to our young man, who had been able to observe that he multiplied the attentions which his wife had brought to the General's notice. Paul Overt had been able to observe further that this lady was not in the least discomposed by these demonstrations and that she gave every sign of an unclouded spirit. She had Lord Masham on one side of her and on the other the accomplished Mr Mulliner, editor of the new high-class, lively evening paper which was expected to meet a want felt in circles increasingly conscious that Conservatism must be made amusing, and unconvinced when assured by those of another political colour that it was already amusing enough. At the end of an hour spent in her company Paul Overt thought her still prettier than she had appeared to him at first, and if her profane allusions to her husband's work had not still rung in his ears he should have liked her—so far as it could be a question of that in connection with a woman to whom he had not yet spoken and to whom probably he should never speak if it were left to her. Pretty women evidently were necessary to Henry St George, and for the moment it was Miss Fancourt who was most indispensable. If Overt had promised himself to take a better look at him the opportunity now was of the best, and it brought consequences which the young man felt to be important. He saw more in his face, and he liked it the better for its not telling its whole story in the first three minutes. That story came out as one read, in little instalments (it was excusable that Overt's mental comparisons should be somewhat professional,) and the text was a style considerably involved—a language not easy to translate at sight. There were shades of meaning in it and a vague perspective of history which receded as you advanced. Of two facts Paul Overt had taken especial notice. The first of these was that he liked the countenance of the

illustrious novelist much better when it was in repose than
when it smiled; the smile displeased him (as much as anything
from that source could,) whereas the quiet face had a charm
which increased in proportion as it became completely quiet.
The change to the expression of gaiety excited on Overt's
part a private protest which resembled that of a person sitting
in the twilight and enjoying it, when the lamp is brought in
too soon. His second reflection was that, though generally he
disliked the sight of a man of that age using arts to make himself agreeable to a pretty girl, he was not struck in this case
by the ugliness of the thing, which seemed to prove that St
George had a light hand or the air of being younger than he
was, or else that Miss Fancourt showed that *she* was not
conscious of an anomaly.

Overt walked with her into the gallery, and they strolled to
the end of it, looking at the pictures, the cabinets, the charming vista, which harmonised with the prospect of the summer
afternoon, resembling it in its long brightness, with great
divans and old chairs like hours of rest. Such a place as that
had the added merit of giving persons who came into it
plenty to talk about. Miss Fancourt sat down with Paul Overt
on a flowered sofa, the cushions of which, very numerous,
were tight, ancient cubes, of many sizes, and presently she
said: "I'm so glad to have a chance to thank you."

"To thank me?"

"I liked your book so much. I think it's splendid."

She sat there smiling at him, and he never asked himself
which book she meant; for after all he had written three or
four. That seemed a vulgar detail, and he was not even
gratified by the idea of the pleasure she told him—her bright,
handsome face told him—he had given her. The feeling she
appealed to, or at any rate the feeling she excited, was something larger—something that had little to do with any quickened pulsation of his own vanity. It was responsive admiration
of the life she embodied, the young purity and richness of

which appeared to imply that real success was to resemble
that, to live, to bloom, to present the perfection of a fine type,
not to have hammered out headachy fancies with a bent back
at an ink-stained table. While her grey eyes rested on him
(there was a wideish space between them, and the division of
her rich-coloured hair, which was so thick that it ventured
to be smooth, made a free arch above them,) he was almost
ashamed of that exercise of the pen which it was her present
inclination to eulogise. He was conscious that he should have
liked better to please her in some other way. The lines of her
face were those of a woman grown, but there was something
childish in her complexion and the sweetness of her mouth.
Above all she was natural—that was indubitable now—more
natural than he had supposed at first, perhaps on account of
her æsthetic drapery, which was conventionally unconven-
tional, suggesting a tortuous spontaneity. He had feared that
sort of thing in other cases, and his fears had been justified;
though he was an artist to the essence, the modern reactionary
nymph, with the brambles of the woodland caught in her
folds and a look as if the satyrs had toyed with her hair, was
apt to make him uncomfortable. Miss Fancourt was really
more candid than her costume, and the best proof of it was her
supposing that such garments suited her liberal character.
She was robed like a pessimist, but Overt was sure she liked
the taste of life. He thanked her for her appreciation—aware
at the same time that he didn't appear to thank her enough
and that she might think him ungracious. He was afraid she
would ask him to explain something that he had written, and
he always shrank from that (perhaps too timidly,) for to his
own ear the explanation of a work of art sounded fatuous. But
he liked her so much as to feel a confidence that in the long
run he should be able to show her that he was not rudely
evasive. Moreover it was very certain that she was not quick
to take offence; she was not irritable, she could be trusted to
wait. So when he said to her, "Ah! don't talk of anything I

have done, *here;* there is another man in the house who is the actuality!'" when he uttered this short, sincere protest, it was with the sense that she would see in the words neither mock humility nor the ungraciousness of a successful man bored with praise.

"You mean Mr St George—isn't he delightful?"

Paul Overt looked at her a moment; there was a species of morning-light in her eyes.

"Alas, I don't know him. I only admire him at a distance."

"Oh, you must know him—he wants so to talk to you," rejoined Miss Fancourt, who evidently had the habit of saying the things that, by her quick calculation, would give people pleasure. Overt divined that she would always calculate on everything's being simple between others.

"I shouldn't have supposed he knew anything about me," Paul said, smiling.

"He does then—everything. And if he didn't, I should be able to tell him."

"To tell him everything?"

"You talk just like the people in your book!" the girl exclaimed.

"Then they must all talk alike."

"Well, it must be so difficult. Mr St George tells me it is, terribly. I've tried too and I find it so. I've tried to write a novel."

"Mr St George oughtn't to discourage you," said Paul Overt.

"You do much more—when you wear that expression."

"Well, after all, why try to be an artist?" the young man went on. "It's so poor—so poor!"

"I don't know what you mean," said Marian Fancourt, looking grave.

"I mean as compared with being a person of action—as living your works."

"But what is art but a life—if it be real?" asked the girl.
"I think it's the only one—everything else is so clumsy!"
Paul Overt laughed, and she continued: "It's so interesting,
meeting so many celebrated people."

"So I should think; but surely it isn't new to you."

"Why, I have never seen any one—any one: living always
in Asia."

"But doesn't Asia swarm with personages? Haven't you
administered provinces in India and had captive rajahs and
tributary princes chained to your car?"

"I was with my father, after I left school to go out there.
It was delightful being with him—we are alone together in
the world, he and I—but there was none of the society I like
best. One never heard of a picture—never of a book, except
bad ones."

"Never of a picture? Why, wasn't all life a picture?"

Miss Fancourt looked over the delightful place where they
sat. "Nothing to compare with this. I adore England!" she
exclaimed.

"Ah, of course I don't deny that we must do something
with it yet."

"It hasn't been touched, really," said the girl.

"Did Henry St George say that?"

There was a small and, as he felt it, venial intention of
irony in his question; which, however, the girl took very
simply, not noticing the insinuation. "Yes, he says it has not
been touched—not touched comparatively," she answered,
eagerly. "He's so interesting about it. To listen to him makes
one want so to do something."

"It would make me want to," said Paul Overt, feeling
strongly, on the instant, the suggestion of what she said and
of the emotion with which she said it, and what an incentive,
on St George's lips, such a speech might be.

"Oh, you—as if you hadn't! I should like so to hear you
talk together," the girl added, ardently.

"That's very genial of you; but he would have it all his own way. I'm prostrate before him."

Marian Fancourt looked earnest for a moment. "Do you think then he's so perfect?"

"Far from it. Some of his later books seem to me awfully queer."

"Yes, yes—he knows that."

Paul Overt stared. "That they seem to me awfully queer?"

"Well yes, or at any rate that they are not what they should be. He told me he didn't esteem them. He has told me such wonderful things—he's so interesting."

There was a certain shock for Paul Overt in the knowledge that the fine genius they were talking of had been reduced to so explicit a confession and had made it, in his misery, to the first comer; for though Miss Fancourt was charming, what was she after all but an immature girl encountered at a country-house? Yet precisely this was a part of the sentiment that he himself had just expressed; he would make way completely for the poor peccable great man, not because he didn't read him clear, but altogether because he did. His consideration was half composed of tenderness for superficialities which he was sure St George judged privately with supreme sternness and which denoted some tragic intellectual secret. He would have his reasons for his psychology *à fleur de peau,* and these reasons could only be cruel ones, such as would make him dearer to those who already were fond of him. "You excite my envy. I judge him, I discriminate—but I love him," Overt said in a moment. "And seeing him for the first time this way is a great event for me."

"How momentous—how magnificent!" cried the girl. "How delicious to bring you together!"

"*Your* doing it—that makes it perfect," Overt responded.

"He's as eager as you," Miss Fancourt went on. "But it's so odd you shouldn't have met."

"It's not so odd as it seems. I've been out of England so much—repeated absences during all these last years."

"And yet you write of it as well as if you were always here."

"It's just the being away perhaps. At any rate the best bits, I suspect, are those that were done in dreary places abroad."

"And why were they dreary?"

"Because they were health-resorts—where my poor mother was dying."

"Your poor mother?" the girl murmured, kindly.

"We went from place to place to help her to get better. But she never did. To the deadly Riviera (I hate it!) to the high Alps, to Algiers, and far away—a hideous journey—to Colorado."

"And she isn't better?" Miss Fancourt went on.

"She died a year ago."

"Really?—like mine! Only that is far away. Some day you must tell me about your mother," she added.

Overt looked at her a moment. "What right things you say! If you say them to St George I don't wonder he's in bondage."

"I don't know what you mean. He doesn't make speeches and professions at all—he isn't ridiculous."

"I'm afraid you consider that I am."

"No, I don't," the girl replied, rather shortly. "He understands everything."

Overt was on the point of saying jocosely: "And I don't—is that it?" But these words, before he had spoken, changed themselves into others slightly less trivial: "Do you suppose he understands his wife?"

Miss Fancourt made no direct answer to his question; but after a moment's hesitation she exclaimed: "Isn't she charming?"

"Not in the least!"

"Here he comes. Now you must know him," the girl went on. A small group of visitors had gathered at the other end of the gallery and they had been joined for a moment by Henry St George, who strolled in from a neighbouring room. He stood near them a moment, not, apparently, falling into the conversation, but taking up an old miniature from a table and vaguely examining it. At the end of a minute he seemed to perceive Miss Fancourt and her companion in the distance; whereupon, laying down his miniature, he approached them with the same procrastinating air, with his hands in his pockets, looking to right and left at the pictures. The gallery was so long that this transit took some little time, especially as there was a moment when he stopped to admire the fine Gainsborough. "He says she has been the making of him," Miss Fancourt continued, in a voice slightly lowered.

"Ah, he's often obscure!" laughed Paul Overt.

"Obscure?" she repeated, interrogatively. Her eyes rested upon her other friend, and it was not lost upon Paul that they appeared to send out great shafts of softness. "He is going to speak to us!" she exclaimed, almost breathlessly. There was a sort of rapture in her voice; Paul Overt was startled. "Bless my soul, is she so fond of him as that—is she in love with him?" he mentally inquired. "Didn't I tell you he was eager?" she added, to her companion.

"It's eagerness dissimulated," the young man rejoined, as the subject of their observation lingered before his Gainsborough. "He edges toward us shyly. Does he mean that she saved him by burning that book?"

"That book? what book did she burn?" The girl turned her face quickly upon him.

"Hasn't he told you, then?"

"Not a word."

"Then he doesn't tell you everything!" Paul Overt had guessed that Miss Fancourt pretty much supposed he did. The great man had now resumed his course and come nearer; nevertheless Overt risked the profane observation: "St George and the dragon, the anecdote suggests!"

Miss Fancourt, however, did not hear it; she was smiling at her approaching friend. "He *is* eager—he is!" she repeated.

"Eager for you—yes."

The girl called out frankly, joyously: "I know you want to know Mr Overt. You'll be great friends, and it will always be delightful to me to think that I was here when you first met and that I had something to do with it."

There was a freshness of intention in this speech which carried it off; nevertheless our young man was sorry for Henry St George, as he was sorry at any time for any one who was publicly invited to be responsive and delightful. He would have been so contented to believe that a man he deeply admired attached an importance to him that he was determined not to play with such a presumption if it possibly were vain. In a single glance of the eye of the pardonable master he discovered (having the sort of divination that belonged to his talent,) that this personage was full of general good-will, but had not read a word he had written. There was even a relief, a simplification, in that: liking him so much already for what he had done, how could he like him more for having been struck with a certain promise? He got up, trying to show his compassion, but at the same instant he found himself encompassed by St George's happy personal art—a manner of which it was the essence to conjure away false positions. It all took place in a moment. He was conscious that he knew him now, conscious of his handshake and of the very quality of his hand; of his face, seen nearer and consequently seen better, of a general fraternising assurance, and in particular of the circumstance that St George didn't dislike him (as yet at least,) for being imposed by a charming but too gushing girl, valuable enough without such danglers. At any rate no irritation was reflected in the voice with which he questioned Miss Fancourt in respect to some project of a walk—a general walk of the company round the park. He had said something to Overt about a talk—"We must have a

tremendous lot of talk; there are so many things, aren't
there?"—but Paul perceived that this idea would not in the
present case take very immediate effect. All the same he was
extremely happy, even after the matter of the walk had been
settled (the three presently passed back to the other part of
the gallery, where it was discussed with several members of
the party,) even when, after they had all gone out together,
he found himself for half an hour in contact with Mrs St
George. Her husband had taken the advance with Miss Fancourt, and this pair were quite out of sight. It was the prettiest
of rambles for a summer afternoon—a grassy circuit, of immense extent, skirting the limit of the park within. The park
was completely surrounded by its old mottled but perfect red
wall, which, all the way on their left, made a picturesque
accompaniment. Mrs St George mentioned to him the surprising number of acres that were thus enclosed, together
with numerous other facts relating to the property and the
family, and its other properties: she could not too strongly
urge upon him the importance of seeing their other houses.
She ran over the names of these and rang the changes on them
with the facility of practice, making them appear an almost
endless list. She had received Paul Overt very amiably when
he broke ground with her by telling her that he had just had
the joy of making her husband's acquaintance, and struck him
as so alert and so accommodating a little woman that he was
rather ashamed of his *mot* about her to Miss Fancourt; though
he reflected that a hundred other people, on a hundred occasions, would have been sure to make it. He got on with Mrs
St George, in short, better than he expected; but this did not
prevent her from suddenly becoming aware that she was faint
with fatigue and must take her way back to the house by the
shortest cut. She hadn't the strength of a kitten, she said—
she was awfully seedy; a state of things that Overt had been
too preoccupied to perceive—preoccupied with a private
effort to ascertain in what sense she could be held to have been

the making of her husband. He had arrived at a glimmering of the answer when she announced that she must leave him, though this perception was of course provisional. While he was in the very act of placing himself at her disposal for the return the situation underwent a change; Lord Masham suddenly turned up, coming back to them, overtaking them, emerging from the shrubbery—Overt could scarcely have said how he appeared, and Mrs St George had protested that she wanted to be left alone and not to break up the party. A moment later she was walking off with Lord Masham. Paul Overt fell back and joined Lady Watermouth, to whom he presently mentioned that Mrs St George had been obliged to renounce the attempt to go further.

"She oughtn't to have come out at all," her ladyship remarked, rather grumpily.

"Is she so very much of an invalid?"

"Very bad indeed." And his hostess added, with still greater austerity: "She oughtn't to come to stay with one!" He wondered what was implied by this, and presently gathered that it was not a reflection on the lady's conduct or her moral nature: it only represented that her strength was not equal to her aspirations.

III

THE smoking-room at Summersoft was on the scale of the rest of the place; that is it was high and light and commodious, and decorated with such refined old carvings and mouldings that it seemed rather a bower for ladies who should sit at work at fading crewels than a parliament of gentlemen smoking strong cigars. The gentlemen mustered there in considerable force on the Sunday evening, collecting mainly at one end, in front of one of the cool fair fireplaces of white marble, the entablature of which was adorned with a delicate little Italian "subject." There was another in the wall that faced it, and, thanks to the mild summer night, there was no fire in either; but a nucleus for aggregation was furnished on one side by a table in the chimney-corner laden with bottles, decanters and tall tumblers. Paul Overt was an insincere smoker; he puffed cigarettes occasionally for reasons with which tobacco had nothing to do. This was particularly the case on the occasion of which I speak; his motive was the vision of a little direct talk with Henry St George. The "tremendous" communion of which the great man had held out hopes to him earlier in the day had not yet come off, and this saddened him considerably, for the party was to go its several ways immediately after breakfast on the morrow. He had, however, the disappointment of finding that apparently the author of *Shadowmere* was not disposed to prolong his vigil. He was not among the gentlemen assembled in the smoking-room when Overt entered it, nor was he one of those who turned up, in bright habiliments, during the next ten minutes. The young man waited a little, wondering whether he had only gone to put on something extraordinary; this would account for his delay as well as contribute further to Overt's observation of his tendency to do the approved superficial thing. But he didn't arrive—he must have been putting on something more extraordinary than was probable. Paul gave him up, feeling a little injured, a little wounded at his not having managed to say twenty words to him. He was not angry, but he puffed his cigarette sighingly, with the sense of having lost a precious chance. He wandered away with his regret, moved slowly round the room, looking at the old prints on the walls. In this attitude he presently felt a hand laid on his shoulder and a friendly voice in his ear. "This is good. I hoped I should find you. I came down on purpose." St George was there, without a change of dress and with a kind face—his graver one—to which Overt eagerly responded.

He explained that it was only for the Master—the idea of a little talk—that he had sat up and that, not finding him, he had been on the point of going to bed.

"Well, you know, I don't smoke—my wife doesn't let me," said St George, looking for a place to sit down. "It's very good for me—very good for me. Let us take that sofa."

"Do you mean smoking is good for you?"

"No, no, her not letting me. It's a great thing to have a wife who proves to one all the things one can do without. One might never find them out for oneself. She doesn't allow me to touch a cigarette."

They took possession of the sofa, which was at a distance from the group of smokers, and St George went on: "Have you got one yourself?"

"Do you mean a cigarette?"

"Dear no! a wife."

"No; and yet I would give up my cigarette for one."

"You would give up a good deal more than that," said St George. "However, you would get a great deal in return. There is a great deal to be said for wives," he added, folding his arms and crossing his outstretched legs. He declined tobacco altogether and sat there without returning fire. Paul Overt stopped smoking, touched by his courtesy; and after all they were out of the fumes, their sofa was in a far-away corner. It would have been a mistake, St George went on, a great mistake for them to have separated without a little chat; "for I know all about you," he said, "I know you're very remarkable. You've written a very distinguished book."

"And how do you know it?" Overt asked.

"Why, my dear fellow, it's in the air, it's in the papers, it's everywhere," St George replied, with the immediate familiarity of a *confrère*—a tone that seemed to his companion the very rustle of the laurel. "You're on all men's lips and, what's better, you're on all women's. And I've just been reading your book."

"Just? You hadn't read it this afternoon," said Overt.

"How do you know that?"

"You know how I know it," the young man answered, laughing.

"I suppose Miss Fancourt told you."

"No, indeed; she led me rather to suppose that you had."

"Yes; that's much more what she would do. Doesn't she shed a rosy glow over life? But you didn't believe her?" asked St George.

"No, not when you came to us there."

"Did I pretend? did I pretend badly?" But without waiting for an answer to this St George went on: "You ought always to believe such a girl as that—always, always. Some women are meant to be taken with allowances and reserves; but you must take *her* just as she is."

"I like her very much," said Paul Overt.

Something in his tone appeared to excite on his companion's part a momentary sense of the absurd; perhaps it was the air of deliberation attending this judgment. St George broke into a laugh and returned: "It's the best thing you can do with her. She's a rare young lady! In point of fact, however, I confess I hadn't read you this afternoon."

"Then you see how right I was in this particular case not to believe Miss Fancourt."

"How right? how can I agree to that, when I lost credit by it?"

"Do you wish to pass for exactly what she represents you? Certainly you needn't be afraid," Paul said.

"Ah, my dear young man, don't talk about passing—for the likes of me! I'm passing away—nothing else than that. She has a better use for her young imagination (isn't it fine?) than in 'representing' in any way such a weary, wasted, used-up animal!" St George spoke with a sudden sadness which produced a protest on Paul's part; but before the protest could be uttered he went on, reverting to the latter's successful novel: "I had no idea you were so good—one hears of so many things. But you're surprisingly good."

"I'm going to be surprisingly better," said Overt.

"I see that and it's what fetches me. I don't see so much else—as one looks about—that's going to be surprisingly better. They're going to be consistently worse—most of the things. It's so much easier to be worse—heaven knows I've found it so. I'm not in a great glow, you know, about what's being attempted, what's being done. But you *must* be better— you must keep it up. I haven't, of course. It's very difficult— that's the devil of the whole thing; but I see you can. It will be a great disgrace if you don't."

"It's very interesting to hear you speak of yourself; but I don't know what you mean by your allusions to your having fallen off," Paul Overt remarked, with pardonable hypocrisy. He liked his companion so much now that it had ceased for the moment to be vivid to him that there had been any decline.

"Don't say that—don't say that," St George replied gravely, with his head resting on the top of the back of the sofa and his eyes on the ceiling. "You know perfectly what I mean. I haven't read twenty pages of your book without seeing that you can't help it."

"You make me very miserable," Paul murmured.

"I'm glad of that, for it may serve as a kind of warning. Shocking enough it must be, especially to a young, fresh mind, full of faith,—the spectacle of a man meant for better things sunk at my age in such dishonour." St George, in the same contemplative attitude, spoke softly but deliberately, and without perceptible emotion. His tone indeed suggested an impersonal lucidity which was cruel—cruel to himself— and which made Paul lay an argumentative hand on his arm. But he went on, while his eyes seemed to follow the ingenuities of the beautiful Adams ceiling: "Look at me well and take my lesson to heart, for it *is* a lesson. Let that good come of it at least that you shudder with your pitiful impression and that this may help to keep you straight in the future. Don't become in your old age what I am in mine—the depressing, the deplorable illustration of the worship of false gods!"

"What do you mean by your old age?" Paul Overt asked.

"It has made me old. But I like your youth."

Overt answered nothing—they sat for a minute in silence. They heard the others talking about the governmental majority. Then, "What do you mean by false gods?" Paul inquired.

"The idols of the market—money and luxury and 'the world,' placing one's children and dressing one's wife—everything that drives one to the short and easy way. Ah, the vile things they make one do!"

"But surely one is right to want to place one's children."

"One has no business to have any children," St George declared, placidly. "I mean of course if one wants to do something good."

"But aren't they an inspiration—an incentive?"

"An incentive to damnation, artistically speaking."

"You touch on very deep things—things I should like to discuss with you," Paul Overt said. "I should like you to tell me volumes about yourself. This is a festival for *me!*"

"Of course it is, cruel youth. But to show you that I'm still not incapable, degraded as I am, of an act of faith, I'll tie my vanity to the stake for you and burn it to ashes. You must come and see me—you must come and see us. Mrs St George is charming; I don't know whether you have had any opportunity to talk with her. She will be delighted to see you; she likes great celebrities, whether incipient or predominant. You must come and dine—my wife will write to you. Where are you to be found?"

"This is my little address"—and Overt drew out his pocketbook and extracted a visiting-card. On second thoughts, however, he kept it back, remarking that he would not trouble his friend to take charge of it but would come and see him straightway in London and leave it at his door if he should fail to obtain admittance.

"Ah! you probably will fail; my wife's always out, or when she isn't out she's knocked up from having been out. You must come and dine—though that won't do much good either, for my wife insists on big dinners. You must come down and see us in the country, that's the best way; we have plenty of room, and it isn't bad."

"You have a house in the country?" Paul asked, enviously.

"Ah, not like this! But we have a sort of place we go to—an hour from Euston. That's one of the reasons."

"One of the reasons?"

"Why my books are so bad."

"You must tell me all the others!" Paul exclaimed, laughing.

St George made no direct rejoinder to this; he only inquired rather abruptly: "Why have I never seen you before?"

The tone of the question was singularly flattering to his new comrade; it seemed to imply that he perceived now that for years he had missed something. "Partly, I suppose, because there has been no particular reason why you should see me. I haven't lived in the world—in your world. I have spent many years out of England, in different places abroad."

"Well, please don't do it any more. You must do England —there's such a lot of it."

"Do you mean I must write about it?" Paul asked, in a voice which had the note of the listening candour of a child.

"Of course you must. And tremendously well, do you mind? That takes off a little of my esteem for this thing of yours—that it goes on abroad. Hang abroad! Stay at home and do things here—do subjects we can measure."

"I'll do whatever you tell me," said Paul Overt, deeply attentive. "But excuse me if I say I don't understand how you have been reading my book," he subjoined. "I've had you before me all the afternoon, first in that long walk, then at tea on the lawn, till we went to dress for dinner, and all the evening at dinner and in this place."

St George turned his face round with a smile. "I only read for a quarter of an hour."

"A quarter of an hour is liberal, but I don't understand where you put it in. In the drawing-room, after dinner, you were not reading, you were talking to Miss Fancourt."

"It comes to the same thing, because we talked about *Ginistrella*. She described it to me—she lent it to me."

"Lent it to you?"

"She travels with it."

"It's incredible," Paul Overt murmured, blushing.

"It's glorious for you; but it also turned out very well for me. When the ladies went off to bed she kindly offered to send the book down to me. Her maid brought it to me in the hall and I went to my room with it. I hadn't thought of coming here, I do that so little. But I don't sleep early, I always have to read for an hour or two. I sat down to your novel on the spot, without undressing, without taking off anything but my coat. I think that's a sign that my curiosity had been strongly roused about it. I read a quarter of an hour, as I tell you, and even in a quarter of an hour I was greatly struck."

"Ah, the beginning isn't very good—it's the whole thing!" said Overt, who had listened to this recital with extreme interest. "And you laid down the book and came after me?" he asked.

"That's the way it moved me. I said to myself, 'I see it's off his own bat, and he's there, by the way, and the day's over and I haven't said twenty words to him.' It occurred to me that you would probably be in the smoking-room and that it wouldn't be too late to repair my omission. I wanted to do something civil to you, so I put on my coat and came down. I shall read your book again when I go up."

Paul Overt turned round in his place—he was exceedingly

touched by the picture of such a demonstration in his favour. "You're really the kindest of men. *Cela s'est passé comme ça?* and I have been sitting here with you all this time and never apprehended it and never thanked you!"

"Thank Miss Fancourt—it was she who wound me up. She has made me feel as if I had read your novel."

"She's an angel from heaven!" Paul Overt exclaimed.

"She is indeed. I have never seen anyone like her. Her interest in literature is touching—something quite peculiar to herself; she takes it all so seriously. She feels the arts and she wants to feel them more. To those who practise them it's almost humiliating—her curiosity, her sympathy, her good faith. How can anything be as fine as she supposes it?"

"She's a rare organisation," Paul Overt sighed.

"The richest I have ever seen—an artistic intelligence really of the first order. And lodged in such a form!" St George exclaimed.

"One would like to paint such a girl as that," Overt continued.

"Ah, there it is—there's nothing like life! When you're finished, squeezed dry and used up and you think the sack's empty, you're still spoken to, you still get touches and thrills, the idea springs up—out of the lap of the actual—and shows you there's always something to be done. But I shan't do it—she's not for me!"

"How do you mean, not for you?"

"Oh, it's all over—she's for you, if you like."

"Ah, much less!" said Paul Overt. "She's not for a dingy little man of letters; she's for the world, the bright rich world of bribes and rewards. And the world will take hold of her—it will carry her away."

"It will try; but it's just a case in which there may be a fight. It would be worth fighting, for a man who had it in him, with youth and talent on his side."

These words rang not a little in Paul Overt's consciousness

—they held him silent a moment. "It's a wonder she has remained as she is—giving herself away so, with so much to give away."

"Do you mean so ingenuous—so natural? Oh, she doesn't care a straw—she gives away because she overflows. She has her own feelings, her own standards; she doesn't keep remembering that she must be proud. And then she hasn't been here long enough to be spoiled; she has picked up a fashion or two, but only the amusing ones. She's a provincial—a provincial of genius; her very blunders are charming, her mistakes are interesting. She has come back from Asia with all sorts of excited curiosities and unappeased appetites. She's first-rate herself and she expends herself on the second-rate. She's life herself and she takes a rare interest in imitations. She mixes all things up, but there are none in regard to which she hasn't perceptions. She sees things in a perspective—as if from the top of the Himalayas—and she enlarges everything she touches. Above all, she exaggerates—to herself, I mean. She exaggerates you and me!"

There was nothing in this description to allay the excitement produced in the mind of our younger friend by such a sketch of a fine subject. It seemed to him to show the art of St George's admired hand, and he lost himself in it, gazing at the vision (it hovered there before him,) of a woman's figure which should be part of the perfection of a novel. At the end of a moment he became aware that it had turned into smoke, and out of the smoke—the last puff of a big cigar—proceeded the voice of General Fancourt, who had left the others and come and planted himself before the gentlemen on the sofa. "I suppose that when you fellows get talking you sit up half the night."

"Half the night?—*jamais de la vie!* I follow a hygiene," St George replied, rising to his feet.

"I see, you're hothouse plants," laughed the General. "That's the way you produce your flowers."

"I produce mine between ten and one every morning; I bloom with a regularity!" St George went on.

"And with a splendour!" added the polite General, while Paul Overt noted how little the author of *Shadowmere* minded, as he phrased it to himself, when he was addressed as a celebrated story-teller. The young man had an idea that *he* should never get used to that—it would always make him uncomfortable (from the suspicion that people would think they had to,) and he would want to prevent it. Evidently his more illustrious congener had toughened and hardened—had made himself a surface. The group of men had finished their cigars and taken up their bedroom candlesticks; but before they all passed out Lord Watermouth invited St George and Paul Overt to drink something. It happened that they both declined, upon which General Fancourt said: "Is that the hygiene? You don't sprinkle the flowers?"

"Oh, I should drown them!" St George replied; but leaving the room beside Overt he added whimsically, for the latter's benefit, in a lower tone: "My wife doesn't let me."

"Well, I'm glad I'm not one of you fellows!" the General exclaimed.

The nearness of Summersoft to London had this consequence, chilling to a person who had had a vision of sociability in a railway-carriage, that most of the company, after breakfast, drove back to town, entering their own vehicles, which had come out to fetch them, while their servants returned by train with their luggage. Three or four young men, among whom was Paul Overt, also availed themselves of the common convenience; but they stood in the portico of the house and saw the others roll away. Miss Fancourt got into a victoria with her father, after she had shaken hands with Paul Overt and said, smiling in the frankest way in the world—"I *must* see you more. Mrs St George is so nice: she has promised to ask us both to dinner together." This lady and her husband took their places in a perfectly-appointed brougham (she required a closed carriage,) and as our young man waved his hat to them in response to their nods and flourishes he reflected that, taken together, they were an honourable image of success, of the material rewards and the social credit of literature. Such things were not the full measure, but all the same he felt a little proud for literature.

IV

BEFORE a week had elapsed Paul Overt met Miss Fancourt in Bond Street, at a private view of the works of a young artist in "black and white" who had been so good as to invite him to the stuffy scene. The drawings were admirable, but the crowd in the one little room was so dense that he felt as if he were up to his neck in a big sack of wool. A fringe of people at the outer edge endeavoured by curving forward their backs and presenting, below them, a still more convex surface of resistance to the pressure of the mass, to preserve an interval between their noses and the glazed mounts of the pictures; while the central body, in the comparative gloom projected by a wide horizontal screen, hung under the sky-light and allowing only a margin for the day, remained up-right, dense and vague, lost in the contemplation of its own ingredients. This contemplation sat especially in the sad eyes of certain female heads, surmounted with hats of strange con-volution and plumage, which rose on long necks above the others. One of the heads, Paul Overt perceived, was much the most beautiful of the collection, and his next discovery was that it belonged to Miss Fancourt. Its beauty was enhanced by the glad smile that she sent him across surrounding obstructions, a smile which drew him to her as fast as he could make his way. He had divined at Summersoft that the last thing her nature contained was an affectation of indifference;

yet even with this circumspection he had a freshness of pleasure in seeing that she did not pretend to await his arrival with composure. She smiled as radiantly as if she wished to make him hurry, and as soon as he came within earshot she said to him, in her voice of joy: "He's here—he's here—he's coming back in a moment!"

"Ah, your father?" Paul responded, as she offered him her hand.

"Oh dear no, this isn't in my poor father's line. I mean Mr St George. He has just left me to speak to some one—he's coming back. It's he who brought me—wasn't it charming?"

"Ah, that gives him a pull over me—I couldn't have 'brought' you, could I?"

"If you had been so kind as to propose it—why not you as well as he?" the girl asked, with a face which expressed no cheap coquetry, but simply affirmed a happy fact.

"Why, he's a *père de famille*. They have privileges," Paul Overt explained. And then, quickly: "Will you go to see places with *me?*" he broke out.

"Anything you like!" she smiled. "I know what you mean, that girls have to have a lot of people——" She interrupted herself to say: "I don't know; I'm free. I have always been like that," she went on; "I can go anywhere with any one. I'm so glad to meet you," she added, with a sweet distinctness that made the people near her turn round.

"Let me at least repay that speech by taking you out of this squash," said Paul Overt. "Surely people are not happy here!"

"No, they are *mornes*, aren't they? But I am very happy indeed, and I promised Mr St George to remain in this spot till he comes back. He's going to take me away. They send him invitations for things of this sort—more than he wants. It was so kind of him to think of me."

"They also send me invitations of this kind—more than I want. And if thinking of *you* will do it——!" Paul went on.

"Oh, I delight in them—everything that's life—everything that's London!"

"They don't have private views in Asia, I suppose. But what a pity that for this year, in this fertile city, they are pretty well over."

"Well, next year will do, for I hope you believe we are going to be friends always. Here he comes!" Miss Fancourt continued, before Paul had time to respond.

He made out St George in the gaps of the crowd, and this perhaps led to his hurrying a little to say: "I hope that doesn't mean that I'm to wait till next year to see you."

"No, no; are we not to meet at dinner on the 25th?" she answered, with an eagerness greater even than his own.

"That's almost next year. Is there no means of seeing you before?"

She stared, with all her brightness. "Do you mean that you would *come?*"

"Like a shot, if you'll be so good as to ask me!"

"On Sunday, then—this next Sunday?"

"What have I done that you should doubt it?" the young man demanded, smiling.

Miss Fancourt turned instantly to St George, who had now joined them, and announced triumphantly: "He's coming on Sunday—this next Sunday!"

"Ah, my day—my day too!" said the famous novelist, laughing at Paul Overt.

"Yes, but not yours only. You shall meet in Manchester Square; you shall talk—you shall be wonderful!"

"We don't meet often enough," St George remarked, shaking hands with his disciple. "Too many things—ah, too many things! But we must make it up in the country in September. You won't forget that you've promised me that?"

"Why, he's coming on the 25th; you'll see him then," said Marian Fancourt.

"On the 25th?" St George asked, vaguely.

"We dine with you; I hope you haven't forgotten. He's dining out," she added gaily to Paul Overt.

"Oh, bless me, yes; that's charming! And you're coming? My wife didn't tell me," St George said to Paul. "Too many things—too many things!" he repeated.

"Too many people—too many people!" Paul exclaimed, giving ground before the penetration of an elbow.

"You oughtn't to say that; they all read you."

"Me? I should like to see them! Only two or three at most," the young man rejoined.

"Did you ever hear anything like that? he knows how good he is!" St George exclaimed, laughing, to Miss Fancourt. "They read *me*, but that doesn't make me like them any better. Come away from them, come away!" And he led the way out of the exhibition.

"He's going to take me to the Park," the girl said, with elation, to Paul Overt, as they passed along the corridor which led to the street.

"Ah, does he go there?" Paul asked, wondering at the idea as a somewhat unexpected illustration of St George's *moeurs*.

"It's a beautiful day; there will be a great crowd. We're going to look at the people, to look at types," the girl went on. "We shall sit under the trees; we shall walk by the Row."

"I go once a year, on business," said St George, who had overheard Paul's question.

"Or with a country cousin, didn't you tell me? I'm the country cousin!" she went on, over her shoulder, to Paul, as her companion drew her toward a hansom to which he had signalled. The young man watched them get in; he returned, as he stood there, the friendly wave of the hand with which, ensconced in the vehicle beside Miss Fancourt, St George took leave of him. He even lingered to see the vehicle start away and lose itself in the confusion of Bond Street. He followed it with his eyes; it was embarrassingly suggestive.

"She's not for me!" the great novelist had said emphatically at Summersoft; but his manner of conducting himself toward her appeared not exactly in harmony with such a conviction. How could he have behaved differently if she *had* been for him? An indefinite envy rose in Paul Overt's heart as he took his way on foot alone, and the singular part of it was that it was directed to each of the occupants of the hansom. How much he should like to rattle about London with such a girl! How much he should like to go and look at "types" with St George!

The next Sunday, at four o'clock, he called in Manchester Square, where his secret wish was gratified by his finding Miss Fancourt alone. She was in a large, bright, friendly, occupied room, which was painted red all over, draped with the quaint, cheap, florid stuffs that are represented as coming from southern and eastern countries, where they are fabled to serve as the counterpanes of the peasantry, and bedecked with pottery of vivid hues, ranged on casual shelves, and with many water-colour drawings from the hand (as the visitor learned,) of the young lady, commemorating, with courage and skill, the sunsets, the mountains, the temples and palaces of India. Overt sat there an hour—more than an hour, two hours—and all the while no one came in. Miss Fancourt was so good as to remark, with her liberal humanity, that it was delightful they were not interrupted; it was so rare in London, especially at that season, that people got a good talk. But fortunately now, of a fine Sunday, half the world went out of town, and that made it better for those who didn't go, when they were in sympathy. It was the defect of London (one of two or three, the very short list of those she recognised in the teeming world-city that she adored,) that there were too few good chances for talk; one never had time to carry anything far.

"Too many things—too many things!" Paul Overt said, quoting St George's exclamation of a few days before.

"Ah yes, for him there are too many; his life is too complicated."

"Have you seen it *near?* That's what I should like to do; it might explain some mysteries," Paul Overt went on. The girl asked him what mysteries he meant, and he said: "Oh, peculiarities of his work, inequalities, superficialities. For one who looks at it from the artistic point of view it contains a bottomless ambiguity."

"Oh, do describe that more—it's so interesting. There are no such suggestive questions. I'm so fond of them. He thinks he's a failure—fancy!" Miss Fancourt added.

"That depends upon what his ideal may have been. Ah, with his gifts it ought to have been high. But till one knows what he really proposed to himself—— Do *you* know, by chance?" the young man asked, breaking off.

"Oh, he doesn't talk to me about himself. I can't make him. It's too provoking."

Paul Overt was on the point of asking what then he did talk about; but discretion checked this inquiry, and he said instead: "Do you think he's unhappy at home?"

"At home?"

"I mean in his relations with his wife. He has a mystifying little way of alluding to her."

"Not to me," said Marian Fancourt, with her clear eyes. "That wouldn't be right, would it?" she asked, seriously.

"Not particularly; so I am glad he doesn't mention her to you. To praise her might bore you, and he has no business to do anything else. Yet he knows you better than me."

"Ah, but he respects *you!*" the girl exclaimed, enviously.

Her visitor stared a moment; then he broke into a laugh. "Doesn't he respect you?"

"Of course, but not in the same way. He respects what you've done—he told me so, the other day."

"When you went to look at types?"

"Ah, we found so many—he has such an observation of

them! He talked a great deal about your book. He says it's really important."

"Important! Ah! the grand creature," Paul murmured, hilarious.

"He was wonderfully amusing, he was inexpressibly droll, while we walked about. He sees everything; he has so many comparisons, and they are always exactly right. *C'est d'un trouvé!* as they say."

"Yes, with his gifts, such things as he ought to have done!" Paul Overt remarked.

"And don't you think he *has* done them?"

He hesitated a moment. "A part of them—and of course even that part is immense. But he might have been one of the greatest! However, let us not make this an hour of qualifications. Even as they stand, his writings are a mine of gold."

To this proposition Marian Fancourt ardently responded, and for half an hour the pair talked over the master's principal productions. She knew them well—she knew them even better than her visitor, who was struck with her critical intelligence and with something large and bold in the movement in her mind. She said things that startled him and that evidently had come to her directly; they were not picked-up phrases, she placed them too well. St George had been right about her being first-rate, about her not being afraid to gush, not remembering that she must be proud. Suddenly something reminded her, and she said: "I recollect that he did speak of Mrs St George to me once. He said, *à propos* of something or other, that she didn't care for perfection."

"That's a great crime, for an artist's wife," said Paul Overt.

"Yes, poor thing!" and the young lady sighed, with a suggestion of many reflections, some of them mitigating. But she added in a moment, "Ah, perfection, perfection—how one ought to go in for it! I wish I could."

"Every one can, in his way," said Paul Overt.

"In *his* way, yes; but not in hers. Women are so hampered —so condemned! But it's a kind of dishonour if you don't, when you want to *do* something, isn't it?" Miss Fancourt pursued, dropping one train in her quickness to take up another, an accident that was common with her. So these two young persons sat discussing high themes in their eclectic drawing-room, in their London season—discussing, with extreme seriousness, the high theme of perfection. And it must be said, in extenuation of this eccentricity, that they were interested in the business; their tone was genuine, their emotion real; they were not posturing for each other or for some one else.

The subject was so wide that they found it necessary to contract it; the perfection to which for the moment they agreed to confine their speculations was that of which the valid work of art is susceptible. Miss Fancourt's imagination, it appeared, had wandered far in that direction, and her visitor had the rare delight of feeling that their conversation was a full interchange. This episode will have lived for years in his memory and even in his wonder; it had the quality that fortune distils in a single drop at a time—the quality that lubricates ensuing weeks and months. He has still a vision of the room, whenever he likes—the bright, red, sociable, talkative room, with the curtains that, by a stroke of successful audacity, had the note of vivid blue. He remembers where certain things stood, the book that was open on the table and the particular odour of the flowers that were placed on the left, somewhere behind him. These facts were the fringe, as it were, of a particular consciousness which had its birth in those two hours and of which perhaps the most general description would be to mention that it led him to say over and over again to himself: "I had no idea there was any one like this— I had no idea there was any one like this!" Her freedom amazed him and charmed him—it seemed so to simplify the practical question. She was on the footing of an independent

personage—a motherless girl who had passed out of her teens
and had a position, responsibilities, and was not held down to
the limitations of a little miss. She came and went without the
clumsiness of a chaperon; she received people alone and,
though she was totally without hardness, the question of protection or patronage had no relevancy in regard to her. She
gave such an impression of purity combined with naturalness
that, in spite of her eminently modern situation, she suggested no sort of sisterhood with the "fast" girl. Modern
she was, indeed, and made Paul Overt, who loved old colour,
the golden glaze of time, think with some alarm of the
muddled palette of the future. He couldn't get used to her
interest in the arts he cared for; it seemed too good to be
real—it was so unlikely an adventure to tumble into such a
well of sympathy. One might stray into the desert easily—
that was on the cards and that was the law of life; but it was
too rare an accident to stumble on a crystal well. Yet if her
aspirations seemed at one moment too extravagant to be real,
they struck him at the next as too intelligent to be false. They
were both noble and crude, and whims for whims, he liked
them better than any he had met. It was probable enough she
would leave them behind—exchange them for politics, or
"smartness," or mere prolific maternity, as was the custom of
scribbling, daubing, educated, flattered girls, in an age of
luxury and a society of leisure. He noted that the water-
colours on the walls of the room she sat in had mainly the
quality of being *naïves*, and reflected that *naïveté* in art is
like a cipher in a number: its importance depends upon the
figure it is united with. But meanwhile he had fallen in love
with her.

Before he went away he said to Miss Fancourt: "I thought
St George was coming to see you to-day—but he doesn't
turn up."

For a moment he supposed she was going to reply, "*Comment donc?* Did you come here only to meet him?" But the

next he became aware of how little such a speech would have fallen in with any flirtatious element he had as yet perceived in her. She only replied: "Ah yes, but I don't think he'll come. He recommended me not to expect him." Then she added, laughing: "He said it wasn't fair to you. But I think I could manage two."

"So could I," Paul Overt rejoined, stretching the point a little to be humorous. In reality his appreciation of the occasion was so completely an appreciation of the woman before him that another figure in the scene, even so esteemed a one as St George, might for the hour have appealed to him vainly. As he went away he wondered what the great man had meant by its not being fair to him; and, still more than that, whether he had actually stayed away out of the delicacy of such an idea. As he took his course, swinging his stick, through the Sunday solitude of Manchester Square, with a good deal of emotion fermenting in his soul, it appeared to him that he was living in a world really magnanimous. Miss Fancourt had told him that there was an uncertainty about her being, and her father's being, in town on the following Sunday, but that she had the hope of a visit from him if they should not go away. She promised to let him know if they stayed at home, then he could act accordingly. After he had passed into one of the streets that lead out of the square, he stopped, without definite intentions, looking sceptically for a cab. In a moment he saw a hansom roll through the square from the other side and come a part of the way toward him. He was on the point of hailing the driver when he perceived that he carried a fare; then he waited, seeing him prepare to deposit his passenger by pulling up at one of the houses. The house was apparently the one he himself had just quitted; at least he drew that inference as he saw that the person who stepped out of the hansom was Henry St George. Paul Overt turned away quickly, as if he had been caught in the act of spying. He gave up his cab—he preferred to walk; he would go nowhere else.

He was glad St George had not given up his visit altogether—
that would have been too absurd. Yes, the world was magnanimous, and Overt felt so too as, on looking at his watch,
he found it was only six o'clock, so that he could mentally
congratulate his successor on having an hour still to sit in
Miss Fancourt's drawing-room. He himself might use that
hour for another visit, but by the time he reached the Marble
Arch the idea of another visit had become incongruous to
him. He passed beneath that architectural effort and walked
into the Park till he got upon the grass. Here he continued to
walk; he took his way across the elastic turf and came out by
the Serpentine. He watched with a friendly eye the diversions
of the London people, and bent a glance almost encouraging
upon the young ladies paddling their sweethearts on the lake,
and the guardsmen tickling tenderly with their bearskins the
artificial flowers in the Sunday hats of their partners. He prolonged his meditative walk; he went into Kensington Gardens—he sat upon the penny chairs—he looked at the little
sail-boats launched upon the round pond—he was glad he
had no engagement to dine. He repaired for this purpose, very
late, to his club, where he found himself unable to order a
repast and told the waiter to bring whatever he would. He did
not even observe what he was served with, and he spent the
evening in the library of the establishment, pretending to
read an article in an American magazine. He failed to discover
what it was about; it appeared in a dim way to be about
Marian Fancourt.

Quite late in the week she wrote to him that she was not to
go into the country—it had only just been settled. Her father,
she added, would never settle anything—he put it all on her.
She felt her responsibility—she had to—and since she was
forced that was the way she had decided. She mentioned no
reasons, which gave Paul Overt all the clearer field for bold
conjecture about them. In Manchester Square, on this second
Sunday, he esteemed his fortune less good, for she had three

or four other visitors. But there were three or four compensations; the greatest, perhaps, of which was that, learning from her that her father had, after all, at the last hour, gone out of town alone, the bold conjecture I just now spoke of found itself becoming a shade more bold. And then her presence was her presence, and the personal red room was there and was full of it, whatever phantoms passed and vanished, emitting incomprehensible sounds. Lastly, he had the resource of staying till every one had come and gone and of supposing that this pleased her, though she gave no particular sign. When they were alone together he said to her: "But St George did come—last Sunday. I saw him as I looked back."

"Yes; but it was the last time."

"The last time?"

"He said he would never come again."

Paul Overt stared. "Does he mean that he wishes to cease to see you?"

"I don't know what he means," the girl replied, smiling. "He won't, at any rate, see me here."

"And, pray, why not?"

"I don't know," said Marian Fancourt; and her visitor thought he had not yet seen her more beautiful than in uttering these unsatisfactory words.

V

"OH, I say, I want you to remain," Henry St George said to him at eleven o'clock, the night he dined with the head of the profession. The company had been numerous and they were taking their leave; our young man, after bidding good-night to his hostess, had put out his hand in farewell to the master of the house. Besides eliciting from St George the protest I have

quoted this movement provoked a further observation about
such a chance to have a talk, their going into his room, his
having still everything to say. Paul Overt was delighted to be
asked to stay; nevertheless he mentioned jocularly the literal
fact that he had promised to go to another place, at a distance.

"Well then, you'll break your promise, that's all. You
humbug!" St George exclaimed, in a tone that added to
Overt's contentment.

"Certainly, I'll break it; but it was a real promise."

"Do you mean to Miss Fancourt? You're following her?"
St George asked.

Paul Overt answered by a question. "Oh, is *she* going?"

"Base impostor!" his ironic host went on; "I've treated
you handsomely on the article of that young lady: I won't
make another concession. Wait three minutes—I'll be with
you." He gave himself to his departing guests, went with the
long-trained ladies to the door. It was a hot night, the windows were open, the sound of the quick carriages and of the
linkmen's call came into the house. The company had been
brilliant; a sense of festal things was in the heavy air: not only
the influence of that particular entertainment, but the suggestion of the wide hurry of pleasure which, in London, on
summer nights, fills so many of the happier quarters of the
complicated town. Gradually Mrs St George's drawing-room
emptied itself; Paul Overt was left alone with his hostess, to
whom he explained the motive of his waiting. "Ah yes, some
intellectual, some *professional*, talk," she smiled; "at this
season doesn't one miss it? Poor dear Henry, I'm so glad!"
The young man looked out of the window a moment, at the
called hansoms that lurched up, at the smooth broughams that
rolled away. When he turned round Mrs St George had disappeared; her husband's voice came up to him from below—
he was laughing and talking, in the portico, with some lady
who awaited her carriage. Paul had solitary possession, for
some minutes, of the warm, deserted rooms, where the

covered, tinted lamplight was soft, the seats had been pushed about and the odour of flowers lingered. They were large, they were pretty, they contained objects of value; everything in the picture told of a "good house." At the end of five minutes a servant came in with a request from Mr St George that he would join him downstairs; upon which, descending, he followed his conductor through a long passage to an apartment thrown out, in the rear of the habitation, for the special requirements, as he guessed, of a busy man of letters.

St George was in his shirt-sleeves in the middle of a large, high room—a room without windows, but with a wide sky-light at the top, like a place of exhibition. It was furnished as a library, and the serried bookshelves rose to the ceiling, a surface of incomparable tone, produced by dimly-gilt "backs," which was interrupted here and there by the suspension of old prints and drawings. At the end furthest from the door of admission was a tall desk, of great extent, at which the person using it could only write standing, like a clerk in a counting-house; and stretching from the door to this structure was a large plain band of crimson cloth, as straight as a garden-path and almost as long, where, in his mind's eye, Paul Overt immediately saw his host pace to and fro during his hours of composition. The servant gave him a coat, an old jacket with an air of experience, from a cupboard in the wall, retiring afterwards with the garment he had taken off. Paul Overt welcomed the coat; it was a coat for talk and promised con-fidences—it must have received so many—and had pathetic literary elbows. "Ah, we're practical—we're practical!" St George said, as he saw his visitor looking the place over. "Isn't it a good big cage, to go round and round? My wife invented it and she locks me up here every morning."

"You don't miss a window—a place to look out?"

"I did at first, awfully; but her calculation was just. It saves time, it has saved me many months in these ten years. Here I stand, under the eye of day—in London of course, very often, it's rather a bleared old eye—walled in to my trade. I can't get away, and the room is a fine lesson in concentration. I've learned the lesson, I think; look at that big bundle of proof and admit that I have." He pointed to a fat roll of papers, on one of the tables, which had not been undone.

"Are you bringing out another——?" Paul Overt asked, in a tone of whose deficiencies he was not conscious till his companion burst out laughing, and indeed not even then.

"You humbug—you humbug! Don't I know what you think of them?" St George inquired, standing before him with his hands in his pockets and with a new kind of smile. It was as if he were going to let his young votary know him well now.

"Upon my word, in that case you know more than I do!" Paul ventured to respond, revealing a part of the torment of being able neither clearly to esteem him nor distinctly to renounce him.

"My dear fellow," said his companion, "don't imagine I talk about my books, specifically; it isn't a decent subject—*il ne manquerait plus que ça*—I'm not so bad as you may apprehend! About myself, a little, if you like; though it wasn't for that I brought you down here. I want to ask you something— very much indeed—I value this chance. Therefore sit down. We are practical, but there *is* a sofa, you see, for she does humour me a little, after all. Like all really great administrators she knows when to." Paul Overt sank into the corner of a deep leathern couch, but his interlocutor remained standing and said: "If you don't mind, in this room this is my habit. From the door to the desk and from the desk to the door. That shakes up my imagination, gently; and don't you see what a good thing it is that there's no window for her to fly out of? The eternal standing as I write (I stop at that bureau and put it down, when anything comes, and so we go on,) was rather wearisome at first, but we adopted it with an eye to the long run; you're in better order (if your legs don't break down!) and you can keep it up for more years. Oh, we're practical— we're practical!" St George repeated, going to the table and taking up, mechanically, the bundle of proofs. He pulled off the wrapper, he turned the papers over with a sudden change of attention which only made him more interesting to Paul Overt. He lost himself a moment, examining the sheets of his new book, while the younger man's eyes wandered over the room again.

"Lord, what good things I should do if I had such a charming place as this to do them in!" Paul reflected. The outer world, the world of accident and ugliness was so successfully excluded, and within the rich, protecting square, beneath the patronising sky, the figures projected for an artistic purpose could hold their particular revel. It was a prevision of Paul Overt's rather than an observation on actual data, for which the occasions had been too few, that his new friend would have the quality, the charming quality, of surprising him by flashing out in personal intercourse, at moments of suspended, or perhaps even of diminished expectation. A happy relation with him would be a thing proceeding by jumps, not by traceable stages.

"Do you read them—really?" he asked, laying down the proofs on Paul's inquiring of him how soon the work would be published. And when the young man answered, "Oh yes, always," he was moved to mirth again by something he caught in his manner of saying that. "You go to see your grandmother on her birthday—and very proper it is, especially as she won't last for ever. She has lost every faculty and every sense; she neither sees, nor hears, nor speaks; but all customary pieties and kindly habits are respectable. But you're strong if you *do* read 'em! *I* couldn't, my dear fellow. You *are* strong, I know; and that's just a part of what I wanted to say to you. You're very strong indeed. I've been going into your other things—they've interested me exceedingly. Some one ought to have told me about them before—some one I could believe. But whom can one believe? You're wonderfully in the good direction—it's extremely curious work. Now do you mean to keep it up?—that's what I want to ask you."

"Do I mean to do others?" Paul Overt asked, looking up from his sofa at his erect inquisitor and feeling partly like a happy little boy when the schoolmaster is gay and partly like some pilgrim of old who might have consulted the oracle. St George's own performance had been infirm, but as an adviser he would be infallible.

"Others—others? Ah, the number won't matter; one other would do, if it were really a further step—a throb of the same effort. What I mean is, have you it in your mind to go in for some sort of little perfection?"

"Ah, perfection!" Overt sighed, "I talked of that the other Sunday with Miss Fancourt."

"Oh yes, they'll talk of it, as much as you like! But they do mighty little to help one to it. There's no obligation, of course; only you strike me as capable," St George went on. "You must have thought it all over. I can't believe you're without a plan. That's the sensation you give me, and it's so rare that it really stirs up one; it makes you remarkable. If you haven't a plan and you don't mean to keep it up, of course it's all right, it's no one's business, no one can force you, and not more than two or three people will notice that you don't go straight. The others—*all* the rest, every blessed soul in England, will think you do—will think you *are* keeping it up: upon my honour they will! I shall be one of the two or three who know better. Now the question is whether you can do it for two or three. Is that the stuff you're made of?"

"I could do it for one, if you were the one."

"Don't say that—I don't deserve it; it scorches me," St George exclaimed, with eyes suddenly grave and glowing. "The 'one' is of course oneself—one's conscience, one's idea, the singleness of one's aim. I think of that pure spirit as a man thinks of a woman whom, in some detested hour of his youth, he has loved and forsaken. She haunts him with reproachful eyes, she lives for ever before him. As an artist, you know, I've married for money." Paul stared and even blushed a little, confounded by this avowal; whereupon his host, observing the expression of his face, dropped a quick laugh and went on: "You don't follow my figure. I'm not speaking of my dear wife, who had a small fortune, which, however, was not my bribe. I fell in love with her, as many other people have done. I refer to the mercenary muse whom I led to the altar of literature. Don't do that, my boy. She'll lead you a life!"

"Haven't you been happy?"

"Happy? It's a kind of hell."

"There are things I should like to ask you," Paul Overt said, hesitating.

"Ask me anything in all the world. I'd turn myself inside out to save you."

"To save me?" Paul repeated.

"To make you stick to it—to make you see it through. As I said to you the other night at Summersoft, let my example be vivid to you."

"Why, your books are not so bad as that," said Paul, laughing and feeling that he breathed the air of art.

"So bad as what?"

"Your talent is so great that it is in everything you do, in what's less good as well as in what's best. You've some forty volumes to show for it—forty volumes of life, of observation, of magnificent ability."

"I'm very clever, of course I know that," St George replied, quietly. "Lord, what rot they'd all be if I hadn't been! I'm a successful charlatan—I've been able to pass off my system. But do you know what it is? It's *carton-pierre*."

"*Carton-pierre?*"

"Lincrusta-Walton!"

"Ah, don't say such things—you make me bleed!" the younger man protested. "I see you in a beautiful, fortunate home, living in comfort and honour."

"Do you call it honour?" St George interrupted, with an intonation that often comes back to his companion. "That's what I want *you* to go in for. I mean the real thing. This is brummagaem."

"Brummagaem?" Paul ejaculated, while his eyes wandered, by a movement natural at the moment, over the luxurious room.

"Ah, they make it so well to-day; it's wonderfully deceptive!"

"Is it deceptive that I find you living with every appearance of domestic felicity—blessed with a devoted, accomplished wife, with children whose acquaintance I haven't yet had the pleasure of making, but who *must* be delightful young people, from what I know of their parents?"

"It's all excellent, my dear fellow—heaven forbid I should deny it. I've made a great deal of money; my wife has known how to take care of it, to use it without wasting it, to put a good bit of it by, to make it fructify. I've got a loaf on the shelf; I've got everything, in fact, but the great thing——"

"The great thing?"

"The sense of having done the best—the sense, which is the real life of the artist and the absence of which is his death, of having drawn from his intellectual instrument the finest music that nature had hidden in it, of having played it as it should be played. He either does that or he doesn't—and if he doesn't he isn't worth speaking of. And precisely those who really know don't speak of him. He may still hear a great chatter, but what he hears most is the incorruptible silence of Fame. I have squared her, you may say, for my little hour— but what is my little hour? Don't imagine for a moment I'm such a cad as to have brought you down here to abuse or to complain of my wife to you. She is a woman of very distinguished qualities, to whom my obligations are immense; so that, if you please, we will say nothing about her. My boys —my children are all boys—are straight and strong, thank God! and have no poverty of growth about them, no penury of needs. I receive, periodically, the most satisfactory attestation from Harrow, from Oxford, from Sandhurst (oh, we have done the best for them!) of their being living, thriving, consuming organisms."

"It must be delightful to feel that the son of one's loins is at Sandhurst," Paul remarked, enthusiastically.

"It is—it's charming. Oh, I'm a patriot!"

"Then what did you mean—the other night at Summersoft—by saying that children are a curse?"

"My dear fellow, on what basis are we talking?" St George asked, dropping upon the sofa, at a short distance from his visitor. Sitting a little sideways he leaned back against the opposite arm with his hands raised and interlocked behind his head. "On the supposition that a certain perfection is possible and even desirable—isn't it so? Well, all I say is that one's children interfere with perfection. One's wife interferes. Marriage interferes."

"You think then the artist shouldn't marry?"

"He does so at his peril—he does so at his cost."

"Not even when his wife is in sympathy with his work?"

"She never is—she can't be! Women don't know what work is."

"Surely, they work themselves," Paul Overt objected.

"Yes, very badly. Oh, of course, often, they think they understand, they think they sympathise. Then it is that they are most dangerous. Their idea is that you shall do a great lot and get a great lot of money. Their great nobleness and virtue, their exemplary conscientiousness as British females, is in keeping you up to that. My wife makes all my bargains with my publishers for me, and she has done so for twenty years.

She does it consummately well; that's why I'm really pretty well off. Are you not the father of their innocent babes, and will you withhold from them their natural sustenance? You asked me the other night if they were not an immense incentive. Of course they are—there's no doubt of that!"

"For myself, I have an idea I need incentives," Paul Overt dropped.

"Ah well, then, *n'en parlons plus!*" said his companion, smiling.

"You are an incentive, I maintain," the young man went on. "You don't affect me in the way you apparently would like to. Your great success is what I see—the pomp of Ennismore Gardens!"

"Success?—do you call it success to be spoken of as you would speak of me if you were sitting here with another artist—a young man intelligent and sincere like yourself? Do you call it success to make you blush—as you would blush— if some foreign critic (some fellow, of course, I mean, who should know what he was talking about and should have shown you he did, as foreign critics like to show it!) were to say to you: 'He's the one, in this country, whom they consider the most perfect, isn't he?' Is it success to be the occasion of a young Englishman's having to stammer as you would have to stammer at such a moment for old England? No, no; success is to have made people tremble after another fashion. Do try it!"

"Try it?"

"Try to do some really good work."

"Oh, I want to, heaven knows!"

"Well, you can't do it without sacrifices; don't believe that for a moment," said Henry St George. "I've made none. I've had everything. In other words, I've missed everything."

"You've had the full, rich, masculine, human, general life, with all the responsibilities and duties and burdens and sorrows and joys—all the domestic and social initiations and complications. They must be immensely suggestive, immensely amusing."

"Amusing?"

"For a strong man—yes."

"They've given me subjects without number, if that's what you mean; but they've taken away at the same time the power to use them. I've touched a thousand things, but which one of them have I turned into gold? The artist has to do only with that—he knows nothing of any baser metal. I've led the life of the world, with my wife and my progeny; the clumsy, expensive, materialised, brutalised, Philistine, snobbish life of London. We've got everything handsome, even a carriage— we are prosperous, hospitable, eminent people. But, my dear fellow, don't try to stultify yourself and pretend you don't know what we *haven't* got. It's bigger than all the rest. Between artists—come! You know as well as you sit there that you would put a pistol-ball into your brain if you had written my books!"

It appeared to Paul Overt that the tremendous talk promised by the master at Summersoft had indeed come off, and with a promptitude, a fulness, with which his young imagination had scarcely reckoned. His companion made an immense impression on him and he throbbed with the excitement of such deep soundings and such strange confidences. He throbbed indeed with the conflict of his feelings—bewilderment and recognition and alarm, enjoyment and protest and assent, all commingled with tenderness (and a kind of shame in the participation,) for the sores and bruises exhibited by so fine a creature, and with a sense of the tragic secret that he nursed under his trappings. The idea of *his* being made the occasion of such an act of humility made him flush and pant, at the same time that his perception, in certain directions, had been too much awakened to conceal from him anything that St George really meant. It had been his odd fortune to blow upon the deep waters, to make them surge and break in waves of

strange eloquence. He launched himself into a passionate contradiction of his host's last declaration; tried to enumerate to
him the parts of his work he loved, the splendid things he had
found in it, beyond the compass of any other writer of the day.
St George listened awhile, courteously; then he said, laying
his hand on Paul Overt's:

"That's all very well; and if your idea is to do nothing
better there is no reason why you shouldn't have as many
good things as I—as many human and material appendages,
as many sons or daughters, a wife with as many gowns, a
house with as many servants, a stable with as many horses, a
heart with as many aches." He got up when he had spoken
thus, and then stood a moment near the sofa, looking down
on his agitated pupil. "Are you possessed of any money?" it
occurred to him to ask.

"None to speak of."

"Oh, well, there's no reason why you shouldn't make a
goodish income—if you set about it the right way. Study *me*
for that—study me well. You may really have a carriage."

Paul Overt sat there for some moments without speaking.
He looked straight before him—he turned over many things.
His friend had wandered away from him, taking up a parcel
of letters that were on the table where the roll of proofs had
lain. "What was the book Mrs St George made you burn—
the one she didn't like?" he abruptly inquired.

"The book she made me burn—how did you know that?"
St George looked up from his letters.

"I heard her speak of it at Summersoft."

"Ah, yes; she's proud of it. I don't know—it was rather
good."

"What was it about?"

"Let me see." And St George appeared to make an effort
to remember. "Oh, yes, it was about myself." Paul Overt
gave an irrepressible groan for the disappearance of such a
production, and the elder man went on: "Oh, but *you* should

write it—*you* should do me. There's a subject, my boy: no end of stuff in it!"

Again Paul was silent, but after a little he spoke. "Are there no women that really understand—that can take part in a sacrifice?"

"How can they take part? They themselves are the sacrifice. They're the idol and the altar and the flame."

"Isn't there even *one* who sees further?" Paul continued.

For a moment St George made no answer to this; then, having torn up his letters, he stood before his disciple again, ironic. "Of course I know the one you mean. But not even Miss Fancourt."

"I thought you admired her so much."

"It's impossible to admire her more. Are you in love with her?" St George asked.

"Yes," said Paul Overt.

"Well, then, give it up."

Paul stared. "Give up my love?"

"Bless me, no; your idea."

"My idea?"

"The one you talked with her about. The idea of perfection."

"She would help it—she would help it!" cried the young man.

"For about a year—the first year, yes. After that she would be as a millstone round its neck."

"Why, she has a passion for completeness, for good work —for everything you and I care for most."

"'You and I' is charming, my dear fellow! She has it indeed, but she would have a still greater passion for her children; and very proper too. She would insist upon everything's being made comfortable, advantageous, propitious for them. That isn't the artist's business."

"The artist—the artist! Isn't he a man all the same?"

St George hesitated. "Sometimes I really think not. You know as well as I what he has to do: the concentration, the finish, the independence that he must strive for, from the moment that he begins to respect his work. Ah, my young friend, his relation to women, especially in matrimony, is at the mercy of this damning fact—that whereas he can in the nature of things have but one standard, they have about fifty. That's what makes them so superior," St George added, laughing. "Fancy an artist with a plurality of standards," he went on. "To *do* it—to do it and make it divine is the only thing he has to think about. 'Is it done or not?' is his only question. Not 'Is it done as well as a proper solicitude for my dear little family will allow?' He has nothing to do with the relative, nothing to do with a dear little family!"

"Then you don't allow him the common passions and affections of men?"

"Hasn't he a passion, an affection, which includes all the rest? Besides, let him have all the passions he likes—if he only keeps his independence. He must afford to be poor."

Paul Overt slowly got up. "Why did you advise me to make up to her, then?"

St George laid his hand on his shoulder. "Because she would make an adorable wife! And I hadn't read you then."

"I wish you had left me alone!" murmured the young man.

"I didn't know that that wasn't good enough for you," St George continued.

"What a false position, what a condemnation of the artist, that he's a mere disfranchised monk and can produce his effect only by giving up personal happiness. What an arraignment of art!" Paul Overt pursued, with a trembling voice.

"Ah, you don't imagine, by chance, that I'm defending art? Arraignment, I should think so! Happy the societies in which it hasn't made its appearance; for from the moment it comes they have a consuming ache, they have an incurable corruption in their bosom. Assuredly, the artist is in a false position. But I thought we were taking him for granted. Pardon me," St George continued; "*Ginistrella* made me!"

Paul Overt stood looking at the floor—one o'clock struck, in the stillness, from a neighbouring church-tower. "Do you think she would ever look at me?" he asked at last.

"Miss Fancourt—as a suitor? Why shouldn't I think it? That's why I've tried to favour you—I have had a little chance or two of bettering your opportunity."

"Excuse my asking you, but do you mean by keeping away yourself?" Paul said, blushing.

"I'm an old idiot—my place isn't there," St George replied, gravely.

"I'm nothing, yet; I've no fortune; and there must be so many others."

"You're a gentleman and a man of genius. I think you might do something."

"But if I must give that up—the genius?"

"Lots of people, you know, think I've kept mine."

"You have a genius for torment!" Paul Overt exclaimed; but taking his companion's hand in farewell as a mitigation of this judgment.

"Poor child, I do bother you. Try, try, then! I think your chances are good, and you'll win a great prize."

Paul held the other's hand a minute; he looked into his face. "No, I *am* an artist—I can't help it!"

"Ah, show it then!" St George broke out—"let me see before I die the thing I most want, the thing I yearn for—a life in which the passion is really intense. If you can be rare, don't fail of it! Think what it is—how it counts—how it lives!" They had moved to the door and St George had closed both his own hands over that of his companion. Here they paused again and Paul Overt ejaculated—"I want to live!"

"In what sense?"

"In the greatest sense."

"Well then, stick to it—see it through."

"With your sympathy—your help?"

"Count on that—you'll be a great figure to me. Count on

my highest appreciation, my devotion. You'll give me satisfaction!—if that has any weight with you." And as Paul appeared still to waver, St George added: "Do you remember what you said to me at Summersoft?"

"Something infatuated, no doubt!"

" 'I'll do anything in the world you tell me.' You said that."

"And you hold me to it?"

"Ah, what am I?" sighed the master, shaking his head.

"Lord, what things I shall have to do!" Paul almost moaned as he turned away.

VI

"It goes on too much abroad—hang abroad!" These, or something like them, had been St George's remarkable words in relation to the action of *Ginistrella;* and yet, though they had made a sharp impression on Paul Overt, like almost all the master's spoken words, the young man, a week after the conversation I have narrated, left England for a long absence and full of projects of work. It is not a perversion of the truth to say that that conversation was the direct cause of his departure. If the oral utterance of the eminent writer had the privilege of moving him deeply it was especially on his turning it over at leisure, hours and days afterward, that it appeared to yield its full meaning and exhibit its extreme importance. He spent the summer in Switzerland, and having, in September, begun a new task, he determined not to cross the Alps till he should have made a good start. To this end he returned to a quiet corner that he knew well, on the edge of the Lake of Geneva, within sight of the towers of Chillon: a region and a view for which he had an affection springing from old associations, capable of mysterious little revivals and

refreshments. Here he lingered late, till the snow was on the
nearer hills, almost down to the limit to which he could climb
when his stint was done, on the shortening afternoons. The
autumn was fine, the lake was blue, and his book took form
and direction. These circumstances, for the time, embroidered
his life, and he suffered it to cover him with its mantle. At the
end of six weeks he appeared to himself to have learned St
George's lesson by heart—to have tested and proved its doctrine. Nevertheless he did a very inconsistent thing: before
crossing the Alps he wrote to Marian Fancourt. He was aware
of the perversity of this act, and it was only as a luxury, an
amusement, the reward of a strenuous autumn, that he justified it. She had not asked any such favour of him when he
went to see her three days before he left London—three days
after their dinner in Ennismore Gardens. It is true that she
had no reason to, for he had not mentioned that he was on the
eve of such an excursion. He hadn't mentioned it because he
didn't know it; it was that particular visit that made the matter clear. He had paid the visit to see how much he really
cared for her, and quick departure, without so much as a
farewell, was the sequel to this inquiry, the answer to which
had been a distinct superlative. When he wrote to her from
Clarens he noted that he owed her an explanation (more than
three months after!) for the omission of such a form.

She answered him briefly but very promptly, and gave him
a striking piece of news: the death, a week before, of Mrs St
George. This exemplary woman had succumbed, in the
country, to a violent attack of inflammation of the lungs—he
would remember that for a long time she had been delicate.
Miss Fancourt added that she heard her husband was overwhelmed with the blow; he would miss her unspeakably—
she had been everything to him. Paul Overt immediately
wrote to St George. He had wished to remain in communication with him, but had hitherto lacked the right excuse for
troubling so busy a man. Their long nocturnal talk came back

to him in every detail, but this did not prevent his expressing a cordial sympathy with the head of the profession, for had not that very talk made it clear that the accomplished lady was the influence that ruled his life? What catastrophe could be more cruel than the extinction of such an influence? This was exactly the tone that St George took in answering his young friend, upwards of a month later. He made no allusion, of course, to their important discussion. He spoke of his wife as frankly and generously as if he had quite forgotten that occasion, and the feeling of deep bereavement was visible in his words. "She took every thing off my hands—off my mind. She carried on our life with the greatest art, the rarest devotion, and I was free, as few men can have been, to drive my pen, to shut myself up with my trade. This was a rare service—the highest she could have rendered me. Would I could have acknowledged it more fitly!"

A certain bewilderment, for Paul Overt, disengaged itself from these remarks: they struck him as a contradiction, a retractation. He had certainly not expected his correspondent to rejoice in the death of his wife, and it was perfectly in order that the rupture of a tie of more than twenty years should have left him sore. But if she was such a benefactress as that, what in the name of consistency had St George meant by turning *him* upside down that night—by dosing him to that degree, at the most sensitive hour of his life, with the doctrine of renunciation? If Mrs St George was an irreparable loss, then her husband's inspired advice had been a bad joke and renunciation was a mistake. Overt was on the point of rushing back to London to show that, for his part, he was perfectly willing to consider it so, and he went so far as to take the manuscript of the first chapters of his new book out of his table-drawer, to insert it into a pocket of his portmanteau. This led to his catching a glimpse of some pages he had not looked at for months, and that accident, in turn, to his being struck with the high promise they contained—a rare result of such retrospections, which it was his habit to avoid as much as possible. They usually made him feel that the glow of composition might be a purely subjective and a very barren emotion. On this occasion a certain belief in himself disengaged itself whimsically from the serried erasures of his first draft, making him think it best after all to carry out his present experiment to the end. If he could write as well as that under the influence of renunciation, it would be a pity to change the conditions before the termination of the work. He would go back to London of course, but he would go back only when he should have finished his book. This was the vow he privately made, restoring his manuscript to the table-drawer. It may be added that it took him a long time to finish his book, for the subject was as difficult as it was fine and he was literally embarrassed by the fulness of his notes. Something within him told him that he must make it supremely good—otherwise he should lack, as regards his private behaviour, a handsome excuse. He had a horror of this deficiency and found himself as firm as need be on the question of the lamp and the file. He crossed the Alps at last and spent the winter, the spring, the ensuing summer, in Italy, where still, at the end of a twelvemonth, his task was unachieved. "Stick to it—see it through:" this general injunction of St George's was good also for the particular case. He applied it to the utmost, with the result that when in its slow order, the summer had come round again he felt that he had given all that was in him. This time he put his papers into his portmanteau, with the address of his publisher attached, and took his way northward.

He had been absent from London for two years—two years which were a long period and had made such a difference in his own life (through the production of a novel far stronger, he believed, than *Ginistrella*) that he turned out into Piccadilly, the morning after his arrival, with an indefinite expectation of changes, of finding that things had happened. But there were few transformations in Piccadilly (only three or four big red houses where there had been low black ones), and the brightness of the end of June peeped through the rusty railings of the Green Park and glittered in the varnish of the rolling carriages as he had seen it in other, more cursory Junes. It was a greeting that he appreciated; it seemed friendly and pointed, added to the exhilaration of his finished book, of his having his own country and the huge, oppressive, amusing city that suggested everything, that contained everything, under his hand again. "Stay at home and do things here—do subjects we can measure," St George had said; and now it appeared to him that he should ask nothing better than to stay at home for ever. Late in the afternoon he took his way to Manchester Square, looking out for a number he had not forgotten. Miss Fancourt, however, was not within, so that he turned, rather dejectedly, from the door. This movement brought him face to face with a gentleman who was approaching it and whom he promptly perceived to be Miss Fancourt's father. Paul saluted this personage, and the General returned his greeting with his customary good manner—a manner so good, however, that you could never tell whether it meant that he placed you. Paul Overt felt the impulse to speak to him; then, hesitating, became conscious both that he had nothing particular to say and that though the old soldier remembered him he remembered him wrong. He therefore passed on, without calculating on the irresistible effect that his own evident recognition would have upon the General, who never neglected a chance to gossip. Our young man's face was expressive, and observation seldom let it pass. He had not taken ten steps before he heard himself called after with a friendly, semi-articulate "A—I beg your pardon!" He turned round and the General, smiling at him from the steps, said: "Won't you come in? I won't leave you the advantage of me!" Paul declined to come in, and then was sorry he had done so, for Miss Fancourt, so late in the afternoon, might return at any moment. But her father gave him no second chance; he appeared mainly to wish not to have struck him as inhospitable. A further look at the visitor told him more about him, enough at least to enable him to say—"You've come back, you've come back?" Paul was on the point of replying that he had come back the night before, but he bethought himself to suppress this strong light on the immediacy of his visit, and, giving merely a general assent, remarked that he was extremely sorry not to have found Miss Fancourt. He had come late, in the hope that she would be in. "I'll tell her —I'll tell her," said the old man; and then he added quickly, gallantly, "You'll be giving us something new? It's a long time, isn't it?" Now he remembered him right.

"Rather long. I'm very slow," said Paul. "I met you at Summersoft a long time ago."

"Oh, yes, with Henry St George. I remember very well. Before his poor wife——" General Fancourt paused a moment, smiling a little less. "I daresay you know."

"About Mrs St George's death? Oh yes, I heard at the time."

"Oh no; I mean—I mean he's to be married."

"Ah! I've not heard that." Just as Paul was about to add, "To whom?" the General crossed his intention with a question.

"When did you come back? I know you've been away— from my daughter. She was very sorry. You ought to give her something new."

"I came back last night," said our young man, to whom something had occurred which made his speech, for the moment, a little thick.

"Ah, most kind of you to come so soon. Couldn't you turn up at dinner?"

"At dinner?" Paul Overt repeated, not liking to ask whom St George was going to marry, but thinking only of that.

"There are several people, I believe. Certainly St George.

Or afterwards, if you like better. I believe my daughter expects——." He appeared to notice something in Overt's upward face (on his steps he stood higher) which led him to interrupt himself, and the interruption gave him a momentary sense of awkwardness, from which he sought a quick issue. "Perhaps then you haven't heard she's to be married."

"To be married?" Paul stared.

"To Mr St George—it has just been settled. Odd marriage, isn't it?" Paul uttered no opinion on this point: he only continued to stare. "But I daresay it will do—she's so awfully literary!" said the General.

Paul had turned very red. "Oh, it's a surprise—very interesting, very charming! I'm afraid I can't dine—so many thanks!"

"Well, you must come to the wedding!" cried the General. "Oh, I remember that day at Summersoft. He's a very good fellow."

"Charming—charming!" Paul stammered, retreating. He shook hands with the General and got off. His face was red and he had the sense of its growing more and more crimson. All the evening at home—he went straight to his rooms and remained there dinnerless—his cheek burned at intervals as if it had been smitten. He didn't understand what had happened to him, what trick had been played him, what treachery practised. "None, none," he said to himself. "I've nothing to do with it. I'm out of it—it's none of my business." But that bewildered murmur was followed again and again by the incongruous ejaculation—"Was it a plan—was it a plan?" Sometimes he cried to himself, breathless, "Am I a dupe—am I a dupe?" If he was, he was an absurd, and abject one. It seemed to him he had never lost her till now. He had renounced her, yes; but that was another affair—that was a closed but not a locked door. Now he felt as if the door had been slammed in his face. Did he expect her to wait—was she to give him his time like that: two years at a stretch? He didn't know what he had expected—he only knew what he hadn't. It wasn't this—it wasn't this. Mystification, bitterness and wrath rose and boiled in him when he thought of the deference, the devotion, the credulity with which he had listened to St George. The evening wore on and the light was long; but even when it had darkened he remained without a lamp. He had flung himself on the sofa, and he lay there through the hours with his eyes either closed or gazing into the gloom, in the attitude of a man teaching himself to bear something, to bear having been made a fool of. He had made it too easy—that idea passed over him like a hot wave. Suddenly, as he heard eleven o'clock strike, he jumped up, remembering what General Fancourt had said about his coming after dinner. He would go—he would see her at least; perhaps he should see what it meant. He felt as if some of the elements of a hard sum had been given him and the others were wanting: he couldn't do his sum till he was in possession of them all.

He dressed quickly, so that by half-past eleven he was at Manchester Square. There were a good many carriages at the door—a party was going on; a circumstance which at the last gave him a slight relief, for now he would rather see her in a crowd. People passed him on the staircase; they were going away, going "on," with the hunted, herdlike movement of London society at night. But sundry groups remained in the drawing-room, and it was some minutes, as she didn't hear him announced, before he discovered her and spoke to her. In this short interval he had perceived that St George was there, talking to a lady before the fireplace; but he looked away from him, for the moment, and therefore failed to see whether the author of *Shadowmere* noticed him. At all events he didn't come to him. Miss Fancourt did, as soon as she saw him; she almost rushed at him, smiling, rustling, radiant, beautiful. He had forgotten what her head, what her face offered to the sight; she was in white, there were gold figures on her dress, and her hair was like a casque of gold. In a single moment he saw she was happy, happy with a kind of aggressiveness, of splendour. But she would not speak to him of that, she would speak only of himself.

"I'm so delighted; my father told me. How kind of you to come!" She struck him as so fresh and brave, while his eyes moved over her, that he said to himself, irresistibly: "Why to *him*, why not to youth, to strength, to ambition, to a future? Why, in her rich young capacity, to failure, to abdication, to superannuation?" In his thought, at that sharp moment, he blasphemed even against all that had been left of his faith in the peccable master. "I'm so sorry I missed you," she went on. "My father told me. How charming of you to have come so soon!"

"Does that surprise you?" Paul Overt asked.

"The first day? No, from you—nothing that's nice." She was interrupted by a lady who bade her good-night, and he seemed to read that it cost her nothing to speak to one in that tone; it was her old bounteous, demonstrative way, with a certain added amplitude that time had brought; and if it began to operate on the spot, at such a juncture in her history, perhaps in the other days too it had meant just as little or as much—a sort of mechanical charity, with the difference now that she was satisfied, ready to give but asking nothing. Oh, she was satisfied—and why shouldn't she be? Why shouldn't she have been surprised at his coming the first day—for all the good she had ever got from him? As the lady continued to hold her attention Paul Overt turned from her with a strange irritation in his complicated artistic soul and a kind of disinterested disappointment. She was so happy that it was almost stupid—it seemed to deny the extraordinary intelligence he had formerly found in her. Didn't she know how bad St George could be, hadn't she perceived the deplorable thinness——? If she didn't she was nothing, and if she did why such an insolence of serenity? This question expired as our young man's eyes settled at last upon the genius who had advised him in a great crisis. St George was still before the chimney-piece, but now he was alone (fixed, waiting, as if he meant to remain after every one), and he met the clouded gaze of the young friend who was tormented with uncertainty as to whether he had the right (which his resentment would have enjoyed,) to regard himself as his victim. Somehow, the fantastic inquiry I have just noted was answered by St George's aspect. It was as fine in its way as Marian Fancourt's—it denoted the happy human being; but somehow it represented to Paul Overt that the author of *Shadowmere* had now definitively ceased to count—ceased to count as a writer. As he smiled a welcome across the room he was almost *banal*, he was almost smug. Paul had the impression that for a moment he hesitated to make a movement forward, as if he had a bad conscience; but the next they had met in the middle of the room and had shaken hands, expressively, cordially on St George's part. Then they had passed together to where the elder man had been standing, while St George said: "I hope you are never going away again. I have been dining here; the General told me." He was handsome, he was young, he looked as if he had still a great fund of life. He bent the friendliest, most unconfessing eyes upon Paul Overt; asked him about everything, his health, his plans, his late occupations, the new book. "When will it be out—soon, soon, I hope? Splendid, eh? That's right; you're a comfort! I've read you all over again, the last six months." Paul waited to see if he would tell him what the General had told him in the afternoon, and what Miss Fancourt, verbally at least, of course had not. But as it didn't come out he asked at last: "Is it true, the great news I hear, that you're to be married?"

"Ah, you *have* heard it then?"

"Didn't the General tell you?" Paul Overt went on.

"Tell me what?"

"That he mentioned it to me this afternoon?"

"My dear fellow, I don't remember. We've been in the midst of people. I'm sorry, in that case, that I lose the pleasure, myself, of announcing to you a fact that touches me so nearly. It *is* a fact, strange as it may appear. It has only just become one. Isn't it ridiculous?" St George made this speech without confusion, but on the other hand, so far as Paul could see, without latent impudence. It appeared to his interlocutor that, to talk so comfortably and coolly, he must simply have forgotten what had passed between them. His next words, however, showed that he had not, and they had, as an appeal to Paul's own memory, an effect which would have been ludicrous if it had not been cruel. "Do you recollect the talk we had at my house that night, into which Miss Fancourt's name entered? I've often thought of it since."

"Yes—no wonder you said what you did," said Paul, looking at him.

"In the light of the present occasion? Ah! but there was no light then. How could I have foreseen this hour?"

"Didn't you think it probable?"

"Upon my honour, no," said Henry St George. "Certainly, I owe you that assurance. Think how my situation has changed."

"I see—I see," Paul murmured.

His companion went on, as if, now that the subject had been broached, he was, as a man of imagination and tact, perfectly ready to give every satisfaction—being able to enter fully into everything another might feel. "But it's not only that—for honestly, at my age, I never dreamed——a widower, with big boys and with so little else! It has turned out differently from any possible calculation, and I am fortunate beyond all measure. She has been so free, and yet she consents. Better than any one else perhaps—for I remember how you liked her, before you went away, and how she liked you —you can intelligently congratulate me."

"She has been so free!" Those words made a great impression on Paul Overt, and he almost writhed under that irony in them as to which it little mattered whether it was intentional or casual. Of course she had been free and, appreciably perhaps, by his own act; for was not St George's allusion to her having liked him a part of the irony too? "I thought that by your theory you disapproved of a writer's marrying."

"Surely—surely. But you don't call me a writer?"

"You ought to be ashamed," said Paul.

"Ashamed of marrying again?"

"I won't say that—but ashamed of your reasons."

"You must let me judge of them, my friend."

"Yes; why not? For you judged wonderfully of mine."

The tone of these words appeared suddenly, for Henry St George, to suggest the unsuspected. He stared as if he read a bitterness in them. "Don't you think I have acted fair?"

"You might have told me at the time, perhaps."

"My dear fellow, when I say I couldn't pierce futurity!"

"I mean afterwards."

St George hesitated. "After my wife's death?"

"When this idea came to you."

"Ah, never, never! I wanted to save you, rare and precious as you are."

"Are you marrying Miss Fancourt to save me?"

"Not absolutely, but it adds to the pleasure. I shall be the making of you," said St George, smiling. "I was greatly struck, after our talk, with the resolute way you quitted the country and still more, perhaps, with your force of character in remaining abroad. You're very strong—you're wonderfully strong."

Paul Overt tried to sound his pleasant eyes; the strange thing was that he appeared sincere—not a mocking fiend. He turned away, and as he did so he heard St George say something about his giving them the proof, being the joy of his old age. He faced him again, taking another look. "Do you mean to say you've stopped writing?"

"My dear fellow, of course I have. It's too late. Didn't I tell you?"

"I can't believe it!"

"Of course you can't—with your own talent! No, no; for the rest of my life I shall only read you."

"Does she know that—Miss Fancourt?"

"She will—she will." Our young man wondered whether St George meant this as a covert intimation that the assistance he should derive from that young lady's fortune, moderate as it was, would make the difference of putting it in his power to cease to work, ungratefully, an exhausted vein. Somehow, standing there in the ripeness of his successful manhood, he did not suggest that any of his veins were exhausted. "Don't you remember the moral I offered myself to you—that night —as pointing?" St George continued. "Consider, at any rate, the warning I am at present."

This was too much—he *was* the mocking fiend. Paul separated from him with a mere nod for good-night; the sense that he might come back to him some time in the far future but could not fraternise with him now. It was necessary to his sore spirit to believe for the hour that he had a grievance—all the more cruel for not being a legal one. It was doubtless in the attitude of hugging this wrong that he descended the stairs without taking leave of Miss Fancourt, who had not been in view at the moment he quitted the room. He was glad to get out into the honest, dusky, unsophisticating night, to move fast, to take his way home on foot. He walked a long time, missing his way, not thinking of it. He was thinking of too many other things. His steps recovered their direction, however, and at the end of an hour he found himself before his door, in the small, inexpensive, empty street. He lingered, questioning himself still, before going in, with nothing around and above him but moonless blackness, a bad lamp or two and a few far-away dim stars. To these last faint features he raised his eyes; he had been saying to himself that there would have been mockery indeed if now, on his new foundation, at the end of a year, St George should put forth something with his early quality—something of the type of *Shadowmere* and finer than his finest. Greatly as he admired his talent Paul literally hoped such an incident would not occur; it seemed to him just then that he scarcely should be able to endure it. St George's words were still in his ears, "You're very strong—wonderfully strong." Was he really? Certainly, he would have to be; and it would be a sort of revenge. *Is* he? the reader may ask in turn, if his interest has followed the perplexed young man so far. The best answer to that perhaps is that he is doing his best but that it is too soon to say. When the new book came out in the autumn Mr and Mrs St George found it really magnificent. The former still has published nothing, but Paul Overt does not even yet feel safe. I may say for him, however, that if this event were to befall he would really be the very first to appreciate it: which is perhaps a proof that St George was essentially right and that Nature dedicated him to intellectual, not to personal passion.

THE PATAGONIA

I

THE houses were dark in the August night and the perspective of Beacon Street, with its double chain of lamps, was a foreshortened desert. The club on the hill alone, from its semicylindrical front, projected a glow upon the dusky vagueness of the Common, and as I passed it I heard in the hot stillness the click of a pair of billiard balls. As "every one" was out of town perhaps the servants, in the extravagance of their leisure, were profaning the tables. The heat was insufferable and I thought with joy of the morrow, of the deck of the steamer, the freshening breeze, the sense of getting out to sea. I was even glad of what I had learned in the afternoon at the office of the company—that at the eleventh hour an old ship with a lower standard of speed had been put on in place of the vessel in which I had taken my passage. America was roasting, England might very well be stuffy, and a slow passage (which at that season of the year would probably also be a fine one) was a guarantee of ten or twelve days of fresh air.

I strolled down the hill without meeting a creature, though I could see through the palings of the Common that that recreative expanse was peopled with dim forms. I remembered Mrs Nettlepoint's house—she lived in those days (they are not so distant, but there have been changes) on the waterside, a little way beyond the spot at which the Public Garden terminates; and I reflected that like myself she would be spending the night in Boston if it were true that, as had been mentioned to me a few days before at Mount Desert, she was to embark on the morrow for Liverpool. I presently saw this

285

appearance confirmed by a light above her door and in two or three of her windows, and I determined to ask for her, having nothing to do till bedtime. I had come out simply to pass an hour, leaving my hotel to the blaze of its gas and the perspiration of its porters; but it occurred to me that my old friend might very well not know of the substitution of the *Patagonia* for the *Scandinavia*, so that it would be an act of consideration to prepare her mind. Besides, I could offer to help her, to look after her in the morning: lone women are grateful for support in taking ship for far countries.

As I stood on her doorstep I remembered that as she had a son she might not after all be so lone; yet at the same time it was present to me that Jasper Nettlepoint was not quite a young man to lean upon, having (as I at least supposed) a life of his own and tastes and habits which had long since drawn him away from the maternal side. If he did happen just now to be at home my solicitude would of course seem officious; for in his many wanderings—I believed he had roamed all over the globe—he would certainly have learned how to manage. None the less I was very glad to show Mrs Nettlepoint I thought of her. With my long absence I had lost sight of her; but I had liked her of old; she had been a close friend of my sisters; and I had in regard to her that sense which is pleasant to those who, in general, have grown strange or detached— the feeling that she at least knew all about me. I could trust her at any time to tell people what a respectable person I was. Perhaps I was conscious of how little I deserved this indulgence when it came over me that for years I had not communicated with her. The measure of this neglect was given by my vagueness of mind about her son. However, I really belonged nowadays to a different generation: I was more the old lady's contemporary than Jasper's.

Mrs Nettlepoint was at home: I found her in her back drawing-room, where the wide windows opened upon the water. The room was dusky—it was too hot for lamps—and she sat slowly moving her fan and looking out on the little arm of the sea which is so pretty at night, reflecting the lights of Cambridgeport and Charlestown. I supposed she was musing upon the loved ones she was to leave behind, her married daughters, her grandchildren; but she struck a note more specifically Bostonian as she said to me, pointing with her fan to the Back Bay—"I shall see nothing more charming than that over there, you know!" She made me very welcome, but her son had told her about the *Patagonia*, for which she was sorry, as this would mean a longer voyage. She was a poor creature on shipboard and mainly confined to her cabin, even in weather extravagantly termed fine—as if any weather could be fine at sea.

"Ah, then your son's going with you?" I asked.

"Here he comes, he will tell you for himself much better than I am able to do."

Jasper Nettlepoint came into the room at that moment, dressed in white flannel and carrying a large fan.

"Well, my dear, have you decided?" his mother continued, with some irony in her tone. "He hasn't yet made up his mind, and we sail at ten o'clock!"

"What does it matter, when my things are put up?" said the young man. "There is no crowd at this moment; there will be cabins to spare. I'm waiting for a telegram—that will settle it. I just walked up to the club to see if it was come—they'll send it there because they think the house is closed. Not yet, but I shall go back in twenty minutes."

"Mercy, how you rush about in this temperature!" his mother exclaimed, while I reflected that it was perhaps *his* billiard-balls I had heard ten minutes before. I was sure he was fond of billiards.

"Rush? not in the least. I take it uncommonly easy."

"Ah, I'm bound to say you do," Mrs Nettlepoint exclaimed, inconsequently. I divined that there was a certain tension between the pair and a want of consideration on the young man's part, arising perhaps from selfishness. His mother was nervous, in suspense, wanting to be at rest as to whether she should have his company on the voyage or be obliged to make it alone. But as he stood there smiling and slowly moving his fan he struck me somehow as a person on whom this fact would not sit very heavily. He was of the type of those whom other people worry about, not of those who worry about other people. Tall and strong, he had a handsome face, with a round head and close-curling hair; the whites of his eyes and the enamel of his teeth, under his brown moustache gleamed vaguely in the lights of the Back Bay. I made out that he was sunburnt, as if he lived much in the open air, and that he looked intelligent but also slightly brutal, though not in a morose way. His brutality, if he had any, was bright and finished. I had to tell him who I was, but even then I saw that he failed to place me and that my explanations gave me in his mind no great identity or at any rate no great importance. I foresaw that he would in intercourse make me feel sometimes very young and sometimes very old. He mentioned, as if to show his mother that he might safely be left to his own devices, that he had once started from London to Bombay at three-quarters of an hour's notice.

"Yes, and it must have been pleasant for the people you were with!"

"Oh, the people I was with——!" he rejoined; and his tone appeared to signify that such people would always have to come off as they could. He asked if there were no cold drinks in the house, no lemonade, no iced syrups; in such weather something of that sort ought always to be kept going. When his mother remarked that surely at the club they *were* going he went on, "Oh, yes, I had various things there; but you know I have walked down the hill since. One should have something at either end. May I ring and see?" He rang while Mrs Nettlepoint observed that with the people they had in the house—an establishment reduced naturally at such a moment to its simplest expression (they were burning-up candle-ends and there were no luxuries) she would not answer for the service. The matter ended in the old lady's going out of the room in quest of syrup with the female domestic who had appeared in response to the bell and in whom Jasper's appeal aroused no visible intelligence.

She remained away some time and I talked with her son, who was sociable but desultory and kept moving about the room, always with his fan, as if he were impatient. Sometimes he seated himself for an instant on the window-sill, and then I saw that he was in fact very good-looking; a fine brown, clean young athlete. He never told me on what special contingency his decision depended; he only alluded familiarly to an expected telegram, and I perceived that he was probably not addicted to copious explanations. His mother's absence was an indication that when it was a question of gratifying him she had grown used to spare no pains, and I fancied her rummaging in some close storeroom, among old preserve-pots, while the dull maid-servant held the candle awry. I know not whether this same vision was in his own eyes; at all events it did not prevent him from saying suddenly, as he looked at his watch, that I must excuse him, as he had to go back to the club. He would return in half an hour—or in less. He walked away and I sat there alone, conscious, in the dark, dismantled, simplified room, in the deep silence that rests on American towns during the hot season (there was now and then a far cry or a plash in the water, and at intervals the tinkle of the bells of the horse-cars on the long bridge, slow in the suffocating night), of the strange influence, half sweet, half sad, that abides in houses uninhabited or about to become so—in places muffled and bereaved, where the unheeded sofas and patient belittered tables seem to know (like the disconcerted dogs) that it is the eve of a journey.

After a while I heard the sound of voices, of steps, the rustle of dresses, and I looked round, supposing these things to be the sign of the return of Mrs Nettlepoint and her hand-maiden, bearing the refreshment prepared for her son. What I saw however was two other female forms, visitors just admitted apparently, who were ushered into the room. They were not announced—the servant turned her back on them and rambled off to our hostess. They came forward in a wavering, tentative, unintroduced way—partly, I could see, because the place was dark and partly because their visit was in its nature experimental, a stretch of confidence. One of the ladies was stout and the other was slim, and I perceived in a moment that one was talkative and the other silent. I made out further that one was elderly and the other young and that the fact that they were so unlike did not prevent their being mother and daughter. Mrs Nettlepoint reappeared in a very few minutes, but the interval had sufficed to establish a communication (really copious for the occasion) between the strangers and the unknown gentleman whom they found in possession, hat and stick in hand. This was not my doing (for what had I to go upon?) and still less was it the doing of the person whom I supposed and whom I indeed quickly and definitely learned to be the daughter. She spoke but once—when her companion informed me that she was going out to Europe the next day to be married. Then she said, "Oh, mother!" protestingly, in a tone which struck me in the darkness as doubly strange, exciting my curiosity to see her face.

It had taken her mother but a moment to come to that and to other things besides, after I had explained that I myself was waiting for Mrs Nettlepoint, who would doubtless soon come back.

"Well, she won't know me—I guess she hasn't ever heard much about me," the good lady said; "but I have come from Mrs Allen and I guess that will make it all right. I presume you know Mrs Allen?"

I was unacquainted with this influential personage, but I assented vaguely to the proposition. Mrs Allen's emissary was

good-humoured and familiar, but rather appealing than
insistent (she remarked that if her friend *had* found time to
come in the afternoon—she had so much to do, being just up
for the day, that she couldn't be sure—it would be all right);
and somehow even before she mentioned Merrimac Avenue
(they had come all the way from there) my imagination had
associated her with that indefinite social limbo known to the
properly-constituted Boston mind as the South End—a nebu-
lous region which condenses here and there into a pretty
face, in which the daughters are an "improvement" on the
mothers and are sometimes acquainted with gentlemen resident in more distinguished districts of the New England
capital—gentlemen whose wives and sisters in turn are not
acquainted with them.

When at last Mrs Nettlepoint came in, accompanied by
candles and by a tray laden with glasses of coloured fluid which
emitted a cool tinkling, I was in a position to officiate as master
of the ceremonies, to introduce Mrs Mavis and Miss Grace
Mavis, to represent that Mrs Allen had recommended them—
nay, had urged them—to come that way, informally, and
had been prevented only by the pressure of occupations so
characteristic of her (especially when she was up from Matta-
poisett just for a few hours' shopping) from herself calling in
the course of the day to explain who they were and what was
the favour they had to ask of Mrs Nettlepoint. Good-natured
women understand each other even when divided by the line
of topographical fashion, and our hostess had quickly mas-
tered the main facts: Mrs Allen's visit in the morning in
Merrimac Avenue to talk of Mrs Amber's great idea, the
classes at the public schools in vacation (she was interested
with an equal charity to that of Mrs Mavis—even in such
weather!—in those of the South End) for games and exer-
cises and music, to keep the poor unoccupied children out of
the streets; then the revelation that it had suddenly been
settled almost from one hour to the other that Grace should

sail for Liverpool, Mr Porterfield at last being ready. He was taking a little holiday; his mother was with him, they had come over from Paris to see some of the celebrated old buildings in England, and he had telegraphed to say that if Grace would start right off they would just finish it up and be married. It often happened that when things had dragged on that way for years they were all huddled up at the end. Of course in such a case she, Mrs Mavis, had had to fly round. Her daughter's passage was taken, but it seemed too dreadful that she should make her journey all alone, the first time she had ever been at sea, without any companion or escort. *She* couldn't go—Mr Mavis was too sick: she hadn't even been able to get him off to the seaside.

"Well, Mrs Nettlepoint is going in that ship," Mrs Allen had said; and she had represented that nothing was simpler than to put the girl in her charge. When Mrs Mavis had replied that that was all very well but that she didn't know the lady, Mrs Allen had declared that that didn't make a speck of difference, for Mrs Nettlepoint was kind enough for anything. It was easy enough to know her, if that was all the trouble. All Mrs Mavis would have to do would be to go up to her the next morning when she took her daughter to the ship (she would see her there on the deck with her party) and tell her what she wanted. Mrs Nettlepoint had daughters herself and she would easily understand. Very likely she would even look after Grace a little on the other side, in such a queer situation, going out alone to the gentleman she was engaged to; she would just help her to turn round before she was married. Mr Porterfield seemed to think they wouldn't wait long, once she was there: they would have it right over at the American consul's. Mrs Allen had said it would perhaps be better still to go and see Mrs Nettlepoint beforehand, that day, to tell her what they wanted: then they wouldn't seem to spring it on her just as she was leaving. She herself (Mrs Allen) would call and say a word for them if she could save ten minutes before catching her train. If she hadn't come it was because she hadn't saved her ten minutes; but she had made them feel that they must come all the same. Mrs Mavis liked that better, because on the ship in the morning there would be such a confusion. She didn't think her daughter would be any trouble—conscientiously she didn't. It was just to have some one to speak to her and not sally forth like a servant-girl going to a situation.

"I see, I am to act as a sort of bridesmaid and to give her away," said Mrs Nettlepoint. She was in fact kind enough for anything and she showed on this occasion that it was easy enough to know her. There is nothing more tiresome than complications at sea, but she accepted without a protest the burden of the young lady's dependence and allowed her, as Mrs Mavis said, to hook herself on. She evidently had the habit of patience, and her reception of her visitors' story reminded me afresh (I was reminded of it whenever I returned to my native land) that my dear compatriots are the people in the world who most freely take mutual accommodation for granted. They have always had to help themselves, and by a magnanimous extension they confound helping each other with that. In no country are there fewer forms and more reciprocities.

It was doubtless not singular that the ladies from Merrimac Avenue should not feel that they were importunate: what was striking was that Mrs Nettlepoint did not appear to suspect it. However, she would in any case have thought it inhuman to show that—though I could see that under the surface she was amused at everything the lady from the South End took for granted. I know not whether the attitude of the younger visitor added or not to the merit of her good-nature. Mr Porterfield's intended took no part in her mother's appeal, scarcely spoke, sat looking at the Back Bay and the lights on the long bridge. She declined the lemonade and the other mixtures which, at Mrs Nettlepoint's request, I offered her, while her mother partook freely of everything and I reflected (for I as freely consumed the reviving liquid) that Mr Jasper had better hurry back if he wished to profit by the refreshment prepared for him.

Was the effect of the young woman's reserve ungracious, or was it only natural that in her particular situation she should not have a flow of compliment at her command? I noticed that Mrs Nettlepoint looked at her often, and certainly though she was undemonstrative Miss Mavis was interesting. The candle-light enabled me to see that if she was not in the very first flower of her youth she was still a handsome girl. Her eyes and hair were dark, her face was pale and she held up her head as if, with its thick braids, it were an appurtenance she was not ashamed of. If her mother was excellent and common she was not common (not flagrantly so) and perhaps not excellent. At all events she would not be, in appearance at least, a dreary appendage, and (in the case of a person "hooking on") that was always something gained. Is it because something of a romantic or pathetic interest usually attaches to a good creature who has been the victim of a "long engagement" that this young lady made an impression on me from the first—favoured as I had been so quickly with this glimpse of her history? Certainly she made no positive appeal; she only held her tongue and smiled, and her smile corrected whatever suggestion might have forced itself upon me that the spirit was dead—the spirit of that promise of which she found herself doomed to carry out the letter.

What corrected it less, I must add, was an odd recollection which gathered vividness as I listened to it—a mental association which the name of Mr Porterfield had evoked. Surely I had a personal impression, over-smeared and confused, of the gentleman who was waiting at Liverpool, or who would be, for Mrs Nettlepoint's *protégée*. I had met him, known him, some time, somewhere, somehow, in Europe. Was he not studying something—very hard—somewhere, probably in

Paris, ten years before, and did he not make extraordinarily
neat drawings, linear and architectural? Didn't he go to a
table d'hôte, at two francs twenty-five, in the Rue Bonaparte,
which I then frequented, and didn't he wear spectacles and a
Scotch plaid arranged in a manner which seemed to say, "I
have trustworthy information that that is the way they do it
in the Highlands"? Was he not exemplary and very poor,
so that I supposed he had no overcoat and his tartan was what
he slept under at night? Was he not working very hard still,
and wouldn't he be in the natural course, not yet satisfied that
he knew enough to launch out? He would be a man of long
preparations—Miss Mavis's white face seemed to speak to one
of that. It appeared to me that if I had been in love with her
I should not have needed to lay such a train to marry her.
Architecture was his line and he was a pupil of the Ecole des
Beaux Arts. This reminiscence grew so much more vivid
with me that at the end of ten minutes I had a curious sense
of knowing—by implication—a good deal about the young
lady.

Even after it was settled that Mrs Nettlepoint would do
everything for her that she could her mother sat a little, sip-
ping her syrup and telling how "low" Mr Mavis had been. At
this period the girl's silence struck me as still more conscious, partly perhaps because she deprecated her mother's
loquacity (she was enough of an "improvement" to measure
that) and partly because she was too full of pain at the idea of
leaving her infirm, her perhaps dying father. I divined that
they were poor and that she would take out a very small
purse for her trousseau. Moreover for Mr Porterfield to make
up the sum his own case would have had to change. If he had
enriched himself by the successful practice of his profession I
had not encountered the buildings he had reared—his reputation had not come to my ears.

Mrs Nettlepoint notified her new friends that she was a
very inactive person at sea: she was prepared to suffer to the

full with Miss Mavis, but she was not prepared to walk with her, to struggle with her, to accompany her to the table. To this the girl replied that she would trouble her little, she was sure: she had a belief that she should prove a wretched sailor and spend the voyage on her back. Her mother scoffed at this picture, prophesying perfect weather and a lovely time, and I said that if I might be trusted, as a tame old bachelor fairly sea-seasoned, I should be delighted to give the new member of our party an arm or any other countenance whenever she should require it. Both the ladies thanked me for this (taking my description only too literally), and the elder one declared that we were evidently going to be such a sociable group that it was too bad to have to stay at home. She inquired of Mrs Nettlepoint if there were any one else—if she were to be accompanied by some of her family; and when our hostess mentioned her son—there was a chance of his embarking but (wasn't it absurd?) he had not decided yet, she rejoined with extraordinary candour—"Oh dear, I do hope he'll go: that would be so pleasant for Grace."

Somehow the words made me think of poor Mr Porterfield's tartan, especially as Jasper Nettlepoint strolled in again at that moment. His mother instantly challenged him: it was ten o'clock; had he by chance made up his great mind? Apparently he failed to hear her, being in the first place surprised at the strange ladies and then struck with the fact that one of them was not strange. The young man, after a slight hesitation, greeted Miss Mavis with a handshake and an "Oh, good evening, how do you do?" He did not utter her name, and I could see that he had forgotten it; but she immediately pronounced his, availing herself of an American girl's discretion to introduce him to her mother.

"Well, you might have told me you knew him all this time!" Mrs Mavis exclaimed. Then smiling at Mrs Nettlepoint she added, "It would have saved me a worry, an acquaintance already begun."

"Ah, my son's acquaintances——!" Mrs Nettlepoint murmured.

"Yes, and my daughter's too!" cried Mrs Mavis, jovially. "Mrs Allen didn't tell us *you* were going," she continued, to the young man.

"She would have been clever if she had been able to!" Mrs Nettlepoint ejaculated.

"Dear mother, I have my telegram," Jasper remarked, looking at Grace Mavis.

"I know you very little," the girl said, returning his observation.

"I've danced with you at some ball—for some sufferers by something or other."

"I think it was an inundation," she replied, smiling. "But it was a long time ago—and I haven't seen you since."

"I have been in far countries—to my loss. I should have said it was for a big fire."

"It was at the Horticultural Hall. I didn't remember your name," said Grace Mavis.

"That is very unkind of you, when I recall vividly that you had a pink dress."

"Oh, I remember that dress—you looked lovely in it!" Mrs Mavis broke out. "You must get another just like it—on the other side."

"Yes, your daughter looked charming in it," said Jasper Nettlepoint. Then he added to the girl—"Yet you mentioned my name to your mother."

"It came back to me—seeing you here. I had no idea this was your home."

"Well, I confess it isn't, much. Oh, there are some drinks!" Jasper went on, approaching the tray and its glasses.

"Indeed there are and quite delicious," Mrs Mavis declared.

"Won't you have another then?—a pink one, like your daughter's gown."

"With pleasure, sir. Oh, do see them over," Mrs Mavis

continued, accepting from the young man's hand a third tumbler.

"My mother and that gentleman? Surely they can take care of themselves," said Jasper Nettlepoint.

"But my daughter—she has a claim as an old friend."

"Jasper, what does your telegram say?" his mother interposed.

He gave no heed to her question: he stood there with his glass in his hand, looking from Mrs Mavis to Miss Grace.

"Ah, leave her to me, madam; I'm quite competent," I said to Mrs Mavis.

Then the young man looked at me. The next minute he asked of the young lady—"Do you mean you are going to Europe?"

"Yes, to-morrow; in the same ship as your mother."

"That's what we've come here for, to see all about it," said Mrs Mavis.

"My son, take pity on me and tell me what light your telegram throws," Mrs Nettlepoint went on.

"I will, dearest, when I've quenched my thirst." And Jasper slowly drained his glass.

"Well, you're worse than Gracie," Mrs Mavis commented. "She was first one thing and then the other—but only about up to three o'clock yesterday."

"Excuse me—won't you take something?" Jasper inquired of Gracie; who however declined, as if to make up for her mother's copious *consommation*. I made privately the reflection that the two ladies ought to take leave, the question of Mrs Nettlepoint's goodwill being so satisfactorily settled and the meeting of the morrow at the ship so near at hand; and I went so far as to judge that their protracted stay, with their hostess visibly in a fidget, was a sign of a want of breeding. Miss Grace after all then was not such an improvement on her mother, for she easily might have taken the initiative of departure, in spite of Mrs Mavis's imbibing her glass of syrup in little interspaced sips, as if to make it last as long as possible. I watched the girl with an increasing curiosity; I could not help asking myself a question or two about her and even perceiving already (in a dim and general way) that there were some complications in her position. Was it not a complication that she should have wished to remain long enough to assuage a certain suspense, to learn whether or no Jasper were going to sail? Had not something particular passed between them on the occasion or at the period to which they had covertly alluded, and did she really not know that her mother was bringing her to *his* mother's, though she apparently had thought it well not to mention the circumstance? Such things were complications on the part of a young lady betrothed to that curious cross-barred phantom of a Mr Porterfield. But I am bound to add that she gave me no further warrant for suspecting them than by the simple fact of her encouraging her mother, by her immobility, to linger. Somehow I had a sense that *she* knew better. I got up myself to go, but Mrs Nettlepoint detained me after seeing that my movement would not be taken as a hint, and I perceived she wished me not to leave my fellow-visitors on her hands. Jasper complained of the closeness of the room, said that it was not a night to sit in a room—one ought to be out in the air, under the sky. He denounced the windows that overlooked the water for not opening upon a balcony or a terrace, until his mother, whom he had not yet satisfied about his telegram, reminded him that there was a beautiful balcony in front, with room for a dozen people. She assured him we would go and sit there if it would please him.

"It will be nice and cool to-morrow, when we steam into the great ocean," said Miss Mavis, expressing with more vivacity than she had yet thrown into any of her utterances my own thought of half an hour before. Mrs Nettlepoint replied that it would probably be freezing cold, and her son murmured that he would go and try the drawing-room balcony and report upon it. Just as he was turning away he said, smiling, to Miss Mavis—"Won't you come with me and see if it's pleasant?"

"Oh, well, we had better not stay all night!" her mother exclaimed, but without moving. The girl moved, after a moment's hesitation; she rose and accompanied Jasper into the other room. I observed that her slim tallness showed to advantage as she walked and that she looked well as she passed, with her head thrown back, into the darkness of the other part of the house. There was something rather marked, rather surprising (I scarcely knew why, for the act was simple enough) in her doing so, and perhaps it was our sense of this that held the rest of us somewhat stiffly silent as she remained away. I was waiting for Mrs Mavis to go, so that I myself might go; and Mrs Nettlepoint was waiting for her to go so that I might not. This doubtless made the young lady's absence appear to us longer than it really was—it was probably very brief. Her mother moreover, I think, had a vague consciousness of embarrassment. Jasper Nettlepoint presently returned to the back drawing-room to get a glass of syrup for his companion, and he took occasion to remark that it was lovely on the balcony: one really got some air, the breeze was from that quarter. I remembered, as he went away with his tinkling tumbler, that from *my* hand, a few minutes before, Miss Mavis had not been willing to accept this innocent offering. A little later Mrs Nettlepoint said—"Well, if it's so pleasant there we had better go ourselves." So we passed to the front and in the other room met the two young people coming in from the balcony. I wondered in the light of subsequent events exactly how long they had been sitting there together. (There were three or four cane chairs which had been placed there for the summer.) If it had been but five minutes, that only made subsequent events more curious. "We must go, mother," Miss Mavis immediately said; and a moment later, with a little renewal of chatter as to our general meeting on the ship, the visitors had taken leave. Jasper went down with them to the door and as soon as they had gone out Mrs Nettlepoint exclaimed—"Ah, but she'll be a bore—she'll be a bore!"

"Not through talking too much—surely."

"An affectation of silence is as bad. I hate that particular *pose;* it's coming up very much now; an imitation of the English, like everything else. A girl who tries to be statuesque at sea—that will act on one's nerves!"

"I don't know what she tries to be, but she succeeds in being very handsome."

"So much the better for you. I'll leave her to you, for I shall be shut up. I like her being placed under my 'care.'"

"She will be under Jasper's," I remarked.

"Ah, he won't go—I want it too much."

"I have an idea he will go."

"Why didn't he tell me so then—when he came in?"

"He was diverted by Miss Mavis—a beautiful unexpected girl sitting there."

"Diverted from his mother—trembling for his decision?"

"She's an old friend; it was a meeting after a long separation."

"Yes, such a lot of them as he knows!" said Mrs Nettlepoint.

"Such a lot of them?"

"He has so many female friends—in the most varied circles."

"Well, we can close round her then—for I on my side knew, or used to know, her young man."

"Her young man?"

"The *fiancé*, the intended, the one she is going out to. He can't by the way be very young now."

"How odd it sounds!" said Mrs Nettlepoint.

I was going to reply that it was not odd if you knew Mr Porterfield, but I reflected that that perhaps only made it odder. I told my companion briefly who he was—that I had met him in the old days in Paris, when I believed for a fleeting hour that I could learn to paint, when I lived with the *jeunesse des écoles*, and her comment on this was simply— "Well, he had better have come out for her!"

"Perhaps so. She looked to me as she sat there as if she might change her mind at the last moment."

"About her marriage?"

"About sailing. But she won't change now."

Jasper came back, and his mother instantly challenged him. "Well, *are* you going?"

"Yes, I shall go," he said, smiling. "I have got my telegram."

"Oh, your telegram!" I ventured to exclaim. "That charming girl is your telegram."

He gave me a look, but in the dusk I could not make out very well what it conveyed. Then he bent over his mother, kissing her. "My news isn't particularly satisfactory. I am going for *you*."

"Oh, you humbug!" she rejoined. But of course she was delighted.

II

PEOPLE usually spend the first hours of a voyage in squeezing themselves into their cabins, taking their little precautions, either so excessive or so inadequate, wondering how they can pass so many days in such a hole and asking idiotic questions of the stewards, who appear in comparison such men of the world. My own initiations were rapid, as became an old sailor, and so it seemed were Miss Mavis's, for when I mounted to the deck at the end of half an hour I found her there alone, in the stern of the ship, looking back at the dwindling continent. It dwindled very fast for so big a place. I accosted her, having had no conversation with her amid the crowd of leave-takers and the muddle of farewells before we put off; we talked a little about the boat, our fellow-passengers and our prospects, and then I said—"I think you mentioned last night a name I know—that of Mr Porterfield."

"Oh no, I never uttered it," she replied, smiling at me through her closely-drawn veil.

"Then it was your mother."

"Very likely it was my mother." And she continued to smile, as if I ought to have known the difference.

"I venture to allude to him because I have an idea I used to know him," I went on.

"Oh, I see." Beyond this remark she manifested no interest in my having known him.

"That is if it's the same one." It seemed to me it would be silly to say nothing more; so I added "My Mr Porterfield was called David."

"Well, so is ours." "Ours" struck me as clever.

"I suppose I shall see him again if he is to meet you at Liverpool," I continued.

"Well, it will be bad if he doesn't."

It was too soon for me to have the idea that it would be bad if he did: that only came later. So I remarked that I had not seen him for so many years that it was very possible I should not know him.

"Well, I have not seen him for a great many years, but I expect I shall know him all the same."

"Oh, with you it's different," I rejoined, smiling at her. "Hasn't he been back since those days?"

"I don't know what days you mean."

"When I knew him in Paris—ages ago. He was a pupil of the Ecole des Beaux Arts. He was studying architecture."

"Well, he is studying it still," said Grace Mavis.

"Hasn't he learned it yet?"

"I don't know what he has learned. I shall see." Then she

added: "Architecture is very difficult and he is tremendously thorough."

"Oh, yes, I remember that. He was an admirable worker. But he must have become quite a foreigner, if it's so many years since he has been at home."

"Oh, he is not changeable. If he were changeable———" But here my interlocutress paused. I suspect she had been going to say that if he were changeable he would have given her up long ago. After an instant she went on: "He wouldn't have stuck so to his profession. You can't make much by it."

"You can't make much?"

"It doesn't make you rich."

"Oh, of course you have got to practise it—and to practise it long."

"Yes—so Mr Porterfield says."

Something in the way she uttered these words made me laugh—they were so serene an implication that the gentleman in question did not live up to his principles. But I checked myself, asking my companion if she expected to remain in Europe long—to live there.

"Well, it will be a good while if it takes me as long to come back as it has taken me to go out."

"And I think your mother said last night that it was your first visit."

Miss Mavis looked at me a moment. "Didn't mother talk!"

"It was all very interesting."

She continued to look at me. "You don't think that."

"What have I to gain by saying it if I don't?"

"Oh, men have always something to gain."

"You make me feel a terrible failure, then! I hope at any rate that it gives you pleasure—the idea of seeing foreign lands."

"Mercy—I should think so."

"It's a pity our ship is not one of the fast ones, if you are impatient."

She was silent a moment; then she exclaimed, "Oh, I guess it will be fast enough!"

That evening I went in to see Mrs Nettlepoint and sat on her sea-trunk, which was pulled out from under the berth to accommodate me. It was nine o'clock but not quite dark, as our northward course had already taken us into the latitude of the longer days. She had made her nest admirably and lay upon her sofa in a becoming dressing-gown and cap, resting from her labours. It was her regular practice to spend the voyage in her cabin, which smelt good (such was the refinement of her art), and she had a secret peculiar to herself for keeping her port open without shipping seas. She hated what she called the mess of the ship and the idea, if she should go above, of meeting stewards with plates of supererogatory food. She professed to be content with her situation (we promised to lend each other books and I assured her familiarly that I should be in and out of her room a dozen times a day), and pitied me for having to mingle in society. She judged this to be a limited privilege, for on the deck before we left the wharf she had taken a view of our fellow-passengers.

"Oh, I'm an inveterate, almost a professional observer," I replied, "and with that vice I am as well occupied as an old woman in the sun with her knitting. It puts it in my power, in any situation, to *see* things. I shall see them even here and I shall come down very often and tell you about them. You are not interested to-day, but you will be to-morrow, for a ship is a great school of gossip. You won't believe the number of researches and problems you will be engaged in by the middle of the voyage."

"I? Never in the world—lying here with my nose in a book and never seeing any thing."

"You will participate at second hand. You will see through my eyes, hang upon my lips, take sides, feel passions, all sorts of sympathies and indignations. I have an idea that your young lady is the person on board who will interest me most."

"Mine, indeed! She has not been near me since we left the dock."

"Well, she is very curious."

"You have such cold-blooded terms," Mrs Nettlepoint murmured. "*Elle ne sait pas se conduire;* she ought to have come to ask about me."

"Yes, since you are under her care," I said, smiling. "As for her not knowing how to behave—well, that's exactly what we shall see."

"You will, but not I! I wash my hands of her."

"Don't say that—don't say that."

Mrs Nettlepoint looked at me a moment. "Why do you speak so solemnly?"

In return I considered her. "I will tell you before we land. And have you seen much of your son?"

"Oh yes, he has come in several times. He seems very much pleased. He has got a cabin to himself."

"That's great luck," I said, "but I have an idea he is always in luck. I was sure I should have to offer him the second berth in my room."

"And you wouldn't have enjoyed that, because you don't like him," Mrs Nettlepoint took upon herself to say.

"What put that into your head?"

"It isn't in my head—it's in my heart, my *cœur de mère*. We guess those things. You think he's selfish—I could see it last night."

"Dear lady," I said, "I have no general ideas about him at all. He is just one of the phenomena I am going to observe. He seems to me a very fine young man. However," I added, "since you have mentioned last night I will admit that I thought he rather tantalised you. He played with your suspense."

"Why, he came at the last just to please me," said Mrs Nettlepoint.

I was silent a moment. "Are you sure it was for your sake?"

"Ah, perhaps it was for yours!"

"When he went out on the balcony with that girl perhaps she asked him to come," I continued.

"Perhaps she did. But why should he do everything she asks him?"

"I don't know yet, but perhaps I shall know later. Not that he will tell me—for he will never tell me anything: he is not one of those who tell."

"If she didn't ask him, what you say is a great wrong to her," said Mrs Nettlepoint.

"Yes, if she didn't. But you say that to protect Jasper, not to protect her," I continued, smiling.

"You *are* cold-blooded—it's uncanny!" my companion exclaimed.

"Ah, this is nothing yet! Wait a while—you'll see. At sea in general I'm awful—I pass the limits. If I have outraged her in thought I will jump overboard. There are ways of asking (a man doesn't need to tell a woman that) without the crude words."

"I don't know what you suppose between them," said Mrs Nettlepoint.

"Nothing but what was visible on the surface. It transpired, as the newspapers say, that they were old friends."

"He met her at some promiscuous party—I asked him about it afterwards. She is not a person he could ever think of seriously."

"That's exactly what I believe."

"You don't observe—you imagine," Mrs Nettlepoint pursued. "How do you reconcile her laying a trap for Jasper with her going out to Liverpool on an errand of love?"

"I don't for an instant suppose she laid a trap; I believe she acted on the impulse of the moment. She is going out to Liverpool on an errand of marriage; that is not necessarily the same thing as an errand of love, especially for one who happens to have had a personal impression of the gentleman she is engaged to."

"Well, there are certain decencies which in such a situation the most abandoned of her sex would still observe. You apparently judge her capable—on no evidence—of violating them."

"Ah, you don't understand the shades of things," I rejoined. "Decencies and violations—there is no need for such heavy artillery! I can perfectly imagine that without the least immodesty she should have said to Jasper on the balcony, in fact if not in words—'I'm in dreadful spirits, but if you come I shall feel better, and that will be pleasant for you too.'"

"And why is she in dreadful spirits?"

"She isn't!" I replied, laughing.

"What is she doing?"

"She is walking with your son."

Mrs Nettlepoint said nothing for a moment, then she broke out, inconsequently—"Ah, she's horrid!"

"No, she's charming!" I protested.

"You mean she's 'curious'?"

"Well, for me it's the same thing!"

This led my friend of course to declare once more that I was cold-blooded. On the afternoon of the morrow we had another talk, and she told me that in the morning Miss Mavis had paid her a long visit. She knew nothing about anything, but her intentions were good and she was evidently in her own eyes conscientious and decorous. And Mrs Nettlepoint concluded these remarks with the exclamation "Poor young thing!"

"You think she is a good deal to be pitied, then?"

"Well, her story sounds dreary—she told me a great deal of it. She fell to talking little by little and went from one thing to another. She's in that situation when a girl *must* open herself—to some woman."

"Hasn't she got Jasper?" I inquired.

"He isn't a woman. You strike me as jealous of him," my companion added.

"I daresay *he* thinks so—or will before the end. Ah no—
ah no!" And I asked Mrs Nettlepoint if our young lady struck
her as a flirt. She gave me no answer, but went on to remark
that it was odd and interesting to her to see the way a girl
like Grace Mavis resembled the girls of the kind she herself
knew better, the girls of "society," at the same time that she
differed from them; and the way the differences and resem-
blances were mixed up, so that on certain questions you
couldn't tell where you would find her. You would think she
would feel as you did because you had found her feeling so,
and then suddenly, in regard to some other matter (which
was yet quite the same) she would be terribly wanting. Mrs
Nettlepoint proceeded to observe (to such idle speculations
does the vanity of a sea-voyage give encouragement) that
she wondered whether it were better to be an ordinary girl
very well brought up or an extraordinary girl not brought up
at all.

"Oh, I go in for the extraordinary girl under all circumstances."

"It is true that if you are *very* well brought up you are not
ordinary," said Mrs Nettlepoint, smelling her strong salts.
"You are a lady, at any rate. *C'est toujours ça.*"

"And Miss Mavis isn't one—is that what you mean?"

"Well—you have seen her mother."

"Yes, but I think your contention would be that among
such people the mother doesn't count."

"Precisely; and that's bad."

"I see what you mean. But isn't it rather hard? If your
mother doesn't know anything it is better you should be independent of her, and yet if you are that constitutes a bad note."
I added that Mrs Mavis had appeared to count sufficiently two
nights before. She had said and done everything she wanted,
while the girl sat silent and respectful. Grace's attitude (so far
as her mother was concerned) had been eminently decent.

"Yes, but she couldn't bear it," said Mrs Nettlepoint.

"Ah, if you know it I may confess that she has told me as much."

Mrs Nettlepoint stared. "Told you? There's one of the things they do!"

"Well, it was only a word. Won't you let me know whether you think she's a flirt?"

"Find out for yourself, since you pretend to study folks."

"Oh, your judgment would probably not at all determine mine. It's in regard to yourself that I ask it."

"In regard to myself?"

"To see the length of maternal immorality."

Mrs Nettlepoint continued to repeat my words. "Maternal immorality?"

"You desire your son to have every possible distraction on his voyage, and if you can make up your mind in the sense I refer to that will make it all right. He will have no responsibility."

"Heavens, how you analyse! I haven't in the least your passion for making up my mind."

"Then if you chance it you'll be more immoral still."

"Your reasoning is strange," said the poor lady; "when it was you who tried to put it into my head yesterday that she had asked him to come."

"Yes, but in good faith."

"How do you mean in good faith?"

"Why, as girls of that sort do. Their allowance and measure in such matters is much larger than that of young ladies who have been, as you say, *very* well brought up; and yet I am not sure that on the whole I don't think them the more innocent. Miss Mavis is engaged, and she's to be married next week, but it's an old, old story, and there's no more romance in it than if she were going to be photographed. So her usual life goes on, and her usual life consists (and that of ces demoiselles in general) in having plenty of gentlemen's society. Having it I mean without having any harm from it."

"Well, if there is no harm from it what are you talking about and why am I immoral?"

I hesitated, laughing. "I retract—you are sane and clear. I am sure she thinks there won't be any harm," I added. "That's the great point."

"The great point?"

"I mean, to be settled."

"Mercy, we are not trying them! How can *we* settle it?"

"I mean of course in our minds. There will be nothing more interesting for the next ten days for our minds to exercise themselves upon."

"They will get very tired of it," said Mrs Nettlepoint.

"No, no, because the interest will increase and the plot will thicken. It can't help it." She looked at me as if she thought me slightly Mephistophelean, and I went on—"So she told you everything in her life was dreary?"

"Not everything but most things. And she didn't tell me so much as I guessed it. She'll tell me more the next time. She will behave properly now about coming in to see me; I told her she ought to."

"I am glad of that," I said. "Keep her with you as much as possible."

"I don't follow you much," Mrs Nettlepoint replied, "but so far as I do I don't think your remarks are in very good taste."

"I'm too excited, I lose my head, cold-blooded as you think me. Doesn't she like Mr Porterfield?"

"Yes, that's the worst of it."

"The worst of it?"

"He's so good—there's no fault to be found with him. Otherwise she would have thrown it all up. It has dragged on since she was eighteen: she became engaged to him before he went abroad to study. It was one of those childish muddles which parents in America might prevent so much more than they do. The thing is to insist on one's daughter's waiting, on the engagement's being long; and then after you have got that started to take it on every occasion as little seriously as possible—to make it die out. You can easily tire it out. However, Mr Porterfield has taken it seriously for some years. He has done his part to keep it alive. She says he adores her."

"His part? Surely his part would have been to marry her by this time."

"He has absolutely no money."

"He ought to have got some, in seven years."

"So I think she thinks. There are some sorts of poverty that are contemptible. But he has a little more now. That's why he won't wait any longer. His mother has come out, she has something—a little—and she is able to help him. She will live with them and bear some of the expenses, and after her death the son will have what there is."

"How old is she?" I asked, cynically.

"I haven't the least idea. But it doesn't sound very inspiring. He has not been to America since he first went out."

"That's an odd way of adoring her."

"I made that objection mentally, but I didn't express it to her. She met it indeed a little by telling me that he had had other chances to marry."

"That surprises me," I remarked. "And did she say that *she* had had?"

"No, and that's one of the things I thought nice in her; for she must have had. She didn't try to make out that he had spoiled her life. She has three other sisters and there is very little money at home. She has tried to make money; she has written little things and painted little things, but her talent is apparently not in that direction. Her father has had a long illness and has lost his place—he was in receipt of a salary in connection with some waterworks—and one of her sisters has lately become a widow, with children and without means. And so as in fact she never has married any one else, whatever opportunities she may have encountered, she appears to have

just made up her mind to go out to Mr Porterfield as the least
of her evils. But it isn't very amusing."

"That only makes it the more honourable. She will go
through with it, whatever it costs, rather than disappoint him
after he has waited so long. It is true," I continued, "that
when a woman acts from a sense of honour——"

"Well, when she does?" said Mrs Nettlepoint, for I hesitated perceptibly.

"It is so extravagant a course that some one has to pay
for it."

"You are very impertinent. We all have to pay for each
other, all the while; and for each other's virtues as well as
vices."

"That's precisely why I shall be sorry for Mr Porterfield
when she steps off the ship with her little bill. I mean with her
teeth clenched."

"Her teeth are not in the least clenched. She is in perfect
good-humour."

"Well, we must try and keep her so," I said. "You must
take care that Jasper neglects nothing."

I know not what reflections this innocent pleasantry of
mine provoked on the good lady's part; the upshot of them
at all events was to make her say—"Well, I never asked her
to come; I'm very glad of that. It is all their own doing."

"Their own—you mean Jasper's and hers?"

"No indeed. I mean her mother's and Mrs Allen's; the
girl's too of course. They put themselves upon us."

"Oh yes, I can testify to that. Therefore I'm glad too. We
should have missed it, I think."

"How seriously you take it!" Mrs Nettlepoint exclaimed.

"Ah, wait a few days!" I replied, getting up to leave her.

III

THE *Patagonia* was slow, but she was spacious and comfortable, and there was a kind of motherly decency in her long, nursing rock and her rustling, old-fashioned gait. It was as if she wished not to present herself in port with the splashed eagerness of a young creature. We were not numerous enough to squeeze each other and yet we were not too few to entertain—with that familiarity and relief which figures and objects acquire on the great bare field of the ocean, beneath the great bright glass of the sky. I had never liked the sea so much before, indeed I had never liked it at all; but now I had a revelation of how, in a midsummer mood, it could please. It was darkly and magnificently blue and imperturbably quiet—save for the great regular swell of its heart-beats, the pulse of its life, and there grew to be something so agreeable in the sense of floating there in infinite isolation and leisure that it was a positive satisfaction the *Patagonia* was not a racer. One had never thought of the sea as the great place of safety, but now it came over one that there is no place so safe from the land. When it does not give you trouble it takes it away—takes away letters and telegrams and newspapers and visits and duties and efforts, all the complications, all the superfluities and superstitions that we have stuffed into our terrene life. The simple absence of the post, when the particular conditions enable you to enjoy the great fact by which it is produced, becomes in itself a kind of bliss, and the clean stage of the deck shows you a play that amuses, the personal drama of the voyage, the movement and interaction, in the strong sea-light, of figures that end by representing something—something moreover of which the interest is never, even in its keenness, too great to suffer you to go to sleep. I, at any rate, dozed a great deal, lying on my

rug with a French novel, and when I opened my eyes I generally saw Jasper Nettlepoint passing with his mother's *protégée*
on his arm. Somehow at these moments, between sleeping
and waking, I had an inconsequent sense that they were a
part of the French novel. Perhaps this was because I had
fallen into the trick, at the start, of regarding Grace Mavis
almost as a married woman, which, as every one knows, is the
necessary status of the heroine of such a work. Every revolution of our engine at any rate would contribute to the effect
of making her one.

In the saloon, at meals, my neighbour on the right was a
certain little Mrs Peck, a very short and very round person
whose head was enveloped in a "cloud" (a cloud of dirty
white wool) and who promptly let me know that she was
going to Europe for the education of her children. I had already perceived (an hour after we left the dock) that some
energetic step was required in their interest, but as we were
not in Europe yet the business could not be said to have
begun. The four little Pecks, in the enjoyment of untram-
melled leisure, swarmed about the ship as if they had been
pirates boarding her, and their mother was as powerless to
check their license as if she had been gagged and stowed away
in the hold. They were especially to be trusted to run between
the legs of the stewards when these attendants arrived with
bowls of soup for the languid ladies. Their mother was too
busy recounting to her fellow-passengers how many years
Miss Mavis had been engaged. In the blank of a marine existence things that are nobody's business very soon become
everybody's, and this was just one of those facts that are pro-
pagated with a mysterious and ridiculous rapidity. The whis-
per that carries them is very small, in the great scale of things,
of air and space and progress, but it is also very safe, for there
is no compression, no sounding-board, to make speakers
responsible. And then repetition at sea is somehow not repetition; monotony is in the air, the mind is flat and everything

recurs—the bells, the meals, the stewards' faces, the romp of children, the walk, the clothes, the very shoes and buttons of passengers taking their exercise. These things grow at last so insipid that, in comparison, revelations as to the personal history of one's companions have a taste even when one cares little about the people.

Jasper Nettlepoint sat on my left hand when he was not upstairs seeing that Miss Mavis had her repast comfortably on deck. His mother's place would have been next mine had she shown herself, and then that of the young lady under her care. The two ladies, in other words, would have been between us, Jasper marking the limit of the party on that side. Miss Mavis was present at luncheon the first day, but dinner passed without her coming in, and when it was half over Jasper remarked that he would go up and look after her.

"Isn't that young lady coming—the one who was here to lunch?" Mrs Peck asked of me as he left the saloon.

"Apparently not. My friend tells me she doesn't like the saloon."

"You don't mean to say she's sick, do you?"

"Oh no, not in this weather. But she likes to be above."

"And is that gentleman gone up to her?"

"Yes, she's under his mother's care."

"And is his mother up there, too?" asked Mrs Peck, whose processes were homely and direct.

"No, she remains in her cabin. People have different tastes. Perhaps that's one reason why Miss Mavis doesn't come to table," I added—"her chaperon not being able to accompany her."

"Her chaperon?"

"Mrs Nettlepoint—the lady under whose protection she is."

"Protection?" Mrs Peck stared at me a moment, moving some valued morsel in her mouth; then she exclaimed, familiarly, "Pshaw!" I was struck with this and I was on

the point of asking her what she meant by it when she continued: "Are we not going to see Mrs Nettlepoint?"

"I am afraid not. She vows that she won't stir from her
sofa."

"Pshaw!" said Mrs Peck again. "That's quite a disappointment."

"Do you know her then?"

"No, but I know all about her." Then my companion
added—"You don't mean to say she's any relation?"

"Do you mean to me?"

"No, to Grace Mavis."

"None at all. They are very new friends, as I happen to
know. Then you are acquainted with our young lady?" I had
not noticed that any recognition passed between them at
luncheon.

"Is she yours too?" asked Mrs Peck, smiling at me.

"Ah, when people are in the same boat—literally—they
belong a little to each other."

"That's so," said Mrs Peck. "I don't know Miss Mavis but
I know all about her—I live opposite to her on Merrimac
Avenue. I don't know whether you know that part."

"Oh yes—it's very beautiful."

The consequence of this remark was another "Pshaw!" But
Mrs Peck went on—"When you've lived opposite to people
like that for a long time you feel as if you were acquainted.
But she didn't take it up to-day; she didn't speak to me. She
knows who I am as well as she knows her own mother."

"You had better speak to her first—she's shy," I remarked.

"Shy? Why she's nearly thirty years old. I suppose you
know where she's going."

"Oh yes—we all take an interest in that."

"That young man, I suppose, particularly."

"That young man?"

"The handsome one, who sits there. Didn't you tell me he
is Mrs Nettlepoint's son?"

"Oh yes; he acts as her deputy. No doubt he does all he can to carry out her function."

Mrs Peck was silent a moment. I had spoken jocosely, but she received my pleasantry with a serious face. "Well, she might let him eat his dinner in peace!" she presently exclaimed.

"Oh, he'll come back!" I said, glancing at his place. The repast continued and when it was finished I screwed my chair round to leave the table. Mrs Peck performed the same movement and we quitted the saloon together. Outside of it was a kind of vestibule, with several seats, from which you could descend to the lower cabins or mount to the promenade-deck. Mrs Peck appeared to hesitate as to her course and then solved the problem by going neither way. She dropped upon one of the benches and looked up at me.

"I thought you said he would come back."

"Young Nettlepoint? I see he didn't. Miss Mavis then has given him half of her dinner."

"It's very kind of her! She has been engaged for ages."

"Yes, but that will soon be over."

"So I suppose—as quick as we land. Every one knows it on Merrimac Avenue. Every one there takes a great interest in it."

"Ah, of course, a girl like that: she has many friends."

"I mean even people who don't know her."

"I see," I went on: "she is so handsome that she attracts attention, people enter into her affairs."

"She *used* to be pretty, but I can't say I think she's anything remarkable to-day. Anyhow, if she attracts attention she ought to be all the more careful what she does. You had better tell her that."

"Oh, it's none of my business!" I replied, leaving Mrs Peck and going above. The exclamation, I confess, was not perfectly in accordance with my feeling, or rather my feeling was not perfectly in harmony with the exclamation. The very first thing I did on reaching the deck was to notice that Miss Mavis was pacing it on Jasper Nettlepoint's arm and that whatever beauty she might have lost, according to Mrs Peck's insinuation, she still kept enough to make one's eyes follow her. She had put on a sort of crimson hood, which was very becoming to her and which she wore for the rest of the voyage. She walked very well, with long steps, and I remember that at this moment the ocean had a gentle evening swell which made the great ship dip slowly, rhythmically, giving a movement that was graceful to graceful pedestrians and a more awkward one to the awkward. It was the loveliest hour of a fine day, the clear early evening, with the glow of the sunset in the air and a purple colour in the sea. I always thought that the waters ploughed by the Homeric heroes must have looked like that. I perceived on that particular occasion moreover that Grace Mavis would for the rest of the voyage be the most visible thing on the ship; the figure that would count most in the composition of groups. She couldn't help it, poor girl; nature had made her conspicuous—important as the painters say. She paid for it by the exposure it brought with it—the danger that people would, as I had said to Mrs Peck, enter into her affairs.

Jasper Nettlepoint went down at certain times to see his mother, and I watched for one of these occasions (on the third day out) and took advantage of it to go and sit by Miss Mavis. She wore a blue veil drawn tightly over her face, so that if the smile with which she greeted me was dim I could account for it partly by that.

"Well, we are getting on—we are getting on," I said, cheerfully, looking at the friendly, twinkling sea.

"Are we going very fast?"

"Not fast, but steadily. *Ohne Hast, ohne Rast*—do you know German?"

"Well, I've studied it—some."

"It will be useful to you over there when you travel."

"Well yes, if we do. But I don't suppose we shall much. Mr Nettlepoint says we ought," my interlocutress added in a moment.

"Ah, of course *he* thinks so. He has been all over the world."

"Yes, he has described some of the places. That's what I should like. I didn't know I should like it so much."

"Like what so much?"

"Going on this way. I could go on for ever, for ever and ever."

"Ah, you know it's not always like this," I rejoined.

"Well, it's better than Boston."

"It isn't so good as Paris," I said, smiling.

"Oh, I know all about Paris. There is no freshness in that. I feel as if I had been there."

"You mean you have heard so much about it?"

"Oh yes, nothing else for ten years."

I had come to talk with Miss Mavis because she was attractive, but I had been rather conscious of the absence of a good topic, not feeling at liberty to revert to Mr Porterfield. She had not encouraged me, when I spoke to her as we were leaving Boston, to go on with the history of my acquaintance with this gentleman; and yet now, unexpectedly, she appeared to imply (it was doubtless one of the disparities mentioned by Mrs Nettlepoint) that he might be glanced at without indelicacy.

"I see, you mean by letters," I remarked.

"I shan't live in a good part. I know enough to know that," she went on.

"Dear young lady, there are no bad parts," I answered, reassuringly.

"Why, Mr Nettlepoint says it's horrid."

"It's horrid?"

"Up there in the Batignolles. It's worse than Merrimac Avenue."

"Worse—in what way?"

"Why, even less where the nice people live."

"He oughtn't to say that," I returned. "Don't you call Mr Porterfield a nice person?" I ventured to subjoin.

"Oh, it doesn't make any difference." She rested her eyes on me a moment through her veil, the texture of which gave them a suffused prettiness. "Do you know him very well?" she asked.

"Mr Porterfield?"

"No, Mr Nettlepoint."

"Ah, very little. He's a good deal younger than I."

She was silent a moment; after which she said: "He's younger than me, too." I know not what drollery there was in this but it was unexpected and it made me laugh. Neither do I know whether Miss Mavis took offence at my laughter, though I remember thinking at the moment with compunction that it had brought a certain colour to her cheek. At all events she got up, gathering her shawl and her books into her arm. "I'm going down—I'm tired."

"Tired of me, I'm afraid."

"No, not yet."

"I'm like you," I pursued. "I should like it to go on and on."

She had begun to walk along the deck to the companionway and I went with her. "Oh, no, I shouldn't, after all!"

I had taken her shawl from her to carry it, but at the top of the steps that led down to the cabins I had to give it back. "Your mother would be glad if she could know," I observed as we parted.

"If she could know?"

"How well you are getting on. And that good Mrs Allen."

"Oh, mother, mother! She made me come, she pushed me off." And almost as if not to say more she went quickly below.

I paid Mrs Nettlepoint a morning visit after luncheon and another in the evening, before she "turned in." That same day, in the evening, she said to me suddenly, "Do you know what I have done? I have asked Jasper."

"Asked him what?"

"Why, if *she* asked him, you know."

"I don't understand."

"You do perfectly. If that girl really asked him—on the balcony—to sail with us."

"My dear friend, do you suppose that if she did he would tell you?"

"That's just what he says. But he says she didn't."

"And do you consider the statement valuable?" I asked, laughing out. "You had better ask Miss Gracie herself."

Mrs Nettlepoint stared. "I couldn't do that."

"Incomparable friend, I am only joking. What does it signify now?"

"I thought you thought everything signified. You were so full of signification!"

"Yes, but we are farther out now, and somehow in mid-ocean everything becomes absolute."

"What else *can* he do with decency?" Mrs Nettlepoint went on. "If, as my son, he were never to speak to her it would be very rude and you would think that stranger still. Then *you* would do what he does, and where would be the difference?"

"How do you know what he does? I haven't mentioned him for twenty-four hours."

"Why, she told me herself: she came in this afternoon."

"What an odd thing to tell you!" I exclaimed.

"Not as she says it. She says he's full of attention, perfectly devoted—looks after her all the while. She seems to want me to know it, so that I may commend him for it."

"That's charming; it shows her good conscience."

"Yes, or her great cleverness."

Something in the tone in which Mrs Nettlepoint said this caused me to exclaim in real surprise, "Why, what do you suppose she has in her mind?"

"To get hold of him, to make him go so far that he can't retreat, to marry him, perhaps."

"To marry him? And what will she do with Mr Porterfield?"

"She'll ask me just to explain to him—or perhaps you."

"Yes, as an old friend!" I replied, laughing. But I asked more seriously, "Do you see Jasper caught like that?"

"Well, he's only a boy—he's younger at least than she."

"Precisely; she regards him as a child."

"As a child?"

"She remarked to me herself to-day that he is so much younger."

Mrs Nettlepoint stared. "Does she talk of it with you? That shows she has a plan, that she has thought it over!"

I have sufficiently betrayed that I deemed Grace Mavis a singular girl, but I was far from judging her capable of laying a trap for our young companion. Moreover my reading of Jasper was not in the least that he was catchable—could be made to do a thing if he didn't want to do it. Of course it was not impossible that he might be inclined, that he might take it (or already have taken it) into his head to marry Miss Mavis; but to believe this I should require still more proof than his always being with her. He wanted at most to marry her for the voyage. "If you have questioned him perhaps you have tried to make him feel responsible," I said to his mother.

"A little, but it's very difficult. Interference makes him perverse. One has to go gently. Besides, it's too absurd—think of her age. If she can't take care of herself!" cried Mrs Nettlepoint.

"Yes, let us keep thinking of her age, though it's not so prodigious. And if things get very bad you have one resource left," I added.

"What is that?"

"You can go upstairs."

"Ah, never, never! If it takes that to save her she must be lost. Besides, what good would it do? If I were to go up she could come down here."

"Yes, but you could keep Jasper with you."

"Could I?" Mrs Nettlepoint demanded, in the manner of a woman who knew her son.

In the saloon the next day, after dinner, over the red cloth of the tables, beneath the swinging lamps and the racks of tumblers, decanters and wine-glasses, we sat down to whist, Mrs Peck, among others, taking a hand in the game. She played very badly and talked too much, and when the rubber was over assuaged her discomfiture (though not mine—we had been partners) with a Welsh rabbit and a tumbler of something hot. We had done with the cards, but while she waited for this refreshment she sat with her elbows on the table shuffling a pack.

"She hasn't spoken to me yet—she won't do it," she remarked in a moment.

"Is it possible there is any one on the ship who hasn't spoken to you?"

"Not that girl—she knows too well!" Mrs Peck looked round our little circle with a smile of intelligence—she had familiar, communicative eyes. Several of our company had assembled, according to the wont, the last thing in the evening, of those who are cheerful at sea, for the consumption of grilled sardines and devilled bones.

"What then does she know?"

"Oh, she knows that I know."

"Well, we know what Mrs Peck knows," one of the ladies of the group observed to me, with an air of privilege.

"Well, you wouldn't know if I hadn't told you—from the way she acts," said Mrs Peck, with a small laugh.

"She is going out to a gentleman who lives over there—

he's waiting there to marry her," the other lady went on, in the tone of authentic information. I remember that her name was Mrs Gotch and that her mouth looked always as if she were whistling.

"Oh, he knows—I've told him," said Mrs Peck.

"Well, I presume every one knows," Mrs Gotch reflected.

"Dear madam, is it every one's business?" I asked.

"Why, don't you think it's a peculiar way to act?" Mrs Gotch was evidently surprised at my little protest.

"Why, it's right there—straight in front of you, like a play at the theatre—as if you had paid to see it," said Mrs Peck. "If you don't call it public——!"

"Aren't you mixing things up? What do you call public?"

"Why, the way they go on. They are up there now."

"They cuddle up there half the night," said Mrs Gotch. "I don't know when they come down. Any hour you like—when all the lights are out they are up there still."

"Oh, you can't tire them out. They don't want relief—like the watch!" laughed one of the gentlemen.

"Well, if they enjoy each other's society what's the harm?" another asked. "They'd do just the same on land."

"They wouldn't do it on the public streets, I suppose," said Mrs Peck. "And they wouldn't do it if Mr Porterfield was round!"

"Isn't that just where your confusion comes in?" I inquired. "It's public enough that Miss Mavis and Mr Nettlepoint are always together, but it isn't in the least public that she is going to be married."

"Why, how can you say—when the very sailors know it! The captain knows it and all the officers know it; they see them there—especially at night, when they're sailing the ship."

"I thought there was some rule——" said Mrs Gotch.

"Well, there is—that you've got to behave yourself," Mrs Peck rejoined. "So the captain told me—he said they have some rule. He said they have to have, when people are too demonstrative."

"Too demonstrative?"

"When they attract so much attention."

"Ah, it's we who attract the attention—by talking about what doesn't concern us and about what we really don't know," I ventured to declare.

"She said the captain said he would tell on her as soon as we arrive," Mrs Gotch interposed.

"*She* said——?" I repeated, bewildered.

"Well, he did say so, that he would think it his duty to inform Mr Porterfield, when he comes on to meet her—if they keep it up in the same way," said Mrs Peck.

"Oh, they'll keep it up, don't you fear!" one of the gentlemen exclaimed.

"Dear madam, the captain is laughing at you."

"No, he ain't—he's right down scandalised. He says he regards us all as a real family and wants the family to be properly behaved." I could see Mrs Peck was irritated by my controversial tone: she challenged me with considerable spirit. "How can you say I don't know it when all the street knows it and has known it for years—for years and years?" She spoke as if the girl had been engaged at least for twenty. "What is she going out for, if not to marry him?"

"Perhaps she is going to see how he looks," suggested one of the gentlemen.

"He'd look queer—if he knew."

"Well, I guess he'll know," said Mrs Gotch.

"She'd tell him herself—she wouldn't be afraid," the gentleman went on.

"Well, she might as well kill him. He'll jump overboard."

"Jump overboard?" cried Mrs Gotch, as if she hoped then that Mr Porterfield would be told.

"He has just been waiting for this—for years," said Mrs Peck.

"Do you happen to know him?" I inquired.

Mrs Peck hesitated a moment. "No, but I know a lady who does. Are you going up?"

I had risen from my place—I had not ordered supper. "I'm going to take a turn before going to bed."

"Well then, you'll see!"

Outside the saloon I hesitated, for Mrs Peck's admonition made me feel for a moment that if I ascended to the deck I should have entered in a manner into her little conspiracy. But the night was so warm and splendid that I had been intending to smoke a cigar in the air before going below, and I did not see why I should deprive myself of this pleasure in order to seem not to mind Mrs Peck. I went up and saw a few figures sitting or moving about in the darkness. The ocean looked black and small, as it is apt to do at night, and the long mass of the ship, with its vague dim wings, seemed to take up a great part of it. There were more stars than one saw on land and the heavens struck one more than ever as larger than the earth. Grace Mavis and her companion were not, so far as I perceived at first, among the few passengers who were lingering late, and I was glad, because I hated to hear her talked about in the manner of the gossips I had left at supper. I wished there had been some way to prevent it, but I could think of no way but to recommend her privately to change her habits. That would be a very delicate business, and perhaps it would be better to begin with Jasper, though that would be delicate too. At any rate one might let him know, in a friendly spirit, to how much remark he exposed the young lady— leaving this revelation to work its way upon him. Unfortunately I could not altogether believe that the pair were unconscious of the observation and the opinion of the passengers. They were not a boy and a girl; they had a certain social perspective in their eye. I was not very clear as to the details of that behaviour which had made them (according to the version of my good friends in the saloon) a scandal to the ship, for though I looked at them a good deal I evidently had not looked at them so continuously and so hungrily as Mrs Peck. Nevertheless the probability was that they knew what was thought of them—what naturally would be—and simply didn't care. That made Miss Mavis out rather cynical and even a little immodest; and yet, somehow, if she had such qualities I did not dislike her for them. I don't know what strange, secret excuses I found for her. I presently indeed encountered a need for them on the spot, for just as I was on the point of going below again, after several restless turns and (within the limit where smoking was allowed) as many puffs at a cigar as I cared for, I became aware that a couple of figures were seated behind one of the lifeboats that rested on the deck. They were so placed as to be visible only to a person going close to the rail and peering a little sidewise. I don't think I peered, but as I stood a moment beside the rail my eye was attracted by a dusky object which protruded beyond the boat and which, as I saw at a second glance, was the tail of a lady's dress. I bent forward an instant, but even then I saw very little more; that scarcely mattered, however, for I took for granted on the spot that the persons concealed in so snug a corner were Jasper Nettlepoint and Mr Porterfield's intended. Concealed was the word, and I thought it a real pity; there was bad taste in it. I immediately turned away and the next moment I found myself face to face with the captain of the ship. I had already had some conversation with him (he had been so good as to invite me, as he had invited Mrs Nettlepoint and her son and the young lady travelling with them, and also Mrs Peck, to sit at his table) and had observed with pleasure that he had the art, not universal on the Atlantic liners, of mingling urbanity with seamanship.

"They don't waste much time—your friends in there," he said, nodding in the direction in which he had seen me looking.

"Ah well, they haven't much to lose."

"That's what I mean. I'm told *she* hasn't."

I wanted to say something exculpatory but I scarcely knew what note to strike. I could only look vaguely about me at the starry darkness and the sea that seemed to sleep. "Well, with these splendid nights, this perfection of weather, people are beguiled into late hours."

"Yes. We want a nice little blow," the captain said.

"A nice little blow?"

"That would clear the decks!"

The captain was rather dry and he went about his business. He had made me uneasy and instead of going below I walked a few steps more. The other walkers dropped off pair by pair (they were all men) till at last I was alone. Then, after a little, I quitted the field. Jasper and his companion were still behind their lifeboat. Personally I greatly preferred good weather, but as I went down I found myself vaguely wishing, in the interest of I scarcely knew what, unless of decorum, that we might have half a gale.

Miss Mavis turned out, in sea-phrase, early; for the next morning I saw her come up only a little while after I had finished my breakfast, a ceremony over which I contrived not to dawdle. She was alone and Jasper Nettlepoint, by a rare accident, was not on deck to help her. I went to meet her (she was encumbered as usual with her shawl, her sun-umbrella and a book) and laid my hands on her chair, placing it near the stern of the ship, where she liked best to be. But I proposed to her to walk a little before she sat down and she took my arm after I had put her accessories into the chair. The deck was clear at that hour and the morning light was gay; one got a sort of exhilarated impression of fair conditions and an absence of hindrance. I forget what we spoke of first, but it was because I felt these things pleasantly, and not to torment my companion nor to test her, that I could not help exclaiming cheerfully, after a moment, as I have mentioned having done the first day, "Well, we are getting on, we are getting on!"

"Oh yes, I count every hour."

"The last days always go quicker," I said, "and the last hours——"

"Well, the last hours?" she asked; for I had instinctively checked myself.

"Oh, one is so glad then that it is almost the same as if one had arrived. But we ought to be grateful when the elements have been so kind to us," I added. "I hope you will have enjoyed the voyage."

She hesitated a moment, then she said, "Yes, much more than I expected."

"Did you think it would be very bad?"

"Horrible, horrible!"

The tone of these words was strange but I had not much time to reflect upon it, for turning round at that moment I saw Jasper Nettlepoint come towards us. He was separated from us by the expanse of the white deck and I could not help looking at him from head to foot as he drew nearer. I know not what rendered me on this occasion particularly sensitive to the impression, but it seemed to me that I saw him as I had never seen him before—saw him inside and out, in the intense sea-light, in his personal, his moral totality. It was a quick, vivid revelation; if it only lasted a moment it had a simplifying, certifying effect. He was intrinsically a pleasing apparition, with his handsome young face and a certain absence of compromise in his personal arrangements which, more than any one I have ever seen, he managed to exhibit on shipboard. He had none of the appearance of wearing out old clothes that usually prevails there, but dressed straight, as I heard some one say. This gave him a practical, successful air, as of a young man who would come best out of any predicament. I expected to feel my companion's hand loosen itself on my arm, as indication that now she must go to him, and was almost surprised she did not drop me. We stopped as we met and Jasper bade us a friendly good-morning. Of course the

remark was not slow to be made that we had another lovely
day, which led him to exclaim, in the manner of one to whom
criticism came easily, "Yes, but with this sort of thing consider what one of the others would do!"

"One of the other ships?"

"We should be there now, or at any rate to-morrow."

"Well then, I'm glad it isn't one of the others," I said,
smiling at the young lady on my arm. My remark offered her
a chance to say something appreciative and gave him one
even more; but neither Jasper nor Grace Mavis took advantage of the opportunity. What they did do, I perceived, was to
look at each other for an instant; after which Miss Mavis
turned her eyes silently to the sea. She made no movement
and uttered no word, contriving to give me the sense that she
had all at once become perfectly passive, that she somehow
declined responsibility. We remained standing there with
Jasper in front of us, and if the touch of her arm did not suggest that I should give her up, neither did it intimate that we
had better pass on. I had no idea of giving her up, albeit one
of the things that I seemed to discover just then in Jasper's
physiognomy was an imperturbable implication that she was
his property. His eye met mine for a moment, and it was
exactly as if he had said to me, "I know what you think, but I
don't care a rap." What I really thought was that he was selfish
beyond the limits: that was the substance of my little revelation. Youth is almost always selfish, just as it is almost always
conceited, and, after all, when it is combined with health and
good parts, good looks and good spirits, it has a right to be,
and I easily forgive it if it be really youth. Still it is a question
of degree, and what stuck out of Jasper Nettlepoint (if one felt
that sort of thing) was that his egotism had a hardness, his love
of his own way an avidity. These elements were jaunty and
prosperous, they were accustomed to triumph. He was fond,
very fond, of women; they were necessary to him and that
was in his type; but he was not in the least in love with Grace

Mavis. Among the reflections I quickly made this was the one that was most to the point. There was a degree of awkwardness, after a minute, in the way we were planted there, though the apprehension of it was doubtless not in the least with him.

"How is your mother this morning?" I asked.

"You had better go down and see."

"Not till Miss Mavis is tired of me."

She said nothing to this and I made her walk again. For some minutes she remained silent; then, rather unexpectedly, she began: "I've seen you talking to that lady who sits at our table—the one who has so many children."

"Mrs Peck? Oh yes, I have talked with her."

"Do you know her very well?"

"Only as one knows people at sea. An acquaintance makes itself. It doesn't mean very much."

"She doesn't speak to me—she might if she wanted."

"That's just what she says of you—that you might speak to her."

"Oh, if she's waiting for that——!" said my companion, with a laugh. Then she added—"She lives in our street, nearly opposite."

"Precisely. That's the reason why she thinks you might speak; she has seen you so often and seems to know so much about you."

"What does she know about me?"

"Ah, you must ask her—I can't tell you!"

"I don't care what she knows," said my young lady. After a moment she went on—"She must have seen that I'm not very sociable." And then—"What are you laughing at?"

My laughter was for an instant irrepressible—there was something so droll in the way she had said that.

"Well, you are not sociable and yet you are. Mrs Peck is, at any rate, and thought that ought to make it easy for you to enter into conversation with her."

"Oh, I don't care for her conversation—I know what it

amounts to." I made no rejoinder—I scarcely knew what rejoinder to make—and the girl went on, "I know what she thinks and I know what she says." Still I was silent, but the next moment I saw that my delicacy had been wasted, for Miss Mavis asked, "Does she make out that she knows Mr Porterfield?"

"No, she only says that she knows a lady who knows him."

"Yes, I know—Mrs Jeremie. Mrs Jeremie's an idiot!" I was not in a position to controvert this, and presently my young lady said she would sit down. I left her in her chair—I saw that she preferred it—and wandered to a distance. A few minutes later I met Jasper again, and he stopped of his own accord and said to me—

"We shall be in about six in the evening, on the eleventh day—they promise it."

"If nothing happens, of course."

"Well, what's going to happen?"

"That's just what I'm wondering!" And I turned away and went below with the foolish but innocent satisfaction of thinking that I had mystified him.

IV

"I DON'T know what to do, and you must help me," Mrs Nettlepoint said to me that evening, as soon as I went in to see her.

"I'll do what I can—but what's the matter?"

"She has been crying here and going on—she has quite upset me."

"Crying? She doesn't look like that."

"Exactly, and that's what startled me. She came in to see me this afternoon, as she has done before, and we talked about the weather and the run of the ship and the manners of the stewardess and little commonplaces like that, and then suddenly, in the midst of it, as she sat there, *à propos* of nothing, she burst into tears. I asked her what ailed her and tried to comfort her, but she didn't explain; she only said it was nothing, the effect of the sea, of leaving home. I asked her if it had anything to do with her prospects, with her marriage; whether she found as that drew near that her heart was not in it; I told her that she mustn't be nervous, that I could enter into that—in short I said what I could. All that she replied was that she *was* nervous, very nervous, but that it was already over; and then she jumped up and kissed me and went away. Does she look as if she had been crying?" Mrs Nettlepoint asked.

"How can I tell, when she never quits that horrid veil? It's as if she were ashamed to show her face."

"She's keeping it for Liverpool. But I don't like such incidents," said Mrs Nettlepoint. "I shall go upstairs."

"And is that where you want me to help you?"

"Oh, your arm and that sort of thing, yes. But something more. I feel as if something were going to happen."

"That's exactly what I said to Jasper this morning."

"And what did he say?"

"He only looked innocent, as if he thought I meant a fog or a storm."

"Heaven forbid—it isn't that! I shall never be good-natured again," Mrs Nettlepoint went on; "never have a girl put upon me that way. You always pay for it, there are always tiresome complications. What I am afraid of is after we get there. She'll throw up her engagement; there will be dreadful scenes; I shall be mixed up with them and have to look after her and keep her with me. I shall have to stay there with her till she can be sent back, or even take her up to London. *Voyez-vous ça?*"

I listened respectfully to this and then I said: "You are afraid of your son."

"Afraid of him?"

"There are things you might say to him—and with your manner; because you have one when you choose."

"Very likely, but what is my manner to his? Besides, I have said everything to him. That is I have said the great thing, that he is making her immensely talked about."

"And of course in answer to that he has asked you how you know, and you have told him I have told you."

"I had to; and he says it's none of your business."

"I wish he would say that to my face."

"He'll do so perfectly, if you give him a chance. That's where you can help me. Quarrel with him—he's rather good at a quarrel, and that will divert him and draw him off."

"Then I'm ready to discuss the matter with him for the rest of the voyage."

"Very well; I count on you. But he'll ask you, as he asks me, what the deuce you want him to do."

"To go to bed," I replied, laughing.

"Oh, it isn't a joke."

"That's exactly what I told you at first."

"Yes, but don't exult; I hate people who exult. Jasper wants to know why he should mind her being talked about if she doesn't mind it herself."

"I'll tell him why," I replied; and Mrs Nettlepoint said she should be exceedingly obliged to me and repeated that she would come upstairs.

I looked for Jasper above that same evening, but circumstances did not favour my quest. I found him—that is I discovered that he was again ensconced behind the lifeboat with Miss Mavis; but there was a needless violence in breaking into their communion, and I put off our interview till the next day. Then I took the first opportunity, at breakfast, to make sure of it. He was in the saloon when I went in and was preparing to leave the table; but I stopped him and asked if he would give me a quarter of an hour on deck a little later—there was

something particular I wanted to say to him. He said, "Oh
yes, if you like," with just a visible surprise, but no look of an
uncomfortable consciousness. When I had finished my breakfast I found him smoking on the forward-deck and I immediately began : "I am going to say something that you won't
at all like; to ask you a question that you will think impertinent."

"Impertinent? that's bad."

"I am a good deal older than you and I am a friend—of
many years—of your mother. There's nothing I like less
than to be meddlesome, but I think these things give me a
certain right—a sort of privilege. For the rest, my inquiry will
speak for itself."

"Why so many preliminaries?" the young man asked,
smiling.

We looked into each other's eyes a moment. What indeed
was his mother's manner—her best manner—compared with
his? "Are you prepared to be responsible?"

"To you?"

"Dear no—to the young lady herself. I am speaking of
course of Miss Mavis."

"Ah yes, my mother tells me you have her greatly on
your mind."

"So has your mother herself—now."

"She is so good as to say so—to oblige you."

"She would oblige me a great deal more by reassuring me.
I am aware that you know I have told her that Miss Mavis is
greatly talked about."

"Yes, but what on earth does it matter?"

"It matters as a sign."

"A sign of what?"

"That she is in a false position."

Jasper puffed his cigar, with his eyes on the horizon. "I
don't know whether it's *your* business, what you are attempt-
ing to discuss; but it really appears to me it is none of mine.

What have I to do with the tattle with which a pack of old women console themselves for not being sea-sick?"

"Do you call it tattle that Miss Mavis is in love with you?"

"Drivelling."

"Then you are very ungrateful. The tattle of a pack of old women has this importance, that she suspects or knows that it exists, and that nice girls are for the most part very sensitive to that sort of thing. To be prepared not to heed it in this case she must have a reason, and the reason must be the one I have taken the liberty to call your attention to."

"In love with me in six days, just like that?" said Jasper, smoking.

"There is no accounting for tastes, and six days at sea are equivalent to sixty on land. I don't want to make you too proud. Of course if you recognise your responsibility it's all right and I have nothing to say."

"I don't see what you mean," Jasper went on.

"Surely you ought to have thought of that by this time. She's engaged to be married and the gentleman she is engaged to is to meet her at Liverpool. The whole ship knows it (I didn't tell them!) and the whole ship is watching her. It's impertinent if you like, just as I am, but we make a little world here together and we can't blink its conditions. What I ask you is whether you are prepared to allow her to give up the gentleman I have just mentioned for your sake."

"For my sake?"

"To marry her if she breaks with him."

Jasper turned his eyes from the horizon to my own, and I found a strange expression in them. "Has Miss Mavis commissioned you to make this inquiry?"

"Never in the world."

"Well then, I don't understand it."

"It isn't from another I make it. Let it come from yourself—*to* yourself."

"Lord, you must think I lead myself a life! That's a question the young lady may put to me any moment that it pleases her."

"Let me then express the hope that she will. But what will you answer?"

"My dear sir, it seems to me that in spite of all the titles you have enumerated you have no reason to expect I will tell you." He turned away and I exclaimed, sincerely, "Poor girl!" At this he faced me again and, looking at me from head to foot, demanded: "What is it you want me to do?"

"I told your mother that you ought to go to bed."

"You had better do that yourself!"

This time he walked off, and I reflected rather dolefully that the only clear result of my experiment would probably have been to make it vivid to him that she was in love with him. Mrs Nettlepoint came up as she had announced, but the day was half over: it was nearly three o'clock. She was accompanied by her son, who established her on deck, arranged her chair and her shawls, saw that she was protected from sun and wind, and for an hour was very properly attentive. While this went on Grace Mavis was not visible, nor did she reappear during the whole afternoon. I had not observed that she had as yet been absent from the deck for so long a period. Jasper went away, but he came back at intervals to see how his mother got on, and when she asked him where Miss Mavis was he said he had not the least idea. I sat with Mrs Nettlepoint at her particular request: she told me she knew that if I left her Mrs Peck and Mrs Gotch would come to speak to her. She was flurried and fatigued at having to make an effort, and I think that Grace Mavis's choosing this occasion for retirement suggested to her a little that she had been made a fool of. She remarked that the girl's not being there showed her complete want of breeding and that she was really very good to have put herself out for her so; she was a common creature and that was the end of it. I could see that Mrs Nettlepoint's advent quickened the speculative activity of the other ladies; they watched her from the opposite side of the deck, keeping their eyes fixed on her very much as the man at the wheel kept his on the course of the ship. Mrs Peck plainly meditated an approach, and it was from this danger that Mrs Nettlepoint averted her face.

"It's just as we said," she remarked to me as we sat there. "It is like the bucket in the well. When I come up that girl goes down."

"Yes, but you've succeeded, since Jasper remains here."

"Remains? I don't see him."

"He comes and goes—it's the same thing."

"He goes more than he comes. But *n'en parlons plus;* I haven't gained anything. I don't admire the sea at all—what is it but a magnified water-tank? I shan't come up again."

"I have an idea she'll stay in her cabin now," I said. "She tells me she has one to herself." Mrs Nettlepoint replied that she might do as she liked, and I repeated to her the little conversation I had had with Jasper.

She listened with interest, but "Marry her? mercy!" she exclaimed. "I like the manner in which you give my son away."

"You wouldn't accept that."

"Never in the world."

"Then I don't understand your position."

"Good heavens, I have none! It isn't a position to be bored to death"

"You wouldn't accept it even in the case I put to him— that of her believing she had been encouraged to throw over poor Porterfield?"

"Not even—not even. Who knows what she believes?"

"Then you do exactly what I said you would—you show me a fine example of maternal immorality."

"Maternal fiddlesticks! It was she began it."

"Then why did you come up to-day?"

"To keep you quiet."

Mrs Nettlepoint's dinner was served on deck, but I went into the saloon. Jasper was there but not Grace Mavis, as I had half expected. I asked him what had become of her, if she were ill (he must have thought I had an ignoble pertinacity), and he replied that he knew nothing whatever about her. Mrs Peck talked to me about Mrs Nettlepoint and said it had been a great interest to her to see her; only it was a pity she didn't seem more sociable. To this I replied that she had to beg to be excused—she was not well.

"You don't mean to say she's sick, on this pond?"

"No, she's unwell in another way."

"I guess I know the way!" Mrs Peck laughed. And then she added, "I suppose she came up to look after her charge."

"Her charge?"

"Why, Miss Mavis. We've talked enough about that."

"Quite enough. I don't know what that had to do with it. Miss Mavis hasn't been there to-day."

"Oh, it goes on all the same."

"It goes on?"

"Well, it's too late."

"Too late?"

"Well, you'll see. There'll be a row."

This was not comforting, but I did not repeat it above. Mrs Nettlepoint returned early to her cabin, professing herself much tired. I know not what "went on," but Grace Mavis continued not to show. I went in late, to bid Mrs Nettlepoint good-night, and learned from her that the girl had not been to her. She had sent the stewardess to her room for news, to see if she were ill and needed assistance, and the stewardess came back with the information that she was not there. I went above after this; the night was not quite so fair and the deck was almost empty. In a moment Jasper Nettlepoint and our young lady moved past me together. "I hope you are better!" I called after her; and she replied, over her shoulder—

"Oh, yes, I had a headache; but the air now does me good!"

I went down again—I was the only person there but they, and I wished to not appear to be watching them—and returning to Mrs Nettlepoint's room found (her door was open into the little passage) that she was still sitting up.

"She's all right!" I said. "She's on the deck with Jasper."

The old lady looked up at me from her book. "I didn't know you called that all right."

"Well, it's better than something else."

"Something else?"

"Something I was a little afraid of." Mrs Nettlepoint continued to look at me; she asked me what that was. "I'll tell you when we are ashore," I said.

The next day I went to see her, at the usual hour of my morning visit, and found her in considerable agitation. "The scenes have begun," she said; "you know I told you I shouldn't get through without them! You made me nervous last night—I haven't the least idea what you meant; but you made me nervous. She came in to see me an hour ago, and I had the courage to say to her, 'I don't know why I shouldn't tell you frankly that I have been scolding my son about you.' Of course she asked me what I meant by that, and I said—'It seems to me he drags you about the ship too much, for a girl in your position. He has the air of not remembering that you belong to some one else. There is a kind of want of taste and even of want of respect in it.' That produced an explosion; she became very violent."

"Do you mean angry?"

"Not exactly angry, but very hot and excited—at my presuming to think her relations with my son were not the simplest in the world. I might scold him as much as I liked—that was between ourselves; but she didn't see why I should tell her that I had done so. Did I think she allowed him to treat her with disrespect? That idea was not very complimentary to her! He had treated her better and been kinder to her than most other people—there were very few on the ship that hadn't been insulting. She should be glad enough when she got off it, to her own people, to some one whom no one would have a right to say anything about. What was there in her position that was not perfectly natural? what was the idea of making a fuss about her position? Did I mean that she took it too easily—that she didn't think as much as she ought about Mr Porterfield? Didn't I believe she was attached to him— didn't I believe she was just counting the hours until she saw him? That would be the happiest moment of her life. It showed how little I knew her, if I thought anything else."

"All that must have been rather fine—I should have liked to hear it," I said. "And what did you reply?"

"Oh, I grovelled; I told her that I accused her (as regards my son) of nothing worse than an excess of good nature. She helped him to pass his time—he ought to be immensely obliged. Also that it would be a very happy moment for me too when I should hand her over to Mr Porterfield."

"And will you come up to-day?"

"No indeed—she'll do very well now."

I gave a sigh of relief. "All's well that ends well!"

Jasper, that day, spent a great deal of time with his mother. She had told me that she really had had no proper opportunity to talk over with him their movements after disembarking. Everything changes a little, the last two or three days of a voyage; the spell is broken and new combinations take place. Grace Mavis was neither on deck nor at dinner, and I drew Mrs Peck's attention to the extreme propriety with which she now conducted herself. She had spent the day in meditation and she judged it best to continue to meditate.

"Ah, she's afraid," said my implacable neighbour.

"Afraid of what?"

"Well, that we'll tell tales when we get there."

"Whom do you mean by 'we'?"

"Well, there are plenty, on a ship like this."

"Well then, we won't."

"Maybe we won't have the chance," said the dreadful little woman.

"Oh, at that moment a universal geniality reigns."

"Well, she's afraid, all the same."

"So much the better."

"Yes, so much the better."

All the next day, too, the girl remained invisible and Mrs Nettlepoint told me that she had not been in to see her. She had inquired by the stewardess if she would receive her in her own cabin, and Grace Mavis had replied that it was littered up with things and unfit for visitors: she was packing a trunk over. Jasper made up for his devotion to his mother the day before by now spending a great deal of his time in the smoking-room. I wanted to say to him "This is much better," but I thought it wiser to hold my tongue. Indeed I had begun to feel the emotion of prospective arrival (I was delighted to be almost back in my dear old Europe again) and had less to spare for other matters. It will doubtless appear to the critical reader that I had already devoted far too much to the little episode of which my story gives an account, but to this I can only reply that the event justified me. We sighted land, the dim yet rich coast of Ireland, about sunset and I leaned on the edge of the ship and looked at it. "It doesn't look like much, does it?" I heard a voice say, beside me; and turning, I found Grace Mavis was there. Almost for the first time she had her veil up, and I thought her very pale.

"It will be more to-morrow," I said.

"Oh yes, a great deal more."

"The first sight of land, at sea, changes everything," I went on. "I always think it's like waking up from a dream. It's a return to reality."

For a moment she made no response to this; then she said, "It doesn't look very real yet."

"No, and meanwhile, this lovely evening, the dream is still present."

She looked up at the sky, which had a brightness, though the light of the sun had left it and that of the stars had not come out. "It *is* a lovely evening."

"Oh yes, with this we shall do."

She stood there a while longer, while the growing dusk effaced the line of the land more rapidly than our progress made it distinct. She said nothing more, she only looked in front of her; but her very quietness made me want to say something suggestive of sympathy and service. I was unable to think what to say—some things seemed too wide of the mark and others too importunate. At last, unexpectedly, she appeared to give me my chance. Irrelevantly, abruptly she broke out:

"Didn't you tell me that you knew Mr Porterfield?"

"Dear me, yes—I used to see him. I have often wanted to talk to you about him."

She turned her face upon me and in the deepened evening I fancied she looked whiter. "What good would that do?"

"Why, it would be a pleasure," I replied, rather foolishly.

"Do you mean for you?"

"Well, yes—call it that," I said, smiling.

"Did you know him so well?"

My smile became a laugh and I said—"You are not easy to make speeches to."

"I hate speeches!" The words came from her lips with a violence that surprised me; they were loud and hard. But before I had time to wonder at it she went on—"Shall you know him when you see him?"

"Perfectly, I think." Her manner was so strange that one had to notice it in some way, and it appeared to me the best way was to notice it jocularly; so I added, "Shan't you?"

"Oh, perhaps you'll point him out!" And she walked quickly away. As I looked after her I had a singular, a perverse and rather an embarrassed sense of having, during the

previous days, and especially in speaking to Jasper Nettlepoint, interfered with her situation to her loss. I had a sort of
pang in seeing her move about alone; I felt somehow responsible for it and asked myself why I could not have kept my
hands off. I had seen Jasper in the smoking-room more than
once that day, as I passed it, and half an hour before this I had
observed, through the open door, that he was there. He had
been with her so much that without him she had a bereaved,
forsaken air. It was better, no doubt, but superficially it made
her rather pitiable. Mrs Peck would have told me that their
separation was gammon; they didn't show together on deck
and in the saloon, but they made it up elsewhere. The secret
places on shipboard are not numerous; Mrs Peck's "elsewhere" would have been vague and I know not what license
her imagination took. It was distinct that Jasper had fallen off,
but of course what had passed between them on this subject
was not so and could never be. Later, through his mother, I
had *his* version of that, but I may remark that I didn't believe
it. Poor Mrs Nettlepoint did, of course. I was almost capable,
after the girl had left me, of going to my young man and
saying, "After all, do return to her a little, just till we get in!
It won't make any difference after we land." And I don't
think it was the fear he would tell me I was an idiot that prevented me. At any rate the next time I passed the door of the
smoking-room I saw that he had left it. I paid my usual visit
to Mrs Nettlepoint that night, but I troubled her no further
about Miss Mavis. She had made up her mind that everything
was smooth and settled now, and it seemed to me that I had
worried her and that she had worried herself enough. I left
her to enjoy the foretaste of arrival, which had taken possession of her mind. Before turning in I went above and found
more passengers on deck than I had ever seen so late. Jasper
was walking about among them alone, but I forebore to join
him. The coast of Ireland had disappeared, but the night and
the sea were perfect. On the way to my cabin, when I came

down, I met the stewardess in one of the passages and the idea
entered my head to say to her—"Do you happen to know
where Miss Mavis is?"

"Why, she's in her room, sir, at this hour."

"Do you suppose I could speak to her?" It had come into
my mind to ask her why she had inquired of me whether I
should recognise Mr Porterfield.

"No, sir," said the stewardess; "she has gone to bed."

"That's all right." And I followed the young lady's
excellent example.

The next morning, while I was dressing, the steward of my
side of the ship came to me as usual to see what I wanted. But
the first thing he said to me was—"Rather a bad job, sir—a
passenger missing."

"A passenger—missing?"

"A lady, sir. I think you knew her. Miss Mavis, sir."

"*Missing?*" I cried—staring at him, horror-stricken.

"She's not on the ship. They can't find her."

"Then where to God is she?"

I remember his queer face. "Well sir, I suppose you know
that as well as I."

"Do you mean she has jumped overboard?"

"Some time in the night, sir—on the quiet. But it's beyond
every one, the way she escaped notice. They usually sees 'em,
sir. It must have been about half-past two. Lord, but she was
clever, sir. She didn't so much as make a splash. They say
she *'ad* come against her will, sir."

I had dropped upon my sofa—I felt faint. The man went
on, liking to talk, as persons of his class do when they have
something horrible to tell. She usually rang for the stewardess
early, but this morning of course there had been no ring. The
stewardess had gone in all the same about eight o'clock and
found the cabin empty. That was about an hour ago. Her
things were there in confusion—the things she usually wore
when she went above. The stewardess thought she had been

rather strange last night, but she waited a little and then went back. Miss Mavis hadn't turned up—and she didn't turn up. The stewardess began to look for her—she hadn't been seen on deck or in the saloon. Besides, she wasn't dressed—not to show herself; all her clothes were in her room. There was another lady, an old lady, Mrs Nettlepoint—I would know her—that she was sometimes with, but the stewardess had been with *her* and she knew Miss Mavis had not come near her that morning. She had spoken to *him* and they had taken a quiet look—they had hunted everywhere. A ship's a big place, but you do come to the end of it, and if a person ain't there why they ain't. In short an hour had passed and the young lady was not accounted for: from which I might judge if she ever would be. The watch couldn't account for her, but no doubt the fishes in the sea could—poor miserable lady! The stewardess and he, they had of course thought it their duty very soon to speak to the doctor, and the doctor had spoken immediately to the captain. The captain didn't like it —they never did. But he would try to keep it quiet—they always did.

By the time I succeeded in pulling myself together and getting on, after a fashion, the rest of my clothes I had learned that Mrs Nettlepoint had not yet been informed, unless the stewardess had broken it to her within the previous few minutes. Her son knew, the young gentleman on the other side of the ship (he had the other steward); my man had seen him come out of his cabin and rush above, just before he came in to me. He *had* gone above, my man was sure; he had not gone to the old lady's cabin. I remember a queer vision when the steward told me this—the wild flash of a picture of Jasper Nettlepoint leaping with a mad compunction in his young agility over the side of the ship. I hasten to add that no such incident was destined to contribute its horror to poor Grace Mavis's mysterious tragic act. What followed was miserable enough, but I can only glance at it. When I got to

Mrs Nettlepoint's door she was there in her dressing-gown; the stewardess had just told her and she was rushing out to come to me. I made her go back—I said I would go for Jasper. I went for him but I missed him, partly no doubt because it was really, at first, the captain I was after. I found this personage and found him highly scandalised, but he gave me no hope that we were in error, and his displeasure, expressed with seamanlike plainness, was a definite settlement of the question. From the deck, where I merely turned round and looked, I saw the light of another summer day, the coast of Ireland green and near and the sea a more charming colour than it had been at all. When I came below again Jasper had passed back; he had gone to his cabin and his mother had joined him there. He remained there till we reached Liverpool—I never saw him. His mother, after a little, at his request, left him alone. All the world went above to look at the land and chatter about our tragedy, but the poor lady spent the day, dismally enough, in her room. It seemed to me intolerably long; I was thinking so of vague Porterfield and of my prospect of having to face him on the morrow. Now of course I knew why she had asked me if I should recognise him; she had delegated to me mentally a certain pleasant office. I gave Mrs Peck and Mrs Gotch a wide berth—I couldn't talk to them. I could, or at least I did a little, to Mrs Nettlepoint, but with too many reserves for comfort on either side, for I foresaw that it would not in the least do now to mention Jasper to her. I was obliged to assume by my silence that he had had nothing to do with what had happened; and of course I never really ascertained what he *had* had to do. The secret of what passed between him and the strange girl who would have sacrificed her marriage to him on so short an acquaintance remains shut up in his breast. His mother, I know, went to his door from time to time, but he refused her admission. That evening, to be human at a venture, I requested the steward to go in and ask him if he should care to see me, and the attendant returned with an answer which he candidly transmitted. "Not in the least!" Jasper apparently was almost as scandalised as the captain.

At Liverpool, at the dock, when we had touched, twenty people came on board, and I had already made out Mr Porterfield at a distance. He was looking up at the side of the great vessel with disappointment written (to my eyes) in his face—disappointment at not seeing the woman he loved lean over it and wave her handkerchief to him. Every one was looking at him, every one but she (his identity flew about in a moment) and I wondered if he did not observe it. He used to be lean, he had grown almost fat. The interval between us diminished—he was on the plank and then on the deck with the jostling officers of the customs—all too soon for my equanimity. I met him instantly however, laid my hand on him and drew him away, though I perceived that he had no impression of having seen me before. It was not till afterwards that I thought this a little stupid of him. I drew him far away (I was conscious of Mrs Peck and Mrs Gotch looking at us as we passed) into the empty, stale smoking-room; he remained speechless, and that struck me as like him. I had to speak first, he could not even relieve me by saying "Is anything the matter?" I told him first that she was ill. It was an odious moment.

THE SOLUTION

"Oh yes, you may write it down—every one's dead." I profited by my old friend's permission and made a note of the story, which, at the time he told it to me, seemed curious and interesting. Will it strike you in the same light? Perhaps not, but I will run the risk and copy it out for you as I reported it, with just a little amplification from memory. Though every one *is* dead, perhaps you had better not let it go further. My old friend is dead himself, and how can I say how I miss him? He had many merits, and not the least of them was that he was always at home. The infirmities of the last years of his life confined him to London and to his own house, and of an afternoon, between five and six o'clock, I often knocked at his door. He is before me now, as he leans back in his chair, with his eyes wandering round the top of his room as if a thousand ghostly pictures were suspended there. Following his profession in many countries, he had seen much of life and knew much of men. This thing dropped from him piece by piece (one wet, windy spring afternoon, when we happened to be uninterrupted), like a painless belated confession. I have only given it continuity.

I

It was in Rome, a hundred years ago, or as nearly so as it must have been to be an episode of my extreme youth. I was just twenty-three, and attached to our diplomatic agency there; the other secretaries were all my seniors. Is it because I was twenty-three, or because the time and the place were really better, that this period glows in my memory with all sorts of poetic, romantic lights? It seems to me to have consisted of five winters of sunshine without a cloud; of long excursions on the Campagna and in the Alban and Sabine hills; of joyous artists' feasts, spread upon the warm stones of ruined temples and tombs; of splendid Catholic processions and ceremonies; of friendly, familiar evenings, prolonged very late, in the great painted and tapestried saloons of historic palaces. It was the slumberous, pictorial Rome of the Popes, before the Italians had arrived or the local colour departed, and though I have been back there in recent years it is always the early impression that is evoked for me by the name. The yellow steps, where models and beggars lounged in the sun, had a golden tone, and the models and beggars themselves a magnificent brown one, which it looked easy to paint showily. The excavations, in those days, were comparatively few, but the "subjects"—I was an incorrigible sketcher—were many. The carnival lasted a month, the flowers (and even the flower-girls) lasted for ever, and the old statues in the villas and the galleries became one's personal friends.

Of course we had other friends than these, and that is what I am coming to. I have lived in places where the society was perhaps better, but I have lived in none where I liked it better, in spite of the fact that it was considerably pervaded by Mrs Goldie. Mrs Goldie was an English lady, a widow with three daughters, and her name, accompanied not rarely, I fear, with an irreverent objurgation, was inevitably on our lips. She had a house on the Pincian Hill, from winter to winter; she came early in the season and stayed late, and she formed, with her daughters—Rosina, Veronica and Augusta—an uncompromising feature of every entertainment. As the principal object in any view of Rome is the dome of St Peter's, so the most prominent figure in the social prospect was always the Honourable Blanche. She was a daughter of Lord Bolitho, and there were several elderly persons among us who remembered her in the years before her marriage, when her maiden designation was jocosely—I forget what the original joke had been—in people's mouths. They reintroduced it, and it became common in speaking of her. There must have been some public occasion when, as a spinster, she had done battle for her precedence and had roared out her luckless title. She was capable of that.

I was so fond of the place that it appeared to be natural every one else should love it, but I afterwards wondered what could have been the source of Mrs Goldie's interest in it. She didn't know a Raphael from a Caravaggio, and even after many years could not have told you the names of the seven hills. She used to drive her daughters out to sketch, but she would never have done that if she had cared for the dear old ruins. However, it has always been a part of the magic of Rome that the most dissimilar breasts feel its influence; and though it is, or rather it was, the most exquisite place in the world, uncultivated minds have been known to enjoy it as much as students and poets. It has always touched alike the *raffiné* and the barbarian. Mrs Goldie was a good deal of a barbarian, and she had her reasons for liking the Papal city. Her mind was fixed on tea-parties and the "right people to know." She valued the easy sociability, the picnics, the functions, the frequent opportunities for producing her girls. These opportunities indeed were largely of her own making; for she was highly hospitable, in the simple Roman fashion, and held incessant receptions and *conversazioni*. Dinners she never gave, and when she invited you to lunch, *al fresco*, in the shadow of the aqueducts that stride across the plain, she expected you to bring with you a cold chicken and a bottle of wine. No one, however, in those patriarchal times, was thought the worse of in Rome for being frugal. That was another reason why Mrs Goldie had elected to live there; it was the capital in Europe where the least money—and she had but little—would go furthest in the way of grandeur. It cost her nothing to produce her girls, in proportion to the impressiveness of the spectacle.

I don't know what we should have done without her house, for the young men of the diplomatic body, as well as many others, treated it almost as a club. It was largely for our benefit that the Misses Goldie were produced. I sometimes wondered, even in those days, if our sense of honour was quite as fine as it might have been, to have permitted us to amuse ourselves at the expense of this innocent and hospitable group. The jokes we made about them were almost as numerous as the cups of tea that we received from the hands of the young ladies; and though I have never thought that youth is delicate (delicacy is an acquired virtue and comes later), there was this excuse for our esoteric mirth, that it was simply contagious. We laughed at the airs of greatness the Honourable Blanche gave herself and at the rough-and-ready usage to which she subjected the foreign tongues. It even seemed to us droll, in a crowd, to see her push and press and make play with her elbows, followed by the compact wedge of Rosina, Veronica and Augusta, whom she had trained to follow up her advantages. We noted the boldness with which she asked for favours when they were not offered and snatched them when they were refused, and we almost admired the perpetual manœuvres and conspiracies, all of the most public and transparent kind, which did not prevent her from honestly believing that she was the most shrinking and disinterested of women. She was always in a front seat, always flushed with the achievement of getting there, and always looking round and grimacing, signalling and telegraphing, pointing to other places for other people, waving her parasol and fan and marshalling and ordering the girls. She was tall and angular, and held her head very high; it was surmounted with wonderful turbans and plumages, and indeed the four ladies were caparisoned altogether in a manner of their own.

The oddest thing in the mother was that she bragged about the fine people and the fine things she had left behind her in England; she protested too much, and if you had listened to her you would have had the gravest doubts of her origin and breeding. They were genuinely "good," however, and her vulgarity was as incontestable as her connections. It is a mistake to suppose it is only the people who would like to be what they are not who are snobs. That class includes equally many of those who are what the others would like to be. I used to think, of old, that Thackeray overdid his ridicule of certain types; but I always did him justice when I remembered Mrs Goldie. I don't want to finish her off by saying she was good-natured; but she certainly never abused people, and if she was very worldly she was not the only one. She never even thought of the people she didn't like, much less did she speak of them, for all her time was given to talking about her favourites, as she called them, who were usually of princely name (princes in Rome are numerous and *d'un commerce facile*), and her regard for whom was not chilled by the scant pains they sometimes took to encourage it. What was original in her was the candour and, to a certain extent, the brutality with which she played her game.

The girls were not pretty, but they might have been less plain if they had felt less oppressively the responsibility of their looks. You could not say exactly whether they were ugly or only afraid, on every occasion, that their mother would think them so. This expression was naturally the reverse of ornamental. They were good creatures, though they generally had the air of having slept in their clothes in order to be ready in time. Rosina and Augusta were better than Veronica: we had a theory that Veronica had a temper and sometimes "stood up" to her mother. She was the beauty, she had handsome hair, she sang, alas—she quavered out English ditties beneath the Roman *lambris*. She had pretensions individually, in short; the others had not even those that their mother had for them. In general, however, they were bullied and overpowered by their stern parent; all they could do was to follow her like frightened sheep, and they lived with their eyes fixed on her, so as to execute, at a glance from her, the evolutions in which they had been drilled. We were sorry for them, for we were sure that she secretly felt, with rage, that they were not brilliant and sat upon them for it with all her weight, which of course didn't tend to wake them up. None the less we talked of them profanely, and especially of Veronica, who had the habit of addressing us indiscriminately, though so many of us were English, in incomprehensible strange languages.

When I say "we" I must immediately except the young American secretary, with whom we lived much (at least I did, for I liked him, little as the trick I played him may have shown it), and who never was profane about anything: a circumstance to be noticed the more as the conversation of his chief, the representative of the United States *près du Saint-Père* at that time, was apt (though this ancient worthy was not "bearded like the pard," but clean-shaven—once or twice a week) to be full of strange oaths. His name was Henry Wilmerding, he came from some northern State (I am speaking now of the secretary, not of the minister), and he was as fresh and sociable a young fellow as you could wish to see. The minister was the drollest possible type, but we all delighted in him; indeed I think that among his colleagues he was the most popular man in the diplomatic body. He was a product of the Carolinas and always wore a dress-coat and a faded, superannuated neckcloth; his hat and boots were also of a fashion of his own. He talked very slowly, as if he were delivering a public address, used innumerable "sirs," of the forensic, not in the least of the social kind, and always made me feel as if I were the Speaker of the American Congress, though indeed I never should have ventured to call him to order. The curious part of his conversation was that, though it was rich in expletives, it was also extremely sententious: he uttered them with a solemnity which made them patriarchal and scriptural. He used to remind me of the busts of some of the old dry-faced, powerful Roman lawgivers and administrators. He spoke no language but that of his native State, but that mattered little, as we all learned it and practiced it for our amusement. We ended by making constant use of it among ourselves: we talked it to each other in his presence and under his nose. It seems to me, as I look back, that we must have been rare young brutes; but he was an unsuspecting diplomatist. Indeed they were a pair, for I think Wilmerding never knew—he had such a western bloom of his own.

Wilmerding was a gentleman and he was not a fool, but he was not in the least a man of the world. I couldn't fancy in what society he had grown up; I could only see it was something very different from any of our *milieux*. If he had been turned out by one of ours he couldn't have been so innocent without being stupid or so unworldly without being underbred. He was full of natural delicacy, worse luck: if he hadn't been I shouldn't be telling you this little story of my own shame. He once mentioned to me that his ancestors had been Quakers, and though he was not at all what you call a muff (he was a capital rider, and in the exaltation of his ideas of what was due to women a very knight of romance), there was something rather dovelike in his nature, suggestive of drab tints and the smell of lavender. All the Quakers, or people of Quaker origin, of whom I ever heard have been rich, and Wilmerding, happy dog, was not an exception to the rule. I think this was partly the reason why we succumbed to temptation: we should have handled him more tenderly if he had had the same short allowance as ourselves. He never talked of money (I have noticed Americans rarely do—it's a part of their prudery), but he was free-handed and extravagant and evidently had a long purse to draw upon. He used to buy shocking daubs from those of his compatriots who then cultivated "arrt" (they pronounced the word so oddly), in Rome, and I knew a case where he let a fellow have his picture back (it was certainly a small loss), to sell it over again. His family were proprietors of large cotton-mills from which banknotes appeared to flow in inexhaustible streams. They sent him the handsomest remittances and let him know that the question of supplies was the last he need trouble himself about. There was something so enviable, so ideal in such a situation as this that I daresay it aggravated us a little, in spite of our really having such a kindness for him.

It had that effect especially upon one of our little band—a young French attaché, Guy de Montaut, one of the most delightful creatures I have ever known and certainly the Frenchman I have met in the world whom I have liked best. He had all the qualities of his nation and none of its defects —he was born for human intercourse. He loved a joke as well as I, but his jokes as a general thing were better than mine. It is true that this one I am speaking of, in which he had an equal hand, was bad enough. We were united by a community of debt—we owed money at the same places. Montaut's family was so old that they had long ago spent their substance and were not in the habit of pressing unsolicited drafts upon his acceptance. Neither of us quite understood why the diplomatic career should be open to a young Quaker, or the next thing to it, who was a cotton-spinner into the bargain. At the British establishment, at least, no form of dissent less fashionable than the Catholic was recognised, and altogether it was very clear to me that the ways of the Americans were not as our ways. Montaut, as you may believe, was as little as possible of a Quaker; and if he was considerate of women it was in a very different manner from poor Wilmerding. I don't think he respected them much, but he would have insisted that he sometimes spared them. I wondered often how Wilmerding had ever come to be a secretary of legation, as at that period, in America (I don't know how much they have changed it), such posts were obtained by being begged for and "worked" for in various crooked ways. It was impossible to go in less for haughtiness; yet with all Wilmerding's mildness, and his being the model of the nice young man, I couldn't have imagined his asking a favour.

He went to Mrs Goldie's as much as the rest of us, but really no more, I think—no more, certainly, until the summer we all spent at Frascati. During that happy September we were constantly in and out of her house, and it is possible that when the others were out he was sometimes in. I mean that he played backgammon in the loggia of the villa with Rosy and Gussie, and even strolled, or sat, in the dear old Roman garden with them, looking over Veronica's shoulder while her pencil vainly attempted a perspective or a perpendicular. It was a charming, sociable, promiscuous time, and these poor girls were more or less gilded, for all of us, by it. The long, hot Roman summer had driven the strangers away, and the native society had gone into *villeggiatura*. My chief had crossed the Alps, on his annual leave, and the affairs of our house—they were very simple matters, no great international questions—were in the hands of a responsible underling. I forget what had become of Montaut's people; he himself, at any rate, was not to have his holiday till later. We were in the same situation, he and I, save that I had been able to take several bare rooms, for a couple of months, in a rambling old palace in a fold of the Alban hills. The few survivors of our Roman circle were my neighbours there, and I offered hospitality to Montaut, who, as often as he was free, drove out along the Appian Way to stay with me for a day or two at a time. I think he had a little personal tie in Rome which took up a good deal of his time.

The American minister and his lady—she was easily shocked but still more easily reassured—had fled to Switzerland, so that Wilmerding was left to watch over the interests of the United States. He took a furnished villa at Frascati (you could have one for a few *scudi* a month), and gave very pleasant and innocent bachelor parties. If he was often at Mrs Goldie's she returned his visits with her daughters, and I can live over lovely evenings (oh youth, oh memory!) when tables were set for supper in the garden and lighted by the fireflies, when some of the villagers—such voices as one heard there and such natural art!—came in to sing for us, and when we all walked home in the moonlight with the ladies, singing, ourselves, along the road. I am not sure that Mrs Goldie herself didn't warble to the southern night. This is a proof of the humanising, poetising conditions in which we lived. Mrs Goldie had remained near Rome to save money; there was also a social economy in it, as she kept her eye on some of her princesses. Several of these high dames were in residence in our neighbourhood, and we were a happy family together.

I don't quite know why we went to see Mrs Goldie so much if we didn't like her better, unless it be that my immediate colleagues and I inevitably felt a certain loyalty to the principal English house. Moreover we did like the poor lady better in fact than we did in theory and than the irreverent tone we took about her might have indicated. Wilmerding, all the same, remained her best listener, when she poured forth the exploits and alliances of her family. He listened with exaggerated interest—he held it unpardonable to let one's attention wander from a lady, however great a bore she might be. Mrs Goldie thought very well of him, on these and other grounds, though as a general thing she and her daughters didn't like strangers unless they were very great people. In that case they recognised their greatness, but thought they would have been much greater if they had been English. Of the greatness of Americans they had but a limited sense, and they never compared them with the English, the French or even the Romans. The most they did was to compare them with each other; and in this respect they had a sort of measure. They thought the rich ones much less small than the others.

The summer I particularly speak of, Mrs Goldie's was not simply the principal English house but really the only one—that is for the world in general. I knew of another that I had a very different attachment to and was even presumptuous enough to consider that I had an exclusive interest in. It was not exactly a house, however; it was only a big, cool, shabby, frescoed sitting-room in the inn at Albano, a huge, melancholy mansion that had come down in the world. It formed for the time the habitation of a charming woman whom I fondly believed to be more to me than any other human being. This part of my tale is rather fatuous, or it would be if it didn't refer to a hundred years ago. Not that my devotion was of the same order as my friend Montaut's, for the object of it was the most honourable of women, an accomplished English lady. Her name was Mrs Rushbrook, and I should be capable at this hour of telling you a great deal about her. The description that would be most to the purpose, I confess (it puts the matter in a word), is that I was very far gone about her. I was really very bad, and she was some five years my elder, which, given my age, only made my condition more natural. She had been in Rome, for short visits, three or four times during my period there: her little girl was delicate, and her idea was to make a long stay in a southern climate.

She was the widow of an officer in the navy; she spoke of herself as very poor, but I knew enough of her relations in England to be sure that she would suffer no real inconvenience. Moreover she was extravagant, careless, even slightly capricious. If the "Bohemian" had been invented in those days she might possibly have been one—a very small, fresh, dainty one. She was so pretty that she has remained in my mind *the* pretty woman among those I have known, who, thank heaven, have not been few. She had a lovely head, and her chestnut hair was of a shade I have never seen since. And her figure had such grace and her voice such a charm; she was

in short the woman a fellow loves. She was natural and clever
and kind, and though she was five years older than I she
always struck me as an embodiment of youth—of the golden
morning of life. We made such happy discoveries together
when first I knew her: we liked the same things, we disliked
the same people, we had the same favourite statues in the
Vatican, the same secret preferences in regard to views on
the Campagna. We loved Italy in the same way and in the
same degree; that is with the difference that I cared less for it
after I knew her, because I cared so much more for her than
for anything else. She painted, she studied Italian, she collected and noted the songs of the people, and she had the wit
to pick up certain *bibelots* and curiosities—lucky woman—
before other people had thought of them. It was long ago that
she passed out of my ken, and yet I feel that she was very
modern.

Partly as a new-comer (she had been at Sorrento to give her
little girl sea-baths), and partly because she had her own
occupations and lived to herself, she was rather out of our
circle at Frascati. Mrs Goldie had gone to see her, however,
and she had come over to two or three of our parties. Several
times I drove to Albano to fetch her, but I confess that my
quest usually ended in my remaining with her. She joined
more than one of our picnics (it is ridiculous how many we
had), and she was notably present on an important occasion,
the last general meeting before our little colony dispersed.
This was neither more nor less than a tea-party—a regular
five o'clock tea, though the fashion hadn't yet come in—
on the summit of Monte Cavo. It sounds very vulgar, but I
assure you it was delightful. We went up on foot, on ponies,
or donkeys: the animals were for the convenience of the
ladies, and our provisions and utensils were easily carried.
The great heat had abated; besides, it was late in the day. The
Campagna lay beneath us like a haunted sea (if you can
imagine that—the ghosts of dead sentries walking on the

deep) and the glow of the afternoon was divine. You know it all—the way the Alban mount slopes into the plain and the dome of St Peter's rises out of it, the colour of the Sabines, which look so near, the old grey villages, the ruins of cities, of nations, that are scattered on the hills.

Wilmerding was of our party, as a matter of course, and Mrs Goldie and the three girls and Montaut, confound him, with his communicative sense that everything was droll. He hadn't in his composition a grain of respect. Fortunately he didn't need it to make him happy. We had our tea, we looked at the view, we chattered in groups or strolled about in couples: no doubt we desecrated sufficiently a sublime historic spot. We lingered late, but late as it was we perceived, when we gathered ourselves together to descend the little mountain, that Veronica Goldie was missing. So was Henry Wilmerding, it presently appeared; and then it came out that they had been seen moving away together. We looked for them a little; we called for them; we waited for them. We were all there and we talked about them, Mrs Goldie of course rather more loudly than the rest. She qualified their absence, I remember, as a "most extraordinary performance." Montaut said to me, in a lowered voice: "Diable, diable, diable!" I remember his saying also: "You others are very lucky. What would have been thought if it was I?" We waited in a small, a very small, embarrassment, and before long the young lady turned up with her companion. I forget where they had been; they told us, without confusion: they had apparently a perfectly good conscience. They had not really been away long; but it so happened that we all noticed it and that for a quarter of an hour we thought of it. Besides, the dusk had considerably deepened. As soon as they joined us we started homeward. A little later we all separated, and Montaut and I betook ourselves to our own quarters. He said to me that evening, in relation to this little incident: "In my country, you know, he would have to marry her."

"I don't believe it," I answered.

"Well, *he* would believe it, I'm sure."

"I don't believe that."

"Try him and you'll see. He'll believe anything."

The idea of trying him—such is the levity of youth—took possession of me; but at the time I said nothing. Montaut returned to Rome the next day, and a few days later I followed him—my *villeggiatura* was over. Our afternoon at Monte Cavo had had no consequences that I perceived. When I saw Montaut again in Rome one of the first things he said to me was:

"Well, has Wilmerding proposed?"

"Not that I know of."

"Didn't you tell him he ought?"

"My dear fellow, he'd knock me down."

"Never in the world. He'd thank you for the hint—he's so candid." I burst out laughing at this, and he asked if our friend had come back. When I said I had left him at Frascati he exclaimed: "Why, he's compromising her more!"

I didn't quite understand, and I remember asking: "Do you think he really ought to offer her marriage, as a gentleman?"

"Beyond all doubt, in any civilised society."

"What a queer thing, then, is civilisation! Because I'm sure he has done her no harm."

"How can you be sure? However, call it good if you like. It's a benefit one is supposed to pay for the privilege of conferring."

"He won't see it."

"He will if you open his eyes."

"That's not my business. And there's no one to make him see it," I replied.

"Couldn't the Honourable Blanche make him? It seems to me I would trust her."

"Trust her then and be quiet."

"You're afraid of his knocking you down," Montaut said.

I suppose I replied to this remark with another equally derisive, but I remember saying a moment later: "I'm rather curious to see if he would take such a representation seriously."

"I bet you a louis he will!" Montaut declared; and there was something in his tone that led me to accept the bet.

II

In Rome, of a Sunday afternoon, every one went over to St Peter's; I don't know whether the agreeably frivolous habit still prevails: it had little to do, I fear, with the spirit of worship. We went to hear the music—the famous vesper-service of the Papal choir, and also to learn the news, to stroll about and talk and look at each other. If we treated the great church as a public promenade, or rather as a splendid international *salon*, the fault was not wholly our own, and indeed practically there was little profanity in such an attitude. One's attitude was insignificant, and the bright immensity of the place protected conversation and even gossip. It struck one not as a particular temple, but as formed by the very walls of the faith that has no small pruderies to enforce. One early autumn day, in especial, we crossed the Tiber and lifted the ponderous leather curtain of the door to get a general view of the return of our friends to Rome. Half an hour's wandering lighted up the question of who had arrived, as every one, in his degree, went there for a solution of it. At the end of ten minutes I came upon Henry Wilmerding; he was standing still, with his head thrown back and his eyes raised to the far-arching dome as if he had felt its spell for the first time. The body of the church was almost clear of people; the visitors were collected in the chapel where service was held and just outside of it; the splendid chant and the strange high voices of some of the choristers came to us from a great distance. Before Wilmerding saw me I had time to say to him: "I thought you intended to remain at Frascati till the end of the week."

"I did, but I changed my mind."

"You came away suddenly, then?"

"Yes, it was rather sudden."

"Are you going back?" I presently asked.

"There's nothing particular to go back for."

I hesitated a moment. "Was there anything particular to come away for?"

"My dear fellow, not that I know of," he replied, with a slight flush in his cheek—an intimation (not that I needed it), that I had a little the air of challenging his right to go and come as he chose.

"Not in relation to those ladies?"

"Those ladies?"

"Don't be so unnaturally blank. Your dearest friends."

"Do you mean the Goldies?"

"Don't overdo it. Whom on earth should I mean?"

It is difficult to explain, but there was something youthfully bland in poor Wilmerding which operated as a provocation: it made him seem imperturbable, which he really was not. My little discussion with Montaut about the success with which he might be made to take a joke seriously had not, till this moment, borne any fruit in my imagination, but the idea became prolific, or at least it became amusing, as I stood face to face with him on those solemn fields of marble. There was a temptation to see how much he would swallow. He *was* candid, and his candour was like a rather foolish blank page, the gaping, gilt-edged page of an album, presenting itself for the receipt of a quotation or a thought. Why shouldn't one write something on it, to see how it would look? In this case the inscription could only be a covert pleasantry—an impromptu containing a surprise. If Wilmerding was innocent, that, no doubt, ought to have made one kind, and I had not the faintest intention of being cruel. His blandness might have operated to conciliate, and it was only the turn of a hair that it had the other effect. That hair, let me suppose, was simply the intrinsic brutality—or call it the high animal-spirits—of youth. If after the little experiment suggested by Montaut had fixed itself in my fancy I let him off, it would be because I pitied him. But it was absurd to pity Wilmerding—we envied him, as I have hinted, too much. If he was the white album-page seductive to pointed doggerel he was unmistakably gilt-edged.

"Oh, the Goldies," he said in a moment—"I wouldn't have stayed any longer for *them*. I came back because I wanted to—I don't see that it requires so much explanation."

"No more do I!" I laughed. "Come and listen to the singing." I passed my hand into his arm and we strolled toward the choir and the concourse of people assembled before the high doorway. We lingered there a little: till this hour I never can recall without an ache for the old days the way the afternoon light, taking the heavenly music and diffusing it, slants through the golden recesses of the white windows, set obliquely in the walls. Presently we saw Guy de Montaut in the crowd, and he came toward us after having greeted us with a gesture. He looked hard at me, with a smile, as if the sight of us together reminded him of his wager and he wanted to know whether he had lost or won. I let him know with a glance that he was to be quiet or he would spoil everything, and he was as quiet as he knew how to be. This is not saying much, for he always had an itch to play with fire. It was really the desire to keep his hands off Wilmerding that led me to deal with our friend in my own manner. I remember that as we stood there together Montaut made several humorous attempts to treat him as a great conqueror, of which I think Wilmerding honestly failed to perceive the drift. It was Montaut's saying "You ought to bring them back—we miss them too much," that made me prepare to draw our amiable victim away.

"They're not my property," Wilmerding replied, accepting the allusion this time as to the four English ladies.

"Ah, *all* of them, *mon cher*—I never supposed!" the Frenchman cried, with great merriment, as I broke up our colloquy. I laughed, too—the image he presented seemed comical then—and judged that we had better leave the church. I proposed we should take a turn on the Pincian, crossing the Tiber by the primitive ferry which in those days still plied at the marble steps of the Ripetta, just under the back-windows of the Borghese palace.

"Montaut was talking nonsense just then, but *have* they refused you?" I asked as we took our way along the rustic lane that used to wander behind the castle of St Angelo, skirting the old grassy fortifications and coming down to the Tiber between market-gardens, vineyards and dusty little trellised suburban drinking-shops which had a withered bush over the gate.

"Have *who* refused me?"

"Ah, you keep it up too long!" I answered; and I was silent a little.

"What's the matter with you this afternoon?" he asked. "Why can't you leave the poor Goldies alone?"

"Why can't *you*, my dear fellow—that seems to me the natural inquiry. Excuse my having caught Montaut's tone just now. I don't suppose you proposed for all of them."

"Proposed?—I've proposed for none of them!"

"Do you mean that Mrs Goldie hasn't seemed to expect it?"

"I don't know what she has seemed to expect."

"Can't you imagine what she would naturally look for? If you can't, it's only another proof of the different way you people see things. Of course you have a right to your own way."

"I don't think I know what you are talking about," said poor Wilmerding.

"My dear fellow, I don't want to be offensive, dotting my i's so. You can so easily tell me it's none of my business."

"It isn't your being plain that would be offensive—it's your kicking up such a dust."

"You're very right," I said; "I've taken a liberty and I beg your pardon. We'll talk about something else."

We talked about nothing, however; we went our way in silence and reached the bank of the river. We waited for the ferryman without further speech, but I was conscious that a bewilderment was working in my companion. As I relate my behaviour to you it strikes me, at this distance of time, as that of a very demon. All I can say is that it seemed to me innocent then: youth and gaiety and reciprocity, and something in the sophisticating Roman air which converted all life into a pleasant comedy, apologised for me as I went. Besides, I had no vision of consequences: my part was to prove, as against the too mocking Montaut, that there would be no consequences at all. I remember the way Wilmerding, as we crossed, sat on the edge of the big flat boat, looking down at the yellow swirl of the Tiber. He didn't meet my eye, and he was serious; which struck me as a promise of further entertainment. From the Ripetta we strolled to the Piazza del Popolo, and then began to mount one of the winding ways that diversify the slope of the Pincian. Before we got to the top Wilmerding said to me: "What do you mean by the different way 'we people' see things? Whom do you mean by us people?"

"You innocent children of the west, most unsophisticated of Yankees. Your ideas, your standards, your measures, your manners are different."

"The ideas and the manners of gentlemen are the same all the world over."

"Yes—I fear I can't gainsay you there," I replied.

"I don't ask for the least allowance on the score of being

a child of the west. I don't propose to be a barbarian any-where."

"You're the best fellow in the world," I continued; "but it's nevertheless true—I have been impressed with it on various occasions—that your countrypeople have, in perfect good faith, a different attitude toward women. They think certain things possible that we Europeans, cynical and cor-rupt, look at with a suspicious eye."

"What things do you mean?"

"Oh, don't you know them? You have more freedom than we."

"Ah, never!" my companion cried, in a tone of conviction that still rings in my ears.

"What I mean is that you have less," I said, laughing. "Evidently women, *chez vous*, are not so easily compromised. You must live, over there, in a state of Arcadian, or rather of much more than Arcadian innocence. You can do all sorts of things without committing yourselves. With a quarter of them, in this uncomfortable hemisphere, one is up to one's neck in engagements."

"In engagements?"

"One has given pledges that have in honour to be re-deemed—unless a fellow chooses to wriggle out of them. There is the question of intentions, and the question of how far, in the eyes of the world, people have really gone. Here it's the fashion to assume, if there is the least colour for it, that they have gone pretty far. I daresay often they haven't. But they get the credit of it. That's what makes them often ask themselves—or each other—why they mayn't as well die for sheep as for lambs."

"I know perfectly well what you mean: that's precisely what makes me so careful," said Wilmerding.

I burst into mirth at this—I liked him even better when he was subtle than when he was simple. "You're a dear fellow and a gentleman to the core, and it's all right, and you have

only to trust your instincts. There goes the Boccarossa," I
said, as we entered the gardens which crown the hill and
which used to be as pleasantly neglected of old as they are
regulated and cockneyfied to-day. The lovely afternoon was
waning and the good-humoured, *blasé* crowd (it has seen so
much, in its time) formed a public to admire the heavy
Roman coaches, laden with yellow principessas, which
rumbled round the contracted circle. The old statues in the
shrubbery, the colour of the sunset, the view of St Peter's, the
pines against the sky on Monte Mario, and all the roofs and
towers of Rome between—these things are doubtless a still
fresher remembrance with you than with me. I leaned with
Wilmerding against the balustrade of one of the terraces and
we gave the usual tribute of a gaze to the dome of Michael
Angelo. Then my companion broke out, with perfect
irrelevance:

"Don't you think I've been careful enough?"

It's needless—it would be odious—to tell you in detail
what advantage I took of this. I hated (I told him) the slang
of the subject, but I was bound to say he would be generally
judged—in any English, in any French circle—to have shown
what was called marked interest.

"Marked interest in what? Marked interest in whom?
You can't appear to have been attentive to four women at
once."

"Certainly not. But isn't there one whom you may be held
particularly to have distinguished?"

"One?" Wilmerding stared. "You don't mean the old
lady?"

"*Commediante!* Does your conscience say absolutely
nothing to you?"

"My conscience? What has that got to do with it?"

"Call it then your sense of the way that—to effete prejudice—the affair may have looked."

"The affair—what affair?"

"Honestly, can't you guess? Surely there is one of the young ladies to whom the proprieties point with a tolerably straight finger."

He hesitated; then he cried: "Heaven help me—you don't mean Veronica?"

The pleading wail with which he uttered this question was almost tragic, and for a moment his fate trembled in the balance. I was on the point of letting him off, as I may say, if he disliked the girl so much as that. It was a revelation—I didn't know how much he did dislike her. But at this moment a carriage stopped near the place where we had rested, and, turning round, I saw it contained two ladies whom I knew. They greeted me and prepared to get out, so that I had to go and help them. But before I did this I said to my companion: "Don't worry, after all. It will all blow over."

"Upon my word, it will have to!" I heard him ejaculate as I left him. He turned back to the view of St Peter's. My ladies alighted and wished to walk a little, and I spent five minutes with them; after which, when I looked for Wilmerding, he had disappeared. The last words he had spoken had had such a sharp note of impatience that I was reassured. I had ruffled him, but I had won my bet of Montaut.

Late that night (I had just come in—I was never at home in the evening) there was a tinkle of my bell, and my servant informed me that the signorino of the "American embassy" wished to speak to me. Wilmerding was ushered in, very pale, so pale that I thought he had come to demand satisfaction of me for having tried to make a fool of him. But he hadn't, it soon appeared; he hadn't in the least: he wanted explanations, but they were quite of another kind. He only wished to arrive at the truth—to ask me two or three earnest questions. I ought of course to have told him on the spot that I had only been making use of him for a slight psychological experiment. But I didn't, and this omission was my great fault. I can only declare, in extenuation of it, that I had scruples about betraying Montaut. Besides, I did cling a little to my experiment. There was something that fascinated me in the idea of the supreme sacrifice he was ready to make if it should become patent to him that he had put upon an innocent girl, or upon a confiding mother, a slight, a disappointment even purely conventional. I urged him to let me lay the ghost I had too inconsiderately raised, but at the same time I was curious to see what he would do if the idea of reparation should take possession of him. He would be consistent, and it would be strange to see that. I remember saying to him before he went away: "Have you really a very great objection to Veronica Goldie?" I thought he was going to reply "I loathe her!" But he answered:

"A great objection? I pity her, if I've deceived her."

"Women must have an easy time in your country," I said; and I had an idea the remark would contribute to soothe him.

Nevertheless, the next day, early in the afternoon, being still uneasy, I went to his lodgings. I had had, by a rare chance, a busy morning, and this was the first moment I could spare. Wilmerding had delightful quarters in an old palace with a garden—an old palace with old busts ranged round an old loggia and an old porter in an old cocked hat and a coat that reached to his heels leaning against the *portone*. From this functionary I learned that the signorino had quitted Rome in a two-horse carriage an hour before: he had gone back to Frascati—he had taken a servant and a portmanteau. This news did not confirm my tranquillity in exactly the degree I could have wished, and I stood there looking, and I suppose feeling, rather blank while I considered it. A moment later I was surprised in this attitude by Guy de Montaut, who turned into the court with the step of a man bent on the same errand as myself. We looked at each other—he with a laugh, I with a frown—and then I said: "I don't like it—he's gone."

"Gone?—to America?"

"On the contrary—back to the hills."

Montaut's laugh rang out, and he exclaimed: "Of course you don't like it! Please to hand me over the sum of money that I have had the honour of winning from you."

"Not so fast. What proves to you that you've won it?"

"Why, his going like this—after the talk I had with him this morning."

"What talk had you with him this morning?"

Montaut looked at the old porter, who of course couldn't understand us, but, as if he scented the drift of things, was turning his perceptive Italian eye from one of us to the other. "Come and walk with me, and I'll tell you. The drollest thing!" he went on, as we passed back to the street. "The poor child has been to see me."

"To propose to you a meeting?"

"Not a bit—to ask my advice."

"Your advice?"

"As to how to act in the premises. *Il est impayable.*"

"And what did you say to him?"

"I said Veronica was one of the most charming creatures I had ever seen."

"You ought to be ashamed of yourself."

"*Tudieu, mon cher,* so ought you, if you come to that!" Montaut replied, taking his hand out of my arm.

"It's just what I am. We're a pair of scoundrels."

"Speak for yourself. I wouldn't have missed it for the world."

"You wouldn't have missed what?"

"His visit to me to-day—such an exhibition!"

"What did he exhibit?"

"The desire to be correct—but in a degree! You're a race apart, *vous autres.*"

"Don't lump him and me together," I said: "the immeasurable ocean divides us. Besides, it's you who were stickling for correctness. It was your insistence to me on what he ought to do—on what the family would have a right to expect him to do—that was the origin of the inquiry in which (yesterday, when I met him at St Peter's,) I so rashly embarked."

"My dear fellow, the beauty of it is that the family have brought no pressure: that's an element I was taking for granted. He has no claim to recognise, because none has been made. He tells me that the Honourable Blanche, after her daughter's escapade with him, didn't open her mouth. *Ces Anglaises!*"

"Perhaps that's the way she made her claim," I suggested. "But why the deuce, then, couldn't *he* be quiet?"

"It's exactly what he thinks—that she may have been quiet out of delicacy. He's inimitable!"

"Fancy, in such a matter, his wanting advice!" I groaned, much troubled. We had stopped outside, under the palace windows; the sly porter, from the doorway, was still looking at us.

"Call it information," said Montaut.

"But I gave him lots, last night. He came to me."

"He wanted more—he wanted to be sure! He wanted an honest impression; he begged me, as a favour to him, to be very frank. Had he definitely, yes or no, according to my idea, excited expectations? I told him, definitely, yes—according to my idea!"

"I shall go after him," I declared; "I shall overtake him—I shall bring him back."

"You'll not play fair, then."

"Play be hanged! The fellow mustn't sacrifice his life."

"Where's the sacrifice?—she's quite as good as he. I don't detest poor Veronica—she has possibilities, and also very pretty hair. What pretensions can *he* have? He's touching, but he's only a cotton-spinner and a blockhead. Besides, it offends an *aimable Français* to see three unmated virgins withering in a row. You people don't mind that sort of thing, but it violates our sense of form—of proper arrangement. Girls marry, *que diable!*"

"I notice they don't marry you!" I cried.

"I don't go and hide in the bushes with them. Let him arrange it—I like to see people act out their character. Don't spoil this—it will be perfect. Such a story to tell!"

"*To tell?* We shall blush for it for ever. Besides, we can tell it even if he does nothing."

"Not I—I shall boast of it. I shall have done a good action, I shall have *assuré un sort* to a portionless girl." Montaut took hold of me again, for I threatened to run after Wilmerding, and he made me walk about with him for half an hour. He took some trouble to persuade me that further interference would be an unwarranted injury to Veronica Goldie. She had apparently got a husband—I had no right to dash him from her lips.

"Getting her a husband was none of my business."

"You did it by accident, and so you can leave it."

"I had no business to try him."

"You believed he would resist."

"I don't find it so amusing as you," I said, gloomily.

"What's amusing is that he has had no equivalent," Montaut broke out.

"No equivalent?"

"He's paying for what he didn't have, I gather, eh? *L'imbécile!* It's a reparation without an injury."

"It's an injury without a provocation!" I answered, breaking away from him.

I went straight to the stables at which I kept my horse—we all kept horses in Rome, in those days, for the Campagna was an incomparable riding-ground—and ordered the animal to be brought immediately to Porta San Giovanni. There was some delay, for I reached this point, even after the time it took me to change my dress, a good while before he came. When he did arrive I sprang into the saddle and dashed out of the

gate. I soon got upon the grass and put the good beast to his
speed, and I shall never forget that rich afternoon's ride. It
seemed to me almost historic, at the time, and I thought of
all the celebrated gallops, or those of poetry and fiction, that
had been taken to bring good news or bad, to warn of dangers,
to save cities, to stay executions. I felt as if staying an execution were now the object of mine. I took the direction of the
Appian Way, where so many panting steeds, in the succession
of ages, had struck fire from the stones; the ghostly aqueducts
watched me as I passed, and these romantic associations gave
me a sense of heroism. It was dark when I strained up the hill
to Frascati, but there were lights in the windows of Wilmerding's villa, toward which I first pressed my course. I rode
straight into the court, and called up to him—there was a
window open; and he looked out and asked in unconcealed
surprise what had brought me from Rome. "Let me in and
I'll tell you," I said; and his servant came down and admitted
me, summoning another member of the establishment to look
after my horse.

It was very well to say to Wilmerding that I would tell him
what had brought me: that was not so easy after I had been
introduced into his room. Then I saw that something very
important had happened: his whole aspect instantly told me
so. He was half undressed—he was preparing for dinner—he
was to dine at Mrs Goldie's. This he explained to me without
any question of mine, and it led me to say to him, with, I suspect, a tremor in my voice: "Then you have not yet seen her?"

"On the contrary: I drove to their villa as soon as I got
here. I've been there these two hours. I promised them to go
back to dine—I only came round here to tidy myself a little."
I looked at him hard, and he added: "I'm engaged to be
married."

"To which of them?" I asked; and the question seemed to
me absurd as soon as I had spoken it.

"Why, to Veronica."

"Any of them would do," I rejoined, though this was not much better. And I turned round and looked out of the window into the dark. The tears rose to my eyes—I had ridden heroically, but I had not saved the city.

"What did you desire to say to me?" Wilmerding went on.

"Only that I wish you all the happiness you deserve," I answered, facing him again.

"Did you gallop out here for *that?*" he inquired.

"I might have done it for less!" I laughed, awkwardly; but he was very mild—he didn't fly at me. They had evidently been very nice to him at the other house—well they might be! Veronica had shaken her hair in his eyes, and for the moment he had accepted his fate.

"You had better come back and dine with me," he said.

"On an occasion so private—so peculiar—when you want them all to yourself? Never in the world."

"What then will you do here—alone?"

"I'll wash and dress first, if you'll lend me some things."

"My man will give you everything you need."

His kindness, his courtesy, his extraordinary subjection to his unnecessary doom filled me with a kind of anguish, and I determined that I would save him even yet. I had a sudden inspiration—it was at least an image of help. "To tell the truth, I didn't ride from Rome at such a rate only to be the first to congratulate you. I've taken you on the way; but a considerable part of my business is to go and see Mrs Rushbrook."

"Mrs Rushbrook? Do you call this on your way? She lives at Albano."

"Precisely; and when I've brushed myself up a bit and had a little bread and wine I shall drive over there."

"It will take you a full hour, in the dark."

"I don't care for that—I want to see her. It came over me this afternoon."

Wilmerding looked at me a moment—without any visible

irony—and demanded, with positive solemnity: "Do you wish to propose to her?"

"Oh, if she'd marry me it would suit me! But she won't. At least she won't yet. She makes me wait too long. All the same, I want to see her."

"She's very charming," said Wilmerding, simply. He finished dressing and went off to dine with Veronica, while I passed into another room to repair my own disorder. His servant gave me some things that would serve me for the night; for it was my purpose, at Albano, to sleep at the inn. I was so horrified at what I had done, or at what I had not succeeded in undoing, that I hungered for consolation, or at least for advice. Mrs Rushbrook shone before me in the gloom as a generous dispenser of that sort of comfort.

III

THERE was nothing extraordinary in my going to see her, but there was something very extraordinary in my taking such an hour for the purpose. I was supposed to be settled in Rome again, but it was ten o'clock at night when I turned up at the old inn at Albano. Mrs Rushbrook had not gone to bed, and she greeted me with a certain alarm, though the theory of our intercourse was that she was always glad to see me. I ordered supper and a room for the night, but I couldn't touch the repast before I had been ushered into the vast and vaulted apartment which she used as a parlour, the florid bareness of which would have been vulgar in any country but Italy. She asked me immediately if I had brought bad news, and I replied: "Yes, but only about myself. That's not exactly it," I added; "it's about Henry Wilmerding."

"Henry Wilmerding?" She appeared for the moment not to recognise the name.

"He's going to marry Veronica Goldie."

Mrs Rushbrook stared. "*Que me contez-vous là?* Have you come all this way to tell me that?"

"But he is—it's all settled—it's awful!" I went on.

"What do I care, and what do you mean?"

"I've got into a mess, and I want you to advise me and to get me out of it," I persisted.

"My poor friend, you must make it a little clearer then," she smiled. "Sit down, please—and have you had your dinner?"

She had been sitting at one end of her faded saloon, where, as the autumn night was fresh at Albano, a fire of faggots was crackling in the big marble-framed cavern of the chimney. Her books, her work, her materials for writing and sketching, were scattered near: the place was a comfortable lamplit corner in the general blankness. There was a piano near at hand, and beyond it were the doors of further chambers, in one of which my hostess's little daughter was asleep. There was always something vaguely annoying to me in these signs of occupation and independence: they seemed to limit the ground on which one could appeal to her for oneself.

"I'm tired and I'm hungry," I said, "but I can't think of my dinner till I've talked to you."

"Have you come all the way from Rome?"

"More than all the way, because I've been at Frascati."

"And how did you get here?"

"I hired a chaise and pair at Frascati—the man drove me over."

"At this hour? You weren't afraid of brigands?"

"Not when it was a question of seeing you. You must do something for me—you must stop it."

"What must I do, and what must I stop?" said Mrs Rushbrook, sitting down.

"This odious union—it's too unnatural."

"I see, then. Veronica's to marry some one, and you want her for yourself."

"Don't be cruel, and don't torment me—I'm sore enough already. You know well enough whom I want to marry!" I broke out.

"How can I stop anything?" Mrs Rushbrook asked.

"When I see you this way, at home, between the fire and the lamp, with the empty place beside you—an image of charming domesticity—do you suppose I have any doubt as to what I want?"

She rested her eyes on the fire, as if she were turning my words over as an act of decent courtesy and of pretty form. But immediately afterwards she said: "If you've come out here to make love to me, please say so at once, so that we may have it over on the spot. You will gain nothing whatever by it."

"I'm not such a fool as to have given you such a chance to snub me. That would have been presumptuous, and what is at the bottom of my errand this evening is extreme humility. Don't therefore think you've gained the advantage of putting me in my place. You've done nothing of the sort, for I haven't come out of it—except, indeed, so far as to try a bad joke on Wilmerding. It has turned out even worse than was probable. You're clever, you're sympathetic, you're kind."

"What has Wilmerding to do with that?"

"Try and get him off. That's the sort of thing a woman can do."

"I don't in the least follow you, you know. Who is Wilmerding?"

"Surely you remember him—you've seen him at Frascati, the young American secretary—you saw him a year ago in Rome. The fellow who is always opening the door for you and finding the things you lose."

"The things I lose?"

"I mean the things women lose. He went with us the other day to Monte Cavo."

"And got himself lost with the girl? Oh yes, I recall him," said Mrs Rushbrook.

"It was the darkest hour of his life—or rather of mine. I told him that after that the only thing he could do was to marry Veronica. And he has believed me."

"Does he believe everything you tell him?" Mrs Rushbrook asked.

"Don't be impertinent, because I feel very wretched. He loathes Veronica."

"Then why does he marry her?"

"Because I worked upon him. It's comical—yet it's dreadful."

"Is he an idiot—can't he judge for himself?" said Mrs Rushbrook.

"He's marrying her for good manners. I persuaded him they require it."

"And don't they, then?"

"Not the least in the world!"

"Was that *your* idea of good manners? Why did you do it?"

"I didn't—I backed out, as soon as I saw he believed me. But it was too late. Besides, a friend of mine had a hand in it—he went further than I. I may as well tell you that it's Guy de Montaut, the little Frenchman of the embassy, whom you'll remember—he was of our party at Monte Cavo. Between us, in pure sport and without meaning any harm, we have brought this thing on. And now I'm devoured with remorse—it wasn't a creditable performance."

"What was the beauty of the joke?" Mrs Rushbrook inquired, with exasperating serenity.

"Don't ask me now—I don't see it! It seems to me hideous."

"And M. de Montaut—has he any compunction?"

"Not a bit—he looks at it from the point of view of the Goldies. Veronica is a *fille sans dot*, and not generally liked;

therefore with poor prospects. He has put a husband in her way—a rich, good-natured young man, without encumbrances and of high character. It's a service, where a service was needed, of which he is positively proud."

Mrs Rushbrook looked at me reflectively, as if she were trying to give me her best attention and to straighten out this odd story.

"Mr Wilmerding is rich?" she asked in a moment.

"Dear me, yes—very well off."

"And of high character?"

"An excellent fellow—without a fault."

"I don't understand him, then."

"No more do I!"

"Then what can we do? How can we interfere?" my companion went on.

"That's what I want you to tell me. It's a woman's business—that's why I've tumbled in on you here. You must invent something, you must attempt something."

"My dear friend, what on earth do I care for Mr Wilmerding?"

"You ought to care—he's a knight of romance. Do it for me, then."

"Oh, for you!" my hostess laughed.

"Don't you pity me—doesn't my situation appeal to you?"

"Not a bit! It's grotesque."

"That's because you don't know."

"What is it I don't know?"

"Why, in the first place, what a particularly shabby thing it was to play such a trick on Wilmerding—a gentleman and a man that never injured a fly; and, in the second place, how miserable he'll be and how little comfort he'll have with Veronica."

"What's the matter with Veronica—is she so bad?"

"You know them all—one doesn't want to marry them.

Fancy putting oneself deliberately under Mrs Goldie's heel!
The great matter with Veronica is that, left to himself, he
would never have dreamed of her. That's enough."

"You say he hasn't a fault," Mrs Rushbrook replied. "But
isn't it rather a fault that he's such a booby?"

"I don't know whether it's because I'm rather exalted,
rather morbid, in my reaction against my momentary levity,
that he strikes me as so far from being a booby that I really
think what he has engaged to do is very fine. If without intending it, and in ignorance of the social perspective of a
country not his own, he has appeared to go so far that they
have had a right to expect he would go further, he's willing
to pay the penalty. Poor fellow, he pays for all of us."

"Surely he's very meek," said Mrs Rushbrook. "He's what
you call a muff."

"*Que voulez-vous?* He's simple—he's generous."

"I see what you mean—I like that."

"You would like him if you knew him. He has acted like a
gallant gentleman—from a sense of duty."

"It *is* rather fine," Mrs Rushbrook murmured.

"He's too good for Veronica," I continued.

"And you want me to tell her so?"

"Well, something of that sort. I want you to arrange it."

"I'm much obliged—that's a fine large order!" my companion laughed.

"Go and see Mrs Goldie, intercede with her, entreat her to
let him go, tell her that they really oughtn't to take advantage
of a momentary aberration, an extravagance of magnanimity."

"Don't you think it's *your* place to do all that?"

"Do you imagine it would do any good—that they would
release him?" I demanded.

"How can I tell? You could try. Is Veronica very fond of
him?" Mrs Rushbrook pursued.

"I don't think any of them can really be very fond of any
one who isn't 'smart.' They want certain things that don't

belong to Wilmerding at all—to his nationality or his type. He isn't at all 'smart,' in their sense."

"Oh yes, *their* sense: I know it. It's not a nice sense!" Mrs Rushbrook exclaimed, with a critical sigh.

"At the same time Veronica is dying to be married, and they are delighted with his money. It makes up for deficiencies," I explained.

"And is there so much of it?"

"Lots and lots. I know by the way he lives."

"An American, you say? One doesn't know Americans."

"How do you mean, one doesn't know them?"

"They're vague to me. One doesn't meet many."

"More's the pity, if they're all like Wilmerding. But they can't be. You must know him—I'm sure you'll like him."

"He comes back to me; I see his face now," said Mrs Rushbrook. "Isn't he rather good-looking?"

"Well enough; but I'll say he's another Antinous if it will interest you for him."

"What I don't understand is *your* responsibility," my friend remarked after a moment. "If he insists and persists, how is it your fault?"

"Oh, it all comes back to that. I put it into his head—I perverted his mind. I started him on the fatal course—I administered the primary push."

"Why can't you confess your misdemeanour to him, then?"

"I *have* confessed—that is, almost. I attenuated, I retracted, when I saw how seriously he took it; I did what I could to pull him back. I rode after him to-day and almost killed my horse. But it was no use—he had moved so abominably fast."

"How fast do you mean?"

"I mean that he had proposed to Veronica a few hours after I first spoke to him. He couldn't bear it a moment longer—I mean the construction of his behaviour as shabby."

"He *is* rather a knight!" murmured Mrs Rushbrook.

"*Il est impayable*, as Montaut says. Montaut practiced upon

him without scruple. I really think it was Montaut who
settled him."

"Have you told him, then, it was a trick?" my hostess
demanded.

I hesitated. "No, not quite that."

"Are you afraid he'll cut your throat?"

"Not in the least. I would give him my throat if it would
do any good. But he would cut it and then cut his own. I
mean he'd still marry the girl."

"Perhaps he *does* love her," Mrs Rushbrook suggested.

"I wish I could think it!"

She was silent a moment; then she asked: "Does he love
some one else?"

"Not that I know of."

"Well then," said Mrs Rushbrook, "the only thing for you
to do, that I can see, is to take her off his hands."

"To take Veronica off?"

"That would be the only real reparation. Go to Mrs Goldie
to-morrow and tell her your little story. Say: 'I want to
prevent the marriage, and I've thought of the most effective
thing. If *I* will take her, she will let him go, won't she?
Therefore consider that I *will* take her.'"

"I would almost do that; I have really thought of it," I
answered. "But Veronica wouldn't take *me*."

"How do you know? It's your duty to try."

"I've no money."

"No, but you're 'smart.' And then you're charming."

"Ah, you're cruel—you're not so sorry for me as I should
like!" I returned.

"I thought that what you wanted was that I should be
sorry for Mr Wilmerding. You must bring him to see me,"
said Mrs Rushbrook.

"And do you care so little about me that you could be
witness of my marrying another woman? I enjoy the way you
speak of it!" I cried.

"Wouldn't it all be for your honour? That's what I care about," she laughed.

"I'll bring Wilmerding to see you to-morrow: *he'll* make you serious," I declared.

"Do; I shall be delighted to see him. But go to Mrs Goldie, too—it *is* your duty."

"Why mine only? Why shouldn't Montaut marry her?"

"You forget that he has no compunction."

"And is that the only thing you can recommend?"

"I'll think it over—I'll tell you to-morrow," Mrs Rushbrook said. "Meanwhile, I do like your American—he sounds so unusual." I remember her exclaiming further, before we separated: "Your poor Wilmerding—he *is* a knight! But for a diplomatist—fancy!"

It was agreed between us the next day that she should drive over to Frascati with me; and the vehicle which had transported me to Albano and remained the night at the hotel conveyed us, before noon, in the opposite sense, along the side of the hills and the loveliest road in the world—through the groves and gardens, past the monuments and ruins and the brown old villages with feudal and papal gateways that overhang the historic plain. If I begged Mrs Rushbrook to accompany me there was always reason enough for that in the extreme charm of her society. The day moreover was lovely, and a drive in those regions was always a drive. Besides, I still attached the idea of counsel and aid to Mrs Rushbrook's presence, in spite of her not having as yet, in regard to my difficulty, any acceptable remedy to propose. She had told me she would try to think of something, and she now assured me she had tried, but the happy idea that would put everything right had not descended upon her. The most she could say was that probably the marriage wouldn't really take place. There was time for accidents; I should get off with my fright; the girl would see how little poor Wilmerding's heart was in it and wouldn't have the ferocity to drag him to the altar.

I endeavoured to take that view, but through my magnifying spectacles I could only see Veronica as ferocious, and I remember saying to Mrs Rushbrook, as we journeyed together: "I wonder if they would take money."

"Whose money—yours?"

"Mine—what money have I? I mean poor Wilmerding's."

"You can always ask them—it's a possibility," my companion answered; from which I saw that she quite took for granted I would intercede with the Honourable Blanche. This was a formidable prospect, a meeting on such delicate ground, but I steeled myself to it in proportion as I seemed to perceive that Mrs Rushbrook held it to be the least effort I could reputably make. I desired so to remain in her good graces that I was ready to do anything that would strike her as gallant—I didn't want to be so much less of a "knight" than the wretched Wilmerding. What I most hoped for—secretly, however, clinging to the conception of a clever woman's tact as infinite —was that she would speak for me either to Mrs Goldie or to Veronica herself. She had powers of manipulation and she would manipulate. It was true that she protested against any such expectation, declaring that intercession on her part would be in the worst possible taste and would moreover be attributed to the most absurd motives: how could I fail to embrace a truth so flagrant? If she was still supposed to be trying to think of something, it was something that *I* could do. Fortunately she didn't say again to me that the solution was that I should "take over" Veronica; for I could scarcely have endured that. You may ask why, if she had nothing to suggest and wished to be out of it, if above all she didn't wish, in general, to encourage me, she should have gone with me on this occasion to Frascati. I can only reply that that was her own affair, and I was so far from quarrelling with such a favour that as we rolled together along the avenues of ilex, in the exquisite Roman weather, I was almost happy.

I went straight to Mrs Goldie's residence, as I should have

gone to a duel, and it was agreed that Mrs Rushbrook should drive on to the Villa Mondragone, where I would rejoin her after the imperfect vindication of my honour. The Villa Mondragone—you probably remember its pompous, painted, faded extent and its magnificent terrace—was open to the public, and any lover of old Rome was grateful for a pretext for strolling in its picturesque, neglected, enchanted grounds. It had been a resource for all of us at Frascati, but Mrs Rushbrook had not seen so much of it as the rest of us, or as she desired.

I may as well say at once that I shall not attempt to make my encounter with the terrible dowager a vivid scene to you, for to this day I see it only through a blur of embarrassment and confusion, a muddle of difficulties suspended like a sort of enlarging veil before a monstrous Gorgon face. What I had to say to Mrs Goldie was in truth neither easy nor pleasant, and my story was so abnormal a one that she may well have been excused for staring at me, with a stony refusal to comprehend, while I stammered it forth. I was even rather sorry for her, inasmuch as it was not the kind of appeal that she had reason to expect, and as her imagination had surely never before been led such a dance. I think it glimmered upon her at first, from my strange manner, that I had come to ask for one of the other girls; but that illusion cannot have lasted long. I have no idea of the order or succession of the remarks that we exchanged; I only recall that at a given moment Mrs Goldie rose, in righteous wrath, to cast me out of her presence. Everything was a part of the general agitation; for the house had been startled by the sudden determination of its mistress to return to Rome. Of this she informed me as soon as I presented myself, and she apprised me in the same breath, you may be sure, of the important cause. Veronica's engagement had altered all their plans; she was to be married immediately, absence and delay being incompatible with dear Henry's official work (I winced at "dear Henry"), and they had no time to lose for conference with dressmakers and shop-keepers. Veronica had gone out for a walk with dear Henry; and the other girls, with one of the maids, had driven to Rome, at an early hour, to see about putting to rights the apartment in Via Babuino. It struck me as characteristic of the Honourable Blanche that *she* had remained on the spot, as if to keep hold of dear Henry.

These announcements gave me, of course, my opening. "Can't you see he is only going through with it as a duty? Do you mean to say you were not very much surprised when he proposed?" I fearlessly demanded.

I maintained that it was *not* a duty—that Wilmerding had a morbid sense of obligation and that at that rate any one of us might be hauled up for the simple sociability, the innocent conviviality of youth. I made a clean breast of it and tried to explain the little history of my unhappy friend's mistake. I am not very proud of any part of my connection with this episode; but though it was a delicate matter to tell a lady that it had been a blunder to offer marriage to her daughter, what I am on the whole least ashamed of is the manner in which I fronted the Honourable Blanche. I was supported by the sense that she was dishonest in pretending that she had not been surprised—that she had regarded our young man as committed to such a step. This was rubbish—her surprise had been at least equal to her satisfaction. I was irritated by her quick assumption, at first, that if I wanted the engagement broken it was because I myself was secretly enamoured of the girl.

Before I went away she put me to the real test, so that I was not able to say afterwards to Mrs Rushbrook that the opportunity to be fully heroic had not been offered me. She gave me the queerest look I had ever seen a worldly old woman give, and proffered an observation of which the general copious sense was this:

"Come, I do see what you mean, and though you have made a pretty mess with your French monkey-tricks, it may

be that if dear Henry's heart isn't in it it simply isn't, and that
my sweet, sensitive girl will in the long run have to pay too
much for what looks now like a tolerably good match. It isn't
so brilliant after all, for what do we really know about him
or about his obscure relations in the impossible country to
which he may wish to transplant my beloved? He has money,
or rather expectations, but he has nothing else, and who
knows about American fortunes? Nothing appears to be
settled or entailed. Take her yourself and you may have her—
I'll engage to make it straight with Mr Wilmerding. You're
impecunious and you're disagreeable, but you're clever and
well-connected; you'll rise in your profession—you'll become
an ambassador."

All this (it was a good deal), Mrs Goldie communicated to
me in the strange, prolonged, confidential leer with which
she suddenly honoured me. It was a good deal, but it was not
all, for I understood her still to subjoin: "That will show
whether you are sincere or not in wishing to get your friend
out of this scrape. It's the only condition on which you can
do it. Accept this condition and I will kindly overlook the
outrage of your present intrusion and your inexpressible
affront to my child."

No, I couldn't tell Mrs Rushbrook that I had not had my
chance to do something fine, for I definitely apprehended this
proposition, I looked it well in the face and I sadly shook my
head. I wanted to get Wilmerding off, but I didn't want to
get him off so much as that.

"Pray, is he aware of your present extraordinary proceeding?" Mrs Goldie demanded, as she stood there to give me
my *congé*.

"He hasn't the faintest suspicion of it."

"And may I take the liberty of inquiring whether it is your
design to acquaint him with the scandalous manner in which
you have betrayed his confidence?" She was wonderfully
majestic and *digne*.

"How can I?" I asked, piteously. "How can I, without uttering words not respectful to the young lady he now stands pledged to marry? Don't you see how that has altered my position?" I wailed.

"Yes, it has given you a delicacy that is wondrous indeed!" cried my hostess, with a laugh of derision which rang in my ears as I withdrew—which rings in my ears at this hour.

I went to the Villa Mondragone, and there, at the end of a quarter of an hour's quest, I saw three persons—two ladies and a gentleman—coming toward me in the distance. I recognised them in a moment as Mrs Rushbrook, Veronica Goldie, and Wilmerding. The combination amused and even gratified me, as it fell upon my sight, for it immediately suggested that, by the favour of accident, Mrs Rushbrook would already have had the advantage of judging for herself how little one of her companions was pleased with his bargain, and be proportionately stimulated to come to his rescue. Wilmerding had turned out to spend a perfunctory hour with his betrothed; Mrs Rushbrook, strolling there and waiting for me, had met them, and she had remained with them on perceiving how glad they were to be relieved of the grimness of their union. I pitied the mismated couple, pitied Veronica almost as much as my more particular victim, and reflected as they came up to me that unfortunately our charming friend would not always be there to render them this delicate service. She seemed pleased, however, with the good turn she had already done them and even disposed to continue the benevolent work. I looked at her hard, with a perceptible headshake, trying to communicate in this way the fact that nothing had come of my attack on Mrs Goldie; and she smiled back as if to say: "Oh, no matter; I daresay I shall think of something now."

Wilmerding struck me as rather less miserable than I had expected; though of course I knew that he was the man to make an heroic effort not to appear miserable. He immediately proposed that we should all go home with him to luncheon;

upon which Veronica said, hesitating with responsibility: "Do you suppose, for me, mamma will mind?" Her intended made no reply to this; his silence was almost a suggestion that if she were in doubt she had perhaps better go home. But Mrs Rushbrook settled the question by declaring that it was, on the contrary, exactly what mamma would like. Besides, was not she, Mrs Rushbrook, the most satisfactory of duennas? We walked slowly together to Wilmerding's villa, and I was not surprised at his allowing me complete possession of Veronica. He fell behind us with Mrs Rushbrook and succeeded, at any rate, in shaking off his gloom sufficiently to manifest the proper elation at her having consented to partake of his hospitality. As I moved beside Veronica I wondered whether she had an incipient sense that it was to me she owed her sudden prospect of a husband. I think she must have wondered to what she owed it. I said nothing to awaken that conjecture: I didn't even allude to her engagement—much less did I utter hollow words of congratulation. She had a right to expect something of that sort, and my silence disconcerted her and made her stiff. She felt important now, and she was the kind of girl who likes to show the importance that she feels. I was sorry for her—it was not *her* fault, poor child— but I couldn't flatly lie to her, couldn't tell her I was "delighted." I was conscious that she was waiting for me to speak, and I was even afraid that she would end by asking me if I didn't know what had happened to her. Her pride, however, kept her from this, and I continued to be dumb and to pity her—to pity her the more as I was sure her mystification would not be cleared up by any revelation in regard to my visit to her mother. Mrs Goldie would never tell her of that.

Our extemporised repast at Wilmerding's was almost merry; our sociability healed my soreness and I forgot for the moment that I had grounds of discomposure. Wilmerding had always the prettiest courtesy in his own house, with pressing, preoccupied, literal ways of playing the master, and

Mrs Rushbrook enjoyed anything that was unexpected and casual. Our carriage was in waiting, to convey us back to Albano, and we offered our companions a lift, as it was time for Wilmerding to take Veronica home. We put them down at the gate of Mrs Goldie's villa, after I had noticed the double-dyed sweetness with which Mrs Rushbrook said to Veronica, as the carriage stopped: "You must bring him over to Albano to return my visit." This was spoken in my interest, but even then the finished feminine hypocrisy of it made me wince a little. I should have winced still more had I foreseen what was to follow.

Mrs Rushbrook was silent during much of the rest of our drive. She had begun by saying: "Now that I see them together I understand what you mean"; and she had also requested me to tell her all I could about poor Wilmerding—his situation in life, his character, his family, his history, his prospects—since, if she were really to go into the matter, she must have the facts in her hand. When I had told her everything I knew, she sat turning my instructions over in her mind, as she looked vaguely at the purple Campagna: she was lovely with that expression. I intimated to her that there was very little time to lose: every day that we left him in his predicament he would sink deeper and be more difficult to extricate.

"Don't you like him—don't you think he's worthy to marry some woman he's really fond of?" I remember asking.

Her answer was rather short: "Oh yes, he's a good creature." But before we reached Albano she said to me: "And is he really rich?"

"I don't know what you call 'really'—I only wish I had his pocket-money."

"And is he generous—free-handed?"

"Try him and you'll see."

"How can I try him?"

"Well then, ask Mrs Goldie."

"Perhaps he'd pay to get off," mused Mrs Rushbrook.

"Oh, they'd ask a fortune!"

"Well, he's perfect to her." And Mrs Rushbrook repeated that he was a good creature.

That afternoon I rode back to Rome, having reminded my friend at Albano that I gave her *carte-blanche* and that delay would not improve matters. We had a little discussion about this, she maintaining, as a possible view, that if one left the affair alone a rupture would come of itself.

"Why should it come when, as you say, he's perfect?"

"Yes, he's very provoking," said Mrs Rushbrook: which made me laugh as I got into the saddle.

IV

IN Rome I kept quiet three or four days, hoping to hear from Mrs Rushbrook; I even removed myself as much as possible from the path of Guy de Montaut. I observed preparations going forward in the house occupied during the winter by Mrs Goldie, and, in passing, I went so far as to question a servant who was tinkering a flower-stand in the doorway and from whom I learned that the *padrona* was expected at any hour. Wilmerding, however, returned to Rome without her; I perceived it from meeting him in the Corso—he didn't come to see me. This might have been accidental, but I was willing to consider that he avoided me, for it saved me the trouble of avoiding him. I couldn't bear to see him—it made me too uncomfortable; I was always thinking that I ought to say something to him that I couldn't say, or that he would say something to me that he didn't. As I had remarked to Mrs Goldie, it was impossible for me now to allude in invidious terms to Veronica, and the same licence on his side would have been still less becoming. And yet it hardly seemed as if we could go on like that. He couldn't quarrel with me avowedly about his prospective wife, but he might have quarrelled with me ostensibly about something else. Such subtleties however (I began to divine), had no place in his mind, which was presumably occupied with the conscientious effort to like Veronica—as a matter of duty—since he was doomed to spend his life with her. Wilmerding was capable, for a time, of giving himself up to this effort: I don't know how long it would have lasted. Our relations were sensibly changed, inasmuch as after my singular interview with Mrs Goldie, the day following her daughter's betrothal, I had scruples about presenting myself at her house as if on the old footing.

She came back to town with the girls, immediately showing herself in her old cardinalesque chariot of the former winters, which was now standing half the time before the smart shops in the Corso and Via Condotti. Wilmerding perceived of course that I had suddenly begun to stay away from his future mother-in-law's; but he made no observation about it—a reserve of which I afterwards understood the reason. This was not, I may say at once, any revelation from Mrs Goldie of my unmannerly appeal to her. Montaut amused himself with again taking up his habits under her roof; the entertainment might surely have seemed mild to a man of his temper, but he let me know that it was richer than it had ever been before—poor Wilmerding showed such a face there. When I answered that it was just his face that I didn't want to see, he declared that I was the best sport of all, with my tergiversations and superstitions. He pronounced Veronica *très-embellie* and said that he was only waiting for her to be married to make love to her himself. I wrote to Mrs Rushbrook that I couldn't say she had served me very well, and that now the Goldies had quitted her neighbourhood I was in despair of her doing anything. She took no notice of my letter, and I availed myself of the very first Sunday to drive

out to Albano and breakfast with her. Riding across the
Campagna now suddenly appeared to me too hot and too
vain.

Mrs Rushbrook told me she had not replied to me because
she was about to return to Rome: she expected to see me
almost as soon as, with the Holy Father's postal arrangements, a letter would be delivered to me. Meanwhile she
couldn't pretend that she had done anything for me: and she
confessed that the more she thought of what I wanted the
more difficult it seemed. She added however that she now
had a project, which she declined to disclose to me. She contradicted herself a little, for she said at one moment that she
hadn't the heart to spoil poor Veronica's happiness and at the
next that it was precisely to carry out her device (such a
secret as it was, even from the girl!) that she had decided to
quit Albano earlier than she had intended.

"How can you spoil Veronica's happiness when she won't
have any happiness? How can she have any happiness with
a man who will have married her in such absurd conditions?"

"Oh, he's charming, Mr Wilmerding—everything you
told me of him is true: it's a case of pure chivalry. He'll be
very kind to her—he'll be sorry for her. Besides, when once
he takes her away from her mother Veronica will be all right.
Seeing more of them that way, before they left Frascati, I
became ever so much interested in them. There's something in
Veronica; when once she's free it will come out."

"How will she ever be free? Her mother will be on top of
them—she'll stick to them—she'll live with them."

"Why so, when she has her other daughters to work
for?"

"Veronica will be rich—I'm sure Mrs Goldie will want to
enjoy that."

"They'll give her money—Mr Wilmerding won't haggle!"

"How do you know—have you asked him?"

"Oh, I know," smiled Mrs Rushbrook. "You know I saw them again. Besides," she added, "he'll escape with his wife —he'll take her to America."

"Veronica won't go—she'll hate that part of it."

"Why will she hate it?"

"Oh, it isn't 'smart.'"

"So much the better. I should like to go there."

"Very good," said I. "I daresay I shall be sent there by the Foreign Office some day. I'll take you over."

"Oh, I don't want to go with *you*," said Mrs Rushbrook, plainly. And then she added that she should try to get back to Rome by the Thursday.

"How was it you saw so much of them before they went away?" I suddenly inquired.

"Why, they returned my visit—the queer young couple. Mr Wilmerding brought her over to see me the day after we breakfasted with him. They stayed three or four hours—they were charming."

"Oh, I see; he didn't tell me."

Mrs Rushbrook coloured a little. "You say that in a tone! *I* didn't ask him not to."

"I didn't say you did. However, he has had very little chance: we've scarcely spoken since that day."

"You're very wrong—he's such a good fellow."

"I like the way you give me information about him, because you've seen him three times."

"I've seen him four—I've seen him five," Mrs Rushbrook protested. "After they had been here I went over to Mrs Goldie's."

"Oh, to speak to her?" I cried, eagerly.

"I spoke to her, of course—it was to bid her good-bye. Mr Wilmerding was there—that made another time. Then he came here once again. In fact, the next day——" Mrs Rushbrook continued.

"He came alone?"

She hesitated a moment. "Yes, he walked over. He said he was so nervous."

"Ah, to talk it over, you mean?" I exclaimed.

"To talk it over?"

"Your interference, your rescue."

Mrs Rushbrook stared; then she burst into merriment. "You don't suppose we've spoken of that! Imagine his knowing it!"

I stood corrected—I perceived that wouldn't have done. "But what then did he come for?" I asked.

"He came to see me—as you do."

"Oh, as I do!" I laughed.

"He came because he feels so awkward with the girl."

"Did he tell you that?"

"You told me yourself! We never spoke of Veronica."

"Then what *did* you speak of?"

"Of other things. How you catechise!"

"If I catechise it's because I thought it was all for me."

"For you—and for him. I went to Frascati again," said Mrs Rushbrook.

"Lord, and what was that for?"

"It was for you," she smiled. "It was a kindness, if they're so uncomfortable together. I relieve them, I know I do!"

"Gracious, you might live with them! Perhaps that's the way out of it."

"We took another walk to Villa Mondragone," my hostess continued. "Augusta Goldie went with us. It went off beautifully."

"Oh, then it's all right," I said, picking up my hat.

Before I took leave of her Mrs Rushbrook told me that she certainly would move to Rome on the Thursday—or on the Friday. She would give me a sign as soon as she was settled. And she added: "I daresay I shall be able to put my idea into execution. But I shall tell you only if it succeeds."

I don't know why I felt, at this, a slight movement of contrariety; at any rate I replied: "Oh, you had better leave them alone."

On the Wednesday night of that week I found, on coming in to go to bed, Wilmerding's card on my table, with "Goodbye—I'm off to-morrow for a couple of months" scrawled on it. I thought it an odd time for him to be "off"—I wondered whether anything had happened. My servant had not seen him; the card had been transmitted by the porter, and I was obliged to sleep upon my mystification. As soon as possible the next morning I went to his house, where I found a postchaise, in charge of one of the old *vetturini* and prepared for a journey, drawn up at the door. While I was in the act of asking for him Wilmerding came down, but to my regret, for it was an obstacle to explanations, he was accompanied by his venerable chief. The American Minister had lately come back, and he leaned affectionately on his young secretary's shoulder. He took, or almost took, the explanations off our hands; he was oratorically cheerful, said that his young friend wanted to escape from the Roman past—to breathe a less tainted air, that he had fixed it all right and was going to see him off, to ride with him a part of the way. The General (have I not mentioned that he was a general?) climbed into the vehicle and waited, like a sitting Cicero, while Wilmerding gave directions for the stowage of two or three more parcels. I looked at him hard as he did this and thought him flushed and excited. Then he put out his hand to me and I held it, with my eyes still on his face. We were a little behind the carriage, out of sight of the General.

"Frankly—what's the matter?" I asked.

"It's all over—they don't want me."

"Don't want you?"

"Veronica can't—she told me yesterday. I mean she can't marry me," Wilmerding explained, with touching lucidity. "She doesn't care for me enough."

"Ah, thank God!" I murmured, with great relief, pressing his hand.

The General put his head out of the chaise. "If there was a railroad in this queer country I guess we should miss the train."

"All the same, I'm glad," said Wilmerding.

"I should think you would be."

"I mean I'm glad I did it."

"You're a *preux chevalier*."

"No, I ain't." And, blushing, he got into the carriage, which rolled away.

Mrs Rushbrook failed to give me the "sign" she promised, and two days after this I went, to get news of her, to the small hotel at which she intended to alight and to which she had told me, on my last seeing her at Albano, that she had sent her maid to make arrangements. When I asked if her advent had been postponed the people of the inn exclaimed that she was already there—she had been there since the beginning of the week. Moreover she was at home, and on my sending up my name she responded that she should be happy to see me. There was something in her face, when I came in, that I didn't like, though I was struck with her looking unusually pretty. I can't tell you now why I should have objected to that. The first words I said to her savoured, no doubt, of irritation: "Will you kindly tell me why you have been nearly a week in Rome without letting me know?"

"Oh, I've been occupied—I've had other things to do."

"You don't keep your promises."

"Don't I? You shouldn't say that," she answered, with an amused air.

"Why haven't I met you out—in this place where people meet every day?"

"I've been busy at home—I haven't been running about."

I looked round me, asked about her little girl, congratulated her on the brightness she imparted to the most *banal*

room as soon as she began to live in it, took up her books,
fidgeted, waited for her to say something about Henry Wilmerding. For this, however, I waited in vain; so that at last
I broke out: "I suppose you know he's gone?"

"Whom are you talking about?"

"Veronica's *promesso sposo*. He quitted Rome yesterday."

She was silent a moment; then she replied—"I didn't
know it."

I thought this odd, but I believed what she said, and even
now I have no doubt it was true. "It's all off," I went on: "I
suppose you know that."

"How do *you* know it?" she smiled.

"From his own lips; he told me, at his door, when I bade
him good-bye. Didn't you really know he had gone?" I
continued.

"My dear friend, do you accuse me of lying?"

"*Jamais de la vie*—only of joking. I thought you and he
had become so intimate."

"Intimate—in three or four days? We've had very little
communication."

"How then did you know his marriage was off?"

"How you cross-examine one! I knew it from Veronica."

"And is it *your* work?"

"Ah, mine—call it rather yours: you set me on."

"Is that what you've been so busy with that you couldn't
send me a message?" I asked.

"What shall I say? It didn't take long."

"And how did you do it?"

"How shall I tell you—how shall I tell?"

"You said you would tell me. Did you go to Mrs Goldie?"

"No, I went to the girl herself."

"And what did you say?"

"Don't ask me—it's my secret. Or rather it's hers."

"Ah, but you promised to let me know if you succeeded."

"Who can tell? It's too soon to speak of success."

"Why so—if he's gone away?"

"He may come back."

"What will that matter if she won't take him?"

"Very true—she won't."

"Ah, what did you do to her?" I demanded, very curious. Mrs Rushbrook looked at me with strange, smiling eyes. "I played a bold game."

"Did you offer her money?"

"I offered her yours."

"Mine? I have none. The bargain won't hold."

"I offered her mine, then."

"You might be serious—you promised to tell me," I repeated.

"Surely not. All I said was that if my attempt didn't succeed I wouldn't tell you."

"That's an equivocation. If there was no promise and it was so disagreeable, why did you make the attempt?"

"It was disagreeable to me, but it was agreeable to you. And now, though you goaded me on, you don't seem delighted."

"Ah, I'm too curious—I wonder too much!"

"Well, be patient," said Mrs Rushbrook, "and with time everything will probably be clear to you."

I endeavoured to conform to this injunction, and my patience was so far rewarded that a month later I began to have a suspicion of the note that Mrs Rushbrook had sounded. I quite gave up Mrs Goldie's house, but Montaut was in and out of it enough to give me occasional news of *ces dames*. He had been infinitely puzzled by Veronica's retractation and Wilmerding's departure: he took it almost as a personal injury, the postponement of the event that would render it proper for him to make love to the girl. Poor Montaut was destined never to see that attitude legitimated, for Veronica Goldie never married. Mrs Rushbrook, somewhat to my surprise, accepted on various occasions the hospitality of the Honourable

Blanche—she became a frequent visitor at Casa Goldie. I was therefore in a situation not to be ignorant of matters relating to it, the more especially as for many weeks after the conversation I have last related my charming friend was remarkably humane in her treatment of me—kind, communicative, sociable, encouraging me to come and see her and consenting often to some delightful rummaging Roman stroll. But she would never tolerate, on my lips, the slightest argument in favour of a union more systematic; she once said, laughing: "How can we possibly marry when we're so impoverished? Didn't we spend every penny we possess to buy off Veronica?" This was highly fantastic, of course, but there was just a sufficient symbolism in it to minister to my unsatisfied desire to know what had really taken place.

I seemed to make that out a little better when, before the winter had fairly begun, I learned from both of my friends that Mrs Goldie had decided upon a change of base, a new campaign altogether. She had got some friends to take her house off her hands; she was quitting Rome, embarking on a scheme of foreign travel, going to Naples, proposing to visit the East, to get back to England for the summer, to *promener* her daughters, in short, in regions hitherto inaccessible and unattempted. This news pointed to a considerable augmentation of fortune on the part of the Honourable Blanche, whose conspicuous thrift we all knew to be funded on slender possessions. If she was undertaking expensive journeys it was because she had "come into" money—a reflection that didn't make Mrs Rushbrook's refusal to enlighten my ignorance a whit less tormenting. When I said to this whimsical woman, as I did several times, that she really oughtn't to leave me so in the dark, her reply was always the same, that the matter was all too delicate—she didn't know how she had done, there were some transactions so tacit, so made up of subtle *sousentendus*, that you couldn't describe them. So I groped for the missing link without finding it—the secret of how it had been possible for Mrs Rushbrook to put the key of Wilmerding's coffers into Mrs Goldie's hand.

I was present at the large party the latter lady gave as her leave-taking of her Roman friends, and as soon as I stood face to face with her I recognised that she had had much less "feeling" than I about our meeting again. I might have come at any time. She was good-natured, in her way, she forgot things and was not rancorous: it had now quite escaped her that she had turned me out of the house. The air of prosperity was in the place, the shabby past was sponged out. The tea was potent, the girls had all new frocks, and Mrs Goldie looked at me with an eye that seemed to say that I might still have Veronica if I wanted. Veronica was now a fortune, but I didn't take it up.

Wilmerding came back to Rome in February, after Casa Goldie, as we had known it, was closed. In his absence I had been at the American Legation on various occasions—no *chancellerie* in Europe was steeped in dustier leisure—and the good General confided to me that he missed his young friend *as* a friend, but so far as missing him as a worker went (there *was* no work), "Uncle Sam" might save his salary. He repeated that he had fixed it all right: Wilmerding had taken three months to cross the Atlantic and see his people. He had doubtless important arrangements to make and copious drafts to explain. They must have been extraordinarily obliging, his people, for Mrs Goldie (to finish with her), was for the rest of her days able to abjure cheap capitals and follow the chase where it was doubtless keenest—among the lordly herds of her native land. If Veronica never married the other girls did, and Miss Goldie, disencumbered and bedizened, reigned as a beauty, a good deal contested, for a great many years. I think that after her sisters went off she got her mother much under control, and she grew more and more to resemble her. She is dead, poor girl, her mother is dead—I told you every one is dead. Wilmerding is dead—his wife is dead.

The subsequent life of this ingenious woman was short: I doubt whether she liked America as well as she had had an idea she should, or whether it agreed with her. She had put me off my guard that winter, and she put Wilmerding a little off his, too, I think, by going down to Naples just before he came back to Rome. She reappeared there, however, late in the spring—though I don't know how long she stayed. At the end of May, that year, my own residence in Rome terminated. I was assigned to a post in the north of Europe, with orders to proceed to it with speed. I saw them together before I quitted Italy, my two good friends, and then the truth suddenly came over me. As she said herself—for I had it out with her fearfully before I left—I had only myself to thank for it. I had made her think of him, I had made her look at him, I had made her do extraordinary things. You won't be surprised to hear they were married less than two years after the service I had induced her to render me.

Ah, don't ask me what really passed between them—that was their own affair. There are "i's" in the matter that have never been dotted, and in later years, when my soreness had subsided sufficiently to allow me a certain liberty of mind, I often wondered and theorised. I was sore for a long time and I never even thought of marrying another woman: that "i" at least I can dot. It made no difference that she probably never would have had me. She fell in love with him, of course —with the idea of him, secretly, in her heart of hearts—the hour I told her, in my distress, of the *beau trait* of which he had been capable. She didn't know him, hadn't seen him, positively speaking; but she took a fancy to the man who had that sort of sense of conduct. Some women would have despised it, but I was careful to pick out the one to whom it happened most to appeal. I dragged them together, I kept them together. When they met he liked her for the interest he was conscious she already took in him, and it all went as softly as when you tread on velvet. Of course I had myself to thank for it, for I not only shut her up with Wilmerding—I shut her up with Veronica.

What she said to Veronica in this situation was no doubt that it was all a mistake (she appealed to the girl's conscience to justify her there), but that he would pay largely for his mistake. Her warrant for that was simply one of the subtle *sousentendus* of which she spoke to me when I attacked her and which are the medium of communication of people in love. She took upon herself to speak for him—she despoiled him, at a stroke, in advance, so that when she married him she married a man of relatively small fortune. This was disinterested at least. There was no bargain between them, as I read it—it all passed in the air. He divined what she had promised for him and he immediately performed. Fancy how she must have liked him then! Veronica believed, her mother believed, because he had already given them a specimen of his disposition to do the handsome thing. I had arranged it all in perfection. My only consolation was that I had done what I wanted; but do you suppose that was sufficient?

THE PUPIL

I

THE poor young man hesitated and procrastinated: it cost
him such an effort to broach the subject of terms, to speak of
money to a person who spoke only of feelings and, as it were,
of the aristocracy. Yet he was unwilling to take leave, treating his engagement as settled, without some more conventional glance in that direction than he could find an opening
for in the manner of the large, affable lady who sat there
drawing a pair of soiled *gants de Suède* through a fat, jewelled
hand and, at once pressing and gliding, repeated over and
over everything but the thing he would have liked to hear. He
would have liked to hear the figure of his salary; but just as
he was nervously about to sound that note the little boy came
back—the little boy Mrs Moreen had sent out of the room to
fetch her fan. He came back without the fan, only with the
casual observation that he couldn't find it. As he dropped this
cynical confession he looked straight and hard at the candidate
for the honour of taking his education in hand. This personage reflected, somewhat grimly, that the first thing he should
have to teach his little charge would be to appear to address
himself to his mother when he spoke to her—especially not to
make her such an improper answer as that.

When Mrs Moreen bethought herself of this pretext for
getting rid of their companion, Pemberton supposed it was
precisely to approach the delicate subject of his remuneration.
But it had been only to say some things about her son which
it was better that a boy of eleven shouldn't catch. They were
extravagantly to his advantage, save when she lowered her voice
to sigh, tapping her left side familiarly: "And all overclouded

by *this*, you know—all at the mercy of a weakness—!"
Pemberton gathered that the weakness was in the region of
the heart. He had known the poor child was not robust:
this was the basis on which he had been invited to treat,
through an English lady, an Oxford acquaintance, then at
Nice, who happened to know both his needs and those of
the amiable American family looking out for something really
superior in the way of a resident tutor.

The young man's impression of his prospective pupil, who
had first come into the room, as if to see for himself, as soon as
Pemberton was admitted, was not quite the soft solicitation
the visitor had taken for granted. Morgan Moreen was, somehow, sickly without being delicate, and that he looked intelligent (it is true Pemberton wouldn't have enjoyed his being
stupid), only added to the suggestion that, as with his big
mouth and big ears he really couldn't be called pretty, he
might be unpleasant. Pemberton was modest—he was even
timid; and the chance that his small scholar might prove
cleverer than himself had quite figured, to his nervousness,
among the dangers of an untried experiment. He reflected,
however, that these were risks one had to run when one
accepted a position, as it was called, in a private family; when
as yet one's University honours had, pecuniarily speaking,
remained barren. At any rate, when Mrs Moreen got up as if
to intimate that, since it was understood he would enter upon
his duties within the week she would let him off now, he
succeeded, in spite of the presence of the child, in squeezing
out a phrase about the rate of payment. It was not the fault of
the conscious smile which seemed a reference to the lady's
expensive identity, if the allusion did not sound rather vulgar.
This was exactly because she became still more gracious to
reply: "Oh! I can assure you that all that will be quite
regular."

Pemberton only wondered, while he took up his hat, what
"all that" was to amount to—people had such different ideas.

Mrs Moreen's words, however, seemed to commit the family to a pledge definite enough to elicit from the child a strange little comment, in the shape of the mocking, foreign ejaculation, "Oh, là-là!"

Pemberton, in some confusion, glanced at him as he walked slowly to the window with his back turned, his hands in his pockets and the air in his elderly shoulders of a boy who didn't play. The young man wondered if he could teach him to play, though his mother had said it would never do and that this was why school was impossible. Mrs Moreen exhibited no discomfiture; she only continued blandly: "Mr Moreen will be delighted to meet your wishes. As I told you, he has been called to London for a week. As soon as he comes back you shall have it out with him."

This was so frank and friendly that the young man could only reply, laughing as his hostess laughed: "Oh! I don't imagine we shall have much of a battle."

"They'll give you anything you like," the boy remarked unexpectedly, returning from the window. "We don't mind what anything costs—we live awfully well."

"My darling, you're too quaint!" his mother exclaimed, putting out to caress him a practiced but ineffectual hand. He slipped out of it, but looked with intelligent, innocent eyes at Pemberton, who had already had time to notice that from one moment to the other his small satiric face seemed to change its time of life. At this moment it was infantine; yet it appeared also to be under the influence of curious intuitions and knowledges. Pemberton rather disliked precocity, and he was disappointed to find gleams of it in a disciple not yet in his teens. Nevertheless he divined on the spot that Morgan wouldn't prove a bore. He would prove on the contrary a kind of excitement. This idea held the young man, in spite of a certain repulsion.

"You pompous little person! We're not extravagant!" Mrs Moreen gayly protested, making another unsuccessful attempt to draw the boy to her side. "You must know what to expect," she went on to Pemberton.

"The less you expect the better!" her companion interposed. "But we *are* people of fashion."

"Only so far as *you* make us so!" Mrs Moreen mocked, tenderly. "Well, then, on Friday—don't tell me you're superstitious—and mind you don't fail us. Then you'll see us all. I'm so sorry the girls are out. I guess you'll like the girls. And, you know, I've another son, quite different from this one."

"He tries to imitate me," said Morgan to Pemberton.

"He tries? Why, he's twenty years old!" cried Mrs Moreen.

"You're very witty," Pemberton remarked to the child—a proposition that his mother echoed with enthusiasm, declaring that Morgan's sallies were the delight of the house. The boy paid no heed to this; he only inquired abruptly of the visitor, who was surprised afterwards that he hadn't struck him as offensively forward: "Do you *want* very much to come?"

"Can you doubt it, after such a description of what I shall hear?" Pemberton replied. Yet he didn't want to come at all; he was coming because he had to go somewhere, thanks to the collapse of his fortune at the end of a year abroad, spent on the system of putting his tiny patrimony into a single full wave of experience. He had had his full wave, but he couldn't pay his hotel bill. Moreover, he had caught in the boy's eyes the glimpse of a far-off appeal.

"Well, I'll do the best I can for you," said Morgan; with which he turned away again. He passed out of one of the long windows; Pemberton saw him go and lean on the parapet of the terrace. He remained there while the young man took leave of his mother, who, on Pemberton's looking as if he expected a farewell from him, interposed with: "Leave him, leave him; he's so strange!" Pemberton suspected she was afraid of something he might say. "He's a genius—you'll love him," she added. "He's much the most interesting person in the family." And before he could invent some civility to oppose to this, she wound up with: "But we're all good, you know!"

"He's a genius—you'll love him!" were words that recurred to Pemberton before the Friday, suggesting, among other things that geniuses were not invariably lovable. However, it was all the better if there was an element that would make tutorship absorbing: he had perhaps taken too much for granted that it would be dreary. As he left the villa after his interview, he looked up at the balcony and saw the child leaning over it. "We shall have great larks!" he called up.

Morgan hesitated a moment: then he answered, laughing: "By the time you come back I shall have thought of something witty!"

This made Pemberton say to himself: "After all he's rather nice."

II

ON the Friday he saw them all, as Mrs Moreen had promised, for her husband had come back and the girls and the other son were at home. Mr Moreen had a white moustache, a confiding manner and, in his buttonhole, the ribbon of a foreign order —bestowed, as Pemberton eventually learned, for services. For what services he never clearly ascertained: this was a point—one of a large number—that Mr Moreen's manner never confided. What it emphatically did confide was that he was a man of the world. Ulick, the firstborn, was in visible training for the same profession—under the disadvantage as yet, however, of a buttonhole only feebly floral and a moustache with no pretensions to type. The girls had hair and

figures and manners and small fat feet, but had never been
out alone. As for Mrs Moreen, Pemberton saw on a nearer
view that her elegance was intermittent and her parts didn't
always match. Her husband, as she had promised, met with
enthusiasm Pemberton's ideas in regard to a salary. The young
man had endeavoured to make them modest, and Mr Moreen
confided to him that *he* found them positively meagre. He
further assured him that he aspired to be intimate with his
children, to be their best friend, and that he was always looking out for them. That was what he went off for, to London
and other places—to look out; and this vigilance was the
theory of life, as well as the real occupation, of the whole
family. They all looked out, for they were very frank on the
subject of its being necessary. They desired it to be understood that they were earnest people, and also that their fortune, though quite adequate for earnest people, required the
most careful administration. Mr Moreen, as the parent bird,
sought sustenance for the nest. Ulick found sustenance mainly
at the club, where Pemberton guessed that it was usually
served on green cloth. The girls used to do up their hair and
their frocks themselves, and our young man felt appealed to
to be glad, in regard to Morgan's education, that, though it
must naturally be of the best, it didn't cost too much. After a
little he *was* glad, forgetting at times his own needs in the
interest inspired by the child's nature and education and the
pleasure of making easy terms for him.

During the first weeks of their acquaintance Morgan had
been as puzzling as a page in an unknown language—altogether different from the obvious little Anglo-Saxons who had
misrepresented childhood to Pemberton. Indeed the whole
mystic volume in which the boy had been bound demanded
some practice in translation. To-day, after a considerable interval, there is something phantasmagoric, like a prismatic
reflection or a serial novel, in Pemberton's memory of the
queerness of the Moreens. If it were not for a few tangible

tokens—a lock of Morgan's hair, cut by his own hand, and the
half-dozen letters he got from him when they were separated
—the whole episode and the figures peopling it would seem
too inconsequent for anything but dreamland. The queerest
thing about them was their success (as it appeared to him for
a while at the time), for he had never seen a family so bril-
liantly equipped for failure. Wasn't it success to have kept
him so hatefully long? Wasn't it success to have drawn him
in that first morning at *déjeuner*, the Friday he came—it was
enough to *make* one superstitious—so that he utterly committed himself, and this not by calculation or a *mot d'ordre*,
but by a happy instinct which made them, like a band of
gipsies, work so neatly together? They amused him as much
as if they had really been a band of gipsies. He was still young
and had not seen much of the world—his English years had
been intensely usual; therefore the reversed conventions of
the Moreens (for they had their standards), struck him as
topsyturvy. He had encountered nothing like them at Oxford;
still less had any such note been struck to his younger American ear during the four years at Yale in which he had richly
supposed himself to be reacting against Puritanism. The reaction of the Moreens, at any rate, went ever so much further.
He had thought himself very clever that first day in hitting
them all off in his mind with the term "cosmopolite." Later,
it seemed feeble and colourless enough—confessedly, helplessly provisional.

However, when he first applied it to them he had a degree
of joy—for an instructor he was still empirical—as if from
the apprehension that to live with them would really be to see
life. Their sociable strangeness was an intimation of that—their
chatter of tongues, their gaiety and good humour, their infinite
dawdling (they were always getting themselves up, but it took
forever, and Pemberton had once found Mr Moreen shaving
in the drawing-room), their French, their Italian and, in the
spiced fluency, their cold, tough slices of American. They

lived on macaroni and coffee (they had these articles prepared
in perfection), but they knew recipes for a hundred other
dishes. They overflowed with music and song, were always
humming and catching each other up, and had a kind of professional acquaintance with continental cities. They talked of
"good places" as if they had been strolling players. They had
at Nice a villa, a carriage, a piano and a banjo, and they went
to official parties. They were a perfect calendar of the "days"
of their friends, which Pemberton knew them, when they
were indisposed, to get out of bed to go to, and which made
the week larger than life when Mrs Moreen talked of them with
Paula and Amy. Their romantic initiations gave their new
inmate at first an almost dazzling sense of culture. Mrs
Moreen had translated something, at some former period—an
author whom it made Pemberton feel *borné* never to have
heard of. They could imitate Venetian and sing Neapolitan,
and when they wanted to say something very particular they
communicated with each other in an ingenious dialect of their
own—a sort of spoken cipher, which Pemberton at first took
for Volapuk, but which he learned to understand as he would
not have understood Volapuk.

"It's the family language—Ultramoreen," Morgan explained to him drolly enough; but the boy rarely condescen-
ded to use it himself, though he attempted colloquial Latin
as if he had been a little prelate.

Among all the "days" with which Mrs Moreen's memory
was taxed she managed to squeeze in one of her own, which
her friends sometimes forgot. But the house derived a frequented air from the number of fine people who were freely
named there and from several mysterious men with foreign
titles and English clothes whom Morgan called the princes
and who, on sofas with the girls, talked French very loud, as
if to show they were saying nothing improper. Pemberton
wondered how the princes could ever propose in that tone
and so publicly: he took for granted cynically that this was

what was desired of them. Then he acknowledged that even
for the chance of such an advantage Mrs Moreen would never
allow Paula and Amy to receive alone. These young ladies
were not at all timid, but it was just the safeguards that made
them so graceful. It was a houseful of Bohemians who wanted
tremendously to be Philistines.

In one respect, however, certainly, they achieved no rigour
—they were wonderfully amiable and ecstatic about Morgan.
It was a genuine tenderness, an artless admiration, equally
strong in each. They even praised his beauty, which was
small, and were rather afraid of him, as if they recognised that
he was of a finer clay. They called him a little angel and a little
prodigy and pitied his want of health effusively. Pemberton
feared at first that their extravagance would make him hate the
boy, but before this happened he had become extravagant
himself. Later, when he had grown rather to hate the others, it
was a bribe to patience for him that they were at any rate nice
about Morgan, going on tiptoe if they fancied he was showing
symptoms, and even giving up somebody's "day" to procure
him a pleasure. But mixed with this was the oddest wish to
make him independent, as if they felt that they were not good
enough for him. They passed him over to Pemberton very
much as if they wished to force a constructive adoption on
the obliging bachelor and shirk altogether a responsibility.
They were delighted when they perceived that Morgan liked
his preceptor, and could think of no higher praise for the
young man. It was strange how they contrived to reconcile
the appearance, and indeed the essential fact, of adoring the
child with their eagerness to wash their hands of him. Did
they want to get rid of him before he should find them out?
Pemberton was finding them out month by month. At any
rate, the boy's relations turned their backs with exaggerated
delicacy, as if to escape the charge of interfering. Seeing in
time how little he had in common with them (it was by *them*
he first observed it—they proclaimed it with complete

humility), his preceptor was moved to speculate on the mysteries of transmission, the far jumps of heredity. Where his detachment from most of the things they represented had come from was more than an observer could say—it certainly had burrowed under two or three generations.

As for Pemberton's own estimate of his pupil, it was a good while before he got the point of view, so little had he been prepared for it by the smug young barbarians to whom the tradition of tutorship, as hitherto revealed to him, had been adjusted. Morgan was scrappy and surprising, deficient in many properties supposed common to the *genus* and abounding in others that were the portion only of the supernaturally clever. One day Pemberton made a great stride: it cleared up the question to perceive that Morgan *was* supernaturally clever and that, though the formula was temporarily meagre, this would be the only assumption on which one could successfully deal with him. He had the general quality of a child for whom life had not been simplified by school, a kind of homebred sensibility which might have been bad for himself but was charming for others, and a whole range of refinement and perception—little musical vibrations as taking as picked-up airs—begotten by wandering about Europe at the tail of his migratory tribe. This might not have been an education to recommend in advance, but its results with Morgan were as palpable as a fine texture. At the same time he had in his composition a sharp spice of stoicism, doubtless the fruit of having had to begin early to bear pain, which produced the impression of pluck and made it of less consequence that he might have been thought at school rather a polyglot little beast. Pemberton indeed quickly found himself rejoicing that school was out of the question: in any million of boys it was probably good for all but one, and Morgan was that millionth. It would have made him comparative and superior—it might have made him priggish. Pemberton would try to be school himself—a bigger seminary than five hundred grazing donkeys;

so that, winning no prizes, the boy would remain unconscious and irresponsible and amusing—amusing, because,
though life was already intense in his childish nature, freshness still made there a strong draught for jokes. It turned out
that even in the still air of Morgan's various disabilities jokes
flourished greatly. He was a pale, lean, acute, undeveloped
little cosmopolite, who liked intellectual gymnastics and who,
also, as regards the behaviour of mankind, had noticed more
things than you might suppose, but who nevertheless had his
proper playroom of superstitions, where he smashed a dozen
toys a day.

III

At Nice once, towards evening, as the pair sat resting in the
open air after a walk, looking over the sea at the pink western
lights, Morgan said suddenly to his companion: "Do you
like it—you know, being with us all in this intimate way?"

"My dear fellow, why should I stay if I didn't?"

"How do I know you will stay? I'm almost sure you won't,
very long."

"I hope you don't mean to dismiss me," said Pemberton.

Morgan considered a moment, looking at the sunset. "I
think if I did right I ought to."

"Well, I know I'm supposed to instruct you in virtue; but
in that case don't do right."

"You're very young—fortunately," Morgan went on,
turning to him again.

"Oh yes, compared with you!"

"Therefore, it won't matter so much if you do lose a lot
of time."

"That's the way to look at it," said Pemberton accom-
modatingly.

They were silent a minute; after which the boy asked: "Do you like my father and mother very much?"

"Dear me, yes. They're charming people."

Morgan received this with another silence; then, unexpectedly, familiarly, but at the same time affectionately, he remarked: "You're a jolly old humbug!"

For a particular reason the words made Pemberton change colour. The boy noticed in an instant that he had turned red, whereupon he turned red himself and the pupil and the master exchanged a longish glance in which there was a consciousness of many more things than are usually touched upon, even tacitly, in such a relation. It produced for Pemberton an embarrassment; it raised, in a shadowy form, a question (this was the first glimpse of it), which was destined to play as singular and, as he imagined, owing to the altogether peculiar conditions, an unprecedented part in his intercourse with his little companion. Later, when he found himself talking with this small boy in a way in which few small boys could ever have been talked with, he thought of that clumsy moment on the bench at Nice as the dawn of an understanding that had broadened. What had added to the clumsiness then was that he thought it his duty to declare to Morgan that he might abuse him (Pemberton) as much as he liked, but must never abuse his parents. To this Morgan had the easy reply that he hadn't dreamed of abusing them; which appeared to be true: it put Pemberton in the wrong.

"Then why am I a humbug for saying *I* think them charming?" the young man asked, conscious of a certain rashness.

"Well—they're not *your* parents."

"They love you better than anything in the world—never forget that," said Pemberton.

"Is that why you like them so much?"

"They're very kind to me," Pemberton replied, evasively.

"You *are* a humbug!" laughed Morgan, passing an arm into

his tutor's. He leaned against him, looking off at the sea again and swinging his long, thin legs.

"Don't kick my shins," said Pemberton, while he reflected: "Hang it, I can't complain of them to the child!"

"There's another reason, too," Morgan went on, keeping his legs still.

"Another reason for what?"

"Besides their not being your parents."

"I don't understand you," said Pemberton.

"Well, you will before long. All right!"

Pemberton did understand, fully, before long; but he made a fight even with himself before he confessed it. He thought it the oddest thing to have a struggle with the child about. He wondered he didn't detest the child for launching him in such a struggle. But by the time it began the resource of detesting the child was closed to him. Morgan was a special case, but to know him was to accept him on his own odd terms. Pemberton had spent his aversion to special cases before arriving at knowledge. When at last he did arrive he felt that he was in an extreme predicament. Against every interest he had attached himself. They would have to meet things together. Before they went home that evening, at Nice, the boy had said, clinging to his arm:

"Well, at any rate you'll hang on to the last."

"To the last?"

"Till you're fairly beaten."

"*You* ought to be fairly beaten!" cried the young man, drawing him closer.

IV

A YEAR after Pemberton had come to live with them Mr
and Mrs Moreen suddenly gave up the villa at Nice. Pemberton had got used to suddenness, having seen it practiced on a
considerable scale during two jerky little tours—one in
Switzerland the first summer, and the other late in the winter,
when they all ran down to Florence and then, at the end of
ten days, liking it much less than they had intended, straggled
back in mysterious depression. They had returned to Nice
"for ever," as they said; but this didn't prevent them from
squeezing, one rainy, muggy May night, into a second-class
railway-carriage—you could never tell by which class they
would travel—where Pemberton helped them to stow away
a wonderful collection of bundles and bags. The explanation
of this manœuvre was that they had determined to spend the
summer "in some bracing place;" but in Paris they dropped
into a small furnished apartment—a fourth floor in a third-
rate avenue, where there was a smell on the staircase and the
portier was hateful—and passed the next four months in
blank indigence.

The better part of this baffled sojourn was for the preceptor
and his pupil, who, visiting the Invalides and Notre Dame,
the Conciergerie and all the museums, took a hundred re-
munerative rambles. They learned to know their Paris, which
was useful, for they came back another year for a longer stay,
the general character of which in Pemberton's memory to-day
mixes pitiably and confusedly with that of the first. He sees
Morgan's shabby knickerbockers—the everlasting pair that
didn't match his blouse and that as he grew longer could only
grow faded. He remembers the particular holes in his three or
four pair of coloured stockings.

Morgan was dear to his mother, but he never was better dressed than was absolutely necessary—partly, no doubt, by his own fault, for he was as indifferent to his appearance as a German philosopher. "My dear fellow, you *are* coming to pieces," Pemberton would say to him in sceptical remonstrance; to which the child would reply, looking at him serenely up and down: "My dear fellow, so are you! I don't want to cast you in the shade." Pemberton could have no rejoinder for this—the assertion so closely represented the fact. If however the deficiencies of his own wardrobe were a chapter by themselves he didn't like his little charge to look too poor. Later he used to say: "Well, if we are poor, why, after all, shouldn't we look it?" and he consoled himself with thinking there was something rather elderly and gentlemanly in Morgan's seediness—it differed from the untidiness of the urchin who plays and spoils his things. He could trace perfectly the degrees by which, in proportion as her little son confined himself to his tutor for society, Mrs Moreen shrewdly forbore to renew his garments. She did nothing that didn't show, neglected him because he escaped notice, and then, as he illustrated this clever policy, discouraged at home his public appearances. Her position was logical enough—those members of her family who did show had to be showy.

During this period and several others Pemberton was quite aware of how he and his comrade might strike people; wandering languidly through the Jardin des Plantes as if they had nowhere to go, sitting, on the winter days, in the galleries of the Louvre, so splendidly ironical to the homeless, as if for the advantage of the *calorifère*. They joked about it sometimes: it was the sort of joke that was perfectly within the boy's compass. They figured themselves as part of the vast, vague, hand-to-mouth multitude of the enormous city and pretended they were proud of their position in it—it showed them such a lot of life and made them conscious of a sort of democratic brotherhood. If Pemberton could not feel a

sympathy in destitution with his small companion (for after all
Morgan's fond parents would never have let him really suffer),
the boy would at least feel it with him, so it came to the same
thing. He used sometimes to wonder what people would
think they were—fancy they were looked askance at, as if it
might be a suspected case of kidnapping. Morgan wouldn't
be taken for a young patrician with a preceptor—he wasn't
smart enough; though he might pass for his companion's
sickly little brother. Now and then he had a five-franc piece,
and except once, when they bought a couple of lovely neckties, one of which he made Pemberton accept, they laid it out
scientifically in old books. It was a great day, always spent on
the quays, rummaging among the dusty boxes that garnish
the parapets. These were occasions that helped them to live,
for their books ran low very soon after the beginning of their
acquaintance. Pemberton had a good many in England, but
he was obliged to write to a friend and ask him kindly to get
some fellow to give him something for them.

If the bracing climate was untasted that summer the young
man had an idea that at the moment they were about to make
a push the cup had been dashed from their lips by a movement of his own. It had been his first blow-out, as he called
it, with his patrons; his first successful attempt (though there
was little other success about it), to bring them to a consideration of his impossible position. As the ostensible eve of a
costly journey the moment struck him as a good one to put
in a signal protest—to present an ultimatum. Ridiculous as it
sounded he had never yet been able to compass an uninterrupted private interview with the elder pair or with either of
them singly. They were always flanked by their elder children, and poor Pemberton usually had his own little charge
at his side. He was conscious of its being a house in which the
surface of one's delicacy got rather smudged; nevertheless he
had kept the bloom of his scruple against announcing to Mr
and Mrs Moreen with publicity that he couldn't go on longer

without a little money. He was still simple enough to suppose Ulick and Paula and Amy might not know that since his arrival he had only had a hundred and forty francs; and he was magnanimous enough to wish not to compromise their parents in their eyes. Mr Moreen now listened to him, as he listened to every one and to everything, like a man of the world, and seemed to appeal to him—though not of course too grossly—to try and be a little more of one himself. Pemberton recognised the importance of the character from the advantage it gave Mr Moreen. He was not even confused, whereas poor Pemberton was more so than there was any reason for. Neither was he surprised—at least any more than a gentleman had to be who freely confessed himself a little shocked, though not, strictly, at Pemberton.

"We must go into this, mustn't we, dear?" he said to his wife. He assured his young friend that the matter should have his very best attention; and he melted into space as elusively as if, at the door, he were taking an inevitable but deprecatory precedence. When, the next moment, Pemberton found himself alone with Mrs Moreen it was to hear her say: "I see, I see," stroking the roundness of her chin and looking as if she were only hesitating between a dozen easy remedies. If they didn't make their push Mr Moreen could at least disappear for several days. During his absence his wife took up the subject again spontaneously, but her contribution to it was merely that she had thought all the while they were getting on so beautifully. Pemberton's reply to this revelation was that unless they immediately handed him a substantial sum he would leave them for ever. He knew she would wonder how he would get away, and for a moment expected her to inquire. She didn't, for which he was almost grateful to her, so little was he in a position to tell.

"You won't, you know you won't—you're too interested," she said. "You *are* interested, you know you are, you dear, kind man!" She laughed, with almost condemnatory archness, as if it were a reproach (but she wouldn't insist), while she flirted a soiled pocket-handkerchief at him.

Pemberton's mind was fully made up to quit the house the following week. This would give him time to get an answer to a letter he had despatched to England. If he did nothing of the sort—that is, if he stayed another year and then went away only for three months—it was not merely because before the answer to his letter came (most unsatisfactory when it did arrive), Mr Moreen generously presented him—again with all the precautions of a man of the world—three hundred francs. He was exasperated to find that Mrs Moreen was right, that he couldn't bear to leave the child. This stood out clearer for the very reason that, the night of his desperate appeal to his patrons, he had seen fully for the first time where he was. Wasn't it another proof of the success with which those patrons practiced their arts that they had managed to avert for so long the illuminating flash? It descended upon Pemberton with a luridness which perhaps would have struck a spectator as comically excessive, after he had returned to his little servile room, which looked into a close court where a bare, dirty opposite wall took, with the sound of shrill clatter, the reflection of lighted back-windows. He had simply given himself away to a band of adventurers. The idea, the word itself, had a sort of romantic horror for him—he had always lived on such safe lines. Later it assumed a more interesting, almost a soothing, sense: it pointed a moral, and Pemberton could enjoy a moral. The Moreens were adventurers not merely because they didn't pay their debts, because they lived on society, but because their whole view of life, dim and confused and instinctive, like that of clever colour-blind animals, was speculative and rapacious and mean. Oh! they were "respectable," and that only made them more *immondes*. The young man's analysis of them put it at last very simply—they were adventurers because they were abject snobs. That was the completest account of them—it was the law of their being.

Even when this truth became vivid to their ingenious inmate he remained unconscious of how much his mind had been prepared for it by the extraordinary little boy who had now become such a complication in his life. Much less could he then calculate on the information he was still to owe to the extraordinary little boy.

V

BUT it was during the ensuing time that the real problem came up—the problem of how far it was excusable to discuss the turpitude of parents with a child of twelve, of thirteen, of fourteen. Absolutely inexcusable and quite impossible it of course at first appeared; and indeed the question didn't press for a while after Pemberton had received his three hundred francs. They produced a sort of lull, a relief from the sharpest pressure. Pemberton frugally amended his wardrobe and even had a few francs in his pocket. He thought the Moreens looked at him as if he were almost too smart, as if they ought to take care not to spoil him. If Mr Moreen hadn't been such a man of the world he would perhaps have said something to him about his neckties. But Mr Moreen was always enough a man of the world to let things pass—he had certainly shown that. It was singular how Pemberton guessed that Morgan, though saying nothing about it, knew something had happened. But three hundred francs, especially when one owed money, couldn't last for ever; and when they were gone—the boy knew when they were gone—Morgan did say something. The party had returned to Nice at the beginning of the winter, but not to the charming villa. They went to an hotel, where they stayed three months, and then they went to another hotel, explaining that they had left the first because they had waited and waited and couldn't get the rooms they wanted. These apartments, the rooms they wanted, were generally very splendid; but fortunately they never *could* get them—fortunately, I mean, for Pemberton, who reflected always that if they had got them there would have been still less for educational expenses. What Morgan said at last was said suddenly, irrelevantly, when the moment came, in the middle of a lesson, and consisted of the apparently unfeeling words: "You ought to *filer*, you know—you really ought."

Pemberton stared. He had learnt enough French slang from Morgan to know that to *filer* meant to go away. "Ah, my dear fellow, don't turn me off!"

Morgan pulled a Greek lexicon toward him (he used a Greek-German), to look out a word, instead of asking it of Pemberton. "You can't go on like this, you know."

"Like what, my boy?"

"You know they don't pay you up," said Morgan, blushing and turning his leaves.

"Don't pay me?" Pemberton stared again and feigned amazement. "What on earth put that into your head?"

"It has been there a long time," the boy replied, continuing his search.

Pemberton was silent, then he went on: "I say, what are you hunting for? They pay me beautifully."

"I'm hunting for the Greek for transparent fiction," Morgan dropped.

"Find that rather for gross impertinence, and disabuse your mind. What do I want of money?"

"Oh, that's another question!"

Pemberton hesitated—he was drawn in different ways. The severely correct thing would have been to tell the boy that such a matter was none of his business and bid him go on with his lines. But they were really too intimate for that; it was not the way he was in the habit of treating him; there had been no reason it should be. On the other hand Morgan had quite lighted on the truth—he really shouldn't be able to keep it up much longer; therefore why not let him know one's real motive for forsaking him? At the same time it wasn't decent to abuse to one's pupil the family of one's pupil; it was better to misrepresent than to do that. So in reply to Morgan's last exclamation he just declared, to dismiss the subject, that he had received several payments.

"I say—I say!" the boy ejaculated, laughing.

"That's all right," Pemberton insisted. "Give me your written rendering."

Morgan pushed a copybook across the table, and his companion began to read the page, but with something running in his head that made it no sense. Looking up after a minute or two he found the child's eyes fixed on him, and he saw something strange in them. Then Morgan said: "I'm not afraid of the reality."

"I haven't yet seen the thing that you *are* afraid of—I'll do you that justice!"

This came out with a jump (it was perfectly true), and evidently gave Morgan pleasure. "I've thought of it a long time," he presently resumed.

"Well, don't think of it any more."

The child appeared to comply, and they had a comfortable and even an amusing hour. They had a theory that they were very thorough, and yet they seemed always to be in the amusing part of lessons, the intervals between the tunnels, where there were waysides and views. Yet the morning was brought to a violent end by Morgan's suddenly leaning his arms on the table, burying his head in them and bursting into tears. Pemberton would have been startled at any rate; but he was doubly startled because, as it then occurred to him, it was the first time he had ever seen the boy cry. It was rather awful.

The next day, after much thought, he took a decision and, believing it to be just, immediately acted upon it. He cornered Mr and Mrs Moreen again and informed them that if, on the spot, they didn't pay him all they owed him, he would not only leave their house, but would tell Morgan exactly what had brought him to it.

"Oh, you *haven't* told him?" cried Mrs Moreen, with a pacifying hand on her well-dressed bosom.

"Without warning you? For what do you take me?"

Mr and Mrs Moreen looked at each other, and Pemberton could see both that they were relieved and that there was a certain alarm in their relief. "My dear fellow," Mr Moreen demanded, "what use *can* you have, leading the quiet life we all do, for such a lot of money?"—an inquiry to which Pemberton made no answer, occupied as he was in perceiving that what passed in the mind of his patrons was something like: "Oh, then, if we've felt that the child, dear little angel, has judged us and how he regards us, and we haven't been betrayed, he must have guessed—and, in short, it's *general!*" an idea that rather stirred up Mr and Mrs Moreen, as Pemberton had desired that it should. At the same time, if he had thought that his threat would do something towards bringing them round, he was disappointed to find they had taken for granted (how little they appreciated his delicacy!) that he had already given them away to his pupil. There was a mystic uneasiness in their parental breasts, and that was the way they had accounted for it. None the less his threat did touch them; for if they had escaped it was only to meet a new danger. Mr Moreen appealed to Pemberton, as usual, as a man of the world; but his wife had recourse, for the first time since the arrival of their inmate, to a fine *hauteur*, reminding him that a devoted mother, with her child, had arts that protected her against gross misrepresentation.

"I should misrepresent you grossly if I accused you of common honesty!" the young man replied; but as he closed the door behind him sharply, thinking he had not done himself much good, while Mr Moreen lighted another cigarette, he heard Mrs Moreen shout after him, more touchingly:

"Oh, you do, you *do*, put the knife to one's throat!"

The next morning, very early, she came to his room. He recognised her knock, but he had no hope that she brought him money; as to which he was wrong, for she had fifty francs in her hand. She squeezed forward in her dressing-gown, and he received her in his own, between his bath-tub and his bed. He had been tolerably schooled by this time to the "foreign ways" of his hosts. Mrs Moreen was zealous, and when she was zealous she didn't care what she did; so she now sat down on his bed, his clothes being on the chairs, and, in her preoccupation, forgot, as she glanced round, to be ashamed of giving him such a nasty room. What Mrs Moreen was zealous about on this occasion was to persuade him that in the first place she was very good-natured to bring him fifty francs, and, in the second, if he would only see it, he was really too absurd to expect to be *paid*. Wasn't he paid enough, without perpetual money—wasn't he paid by the comfortable, luxurious home that he enjoyed with them all, without a care, an anxiety, a solitary want? Wasn't he sure of his position, and wasn't that everything to a young man like him, quite unknown, with singularly little to show, the ground of whose exorbitant pretensions it was not easy to discover? Wasn't he paid, above all, by the delightful relation he had established with Morgan—quite ideal, as from master to pupil—and by the simple privilege of knowing and living with so amazingly gifted a child, than whom really—she meant literally what she said—there was no better company in Europe? Mrs Moreen herself took to appealing to him as a man of the world; she said "Voyons, mon cher," and "My dear sir, look here now;" and urged him to be reasonable, putting it before him that it was really a chance for him. She spoke as if, according as he *should* be reasonable, he would prove himself worthy to be her son's tutor and of the extraordinary confidence they had placed in him.

After all, Pemberton reflected, it was only a difference of

theory, and the theory didn't matter much. They had hitherto gone on that of remunerated, as now they would go on
that of gratuitous, service; but why should they have so
many words about it? Mrs Moreen, however, continued to be
convincing; sitting there with her fifty francs she talked and
repeated, as women repeat, and bored and irritated him, while
he leaned against the wall with his hands in the pockets of his
wrapper, drawing it together round his legs and looking over
the head of his visitor at the grey negations of his window.
She wound up with saying: "You see I bring you a definite
proposal."

"A definite proposal?"

"To make our relations regular, as it were—to put them
on a comfortable footing."

"I see—it's a system," said Pemberton. "A kind of blackmail."

Mrs Moreen bounded up, which was what the young man
wanted.

"What do you mean by that?"

"You practice on one's fears—one's fears about the child
if one should go away."

"And, pray, what would happen to him in that event?"
demanded Mrs Moreen, with majesty.

"Why, he'd be alone with *you*."

"And pray, with whom *should* a child be but with those
whom he loves most?"

"If you think that, why don't you dismiss me?"

"Do you pretend that he loves you more than he loves
us?" cried Mrs Moreen.

"I think he ought to. I make sacrifices for him. Though
I've heard of those *you* make, I don't see them."

Mrs Moreen stared a moment; then, with emotion, she
grasped Pemberton's hand. "*Will* you make it—the sacrifice?"

Pemberton burst out laughing. "I'll see—I'll do what I

THE PUPIL

can—I'll stay a little longer. Your calculation is just—I *do* hate intensely to give him up; I'm fond of him and he interests me deeply, in spite of the inconvenience I suffer. You know my situation perfectly; I haven't a penny in the world, and, occupied as I am with Morgan, I'm unable to earn money."

Mrs Moreen tapped her undressed arm with her folded bank-note. "Can't you write articles? Can't you translate, as *I* do?"

"I don't know about translating; it's wretchedly paid."

"I am glad to earn what I can," said Mrs Moreen virtuously, with her head high.

"You ought to tell me who you do it for." Pemberton paused a moment, and she said nothing; so he added: "I've tried to turn off some little sketches, but the magazines won't have them—they're declined with thanks."

"You see then you're not such a phœnix—to have such pretensions," smiled his interlocutress.

"I haven't time to do things properly," Pemberton went on. Then as it came over him that he was almost abjectly good-natured to give these explanations he added: "If I stay on longer it must be on one condition—that Morgan shall know distinctly on what footing I am."

Mrs Moreen hesitated. "Surely you don't want to show off to a child?"

"To show *you* off, do you mean?"

Again Mrs Moreen hesitated, but this time it was to produce a still finer flower. "And *you* talk of blackmail!"

"You can easily prevent it," said Pemberton.

"And *you* talk of practicing on fears," Mrs Moreen continued.

"Yes, there's no doubt I'm a great scoundrel."

His visitor looked at him a moment—it was evident that she was sorely bothered. Then she thrust out her money at him. "Mr Moreen desired me to give you this on account."

"I'm much obliged to Mr Moreen; but we have no account."

"You won't take it?"

"That leaves me more free," said Pemberton.

"To poison my darling's mind?" groaned Mrs Moreen.

"Oh, your darling's mind!" laughed the young man.

She fixed him a moment, and he thought she was going to break out tormentedly, pleadingly: "For God's sake, tell me what *is* in it!" But she checked this impulse—another was stronger. She pocketed the money—the crudity of the alternative was comical—and swept out of the room with the desperate concession: "You may tell him any horror you like!"

VI

A COUPLE of days after this, during which Pemberton had delayed to profit by Mrs Moreen's permission to tell her son any horror, the two had been for a quarter of an hour walking together in silence when the boy became sociable again with the remark: "I'll tell you how I know it; I know it through Zénobie."

"Zénobie? Who in the world is *she?*"

"A nurse I used to have—ever so many years ago. A charming woman. I liked her awfully, and she liked me."

"There's no accounting for tastes. What is it you know through her?"

"Why, what their idea is. She went away because they didn't pay her. She did like me awfully, and she stayed two years. She told me all about it—that at last she could never get her wages. As soon as they saw how much she liked me they stopped giving her anything. They thought she'd stay for nothing, out of devotion. And she did stay ever so long—

as long as she could. She was only a poor girl. She used to
send money to her mother. At last she couldn't afford it any
longer, and she went away in a fearful rage one night—I
mean of course in a rage against *them*. She cried over me
tremendously, she hugged me nearly to death. She told me all
about it," Morgan repeated. "She told me it was their idea. So
I guessed, ever so long ago, that they have had the same idea
with you."

"Zénobie was very shrewd," said Pemberton. "And she
made you so."

"Oh, that wasn't Zénobie; that was nature. And experience!" Morgan laughed.

"Well, Zénobie was a part of your experience."

"Certainly I was a part of hers, poor dear!" the boy
exclaimed. "And I'm a part of yours."

"A very important part. But I don't see how you know
that I've been treated like Zénobie."

"Do you take me for an idiot?" Morgan asked. "Haven't
I been conscious of what we've been through together?"

"What we've been through?"

"Our privations—our dark days."

"Oh, our days have been bright enough."

Morgan went on in silence for a moment. Then he said:
"My dear fellow, you're a hero!"

"Well, you're another!" Pemberton retorted.

"No, I'm not; but I'm not a baby. I won't stand it any
longer. You must get some occupation that pays. I'm
ashamed, I'm ashamed!" quavered the boy in a little passionate voice that was very touching to Pemberton.

"We ought to go off and live somewhere together," said
the young man.

"I'll go like a shot if you'll take me."

"I'd get some work that would keep us both afloat," Pemberton continued.

"So would I. Why shouldn't *I* work? I ain't such a *crétin!*"

"The difficulty is that your parents wouldn't hear of it," said Pemberton. "They would never part with you; they worship the ground you tread on. Don't you see the proof of it? They don't dislike me; they wish me no harm; they're very amiable people; but they're perfectly ready to treat me badly for your sake."

The silence in which Morgan received this graceful sophistry struck Pemberton somehow as expressive. After a moment Morgan repeated: "You *are* a hero!" Then he added: "They leave me with you altogether. You've all the responsibility. They put me off on you from morning till night. Why, then, should they object to my taking up with you completely? I'd help you."

"They're not particularly keen about my being helped, and they delight in thinking of you as *theirs*. They're tremendously proud of you."

"I'm not proud of them. But you know *that*," Morgan returned.

"Except for the little matter we speak of they're charming people," said Pemberton, not taking up the imputation of lucidity, but wondering greatly at the child's own, and especially at this fresh reminder of something he had been conscious of from the first—the strangest thing in the boy's large little composition, a temper, a sensibility, even a sort of ideal, which made him privately resent the general quality of his kinsfolk. Morgan had in secret a small loftiness which begot an element of reflection, a domestic scorn not imperceptible to his companion (though they never had any talk about it), and absolutely anomalous in a juvenile nature, especially when one noted that it had not made this nature "old-fashioned," as the word is of children—quaint or wizened or offensive. It was as if he had been a little gentleman and had paid the penalty by discovering that he was the only such person in the family. This comparison didn't make him vain; but it could make him melancholy and a trifle

austere. When Pemberton guessed at these young dimnesses
he saw him serious and gallant, and was partly drawn on and
partly checked, as if with a scruple, by the charm of attempt-
ing to sound the little cool shallows which were quickly
growing deeper. When he tried to figure to himself the morning twilight of childhood, so as to deal with it safely, he perceived that it was never fixed, never arrested, that ignorance,
at the instant one touched it, was already flushing faintly into
knowledge, that there was nothing that at a given moment
you could say a clever child didn't know. It seemed to him
that *he* both knew too much to imagine Morgan's simplicity
and too little to disembroil his tangle.

The boy paid no heed to his last remark; he only went on:
"I should have spoken to them about their idea, as I call it,
long ago, if I hadn't been sure what they would say."

"And what would they say?"

"Just what they said about what poor Zénobie told me—
that it was a horrid, dreadful story, that they had paid her
every penny they owed her."

"Well, perhaps they had," said Pemberton.

"Perhaps they've paid you!"

"Let us pretend they have, and *n'en parlons plus*."

"They accused her of lying and cheating," Morgan insisted
perversely. "That's why I don't want to speak to them."

"Lest they should accuse me, too?"

To this Morgan made no answer, and his companion, looking down at him (the boy turned his eyes, which had filled,
away), saw that he couldn't have trusted himself to utter.

"You're right. Don't squeeze them," Pemberton pursued.
"Except for that, they *are* charming people."

"Except for *their* lying and *their* cheating?"

"I say—I say!" cried Pemberton, imitating a little tone of
the lad's which was itself an imitation.

"We must be frank, at the last; we *must* come to an understanding," said Morgan, with the importance of the small boy

who lets himself think he is arranging great affairs—almost playing at shipwreck or at Indians. "I know all about everything," he added.

"I daresay your father has his reasons," Pemberton observed, too vaguely, as he was aware.

"For lying and cheating?"

"For saving and managing and turning his means to the best account. He has plenty to do with his money. You're an expensive family."

"Yes, I'm very expensive," Morgan rejoined, in a manner which made his preceptor burst out laughing.

"He's saving for *you*," said Pemberton. "They think of you in everything they do."

"He might save a little——" The boy paused. Pemberton waited to hear what. Then Morgan brought out oddly: "A little reputation."

"Oh, there's plenty of that. That's all right!"

"Enough of it for the people they know, no doubt. The people they know are awful."

"Do you mean the princes? We mustn't abuse the princes."

"Why not? They haven't married Paula—they haven't married Amy. They only clean out Ulick."

"You *do* know everything!" Pemberton exclaimed.

"No, I don't, after all. I don't know what they live on, or how they live, or *why* they live! What have they got and how did they get it? Are they rich, are they poor, or have they a *modeste aisance?* Why are they always chiveying about—living one year like ambassadors and the next like paupers? Who are they, any way, and what are they? I've thought of all that—I've thought of a lot of things. They're so beastly worldly. That's what I hate most—oh, I've *seen* it! All they care about is to make an appearance and to pass for something or other. What do they want to pass for? What *do* they, Mr Pemberton?"

"You pause for a reply," said Pemberton, treating the

inquiry as a joke, yet wondering too, and greatly struck with the boy's intense, if imperfect, vision. "I haven't the least idea."

"And what good does it do? Haven't I seen the way people treat them—the 'nice' people, the ones they want to know? They'll take anything from them—they'll lie down and be trampled on. The nice ones hate that—they just sicken them. You're the only really nice person we know."

"Are you sure? They don't lie down for me!"

"Well, you shan't lie down for them. You've got to go— that's what you've got to do," said Morgan.

"And what will become of you?"

"Oh, I'm growing up. I shall get off before long. I'll see you later."

"You had better let me finish you," Pemberton urged, lending himself to the child's extraordinarily competent attitude.

Morgan stopped in their walk, looking up at him. He had to look up much less than a couple of years before—he had grown, in his loose leanness, so long and high. "Finish me?" he echoed.

"There are such a lot of jolly things we can do together yet. I want to turn you out—I want you to do me credit."

Morgan continued to look at him. "To give you credit— do you mean?"

"My dear fellow, you're too clever to live."

"That's just what I'm afraid you think. No, no; it isn't fair—I can't endure it. We'll part next week. The sooner it's over the sooner to sleep."

"If I hear of anything—any other chance, I promise to go," said Pemberton.

Morgan consented to consider this. "But you'll be honest," he demanded; "you won't pretend you haven't heard?"

"I'm much more likely to pretend I have."

"But what can you hear of, this way, stuck in a hole with

us? You ought to be on the spot, to go to England—you ought to go to America."

"One would think you were *my* tutor!" said Pemberton.

Morgan walked on, and after a moment he began again: "Well, now that you know that I know and that we look at the facts and keep nothing back—it's much more comfortable, isn't it?"

"My dear boy, it's so amusing, so interesting, that it surely will be quite impossible for me to forego such hours as these."

This made Morgan stop once more. "You *do* keep something back. Oh, you're not straight—*I* am!"

"Why am I not straight?"

"Oh, you've got your idea!"

"My idea?"

"Why, that I probably sha'n't live, and that you can stick it out till I'm removed."

"You *are* too clever to live!" Pemberton repeated.

"I call it a mean idea," Morgan pursued. "But I shall punish you by the way I hang on."

"Look out or I'll poison you!" Pemberton laughed.

"I'm stronger and better every year. Haven't you noticed that there hasn't been a doctor near me since you came?"

"*I'm* your doctor," said the young man, taking his arm and drawing him on again.

Morgan proceeded, and after a few steps he gave a sigh of mingled weariness and relief. "Ah, now that we look at the facts, it's all right!"

VII

THEY looked at the facts a good deal after this; and one of the first consequences of their doing so was that Pemberton stuck it out, as it were, for the purpose. Morgan made the facts so vivid and so droll, and at the same time so bald and so ugly,

that there was fascination in talking them over with him, just
as there would have been heartlessness in leaving him alone
with them. Now that they had such a number of perceptions
in common it was useless for the pair to pretend that they
didn't judge such people; but the very judgment, and the
exchange of perceptions, created another tie. Morgan had
never been so interesting as now that he himself was made
plainer by the sidelight of these confidences. What came out
in it most was the soreness of his characteristic pride. He had
plenty of that, Pemberton felt—so much that it was perhaps
well it should have had to take some early bruises. He would
have liked his people to be gallant, and he had waked up too
soon to the sense that they were perpetually swallowing
humble-pie. His mother would consume any amount, and his
father would consume even more than his mother. He had a
theory that Ulick had wriggled out of an "affair" at Nice:
there had once been a flurry at home, a regular panic, after
which they all went to bed and took medicine, not to be
accounted for on any other supposition. Morgan had a romantic imagination, fed by poetry and history, and he would have
liked those who "bore his name" (as he used to say to Pemberton with the humour that made his sensitiveness manly),
to have a proper spirit. But their one idea was to get in with
people who didn't want them and to take snubs as if they were
honourable scars. Why people didn't want them more he
didn't know—that was people's own affair; after all they were
not superficially repulsive—they were a hundred times
cleverer than most of the dreary grandees, the "poor swells"
they rushed about Europe to catch up with. "After all, they
are amusing—they are!" Morgan used to say, with the wisdom of the ages. To which Pemberton always replied:
"Amusing—the great Moreen troupe? Why, they're altogether delightful; and if it were not for the hitch that you and
I (feeble performers!) make in the *ensemble*, they would carry
everything before them."

What the boy couldn't get over was that this particular blight seemed, in a tradition of self-respect, so undeserved and so arbitrary. No doubt people had a right to take the line they liked; but why should *his* people have liked the line of pushing and toadying and lying and cheating? What had their forefathers—all decent folk, so far as he knew—done to them, or what had *he* done to them? Who had poisoned their blood with the fifth-rate social ideal, the fixed idea of making smart acquaintances and getting into the *monde chic*, especially when it was foredoomed to failure and exposure? They showed so what they were after; that was what made the people they wanted not want *them*. And never a movement of dignity, never a throb of shame at looking each other in the face, never any independence or resentment or disgust. If his father or his brother would only knock some one down once or twice a year! Clever as they were they never guessed how they appeared. They were good-natured, yes—as good-natured as Jews at the doors of clothing-shops! But was that the model one wanted one's family to follow? Morgan had dim memories of an old grandfather, the maternal, in New York, whom he had been taken across the ocean to see, at the age of five: a gentleman with a high neckcloth and a good deal of pronunciation, who wore a dress-coat in the morning, which made one wonder what he wore in the evening, and had, or was supposed to have, "property" and something to do with the Bible Society. It couldn't have been but that *he* was a good type. Pemberton himself remembered Mrs Clancy, a widowed sister of Mr Moreen's, who was as irritating as a moral tale and had paid a fortnight's visit to the family at Nice shortly after he came to live with them. She was "pure and refined," as Amy said, over the banjo, and had the air of not knowing what they meant and of keeping something back. Pemberton judged that what she kept back was an approval of many of their ways; therefore it was to be supposed that she too was of a good type, and that Mr and

Mrs Moreen and Ulick and Paula and Amy might easily have been better if they would.

But that they wouldn't was more and more perceptible from day to day. They continued to "chivey," as Morgan called it, and in due time became aware of a variety of reasons for proceeding to Venice. They mentioned a great many of them—they were always strikingly frank, and had the brightest friendly chatter, at the late foreign breakfast in especial, before the ladies had made up their faces, when they leaned their arms on the table, had something to follow the *demi-tasse*, and, in the heat of familiar discussion as to what they "really ought" to do, fell inevitably into the languages in which they could *tutoyer*. Even Pemberton liked them, then; he could endure even Ulick when he heard him give his little flat voice for the "sweet sea-city." That was what made him have a sneaking kindness for them—that they were so out of the workaday world and kept him so out of it. The summer had waned when, with cries of ecstasy, they all passed out on the balcony that overhung the Grand Canal; the sunsets were splendid—the Dorringtons had arrived. The Dorringtons were the only reason they had not talked of at breakfast; but the reasons that they didn't talk of at breakfast always came out in the end. The Dorringtons, on the other hand, came out very little; or else, when they did, they stayed—as was natural —for hours, during which periods Mrs Moreen and the girls sometimes called at their hotel (to see if they had returned) as many as three times running. The gondola was for the ladies; for in Venice too there were "days," which Mrs Moreen knew in their order an hour after she arrived. She immediately took one herself, to which the Dorringtons never came, though on a certain occasion when Pemberton and his pupil were together at St Mark's—where, taking the best walks they had ever had and haunting a hundred churches, they spent a great deal of time—they saw the old lord turn up with Mr Moreen and Ulick, who showed him the dim basilica as if it belonged to them. Pemberton noted how much less, among its curiosities, Lord Dorrington carried himself as a man of the world; wondering too whether, for such services, his companions took a fee from him. The autumn, at any rate, waned, the Dorringtons departed, and Lord Verschoyle, the eldest son, had proposed neither for Amy nor for Paula.

One sad November day, while the wind roared round the old palace and the rain lashed the lagoon, Pemberton, for exercise and even somewhat for warmth (the Moreens were horribly frugal about fires—it was a cause of suffering to their inmate), walked up and down the big bare *sala* with his pupil. The scagliola floor was cold, the high battered casements shook in the storm, and the stately decay of the place was unrelieved by a particle of furniture. Pemberton's spirits were low, and it came over him that the fortune of the Moreens was now even lower. A blast of desolation, a prophecy of disaster and disgrace, seemed to draw through the comfortless hall. Mr Moreen and Ulick were in the Piazza, looking out for something, strolling drearily, in mackintoshes, under the arcades; but still, in spite of mackintoshes, unmistakable men of the world. Paula and Amy were in bed—it might have been thought they were staying there to keep warm. Pemberton looked askance at the boy at his side, to see to what extent he was conscious of these portents. But Morgan, luckily for him, was now mainly conscious of growing taller and stronger and indeed of being in his fifteenth year. This fact was intensely interesting to him—it was the basis of a private theory (which, however, he had imparted to his tutor) that in a little while he should stand on his own feet. He considered that the situation would change—that, in short, he should be "finished," grown up, producible in the world of affairs and ready to prove himself of sterling ability. Sharply as he was capable, at times, of questioning his circumstances, there were happy hours when he was as superficial as a child; the proof of which was his fundamental assumption that he should presently go to Oxford, to Pemberton's college, and, aided and abetted by Pemberton, do the most wonderful things. It vexed Pemberton to see how little, in such a project, he took account of ways and means: on other matters he was so sceptical about them. Pemberton tried to imagine the Moreens at Oxford, and fortunately failed; yet unless they were to remove there as a family there would be no *modus vivendi* for Morgan. How could he live without an allowance, and where was the allowance to come from? He (Pemberton) might live on Morgan; but how could Morgan live on him? What was to become of him anyhow? Somehow, the fact that he was a big boy now, with better prospects of health, made the question of his future more difficult. So long as he was frail the consideration that he inspired seemed enough of an answer to it. But at the bottom of Pemberton's heart was the recognition of his probably being strong enough to live and not strong enough to thrive. He himself, at any rate, was in a period of natural, boyish rosiness about all this, so that the beating of the tempest seemed to him only the voice of life and the challenge of fate. He had on his shabby little overcoat, with the collar up, but he was enjoying his walk.

It was interrupted at last by the appearance of his mother at the end of the *sala*. She beckoned to Morgan to come to her, and while Pemberton saw him, complacent, pass down the long vista, over the damp false marble, he wondered what was in the air. Mrs Moreen said a word to the boy and made him go into the room she had quitted. Then, having closed the door after him, she directed her steps swiftly to Pemberton. There *was* something in the air, but his wildest flight of fancy wouldn't have suggested what it proved to be. She signified that she had made a pretext to get Morgan out of the way, and then she inquired—without hesitation—if the young man could lend her sixty francs. While, before bursting into a laugh, he stared at her with surprise, she declared that she was awfully pressed for the money; she was desperate for it—it would save her life.

"Dear lady, *c'est trop fort!*" Pemberton laughed. "Where in the world do you suppose I should get sixty francs, *du train dont vous allez?*"

"I thought you worked—wrote things; don't they pay you?"

"Not a penny."

"Are you such a fool as to work for nothing?"

"You ought surely to know that."

Mrs Moreen stared an instant, then she coloured a little. Pemberton saw she had quite forgotten the terms—if "terms" they could be called—that he had ended by accepting from herself; they had burdened her memory as little as her conscience. "Oh, yes, I see what you mean—you have been very nice about that; but why go back to it so often?" She had been perfectly urbane with him ever since the rough scene of explanation in his room, the morning he made her accept *his* "terms"—the necessity of his making his case known to Morgan. She had felt no resentment, after seeing that there was no danger of Morgan's taking the matter up with her. Indeed, attributing this immunity to the good taste of his influence with the boy, she had once said to Pemberton: "My dear fellow; it's an immense comfort you're a gentleman." She repeated this, in substance, now. "Of course you're a gentleman—that's a bother the less!" Pemberton reminded her that he had not "gone back" to anything; and she also repeated her prayer that, somewhere and somehow, he would find her sixty francs. He took the liberty of declaring that if he could find them it wouldn't be to lend them to *her*—as to which he consciously did himself injustice, knowing that if he had them he would certainly place them in her hand. He accused himself, at bottom and with some truth, of a fantastic, demoralised sympathy with her. If misery made strange bed-fellows it also made strange sentiments. It was moreover a part of the demoralisation and of the general bad effect of living with such people that one had to make rough retorts, quite out of the tradition of good manners. "Morgan, Morgan, to what pass have I come for you?" he privately exclaimed, while Mrs Moreen floated voluminously down the *sala* again, to liberate the boy; groaning, as she went, that everything was too odious.

Before the boy was liberated there came a thump at the door communicating with the staircase, followed by the apparition of a dripping youth who poked in his head. Pemberton recognised him as the bearer of a telegram and recognised the telegram as addressed to himself. Morgan came back as, after glancing at the signature (that of a friend in London), he was reading the words: "Found jolly job for you— engagement to coach opulent youth on own terms. Come immediately." The answer, happily, was paid, and the messenger waited. Morgan, who had drawn near, waited too, and looked hard at Pemberton; and Pemberton, after a moment, having met his look, handed him the telegram. It was really by wise looks (they knew each other so well), that, while the telegraph-boy, in his waterproof cape, made a great puddle on the floor, the thing was settled between them. Pemberton wrote the answer with a pencil against the frescoed wall, and the messenger departed. When he had gone Pemberton said to Morgan:

"I'll make a tremendous charge; I'll earn a lot of money in a short time, and we'll live on it."

"Well, I hope the opulent youth will be stupid—he probably will—" Morgan parenthesised, "and keep you a long time."

"Of course, the longer he keeps me the more we shall have for our old age."

"But suppose *they* don't pay you!" Morgan awfully suggested.

"Oh, there are not two such—!" Pemberton paused, he

was on the point of using an invidious term. Instead of this he said "two such chances."

Morgan flushed—the tears came to his eyes. "*Dites toujours*, two such rascally crews!" Then, in a different tone, he added: "Happy opulent youth!"

"Not if he's stupid!"

"Oh, they're happier then. But you can't have everything, can you?" the boy smiled.

Pemberton held him, his hands on his shoulders. "What will become of *you*, what will you do?" He thought of Mrs Moreen, desperate for sixty francs.

"I shall turn into a man." And then, as if he recognised all the bearings of Pemberton's allusion: "I shall get on with them better when you're not here."

"Ah, don't say that—it sounds as if I set you against them!"

"You do—the sight of you. It's all right; you know what I mean. I shall be beautiful. I'll take their affairs in hand; I'll marry my sisters."

"You'll marry yourself!" joked Pemberton; as high, rather tense pleasantry would evidently be the right, or the safest, tone for their separation.

It was, however, not purely in this strain that Morgan suddenly asked: "But I say—how will you get to your jolly job? You'll have to telegraph to the opulent youth for money to come on."

Pemberton bethought himself. "They won't like that, will they?"

"Oh, look out for them!"

Then Pemberton brought out his remedy. "I'll go to the American Consul; I'll borrow some money of him—just for the few days, on the strength of the telegram."

Morgan was hilarious. "Show him the telegram—then stay and keep the money!"

Pemberton entered into the joke enough to reply that, for

Morgan, he was really capable of that; but the boy, growing more serious, and to prove that he hadn't meant what he said, not only hurried him off to the Consulate (since he was to start that evening, as he had wired to his friend), but insisted on going with him. They splashed through the tortuous perforations and over the humpbacked bridges, and they passed through the Piazza, where they saw Mr Moreen and Ulick go into a jeweller's shop. The Consul proved accommodating (Pemberton said it wasn't the letter, but Morgan's grand air), and on their way back they went into St Mark's for a hushed ten minutes. Later they took up and kept up the fun of it to the very end; and it seemed to Pemberton a part of that fun that Mrs Moreen, who was very angry when he had announced to her his intention, should charge him, grotesquely and vulgarly, and in reference to the loan she had vainly endeavoured to effect, with bolting lest they should "get something out" of him. On the other hand he had to do Mr Moreen and Ulick the justice to recognise that when, on coming in, *they* heard the cruel news, they took it like perfect men of the world.

VIII

WHEN Pemberton got at work with the opulent youth, who was to be taken in hand for Balliol, he found himself unable to say whether he was really an idiot or it was only, on his own part, the long association with an intensely living little mind that made him seem so. From Morgan he heard half-a-dozen times: the boy wrote charming young letters, a patchwork of tongues, with indulgent postscripts in the family Volapuk and, in little squares and rounds and crannies of the text, the drollest illustrations—letters that he was divided between the impulse to show his present disciple, as a kind of wasted incentive, and the sense of something in them that was profanable by publicity. The opulent youth went up, in due course, and failed to pass; but it seemed to add to the presumption that brilliancy was not expected of him all at once that his parents, condoning the lapse, which they good-naturedly treated as little as possible as if it were Pemberton's, should have sounded the rally again, begged the young coach to keep his pupil in hand another year.

The young coach was now in a position to lend Mrs Moreen sixty francs, and he sent her a post-office order for the amount. In return for this favour he received a frantic, scribbled line from her: "Implore you to come back instantly —Morgan dreadfully ill." They were on the rebound, once more in Paris—often as Pemberton had seen them depressed he had never seen them crushed—and communication was therefore rapid. He wrote to the boy to ascertain the state of his health, but he received no answer to his letter. Accordingly he took an abrupt leave of the opulent youth and, crossing the Channel, alighted at the small hotel, in the quarter of the Champs Elysées, of which Mrs Moreen had given him the address. A deep if dumb dissatisfaction with this lady and her companions bore him company: they couldn't be vulgarly honest, but they could live at hotels, in velvety *entresols*, amid a smell of burnt pastilles, in the most expensive city in Europe. When he had left them, in Venice, it was with an irrepressible suspicion that something was going to happen; but the only thing that had happened was that they succeeded in getting away. "How is he? where is he?" he asked of Mrs Moreen; but before she could speak, these questions were answered by the pressure round his neck of a pair of arms, in shrunken sleeves, which were perfectly capable of an effusive young foreign squeeze.

"Dreadfully ill—I don't see it!" the young man cried. And then, to Morgan: "Why on earth didn't you relieve me? Why didn't you answer my letter?"

Mrs Moreen declared that when she wrote he was very bad, and Pemberton learned at the same time from the boy that he had answered every letter he had received. This led to the demonstration that Pemberton's note had been intercepted. Mrs Moreen was prepared to see the fact exposed, as Pemberton perceived, the moment he faced her, that she was prepared for a good many other things. She was prepared above all to maintain that she had acted from a sense of duty, that she was enchanted she had got him over, whatever they might say; and that it was useless of him to pretend that he didn't *know*, in all his bones, that his place at such a time was with Morgan. He had taken the boy away from them, and now he had no right to abandon him. He had created for himself the gravest responsibilities; he must at least abide by what he had done.

"Taken him away from you?" Pemberton exclaimed indignantly.

"Do it—do it, for pity's sake; that's just what I want. I can't stand *this*—and such scenes. They're treacherous!" These words broke from Morgan, who had intermitted his embrace, in a key which made Pemberton turn quickly to him, to see that he had suddenly seated himself, was breathing with evident difficulty and was very pale.

"*Now* do you say he's not ill—my precious pet?" shouted his mother, dropping on her knees before him with clasped hands, but touching him no more than if he had been a gilded idol. "It will pass—it's only for an instant; but don't say such dreadful things!"

"I'm all right—all right," Morgan panted to Pemberton, whom he sat looking up at with a strange smile, his hands resting on either side of the sofa.

"Now do you pretend I've been treacherous—that I've deceived?" Mrs Moreen flashed at Pemberton as she got up.

"It isn't *he* says it, it's I!" the boy returned, apparently easier, but sinking back against the wall; while Pemberton, who had sat down beside him, taking his hand, bent over him.

"Darling child, one does what one can; there are so many things to consider," urged Mrs Moreen. "It's his *place*—his only place. You see *you* think it is now."

"Take me away—take me away," Morgan went on, smiling to Pemberton from his white face.

"Where shall I take you, and how—oh, *how*, my boy?" the young man stammered, thinking of the rude way in which his friends in London held that, for his convenience, and without a pledge of instantaneous return, he had thrown them over; of the just resentment with which they would already have called in a successor, and of the little help as regarded finding fresh employment that resided for him in the flatness of his having failed to pass his pupil.

"Oh, we'll settle that. You used to talk about it," said Morgan. "If we can only go, all the rest's a detail."

"Talk about it as much as you like, but don't think you can attempt it. Mr Moreen would never consent—it would be so precarious," Pemberton's hostess explained to him. Then to Morgan she explained: "It would destroy our peace, it would break our hearts. Now that he's back it will be all the same again. You'll have your life, your work and your freedom, and we'll all be happy as we used to be. You'll bloom and grow perfectly well, and we won't have any more silly experiments, will we? They're too absurd. It's Mr Pemberton's place—every one in his place. You in yours, your papa in his, me in mine—*n'est-ce pas, chéri?* We'll all forget how foolish we've been, and we'll have lovely times."

She continued to talk and to surge vaguely about the little draped, stuffy *salon*, while Pemberton sat with the boy, whose colour gradually came back; and she mixed up her reasons, dropping that there were going to be changes, that the other children might scatter (who knew?—Paula had her ideas), and that then it might be fancied how much the poor old parent-birds would want the little nestling. Morgan looked at Pemberton, who wouldn't let him move; and Pemberton

knew exactly how he felt at hearing himself called a little
nestling. He admitted that he had had one or two bad days,
but he protested afresh against the iniquity of his mother's
having made them the ground of an appeal to poor Pemberton. Poor Pemberton could laugh now, apart from the
comicality of Mrs Moreen's producing so much philosophy
for her defence (she seemed to shake it out of her agitated
petticoats, which knocked over the light gilt chairs), so little
did the sick boy strike him as qualified to repudiate any
advantage.

He himself was in for it, at any rate. He should have
Morgan on his hands again indefinitely; though indeed he
saw the lad had a private theory to produce which would be
intended to smooth this down. He was obliged to him for it in
advance; but the suggested amendment didn't keep his heart
from sinking a little, any more than it prevented him from
accepting the prospect on the spot, with some confidence
moreover that he would do so even better if he could have a
little supper. Mrs Moreen threw out more hints about the
changes that were to be looked for, but she was such a mixture of smiles and shudders (she confessed she was very nervous), that he couldn't tell whether she were in high feather
or only in hysterics. If the family were really at last going to
pieces why shouldn't she recognise the necessity of pitching
Morgan into some sort of lifeboat? This presumption was
fostered by the fact that they were established in luxurious
quarters in the capital of pleasure; that was exactly where they
naturally *would* be established in view of going to pieces.
Moreover didn't she mention that Mr Moreen and the others
were enjoying themselves at the opera with Mr Granger, and
wasn't *that* also precisely where one would look for them on
the eve of a smash? Pemberton gathered that Mr Granger was
a rich, vacant American—a big bill with a flourishy heading
and no items; so that one of Paula's "ideas" was probably
that this time she had really done it, which was indeed an

unprecedented blow to the general cohesion. And if the cohesion was to terminate what was to become of poor Pemberton? He felt quite enough bound up with them to figure, to his alarm, as a floating spar in case of a wreck.

It was Morgan who eventually asked if no supper had been ordered for him; sitting with him below, later, at the dim, delayed meal, in the presence of a great deal of corded green plush, a plate of ornamental biscuit and a languor marked on the part of the waiter. Mrs Moreen had explained that they had been obliged to secure a room for the visitor out of the house; and Morgan's consolation (he offered it while Pemberton reflected on the nastiness of lukewarm sauces), proved to be, largely, that this circumstance would facilitate their escape. He talked of their escape (recurring to it often afterwards), as if they were making up a "boy's book" together. But he likewise expressed his sense that there was something in the air, that the Moreens couldn't keep it up much longer. In point of fact, as Pemberton was to see, they kept it up for five or six months. All the while, however, Morgan's contention was designed to cheer him. Mr Moreen and Ulick, whom he had met the day after his return, accepted that return like perfect men of the world. If Paula and Amy treated it even with less formality an allowance was to be made for them, inasmuch as Mr Granger had not come to the opera after all. He had only placed his box at their service, with a bouquet for each of the party; there was even one apiece, embittering the thought of his profusion, for Mr Moreen and Ulick. "They're all like that," was Morgan's comment; "at the very last, just when we think we've got them fast, we're chucked!"

Morgan's comments, in these days, were more and more free; they even included a large recognition of the extraordinary tenderness with which he had been treated while Pemberton was away. Oh, yes, they couldn't do enough to be nice to him, to show him they had him on their mind and

make up for his loss. That was just what made the whole thing
so sad, and him so glad, after all, of Pemberton's return—he
had to keep thinking of their affection less, had less sense of
obligation. Pemberton laughed out at this last reason, and
Morgan blushed and said: "You know what I mean." Pemberton knew perfectly what he meant; but there were a good
many things it didn't make any clearer. This episode of his
second sojourn in Paris stretched itself out wearily, with their
resumed readings and wanderings and maunderings, their
potterings on the quays, their hauntings of the museums, their
occasional lingerings in the Palais Royal, when the first sharp
weather came on and there was a comfort in warm emana-
tions, before Chevet's wonderful succulent window. Morgan
wanted to hear a great deal about the opulent youth—he took
an immense interest in him. Some of the details of his opu-
lence—Pemberton could spare him none of them—evidently
intensified the boy's appreciation of all his friend had given up
to come back to him; but in addition to the greater reciprocity
established by such a renunciation he had always his little
brooding theory, in which there was a frivolous gaiety too,
that their long probation was drawing to a close. Morgan's
conviction that the Moreens couldn't go on much longer
kept pace with the unexpended impetus with which, from
month to month, they did go on. Three weeks after Pemberton had rejoined them they went on to another hotel, a
dingier one than the first; but Morgan rejoiced that his tutor
had at least still not sacrificed the advantage of a room outside. He clung to the romantic utility of this when the day,
or rather the night, should arrive for their escape.

For the first time, in this complicated connection, Pemberton felt sore and exasperated. It was, as he had said to Mrs
Moreen in Venice, *trop fort*—everything was *trop fort*. He
could neither really throw off his blighting burden nor find
in it the benefit of a pacified conscience or of a rewarded
affection. He had spent all the money that he had earned in

England, and he felt that his youth was going and that he was getting nothing back for it. It was all very well for Morgan to seem to consider that he would make up to him for all inconveniences by settling himself upon him permanently—there was an irritating flaw in such a view. He saw what the boy had in his mind; the conception that as his friend had had the generosity to come back to him he must show his gratitude by giving him his life. But the poor friend didn't desire the gift—what could he do with Morgan's life? Of course at the same time that Pemberton was irritated he remembered the reason, which was very honourable to Morgan and which consisted simply of the fact that he was perpetually making one forget that he was after all only a child. If one dealt with him on a different basis one's misadventures were one's own fault. So Pemberton waited in a queer confusion of yearning and alarm for the catastrophe which was held to hang over the house of Moreen, of which he certainly at moments felt the symptoms brush his cheek and as to which he wondered much in what form it would come.

Perhaps it would take the form of dispersal—a frightened *sauve qui peut*, a scuttling into selfish corners. Certainly they were less elastic than of yore; they were evidently looking for something they didn't find. The Dorringtons hadn't reappeared, the princes had scattered; wasn't that the beginning of the end? Mrs Moreen had lost her reckoning of the famous "days;" her social calendar was blurred—it had turned its face to the wall. Pemberton suspected that the great, the cruel, discomfiture had been the extraordinary behaviour of Mr Granger, who seemed not to know what he wanted, or, what was much worse, what *they* wanted. He kept sending flowers, as if to bestrew the path of his retreat, which was never the path of return. Flowers were all very well, but—Pemberton could complete the proposition. It was now positively conspicuous that in the long run the Moreens were a failure; so that the young man was almost grateful the run had not been

short. Mr Moreen, indeed, was still occasionally able to get
away on business, and, what was more surprising, he was also
able to get back. Ulick had no club, but you could not have
discovered it from his appearance, which was as much as ever
that of a person looking at life from the window of such an
institution; therefore Pemberton was doubly astonished at an
answer he once heard him make to his mother, in the desperate tone of a man familiar with the worst privations. Her
question Pemberton had not quite caught; it appeared to be
an appeal for a suggestion as to whom they could get to take
Amy. "Let the devil take her!" Ulick snapped; so that Pemberton could see that not only they had lost their amiability,
but had ceased to believe in themselves. He could also see that
if Mrs Moreen was trying to get people to take her children
she might be regarded as closing the hatches for the storm.
But Morgan would be the last she would part with.

One winter afternoon—it was a Sunday—he and the boy
walked far together in the Bois de Boulogne. The evening was
so splendid, the cold lemon-coloured sunset so clear, the
stream of carriages and pedestrians so amusing and the fascination of Paris so great, that they stayed out later than usual
and became aware that they would have to hurry home to
arrive in time for dinner. They hurried accordingly, arm-in-
arm, good-humoured and hungry, agreeing that there was
nothing like Paris after all and that after all, too, that had come
and gone they were not yet sated with innocent pleasures.
When they reached the hotel they found that, though scan-
dalously late, they were in time for all the dinner they were
likely to sit down to. Confusion reigned in the apartments of
the Moreens (very shabby ones this time, but the best in the
house), and before the interrupted service of the table (with
objects displaced almost as if there had been a scuffle, and a
great wine stain from an overturned bottle), Pemberton
could not blink the fact that there had been a scene of
proprietary mutiny. The storm had come—they were all

seeking refuge. The hatches were down—Paula and Amy
were invisible (they had never tried the most casual art upon
Pemberton, but he felt that they had enough of an eye to him
not to wish to meet him as young ladies whose frocks had
been confiscated), and Ulick appeared to have jumped overboard. In a word, the host and his staff had ceased to "go
on" at the pace of their guests, and the air of embarrassed
detention, thanks to a pile of gaping trunks in the passage,
was strangely commingled with the air of indignant withdrawal.

When Morgan took in all this—and he took it in very
quickly—he blushed to the roots of his hair. He had walked,
from his infancy, among difficulties and dangers, but he had
never seen a public exposure. Pemberton noticed, in a second
glance at him, that the tears had rushed into his eyes and that
they were tears of bitter shame. He wondered for an instant,
for the boy's sake, whether he might successfully pretend not
to understand. Not successfully, he felt, as Mr and Mrs
Moreen, dinnerless by their extinguished hearth, rose before
him in their little dishonoured *salon*, considering apparently
with much intensity what lively capital would be next on their
list. They were not prostrate, but they were very pale, and
Mrs Moreen had evidently been crying. Pemberton quickly
learned however that her grief was not for the loss of her dinner, much as she usually enjoyed it, but on account of a
necessity much more tragic. She lost no time in laying this
necessity bare, in telling him how the change had come, the
bolt had fallen, and how they would all have to turn themselves about. Therefore cruel as it was to them to part with
their darling she must look to him to carry a little further the
influence he had so fortunately acquired with the boy—to
induce his young charge to follow him into some modest
retreat. They depended upon him, in a word, to take their
delightful child temporarily under his protection—it would
leave Mr Moreen and herself so much more free to give the

proper attention (too little, alas! had been given), to the readjustment of their affairs.

"We trust you—we feel that we can," said Mrs Moreen, slowly rubbing her plump white hands and looking, with compunction, hard at Morgan, whose chin, not to take liberties, her husband stroked with a tentative paternal forefinger.

"Oh, yes; we feel that we can. We trust Mr Pemberton fully, Morgan," Mr Moreen conceded.

Pemberton wondered again if he might pretend not to understand; but the idea was painfully complicated by the immediate perception that Morgan had understood.

"Do you mean that he may take me to live with him—for ever and ever?" cried the boy. "Away, away, anywhere he likes?"

"For ever and ever? *Comme vous-y-allez!*" Mr Moreen laughed indulgently. "For as long as Mr Pemberton may be so good."

"We've struggled, we've suffered," his wife went on; "but you've made him so your own that we've already been through the worst of the sacrifice."

Morgan had turned away from his father—he stood looking at Pemberton with a light in his face. His blush had died out, but something had come that was brighter and more vivid. He had a moment of boyish joy, scarcely mitigated by the reflection that, with this unexpected consecration of his hope—too sudden and too violent; the thing was a good deal less like a boy's book—the "escape" was left on their hands. The boyish joy was there for an instant, and Pemberton was almost frightened at the revelation of gratitude and affection that shone through his humiliation. When Morgan stammered "My dear fellow, what do you say to *that?*" he felt that he should say something enthusiastic. But he was still more frightened at something else that immediately followed and that made the lad sit down quickly on the nearest chair.

He had turned very white and had raised his hand to his left side. They were all three looking at him, but Mrs Moreen was the first to bound forward. "Ah, his darling little heart!" she broke out; and this time, on her knees before him and without respect for the idol, she caught him ardently in her arms. "You walked him too far, you hurried him too fast!" she tossed over her shoulder at Pemberton. The boy made no protest, and the next instant his mother, still holding him, sprang up with her face convulsed and with the terrified cry "Help, help! he's going, he's gone!" Pemberton saw, with equal horror, by Morgan's own stricken face, that he *was* gone. He pulled him half out of his mother's hands, and for a moment, while they held him together, they looked, in their dismay, into each other's eyes. "He couldn't stand it, with his infirmity," said Pemberton—"the shock, the whole scene, the violent emotion."

"But I thought he *wanted* to go to you!" wailed Mrs Moreen.

"I *told* you he didn't, my dear," argued Mr Moreen. He was trembling all over, and he was, in his way, as deeply affected as his wife. But, after the first, he took his bereavement like a man of the world.

A NOTE ON THE TEXT

IN preparing these tales for publication, the editor had to choose between James's original magazine texts, those published in book form soon afterwards and those revised and re-written for the New York Edition. The obvious choice, it seemed to him, was the original book form of the story where there was one. In that form it had the benefit of revision from magazine to volume; and in that form it was best known to James's generation. It seemed to the editor that in a chronological edition of James's shorter fictions, the New York Edition texts had no relevance. They belong exclusively to the edition for which they were designed; particularly since the revisions were often made several decades after the original publication.

The original magazine publications of the tales in this volume were as follows:

"The Modern Warning," *Harper's New Monthly Magazine*, June 1888.

"A London Life," *Scribner's Magazine*, June–September 1888.

"The Lesson of the Master," *Universal Review*, 16 July–15 August 1888.

"The Patagonia," *English Illustrated Magazine*, August–September 1888.

"The Solution," *New Review*, December 1889–February 1890.

"The Pupil," *Longman's Magazine*, March–April 1891.

"The Modern Warning" was first reprinted in *The Aspern Papers* (London and New York, 1888), "A London Life" and

"The Patagonia" in *A London Life* (London and New York, 1889) and "The Lesson of the Master," "The Solution" and "The Pupil" in *The Lesson of the Master* (London and New York, 1892). The text of these first book publications has been used here.

For the complete bibliography of the tales the reader is referred to *A Bibliography of the Writings of Henry James* by Leon Edel and Dan H. Laurence (second edition, revised, London, 1961) in the Soho Bibliographies published by Rupert Hart-Davis.